BONE WHITE

RONALD MALFI

PINNACLE BOOKS
Kensington Publishing Corp.
www.kensingtonbooks.com

PINNACLE BOOKS are published by

Kensington Publishing Corp.
119 West 40th Street
New York, NY 10018

All Kensington titles, imprints, and distributed lines are available at special quantity discounts for bulk purchases for sales promotions, premiums, fund-raising, educational, or institutional use. Special book excerpts or customized printings can also be created to fit specific needs. For details, write or phone the office of the Kensington sales manager: Kensington Publishing Corp., 119 West 40th Street, New York, NY 10018, attn: Sales Department; phone 1-800-221-2647.

PINNACLE and the P logo are Reg. U.S. Pat. & TM Off.

ISBN-13: 978-0-7860-4243-2
ISBN-10: 0-7860-4243-5

First Kensington trade paperback printing: August 2017
First Pinnacle mass market paperback printing: October 2018

10 9 8 7 6 5 4 3 2 1

Printed in the United States of America

Pinnacle electronic edition: October 2018

ISBN-13: 978-0-7860-4243-9
ISBN-10: 0-7860-4243-3

For Darin and Jon, my brothers.

"Hell is empty and all the devils are here."

—William Shakespeare

PART ONE
DEAD BODIES

1

The man who walked into Tabby White's luncheonette around seven in the morning on that overcast Tuesday was recognized only by a scant few customers, despite the fact that he had been a resident of that town for the better part of thirty years. He came in on a gust of cold wind, a withered husk of a man in a heavy chamois coat with wool lining. There were bits of leaves and grit in his salt-and-pepper beard, and the tip of his nose and the fleshy pockets beneath his eyes looked red and swollen with chilblains. The thermal undershirt he wore beneath the coat looked stiff with dried blood.

Bill Hopewell, whose family had lived in the town for three generations, was the first to recognize the man, and even that took the accumulation of several minutes' scrutiny. By the time he realized the fellow was old Joe Mallory from up Durham Road, Mallory was seated at the breakfast counter warming his hands around a steaming mug of Tabby's hot cocoa.

"Is that you, Joe?" Bill Hopewell said. Tabby's was a small place, and despite it being breakfast time, there were only about half a dozen customers. A few of them looked up from their meals and over at Bill Hopewell, who was seated by himself at one of the rickety tables before a bowl of oatmeal and a cup of strong coffee. Those same few then glanced over at the scarecrow-thin man in the chamois coat hunched over Tabby's breakfast counter.

The man—Joe Mallory, if it was him—did not turn around. Far as Bill Hopewell could tell, he hadn't even heard him.

It was the look on Tabby White's face that ultimately prompted Bill to climb out of his chair and mosey over to the breakfast counter. Tabby White was about as friendly as they came, and it was rare to catch a glimpse of her when she wasn't smiling. But she wasn't smiling now: She had served the man his requested cup of hot cocoa with dutiful subservience, and was now watching him from the far end of the breakfast counter, backed into the corner as far as she could go, beneath a wall clock in the shape of a cat whose eyes ticked back and forth like the wand of a metronome. There was a look of apprehension on Tabby's face.

"Hey, Joe," Bill Hopewell said as he came up beside the man and leaned one elbow down on the breakfast counter. When the man turned to look at him, Bill momentarily questioned his assumption that this was, in fact, Joseph Mallory from up Durham Road. Mallory was in his fifties, and this guy looked maybe ten years older than that—maybe more. And while Joe Mallory had never been overly concerned with personal hygiene, this guy smelled like he hadn't bathed in the better part of a month.

The man turned and grinned at Bill Hopewell. Through the wiry bristles of his beard, the man's lips were scabbed and wind-chapped. There was a patch of black frostbite, abrasive as tree bark, at one corner of his mouth. The few teeth remaining in Mallory's mouth looked like small wooden pegs.

"Where you been, Joe?" Bill asked. "Ain't nobody seen you in a long time."

"Been years," said Galen Provost, who was watching the exchange from a table near the windows. "Ain't that right, Joe?"

Joseph Mallory turned back around on his stool. With both hands, he brought the mug of hot cocoa to his lips and slurped. A runnel of cocoa spilled down his beard and spattered in splotches on the Formica countertop.

Bill Hopewell and Galen Provost exchanged a disconcerted look. Then Bill turned his gaze toward Tabby, who was still backed into her corner beneath the cat clock with the ticking eyes, gnawing on a thumbnail.

"This is fine cocoa, Tabs," Mallory said, the words coming out in a sandpapery drawl. "Mighty fine."

At the mention of her name, Tabby bumped into a shelf and sent a bottle of ketchup to the floor.

"What you got all over them clothes?" Galen Provost said from across the room. Everyone was watching now.

"Is that blood on your clothes, Joe?" Bill Hopewell asked, his tone less accusatory than Galen's, despite the directness of his query. Perhaps, Bill thought, Galen wouldn't have been so boisterous if he'd been standing right next to Mallory, where he could see the dirt collected in the creases of Mallory's face, the white nits in his hair and beard, and what looked like old blood beneath the man's fingernails. If he could see how *off* Mallory looked. Bill cleared his throat and said, "You been up in them woods, Joe?"

It was at that point that Joseph Mallory started to laugh. Or perhaps he started to cry: Bill Hopewell wasn't sure at that moment which one it was, and he would still be undecided about it much later, once Mallory's face was on the TV news. All he knew was that the noise that juddered from old Joe Mallory's throat sounded much like a stubborn carburetor, and that tears were welling in the man's eyes.

Bill Hopewell pushed himself off the counter and took two steps back.

The laughter—or whatever it was—lasted for just a couple of seconds. When he was done, Mallory swiped the tears from his eyes with a large, callused hand. Then he dug a few damp bills from the inside pocket of his coat and laid them out flat on the countertop. He nodded in Tabby White's direction.

Tabby White just stared at him.

Mallory's stool squealed as he rotated around toward Bill Hopewell. With some difficulty, he climbed down off the stool. His movements were labored and stiff, as if his muscles were wound too tight, his bones like brittle twigs. Those dark streaks across the front of Mallory's shirt were also on his coat and his pants, too, Bill realized.

"Well, they're up there, the whole lot of them," Mallory said. His voice was barely a rasp. Later, Bill would have to relay what he'd heard to Galen Provost and the rest of the patrons of Tabby's luncheonette, who were just out of earshot. "They're all dead, and I killed 'em. But I'm done now, so that's that." He turned away from Bill Hopewell and looked at Tabby. "Val Drammell still the safety officer 'round here?"

Tabby didn't answer. She didn't look capable.

"He is," Bill Hopewell answered for her.

"All right," said Mallory, turning back to Bill. He nodded once, as if satisfied. "One of you folks be kind enough to give him a call? Tell him I'll be sitting out by the church waiting for the staties to come collect me."

"Yeah, okay," Bill said, too stunned to do anything else but agree with the man's request.

"Much obliged," said Mallory, and then he turned and ambled out into the cold, gray morning.

"Tabby," Bill said, not looking at her—in fact, he was staring out the window, watching the gaunt form of Joe Mallory shamble up the road in the direction of the old church. "Best give Val Drammell a call, like he says."

It took Tabby White a few seconds before she understood that she had been spoken to. She moved across the floor toward the portable phone next to the coffee station—one of her white sneakers smeared a streak of ketchup along the linoleum, but she didn't notice—and fumbled with the receiver before bringing it to her ear.

"Val," she said into the phone, her voice reed-thin and bordering on a whine. "It's Tabby down at the luncheonette." There was a pause, then she said, "I think I'll turn you over to Bill Hopewell."

She handed Bill the receiver, and Bill set it against

his ear. He was still watching Joe Mallory as he ambled up the road toward the church. At the horizon, the sky looked bleached and colorless. It promised to be a cold winter. "We got something here I think you should come take a look at," he said, then explained the situation.

2

It was a quarter after eight in the morning when Jill Ryerson's desk phone rang.

"Major Crimes," she said. "This is Ryerson."

"Ms. Ryerson, this is Valerie Drammell, I'm the safety officer up the Hand. I had your card here and figured I'd give you a call on this situation we got out here." It was a man's voice with a woman's name, she realized. He spoke in a rushed, breathless patter that was difficult to understand.

"Where'd you say you're calling from, Mr. Drammell?"

"Up the Hand, ma'am." Then the man cleared his throat and said, "That's Dread's Hand, ma'am."

The name was familiar—it was too unique to forget—but in that moment she couldn't remember how or why she knew it. But something had happened there, maybe within the past year, and she had somehow been involved.

"What's the situation out there, Drammell?"

"Listen, I got a guy here, a local fella, named Joe Mallory," Drammell explained. "Says he killed a bunch of people and buried their bodies in the woods here. He's got . . . well, what looks like blood on his clothes, dried blood. It don't look fresh. He looks . . . he don't look right, Ms. Ryerson—er, Detective. I'm calling the right number, ain't I? This is the right number?"

She assured Drammell that it was, and said she'd be there as soon as possible. After she hung up, she stepped out of her office and peered into the squad room. Mike McHale sat behind the nearest desk.

"Dread's Hand," she said. "Where's that?"

McHale just shrugged his shoulders. There was a road atlas on the credenza behind McHale's desk, and he leaned over and grabbed it, eliciting a grunt as he did so. He opened the atlas on his desk and scrutinized one of the area maps.

"VPSO out there just called. Said he's with some local guy who claims he's killed some people."

McHale looked up from the map, frowning. "Yeah?" he said.

Ryerson shrugged.

"Here it is," McHale said, tapping a finger against an enlarged map of Alaska's interior. "Way out there in the hills. Should take us about an hour and a half, I'd guess," McHale said.

Ryerson curled up one side of her mouth in a partial grin. "Us?"

"What kind of guy would I be, letting you run off chasing murder suspects on your own?"

"Then you're driving," she said.

* * *

They found Drammell seated on a bench outside the village church beside a wasted scarecrow of a man with a frizzy beard that came down past his collarbone. Ryerson and McHale got out of the cruiser and approached the men. Ryerson spotted the coppery-brown streaks of dried blood along the front of Mallory's long johns and around the cuffs of his pants. Not that she put much stock in it right off the bat—this guy could have been butchering critters in the woods for the past couple of days, for all she knew—although there was something in Mallory's gray eyes that chilled her when he first looked up at her.

"I'm here to make my peace with it," Mallory said as they approached.

"What's 'it'?" Ryerson asked.

"C'mon and I'll show y'all," Mallory said. He used Val Drammell's shoulder for support as he hoisted himself off the church bench. Drammell made a face that suggested he was disgusted by the man's touch, although he didn't make a move to shove the man off him. When his eyes shifted toward Ryerson, he looked relieved that they were here and he could transfer this problem to them.

"Just hold on a minute," Ryerson said. "This fella Drammell here called and told us you killed a few people out this way. Is that right?"

"Yes, ma'am," said Mallory.

"Is this something you done recently?"

"Oh no, ma'am. It's been quite some time for me."

"Where are they?"

"That's what I was goin' t' show you, ma'am," Mallory said. He pointed toward the cusp of trees that wreathed the foothills of the White Mountains.

"That's where they are? Up there?"

"The lot of 'em," Mallory said.

"People," Val Drammell interjected. "Says he's buried some *people* up there. Just so we're clear here."

"I understand," she said to Drammell. Looking back at Mallory, she said, "That's what you're telling us, right? That you killed some folks and buried them up there. Is that right?"

"As rain," Mallory said.

She glanced at the tree line before turning her gaze back to Mallory. Those woods were expansive and the foothills could be treacherous. Not to mention that Mallory looked malnourished and about as sturdy as a day-old colt. "How far?" she asked.

"We can walk it, for sure," Mallory responded, although judging by his appearance and by the way he'd utilized Drammell's shoulder as a crutch to lift himself off the bench just a moment ago, Jill Ryerson had serious doubts about that.

"I think maybe you need to see a doctor first," she said to him.

"Time enough for that later," said Mallory. "I ain't gonna expire out here, ma'am. First I'll show you where they are. It's important I show you where they are. This is all very important."

She glanced at McHale, who looked cold and uncertain. He shrugged.

"All right," Ryerson said. For some reason, she believed him—that it was important he show them where they were, right then and there. As if there wouldn't be a chance to do it later. She got an extra coat from the cruiser's trunk, and helped Mallory into it. Mallory peered down at the embroidered badge over the breast, a bemused expression on his wind-burned face.

"Well, lookit that," he muttered, fingering the badge.

Mallory took them up into the woods, a walk that took nearly an hour and covered a distance that Ryerson, in her head, calculated to be just over a mile. Had she gone back for the car, it would have been possible to drive less than halfway up the old mining road: After about fifteen minutes of walking, the road narrowed to maybe three feet in width, and there were times when they had to climb over deadfalls and step around massive boulders in order to keep going. And then the road vanished altogether, surrendering to sparse stands of pines and Sitka spruce and large boulders furred with spongy green moss.

"If this is someone's idea of a practical joke," McHale said to no one in particular midway through the hike, "they're getting brained with my Maglite."

Ryerson let Mallory lead the way. She hadn't cuffed him—it would have been too difficult for the man to climb through the woods with his hands cuffed behind his back—but she had surreptitiously frisked him when she'd helped him into the parka, and she had felt no weapons on him. Besides, she still wasn't convinced this guy wasn't just some crackpot. Lord knew there were enough of them out here. Nonetheless, she kept her eyes on him as they walked.

"How'd you get my name and number?" Ryerson asked Drammell as they climbed toward the cusp of the wooded foothills. "The name of this town sounds familiar, but I've never been out here before."

"Two troopers came out here about a year ago looking for a fella," Drammell said. "Far as I know, they never found the guy. When they left, they gave me your business card. Said I should call you if the fella ever turned up." Drammell frowned and added, "He never did."

Yes, she remembered now. She'd gotten a call about a year ago from the brother of a man who'd gone missing out this way. The man had traced his brother back to Dread's Hand as the last known place he'd been. Ryerson had taken the call and filed the paperwork, but she hadn't come out here herself. Instead, she had dispatched two troopers to Dread's Hand to check things out. She couldn't be positive at the moment, but she believed they managed to recover the man's rental car.

"You guys ever find the fella?" Drammell asked.

"No," said Ryerson.

Despite his weakened physical condition, Mallory appeared to have no difficulties on the walk. McHale and Drammell, on the other hand, were both wheezing by the time they reached a vast clearing. It was right here, Joseph Mallory explained, that he had buried the bodies of eight victims whom he'd murdered over a five-year period. He seemed certain about the number of victims, less certain about how long he'd spent killing. "Time," he suggested, "acts funny out here."

Ryerson and McHale exchanged a glance.

"You understand what you're telling us, don't you?" said McHale.

"Of course." Mallory glared at McHale, indignant. "I ain't stupid, son."

"No, sir," McHale said, and Ryerson detected more than just a hint of sarcasm in his voice.

"This is a big area," Ryerson said. "Is it possible to narrow down a location?"

"There are many locations," Mallory informed her. "Come on, then."

He pointed out the general vicinity of each unmarked grave, which covered an area of just about ten acres of woodland, in Ryerson's estimation. And although Ryerson had been right there standing beside him, inspecting the somber look on Joseph Mallory's wind-chapped face as he murmured, "One soul here, 'nother far yonder," she continued to believe that there were no bodies buried here at all, and that Joseph Mallory was just another backwoods crackpot with dried elk blood on his clothes who wanted his fifteen minutes of fame with the state police out of Fairbanks. After all, it was evident that the old man was one cherry short of an ice cream sundae, as Jill Ryerson's father had been fond of saying.

"That does her," Mallory said once he'd finished walking Ryerson, McHale, and Drammell all over God's green earth (although there was nothing green about this Alaska forest in the middle of September—the ground was as cold and gray as the trunks of the Sitka spruce). The whole thing had taken over two hours—a few times Mallory got confused as to a specific location while other times he just needed to rest—and they still needed to walk back down out of the woods, but despite the cold, Ryerson had overexerted herself and was sweating beneath her uniform and parka. She instructed Mike McHale to mark each spot as Mallory pointed them out, and McHale had jammed sticks into the earth and tied a Kleenex to each one for quick reference.

"You don't really think there's people *buried* here, do you?" McHale asked her at one point, his voice low, his hot, coffee-scented breath against the side of her neck.

"No, I don't," she said. "He just seems confused. But let's do this thing by the book, in case we're wrong, okay?"

"Roger that," said McHale.

"I'm going to cuff you and take you back to Fairbanks for now," Ryerson told Mallory once he finished pointing out all eight unmarked graves. "Would make me feel better if I got a doctor's eyes on you, too."

"I feel fine now," Mallory said, standing there in that clearing. He closed his eyes and tilted his reddened, wind-chapped face to the sky. Sores ran along his cheekbones and suppurated at his lips. It looked like he might have some frostbite in places, too. "But we've been spending too much time out here. I've already scrubbed it off once. Let's get back to town before it gets grabby again."

Jill Ryerson might have asked him to elaborate on what he meant by that statement had Valerie Drammell not spoken up then: "Yeah, let's get back to town. Like, right now." He was looking around, as if expecting someone to walk out of the trees and join them. A ghost, maybe.

"You both should cordon off the area and take some pictures," Ryerson suggested, looking from Drammell to McHale. "Let's treat this as a crime scene. I'll radio for assistance when I get back to the car. I'll contact the ME's office in Anchorage, too, just to put them on notice, in the event that, well . . . our friend here knows what he's talking about."

"Of course I do," grumbled Mallory, scowling.

"Me?" Val Drammell said. "Me stay here, too?"

Ryerson thought he sounded like Tarzan at the moment. "You're not obligated, but we could use the help, Mr. Drammell," she told him.

Drammell nodded, though it was clear he didn't want to be here. The ground speared by McHale's sticks with their Kleenex flags was an unsettling visual, and no doubt the past hour and a half sitting with Mallory on that church bench had creeped the poor guy out. He put a cigarette in his mouth.

"No smoking, please," Ryerson said. "Crime scene."

Drammell stared at her for the length of two heartbeats—long enough for Jill Ryerson to think, *Okay, here we go, let's flex those man muscles now*—but then he took the smoke out of his mouth and propped it up behind his left ear.

"You don't want help taking him back to the car?" McHale asked as Ryerson placed Mallory's hands behind his back and snapped the cuffs on him.

"I can manage," she said. "Let's just secure this place. And let's keep any locals from coming out here, too."

"No locals would come out here," Drammell said, but he did not elaborate.

* * *

Once they got into the police car back in town, Ryerson recited Mallory's Miranda rights.

"Don't have no need for them rights," Mallory said from behind the wire cage in the backseat of the cruiser. "Don't have no need for no lawyers, neither. I confessed all my sins. That's about it, ain't it?"

"I'm just telling you the law, Mr. Mallory," she said, firing up the engine and cranking the heater to full force. A small group of onlookers stood across the road, watching the situation, clouds of vapor spiraling from their open mouths. To Ryerson, they all looked like refugees deposited on the shores of some foreign country.

She drove slowly down the main street, which alternated between rutted dirt and white gravel, while the onlookers all turned their heads in unison to watch their departure.

"You feel like giving me your motive for killing those folks?" she said.

"No," Mallory said.

"No motive?"

"Don't feel like giving it," he clarified.

"How come?"

This time, Mallory didn't answer.

"How 'bout their names?" Ryerson said. "Care to tell me who they are? Were they locals?"

"Don't feel like speakin' their names aloud, ma'am, though I don't expect you to understand," Mallory said. "Don't rightly recall any of their names at the moment, to be honest. That part was never important."

"Is that right," she said.

"I suspect you'll find out in time, though. And that's fine."

"If this is some game you're playing with us, Mr. Mallory, you should just tell me now so we can avoid a lot of unnecessary work."

"Game?" he said.

"If you're trying to fool with us, in other words," she said. "If there are no bodies up there, I mean."

"Oh," he said, "they're up there, all right, ma'am. God help us, they're up there."

Jill Ryerson had her doubts.

Ninety minutes later, Ryerson deposited Mallory at Fairbanks Memorial and into the care of two fresh-faced troopers while McHale and Drammell secured the wooded clearing and awaited the arrival of backup, which included sniffer dogs and a technician schooled in using ground-penetrating radar. Ryerson did not think too much of it until she got a phone call sometime later from McHale, who was still on the scene.

"You better get out here, Jill," McHale said, and she could detect a note of brash excitement in his voice even though he was trying his best to keep himself under control. "We've got a body."

3

Paul Gallo was at Telluride nursing a glass of Johnnie Walker and grading essays on Conrad's *Heart of Darkness* when he first learned of the monster.

Wholly incongruous among the rustic, nautical-themed taverns of downtown Annapolis, the bar known as Telluride was outfitted in a ski lodge motif. There was a pair of skis crossboned above the bar and framed photos of various Colorado slopes on the paneled walls. A cozy stone fireplace stood at the far end of the barroom, fronted by a tattered couch of Navajo design. Stuffed antelope heads hung from lacquered shields, their dead eyes gray and furry with dust.

The proprietor was a retired Baltimore homicide detective named Luther Parnell. Luther had never been skiing in his life, and had admitted to Paul on more than one occasion that he wouldn't know a bunny slope from the bunny hop. He had bought the place following his retirement from the department, and because Telluride's clientele had been plentiful and the place in good shape, he'd left it unchanged, right down to the name.

Paul liked the bar's atmosphere and he liked Lou even more, but he had come here primarily because it was within walking distance of the college campus. His Tuesday and Thursday classes ran late, which put him on the street close to dinnertime. In no hurry to return to his Conduit Street residence for a microwaveable dinner in front of the TV, he'd cultivated the habit of dining at Telluride on those evenings while he graded papers and chatted with Lou.

This evening, Paul had already finished his burger and was halfway through his second glass of Scotch when Luther Parnell, passing by the bar and in a casual tone, said, "Dread's Hand."

Paul looked up from one of the essays he'd been grading and stared at Lou. "What'd you say?"

Luther pointed to the TV that was mounted above the bar. The image on the screen was an aerial shot of a bleak wooded clearing surrounded by tall gray trees. A solitary police car was slotted at an angle between two trees, and a few people were milling about. A strip of yellow police tape flapped about near the lower half of the screen. A yellow backhoe, expelling clouds of bluish exhaust, was carving a trench in the earth. The text at the bottom of the screen identified the location as Dread's Hand, Alaska.

"Some funky name for a town, huh?" Luther said.

But Paul wasn't listening to him now. "What is this? Where's the volume?"

Luther shrugged and made a sound that approximated a grunt. He turned his attention to a balding, middle-aged fellow in a necktie at the far end of the bar. The middle-aged fellow said something and Luther Parnell laughed his great bassoon laugh.

"Lou," Paul called to him. "Can you turn this up? Can you turn the volume up?"

At that moment, a block of text appeared on the lower portion of the screen: UNIDENTIFIED BODY RECOVERED FROM SHALLOW GRAVE.

Paul stood up off his bar stool. The red pen, which he had been using to grade students' essays, rolled off the bar and clattered to the floor, but he hardly noticed. He could focus on nothing but the television screen.

Luther squeezed behind the bar and began searching for the remote.

"Come on, come on," Paul said, waving a hand at him.

"Jeez, son, settle down," Lou said, searching around behind the bar for the TV remote.

On the screen, the block of text was replaced by another declaration. This time, Paul felt an icy finger trace down the base of his spine at the sight of it: LOCAL MAN ADMITS TO MURDER OF UNKNOWN NUMBER OF VICTIMS NEAR REMOTE ALASKA TOWN.

A thudding heartbeat filled Paul Gallo's ears.

"Lou," he said.

"Yeah, yeah, gimme a sec." Lou located the remote and aimed it at the TV.

The voice of a female news reporter burst from the speakers in midsentence: ". . . when a man walked into a local restaurant Tuesday afternoon and confessed to the murders of an unknown number of victims, according to police. Sources say the suspect claims to have buried these victims in a wooded area a few miles from the remote Alaskan town of Dread's Hand, an old mining village about a hundred or so miles northwest of Fairbanks. As you can see from our SkyCrew video, police are on the scene, where they've been working around the clock for the past forty-eight hours. Police have not yet released the identity of the subject, and very little information is known at this time, except that he is in police custody and under the care of medical professionals. One witness has reported that the individual is, or was at one time, a local resident, but the Alaska Bureau of Investigation's Major Crimes Unit, which maintains jurisdiction in this matter, hasn't released an official statement yet."

"A disturbing situation, Sandra," said a male reporter, just as the image on the screen cut away to the studio, where both newscasters sat behind a high desk, looking grim yet also somehow perky. "Just to recap, one unidentified body has been recovered in the approximate location given to police by a suspect claiming to have murdered several individuals here in this isolated Alaskan village."

Paul stood there staring at the TV for what seemed like an eternity, until the broadcast cut to commercial. His heart was banging in his chest, and his hands were shaking. After a time, he was aware of Lou's voice calling out to him.

"Hey, you okay, Paul?"

Paul looked around and noticed that a few of the other patrons were gazing at him from their tables. They turned away as he looked at them.

"Man, what's the matter with you?" Lou said. He jerked his chin toward Paul's stool and suggested he sit down before he fell down.

Paul sat and stared at his drink before knocking the rest of it down his throat.

Lou muted the TV, then stowed the remote back beneath the counter. He leaned over the bar toward Paul, the diamond stud in his left earlobe sparkling. "The hell's the matter with you, man?"

Paul cleared his throat and said, "Dread's Hand is where Danny went missing."

"Danny," Lou said. He spoke the name as if unfamiliar with it. But then recognition dawned on him— Paul watched it overtake Luther Parnell's face like a metamorphosis—and then the retired homicide detective said, "Danny. Your brother. Shit, Paul. You sure?"

"Positive," he said, and thought, *Who could ever forget a name like Dread's Hand?*

Lou glanced back up at the TV, which was now broadcasting a reverse mortgage commercial. Luther Parnell knew the story about Paul's brother. Paul had even come in here a few times with Danny back when Danny had been staying at his place. When Danny disappeared, it had been Lou who'd put Paul in touch with an old colleague of his, a Baltimore city homicide detective named Richard Ridgley. Ridgley had gotten some of Danny's personal records—credit card statements and cell phone toll reports—and had put Paul in touch with Jill Ryerson, an investigator with the Alaska Bureau of Investigation's Major Crimes Unit out of Fairbanks. It had been Ryerson's men who had found

Danny's rental car, abandoned on the side of some nameless dirt road outside of Dread's Hand.

"This is crazy," Paul said. His mind was reeling.

"Just take it easy," Lou said. "Just sit here for a few minutes and take it easy, Paul, okay?"

"I'm okay," he said—a bit disingenuous, he knew, because his body had gone from cold to hot in the span of thirty seconds. He loosened his necktie and undid the top two buttons of his shirt.

"Want me to get Ridge on the line?"

Paul waved a hand. "I'm not sure what good that'll do at this point," he said. He glanced back up at the TV, but it was still on some commercial. "What happens with something like this, Lou? They find this body and . . . and then what?"

Lou arched his eyebrows and refolded his arms. The tattoo of a hula girl flexed on his bicep. At first, Paul thought Lou might be trying to figure that out himself, but then, as Lou spoke, Paul realized the retired homicide detective had only been considering the most delicate way to answer his question.

"I guess it all depends on the . . . well, the condition of the body," Lou said. "If there hasn't been a lot of decomposition, they can lift fingerprints and run them through a database. There are dental records, too, but that's for corroboration once they have a suspected ID of the victim. There are . . . there are identifiers on the body . . ." Lou's voice trailed off. He frowned and said, "You don't want to hear about any of this shit."

"I just want to know how this plays out now," Paul said.

"It plays out with you not jumping to any conclusions for the time being," Lou said. "You said you had some contact up in Alaska, right? Someone Ridge put you in touch with?"

"Ryerson. She's an investigator with Major Crimes."

"Call her."

"What time is it in Alaska right now, anyway?"

"No idea." Lou reached beneath the bar and brought out the bottle of Johnnie Walker. He filled Paul's glass for the third time that evening. "On the house. Drink it."

He wanted it, but he didn't trust himself to pick up the glass. His hands were trembling too badly.

"Four thirty," said the man in the necktie at the far end of the bar.

Paul turned to the man. "What's that?"

"It's currently four thirty in the afternoon in Alaska," the man said. He got off his stool and, carrying a pint of piss-colored beer, came over and sat beside him. He tapped what looked like an expensive wristwatch, then said, "Four thirty-eight, to be exact. They're four hours behind us. I used to live in Anchorage."

"Thanks," Paul said.

"I'm sorry for eavesdropping."

"It's all right."

The man smiled, which made Paul think maybe he hadn't heard most of their conversation after all. He was too jovial. Either that or he was drunk.

"This Dread's Hand place," Paul said, gesturing toward the TV. "Are you familiar with it?"

"No, I'm not. But there are a lot of old mining towns out that way, some so small you'd hardly count them as civilizations. And some that just aren't civilized at all."

Drunk, Paul decided.

The man smiled, then took an almost-dainty sip of his beer. "It's a different world up there, I can tell you that," he continued once he'd set his beer back down on a paper coaster.

"I'll bet," Paul said. He was thinking about the box on the shelf of his bedroom closet at the moment.

"There's an AP article on Yahoo! News," Lou said, staring at his iPhone. "Updated five minutes ago, but there's not much more detail there than what you just heard."

"They're crazy up there, you know," said the man in the necktie.

"Who's that?" Paul asked.

"Everyone," said the man. "Every last one. Even in the big cities. And the farther into the wild you go, the crazier they get. Like bedbugs. High suicide rates, high alcoholism. Domestic violence. They've got a whole rape culture up there, too, you know, although you'd never hear about it in the news. Not down here in the lower forty-eight, anyway." The man nodded at the TV, which was reflecting a soft bluish light against the bald dome of his head. "You don't hear about stuff going on up there until something like this happens. Gets national attention, at least for a little while."

The newscasters were back on the television, but they had already moved on to a different story. Given the current state of the world, with its weekly shootings in the United States and a revolving inventory of terrorist attacks around the world, how much media attention could be spared to some dead bodies up in Alaska?

"I was working up there in the mid-eighties, you

know," the man said. "Going back and forth between Anchorage and Fairbanks, writing claims for an insurance firm that dealt with oil and gas companies. Usually I'd be at some big facility in one of the major cities, and I was stationed in Anchorage, but on occasion I'd get farmed out to some remote village off the beaten path if some ancient piece of machinery broke down or if a tanker truck happened to overturn on some icy road somewhere. That sort of thing happened more than you'd think out there."

"I've seen that TV show," Lou commented. "The one with the truck drivers who drive over the frozen seas."

"A lot of those mountain roads are unpaved and treacherous. Sometimes trees fall across the road and the driver, he doesn't see it until it's too late."

Lou nodded.

"I was in my early twenties back then, so it was something of an adventure for me," the man continued. "This was around '83 or '84, when I was dispatched to Manley Hot Springs, which is maybe a hundred and fifty miles west of Fairbanks on the Tanana River. Nothing out there but these forgotten old mining towns, just like I said before. I think Manley's population was maybe seventy people back then, and a good number of those were probably drifters.

"There's a road, the Elliott Highway, that runs from Fairbanks to Manley Hot Springs. It's a standard paved roadway when it leaves Fairbanks, but for the last eighty or so miles into Manley, it's just an old dirt road. An oil tanker had run off a section outside Manley, and I was sent out there to take pictures and fill out an incident report. This road, it was notorious for accidents, and even more so in the winter, but this particular accident occurred in May, and the weather was nice.

"Anyway, I'm out there taking pictures and filling out my reports, minding my own business, until I hear this old rattletrap engine pull up along the shoulder behind me. Very few cars had passed me on that road all morning, so it struck me as odd, you know? I turn around and see this big brown and white Dodge Monaco with this big aluminum canoe strapped to the roof. It's just idling there, maybe only a couple yards behind my own vehicle. I'm watching it, waiting for the driver to come out, because, look, there's no reason to stop on this stretch of road, unless you need some kind of help or something, know what I mean? Maybe he had a flat tire or maybe . . . I don't know . . . he was having a heart attack or something. Could have been anything."

"How long did he stay there like that?" Lou asked.

"Maybe fifteen, twenty minutes. Also, I don't know if you're familiar with the Dodge Monaco, but the thing was like a poor man's Cadillac, and it's not the type of car you'd use to haul around a canoe. The Monaco's engine is still running, and I can see that there's a figure moving around just behind the glare on the windshield. But the guy, he doesn't get out of the car. Doesn't honk the horn, doesn't roll down the window and wave to get my attention. He doesn't do anything but sit there.

"I finish what I'm doing, then stash my camera and my reports back in my car. And I'm tempted to just drive away . . . but then I look back at the guy's car and figure, ah, what the hell, maybe this knucklehead needs something from me. So, I go on over to the driver's side. The driver rolls down the window, and there's this big, hairy lumberjack face grinning out at me.

"'You need some help?' I ask him.

"'No, sir,' he says, just as polite as you'd please. He looked about my age, although it was difficult to tell, given that scraggly beard of his. And he's grinning at me, some strained grin, and I can't tell if he's making fun of me or just clear off his rocker.

"'Lost?' I ask him.

"'No, sir. Not lost,' he says, still grinning like a wooden puppet. 'In fact, I'm perfectly found.' Those were his words, just like that—*I'm perfectly found*.

"That's when I notice he's got a rifle leaning against the passenger seat, the barrel leaning against the headrest and pointing straight up at the ceiling of the car. The bells and whistles start going off in my head, and I realize that if this guy takes that rifle and shoots me out here, my body might never be found. And in looking at him, I realize that this guy might just be the type to do it. That strange smile hadn't faded from his face, and his eyes looked . . . I don't know . . . too intense, maybe. Like he was trying too hard to look happy and to convince me that he was just, you know, a normal guy. And it wasn't just me thinking this because I saw the gun—this was Alaska, and pretty goddamn far north, and there were guns everywhere, although I can't say I'd ever seen someone just kind of leave it there against the passenger seat of their car while they drove around with it. Anyway, the whole thing was beginning to spook me out.

"'What is it you're doing?' I ask him.

"'Just checking to see if you were white,' he tells me.

"Well, I'd had enough. 'Have a nice day,' I tell him, and get back in my car and drive away.

"Well, something like a week later, I see the guy's big, furry lumberjack face again, only this time it's on the TV news. The guy's name was Michael Silka and he'd murdered nine people in and around the Manley Hot Springs area, including a state trooper, and a pregnant woman and her family. There was a shoot-out and he was gunned down by police just a few days after I ran into him out on the Elliott Highway."

"Jesus," Paul said.

The man in the necktie finished off his beer, then set the empty glass down on its paper coaster.

"To this day," the man said, "I wonder if Silka was just sitting in that car, trying to drum up the nerve to step out and blow my head off with that rifle. Maybe dump my body and steal my car. Maybe make me his tenth victim, you know? A nice, round, even number. If that was his intention—if that was the reason he pulled his rattletrap car behind mine that day and just sat there for twenty minutes, watching me—then only God knows what stopped him from doing it."

"That's the creepiest goddamn thing I've ever heard," Lou said. He was staring at the man with wide, almost comical eyes. "And I've seen some crazy shit in my life."

"I still think about it, sometimes," the man said. Some men might take pride in the retelling of such a story, Paul thought, but this guy looked like he'd just had the wind knocked out of him.

The man took a fifty-dollar bill from his pocket and

placed it on the bar next to his empty beer glass. "It's
been a pleasure, gentlemen. Have a good night. And be
safe." He made a gun with his thumb and forefinger and
*kapow*ed Paul with it.

Paul watched him wobble out of the place.

"That's Tom Justice," Lou informed him. "He lives a
few blocks away. Comes in and gets sauced from time
to time, then walks home." He looked at Paul. "You
okay? You didn't need to hear that spooky-ass story."

"I'm okay," he said, knowing damn well that he
wasn't.

It was a quarter after ten when he arrived home, his
head woozy from too much Scotch, his mind reeling
with one final, terrible possibility. Something like five
thousand miles away, there was a body being extricated
from a slab of arctic tundra. The likelihood of it being Danny was remote, though he couldn't convince
himself that it was an impossibility. It occurred to him,
too, that until tonight and despite not having heard from
Danny since his disappearance over a year ago, there
had always been a part of him—a dimming flicker of
candlelight—that held out hope that Danny was still
alive out there somewhere. That Danny had just flaked
out and went off the grid, and he was alive out there
and living like one of those mountain men, off the land.
Or maybe he had picked up his heels and headed off
into the Yukon or clear across Canada or wherever. It
was even possible that Danny had gotten in trouble with
the law again, and this little disappearing act had been
Danny's plan from the very beginning . . .

Those were optimistic if far-fetched propositions,

but there was a part of Paul that was always able to grasp on to them. They gave him hope. After all, wasn't it just like Danny to do something nutty like that?

But tonight's newscast changed all that. He felt that hope fade, and the absence of it left him feeling hollow. All of a sudden, he felt almost weightless with grief.

Paul Gallo had no wife, no kids, no pets, and was greeted only by a darkened foyer as he stepped through the front door of his Conduit Street bungalow. He dumped his briefcase on the floor and went into the living room, where he dug the television remote out from between two sofa cushions. He turned on the TV, then went into the kitchen, where he made himself a pot of strong coffee.

When the eleven o'clock news started, he sat on the sofa clutching his coffee mug in both hands and waited through reports of never-ending violence in Baltimore, political corruption in DC, and a sports montage that meant very little to him.

The segment about Dread's Hand came near the end of the broadcast.

"In other news, police are still conducting a search for human remains in a remote village in *Alaska* this evening," the news anchor reported, emphasizing the name of the state as if surprised by its very existence, "after an unidentified body was discovered Tuesday evening in a shallow grave. The search began after a local man confessed to the murders of an untold number of individuals in and around the town of Dread's Hand, and then directed police to the wooded area where he claimed to have buried the bodies."

The image on the screen changed to a black-and-white photograph of an unsmiling, stone-faced man who looked to be in his fifties. He wore a checked hunting coat and his hair was parted to one side, suggestive of a comb-over to hide his baldness. The name beneath the photo said JOSEPH ALLEN MALLORY, and the scroll beneath the name read: ALASKA MURDER SUSPECT IDENTIFIED.

"Joseph Mallory was identified by police earlier this evening as the suspect," said the reporter, "and is a local resident of Dread's Hand. Police say Mallory has been taken to a hospital in Anchorage and is being treated for hypothermia and dehydration. Police have not disclosed a specific number of victims, and although police say Mallory is cooperating with investigators, he has not yet given a motive for these crimes, nor has he identified his victims."

The black-and-white photo of Mallory was replaced by the reporter's stoic face. "And this station has just received word that a second body has just been recovered from that same site. Police are expected to continue searching throughout the night."

Paul turned off the TV, set his coffee down on an end table, then went up to his bedroom, where he pulled open the closet door. On the top shelf were binders filled with tax documents and work papers, as well as a few shoe boxes stuffed with random receipts and correspondence. Among the shoe boxes and binders was a flat, unlabeled cardboard box. Paul took the box down from the shelf, sat on his bed, and opened it in his lap.

Inside were the copies of Danny's credit card statements and phone records he'd gotten from Detective Richard Ridgley, a series of postcards Danny had sent him during the early part of his Alaskan sojourn, as

well as a glossy eight-by-ten photo of Danny that Paul
had e-mailed to the state troopers in Fairbanks—Danny
in a ski jacket with sunglasses nesting in his dark
hair. Danny was grinning at the camera, looking like
a magazine advertisement for teeth whitening. There
were also printouts of the last two text messages he'd
received from Danny just before Danny went dark. The
first said **Entering Dread's Hand—Spooky!** The second was
a close-up of Danny's face, a decrepit log cabin in the
background, slightly out of focus. Paul had sent copies
of both transmissions to the police.

Also in the box were copies of the reports Paul had
filed with the Alaska Bureau of Investigation. Stapled
to the top of the reports was Investigator Jill Ryerson's
business card, which she'd sent to him in the mail along
with copies of the reports.

There was no cell number on the card, so he called
the office line. It rang several times before a record-
ing of Ryerson's cool, businesslike voice invited him to
leave a message. *Beep.*

Paul sat there on the edge of his bed with the phone
to his ear, unable to say anything. His mind was too
confused with thoughts, a veritable runaway train of
thought, yet he felt powerless to verbalize a single utterance over the phone.

But it's not just that, he thought, the phone growing
warm against his ear. *You're still the fool holding out
hope. You don't really want to know, do you? It's better
this way, isn't it?*

In the end, he hung up without leaving a message.

4

They had been close when they were young. Tenants of a shared womb, casualties of the same bloodline, Paul Gallo was born seven minutes before his twin brother, Danny. Paul came out quickly, a pinkish, squealing bundle of quivering limbs, toothless mouth agape, eyes squinty and piggish and gummed shut. He was mopped clean and spirited to the opposite end of the delivery room, where two nurses checked his vitals. Everything appeared fine. But there were complications during Danny's delivery.

"Now, let's get that other one," said the doctor, and Paul's mother pushed. Then he said, "Wait. Wait. Hold on."

Another nurse was examining a monitor. "Baby's blood pressure dropped," she said.

"What's that mean?" said Michael Gallo, Paul's father. "What's going on?"

The umbilical cord was wrapped around the other baby's neck inside the womb, the doctor explained.

Whenever his mother pushed, the cord tightened like a noose.

"Let's try repositioning," the doctor suggested. To the nearest nurse, he said, "Get some help in here."

They repositioned Melinda Gallo, but with the next push, Danny's blood pressure plummeted yet again. One of the nurses told Michael Gallo to step aside.

"Doctor!" shouted one of the nurses at the other end of the delivery room. "Blood pressure's *dropped*."

"We're on it," the doctor assured the nurse.

"No," she shouted back. "On *this* baby. Here. Here."

Paul Gallo's tiny body had gone limp on the scale beneath the heating lamps. One of the nurses lifted his legs and smacked him across his narrow, reddened backside. The baby did not cry.

"Doctor—"

"Get some help in here, nurse," the doctor repeated. "STAT."

"What's going on?" demanded Michael Gallo. He went to the scale where little Paul was splayed out on a striped maternity blanket, motionless, one eye open and gazing at nothing. And just as Michael stared at his son, Paul shuddered, then began crying again.

The nurse nearest Michael Gallo whispered, "Thank God."

Across the room, Melinda Gallo grunted, cried out, pushed again.

"No," the doctor told her.

On the monitor, Danny's heartbeat slowed.

On the scale, Paul's tiny body went limp again.

In the end, they performed an emergency caesarean and got Danny out, unharmed. He wailed as his bottom was spanked while, across the room, his older brother joined in the chorus. The doctor, who was a man in his sixties sporting a fiery red beard, later commented on the peculiarity of it all with somewhat of a quizzical smile planted on his lips, but he said nothing more to the new parents about it. No one did.

They were identical twins, and indeed they looked very much alike when they were children—so much so that Melinda Gallo took great joy in exploiting this circumstance, often dressing them in matching outfits so that their neighbors, their classmates, and even their relatives couldn't tell them apart. During this period, the boys took to wearing the same haircuts, combed from left to right with identical parts, happy to add to the confusion. There was a secret magic that existed between them back then, before that brotherly bond weakened under the weight of burgeoning adulthood. *Can you see those boys? Can you see them?* Summers spent racing, barefoot and shirtless, along the muddy riverbanks of the Magothy. Cool summer evenings camped out in the backyard, gazing up at a firmament jeweled with stars, their toes gliding over the damp grass while they whispered and giggled and were happy. It was the magic of youth and of brotherhood, and those were the strongest powers in the known universe. For a while, anyway.

By the time their ages reached double digits, Paul and Danny Gallo's resemblance began to fade. It was apparent that they were brothers, but they were no longer able to trick people into believing they were each other. In fact, they no longer wanted to, intent instead on carving out their own individual identities. Paul kept his hair short while Danny let his grow in long, unruly waves down past his shirt collar. Throughout Paul's entire high school career, he remained clean-shaven and fresh-faced while Danny often sported a wiry black chinstrap or goatee, with sideburns as bushy as foxtails. They were both of average height and build, but Paul walked around at a quick clip and with some apparent purpose—the boys' mother would sometimes call him a hummingbird—whereas Danny had, over time, adopted a casual saunter that aggravated their father and suggested a degree of insolence Danny was more than happy to live up to.

These newfound differences were not just limited to their physical characteristics, either. Throughout school, Paul remained a studious, well-read child. He got good grades and he got them with ease. He was decent at sports, too, although no one would ever mistake him for a natural athlete. Danny, on the other hand, struggled in class and was always in danger of failing one subject or another. He had no interest in books. Unlike Paul, however, Danny *was* a natural-born athlete, although he held no interest in organized sports and rarely participated in neighborhood kickball or baseball games. Once, at the insistence of their father (who perhaps felt Danny's best chance of getting into a decent college might be through receipt of an athletic scholarship), Danny went out for the high school wrestling team. He wrestled in only two matches—and he won them both—before he was kicked off the team for smoking cigarettes in the boys' locker room. Their father hit the roof, but Danny shrugged it off, indifferent. "Hated those fucking unitards," Danny later told Paul, which was the extent of their conversation into the matter.

The summer after their sophomore year of high school, their father fought with Danny about getting a summer job. By that point, Danny's idea of summer vacation involved smoking dope and listening to Van Halen, but he knew that their father wouldn't relent, so he wrangled a job as a cashier at the local Caldor in town. He left the house every morning at eight and returned around five in the evening, and their father kept off his case. But sometime around the beginning of August, while Paul was on lunch break from his own summer job at a nearby hardware store, he saw Danny in the parking lot of Taco Bell. Danny was splayed out on the hood of a friend's car in jean shorts and a T-shirt, mirrored sunglasses on, a kiss-my-ass grin etched across his face as he sucked on a Marlboro. When Paul called his name, Danny sat up, as did his degenerate friends who were hanging around with him, lounging in the grass or perched like buzzards on the curb. But when Danny saw it was Paul, that kiss-my-ass grin broke into an all-out smile. He and his friends were going to the beach for the day, he told Paul, and did Paul want to come? Paul said he had to get back to work, and that he thought Danny did, too. That smile only widened, and Danny didn't have to explain it any further. He'd never had a job and had lied to their old man—and to Paul—for the entire summer.

Except maybe Paul *had* known. Some subconscious part of him, anyway. Because Paul rarely went to that little shopping plaza during his lunch break, opting to save his money and brown-bag it instead. And he never ate Taco Bell. Yet he had arrived there that afternoon in time to catch Danny moments before he departed with his friends for their beach trip. Had it been chance . . . or something more? It was strange, but it seemed that as they grew older, and in spite of their brotherly bond having diminished, some secondary connection had developed between them—a connection that was perhaps more tenuous yet just as powerful as their bloodline.

At sixteen, Paul got his driver's license the first time he took the test. Their father was proud, and when the weekend came around, he handed Paul the keys to the family Plymouth without any provocation on Paul's part. Since Paul didn't want to turn his nose up at their father's generosity, he took the keys, revved up that old Plymouth's engine . . . then puttered at five miles an hour down their street while his parents, waving from the foot of the driveway, watched him go.

He could have been driving a tractor, for all the speed he put behind it. What he couldn't bring himself to admit to his father as his old man had held those shiny brass keys out toward him was that, at sixteen and with a freshly minted license tucked away in his wallet, Paul was terrified at the thought of traveling too far from home. That afternoon, he wound up driving three blocks over to the neighborhood park, where he pulled into a parking space and listened to the radio for forty-five minutes before returning home. It took a good month or so before he was comfortable enough to get out on the highway.

In typical Danny Gallo fashion, Paul's younger brother failed his driver's test enough times that the

DMV made him wait several months before he could take it again. However, that didn't stop him from stealing the Plymouth and driving it into Baltimore one weekend with a carload of his friends. Later that evening, Danny had sauntered back into the house and into the whirlwind of fury that was their father's wrath, unaffected and disinterested and maybe even a little high. Throughout the entirety of their father's ranting and raving, Danny's expression remained deadpan.

Days later, when their father had had time to cool down, the old man suggested that if Danny needed a ride somewhere, he should just ask *Paul* to drive him. This conversation was held at the dinner table, and at the moment of their father's suggestion, Danny's eyes shifted in Paul's direction. Paul glanced up and met his brother's stare. Danny did not look angry; in fact, it looked like he was struggling not to burst out into delirious fits of laughter.

"I'm sure Paul will take you wherever you want to go," their father said. "Isn't that right, Paul?"

"Uh, sure," Paul said.

Under his breath, Danny said, "I guess we could sit in some parking lot, listening to the radio together, huh?"

"What'd you say?" their father said, confused by Danny's barely audible comment, and no doubt wondering whether some punishment was required. "What was that, buddy?"

Danny just rolled his shoulders and said, "Nothing. Never mind. I was just goofing." Yet his eyes clung to Paul's, that smile—or was it a smirk?—still threatening to break out across his face.

As for their father's hope that Danny might secure even a partial athletic scholarship to college, that never happened. Danny attended three semesters of community college before dropping out. Annoyed by their father's constant badgering, Danny moved into an apartment with some friends—and in doing so, inadvertently embarked on the first step of a journey that would lead him through a lifetime of inconsequence and mediocrity, moving from one shitty apartment to the next, from one lousy relationship to another, and from one crappy, underpaid job to yet another. It was a never-ending cycle that Danny not only seemed powerless to break, but also seemed ignorant of the fact that he was actually stuck in it.

"You're going to have to look out for him after we're gone, Paul," their father used to tell him. He said this with enough regularity that Paul grew immune to it, never fully comprehending the sheer magnitude of what he was saying. "Your brother's a screwup who walks around with his head up his can. You're going to have to look out for him after we're gone."

When their parents died in a small plane crash some years later, they left Paul and Danny the house and whatever meager savings they'd managed to salt away in the bank account over the years. Paul sold the house, and after the bank took their cut, he split what remained with his brother—who hadn't even bothered to attend the funeral—in accordance with their parents' wishes. It came to just over a hundred thousand dollars each. Paul took his share and invested it. Danny quit whatever menial job he'd been bumbling through at the time and used his share of the money to travel.

He basked in the sunshine on Catalina Island off the coast of California, spent a few weeks in the Virgin Islands, and wasted a month in the Pacific Northwest, where, according to a series of postcards he'd sent Paul, he spent his time gazing at the night sky for UFOs or searching for Bigfoot.

The brothers were mostly estranged by this point, having maintained minimal contact over the years, and Paul assumed the sending of those postcards was Danny's way of maintaining contact without actually having to talk to him. Paul was fine with it. It seemed that every time they spoke, Danny would ask him for money. When Danny got hemmed up with the police and was facing some trumped-up possession charges, he called and asked if Paul could lend him the money for a proper attorney instead of going with a public defender. Paul would ask him what he'd done with his share of the inheritance, to which Danny provided no suitable answer. "It's just a loan," Danny insisted. "It won't ruin you." But it was never just a loan with Danny, and Paul told him so. He refused to lend his brother the money.

Things went downhill from there.

Danny spent eleven months in a state prison. In all that time, Paul received just one piece of correspondence from his brother. It was written in Danny's unique, elongated handwriting and printed on the title page torn from a John D. MacDonald paperback. The note said, somewhat enigmatically:

Up is down, down is up.
Bigfoot is searching for me now.

Paul considered writing back to him, but in the end, he didn't.

Then, one evening, Paul arrived home from work to find a strange man seated on the steps leading to his front door. Even when the man stood and Paul got a good look at him, he wasn't sure it was Danny until he spoke.

"I know this is an inconvenience," he said, "but I've got nowhere else to go."

Danny stayed with him for three months until he could get back on his feet. During that time, Danny called in a favor of some old acquaintance of his and was offered a job as a roofer. He took it. He would leave the house in the morning and spend the whole day building and repairing roofs. And although he returned home in the evenings visibly exhausted and lathered in roofing tar, there was a part of Paul Gallo that couldn't help but recall that afternoon, so many years ago, when he'd caught Danny lounging on the hood of his friend's car in the parking lot of Taco Bell, smoking a cigarette and planning a beach trip while the rest of their family thought he was ringing up customers at Caldor.

He was surprised to find that he had mixed emotions when Danny found an apartment in Baltimore and moved out. They had bonded again in the brief time Danny had lived with him, and that was good. But also, Paul was hearing his father's voice on a regular basis now, whispering that old mantra into his ear—*You're going to have to look out for him after we're gone, Paul*—so he made it a point to meet with Danny every other week for dinner in the city. Most times, they paid for their own meals, but on a few occasions Danny insisted on paying, and so Paul let him. This little dining ritual lasted for about six months, until one night, halfway through a platter of kitfo and flat bread, Danny set his beer down and said, "I'm going away for a while."

Paul's first thought was that Danny had done something stupid and gotten jammed up with the police again. "Jesus Christ, Danny. Jail?"

Danny laughed. "No, man. That's not what I mean. I quit the roofing gig and I'm rolling up my carpet. I'm tired of this city. I'm tired of Maryland. You've been living in the same thirty-mile radius your whole life, Paul, and I don't know how you do it. It's making me crazy."

"You quit your job?"

Danny dismissed the question with a wave of his hand. "I quit last month. I was gonna tell you sooner. I was spent, man. You feel me?"

"It's a job. Everybody's spent."

"Yeah, well, this ain't for me. I can't keep doing this, you know what I mean? I feel like I'm running around in circles and never getting anywhere." Danny leaned forward so that his shadow fell across the table. He had dark beard stubble covering his chin and the stirrings of a mustache. "Last night I had a dream, Paul. Same dream I've been having for months now. It's me, and I'm standing out in this open field, and everywhere I look, every direction, is freedom. Like, I can run anywhere I want and be free. But when I try—when I go to lift my foot—I can't. My foot is stuck to the ground. And the ground, it's sucking me down, eating me up like quicksand. And I'm sweating and screaming and I try to pull my feet out, but I can't. I just can't. And then

I look down, and I see why—it isn't quicksand at all, but a hand, a rotting hand, coming straight out of the ground, its fingers around my ankle. And even though I don't see the thing's face, I know it's me down there, buried under the ground. It's me down there, and I'm pulling myself down into my own grave."

"It's just a dream," Paul assured him.

"Well, yes and no," Danny said, leaning back again in his chair. "I mean, yeah, it's a dream, but it's also symbolic of the way I feel. You're an English professor, so I know you can dig the symbolism, Paul. It's my subconscious telling me to get out before it's too late."

"Too late for what?"

Danny shrugged. "I have no idea," he said.

"So where are you gonna go?"

"I'm going to Alaska," he said.

"Alaska?" Paul set his own beer down. "What's in Alaska?"

"Nothing, Paul. That's the point. Don't you get it? Or . . . I don't know . . . maybe it's me. Maybe *I'm* in Alaska. Hopefully." Danny chuckled and leaned even farther back in his chair so that the front legs lifted off the floor; it was all Paul could do not to reach over and snatch his brother's arm before he toppled over. Danny ran his hands through his hair, and it reminded Paul of Danny as a child, this simple gesture summoning memories of the summer nights spent gazing up at the stars in their backyard. "I'm going to find myself, Paul. I know that must sound like a bunch of feel-good bullshit to you, but I'm serious. I'm thirty-five years old and I don't know what the fuck I'm supposed to do with my life."

"You're not going to find yourself if you just pick up and leave every time you're faced with responsibility."

"Christ, you sound like Dad."

"And you sound like you're running from something, not trying to find it."

Danny shrugged again, and picked up his beer. "Maybe sometimes they're one and the same, big brother." He took a swig of his beer.

"How long will you be gone?" Paul asked.

"Not sure. A few months, at least. Maybe as long as a year . . ."

"A *year*?" he said.

"No one just picks up and goes to Alaska for a three-day weekend, Paul. Besides, I really want to invest myself in this, and get down into it, you know? Do some real soul-searching."

Danny was right—it *did* sound like feel-good bullshit. But he wouldn't tell Danny that. "And this isn't something I can talk you out of?" he said instead.

"I've already bought the plane ticket. I leave on Tuesday."

Paul sighed. Danny was grinning at him and Paul wanted to join him, but there was a subtle ache that had come alive in the pit of his stomach. "It's not like Catalina Island, you know," he said.

"Come on, Paul. Can't you just have my back for once?"

You're going to have to look out for him after we're gone, his father whispered into his ear.

"All right," he said. "I support you. I hope it's great. I hope you meet an Eskimo, buy a nice igloo, and settle down."

"Oh, boy . . ."

"Seriously. I hope you find what you're looking for out there."

Danny's grin was much more handsome than his own, Paul thought.

"Thanks, bro," Danny said.

"Just promise me you'll keep in touch," he said. After all this time, they were finally in a good place with each other, and Paul guessed he wasn't ready to give that up. Besides, the ghost-voice of his father was already making him feel guilty.

Danny held up three fingers, though unlike Paul, he'd never been a Boy Scout. "I promise," he said. "I'll send you postcards every week."

And he did, in fact. He called on occasion, too, and texted pictures of himself at various landmarks throughout America's Last Frontier. At one point, Paul remembered thinking that maybe he had been wrong, and that this hadn't been such a bad thing for Danny after all. That maybe his younger brother had been right. That he might be "finding himself" out there.

But then sometime during that summer, the phone calls stopped. The text messages and phone pictures stopped, too. The postcards no longer showed up in Paul's mailbox. At first, Paul thought nothing of it. After all, this was Danny Gallo, right? But after several weeks of no contact with his brother—weeks during which he suffered from a bout of soul-crushing insomnia—Paul became certain it wasn't just another one of Danny's flaky episodes. He knew something wasn't right, something wasn't in its place. Something was out of orbit.

He made repeated calls to Danny's cell phone, but each one went to voice mail without ringing. Sometime later, Danny's cell phone service was disconnected altogether. He contacted Danny's cell phone provider and pretended he was his brother. They informed him that the cell service had been discontinued because he had failed to pay his bill for several months.

"If you'd like to work out a payment plan, Mr. Gallo, I can assure you this won't go into collect—"

Paul hung up.

Sometime after that, Luther Parnell put him in touch with a police detective named Richard Ridgley over in Baltimore PD's Homicide Division, and Ridge was able to get his hands on Danny's most recent credit card statements. Paul discovered that, much like Danny's cell phone bill, his brother had an outstanding balance unpaid on his credit card. The last purchase had been made at a gas station located along a stretch of highway just south of an old Alaskan mining town with the ominous name of Dread's Hand. This purchase was made on the same day Paul had received the first of the last two messages he'd received from Danny: Entering Dread's Hand—Spooky!

At Ridge's suggestion, Paul contacted the Alaska Bureau of Investigation and was put in touch with an investigator named Jill Ryerson with ABI's Major Crimes Unit. She walked him through the process of filling out a missing persons report. She also located Danny's rental car, abandoned on the shoulder of a dirt road somewhere on the outskirts of Dread's Hand. Its tires were flat, and it looked as though it hadn't been used in quite a while, Ryerson said. Paul asked whether there were any signs of a struggle in or around his brother's vehicle, and Ryerson assured him that there weren't.

"So where does that leave us?" he asked.

"I'm afraid I don't have a suitable response to that, Mr. Gallo," she said.

After that, Paul Gallo did the only thing there was left for him to do: He waited.

And waited.

And waited.

After a time, something curdled and died inside him. It wasn't just his disheartened spirit, but rather it felt like a physical sensation, like a tiny organ shriveling up and turning hard and black in the center of his gut. *Can you see those boys?* he wondered. Because the image was fading, growing dim, like a bulb burning out in a darkened room. *Can you see those boys? Can you see them?*

The only thing that never stopped and never faded were his father's words, unchanged from all those years ago, yet now tempered with some terrible regret and disappointment: *You're going to have to look out for him after we're gone, Paul.*

Eventually, Paul came to terms with Danny's disappearance. He even considered having a memorial service for him, but since there were no other surviving members of their immediate family and he didn't know any of Danny's friends—did he even *have* friends?—Paul decided against it. Instead, he held his own private ceremony for Danny: One evening, he bought a bottle of Knob Creek—Danny's favorite bourbon—and drank to his brother while an old Van Halen disc played on the stereo. The next morning, Paul dumped the rest of the bourbon down the sink and then hid the empty bottle deep down in the trash.

Danny was gone, and Paul's role in trying to find him was over.

Or so he thought at the time.

5

Jill Ryerson was sitting behind the wheel of her cruiser, the window cracked, the heater pumping hot air from the vents. She was staring past the trees at the run-down structure that was Joseph Mallory's house, a fine rain misting the cruiser's windshield. Hers wasn't the only cop car in the vicinity—in fact, there were quite a few others, as they prepared to execute a search warrant on Mallory's residence—but she preferred to sit in the car and soak up the heat for as long as possible.

Val Drammell has gone radio silent, there's the waitress from the luncheonette leaving me voice mails quoting scripture instead of giving an official statement, and we're short-staffed and working around the clock because half of the department has come down with the flu. Meanwhile, I can't seem to get my core temperature back up into the nineties. What I need is a good vacation. Maybe a cruise somewhere warm.

It was a quarter after three in the afternoon, but it

could have been midnight for all her exhaustion. The rain didn't help any. She closed her eyes and leaned her head against the cool glass of the driver's side window.

She was still thinking about that first body.

After arresting Mallory and dropping him off at the hospital, she had gotten the call from McHale, saying they'd found a body. The news had stunned her; she would have bet the farm that Joseph Mallory was just a local crackpot with a vivid imagination. It was just one more reminder that people were full of surprises.

It was on her drive back out to Dread's Hand that evening that she phoned Captain Ericsson, who subsequently had Mallory transported from Fairbanks Memorial to Anchorage Regional in an effort to keep one step ahead of the media. It was also on this drive that Ryerson realized she didn't much care for the town of Dread's Hand. For one thing, all those wooden crosses flanking the solitary road that led into town made her uneasy. But it wasn't just the crosses—the town itself had a disquieting, claustrophobic vibe about it. She knew nothing about the place except that it had once been an old mining village, and she certainly didn't know any of its residents. As she drove past the old church toward the cusp of forest, she'd noticed a child standing there on the shoulder of the road, a boy or girl no more than eight or nine years old, wearing what she at first assumed was a balaclava over their face. However, as she drove by, she saw that the balaclava was made out of fur and was actually some sort of mask. Ragged eyeholes had been cut into the furry hide. The kid raised a hand and waved as Ryerson drove by. The

sight was so jarring that she'd eased down on the accelerator and sped away.

When she had arrived back on the scene, there was a
backhoe coughing blue diesel exhaust into the air and a
coroner's investigator was scrutinizing the body at the
bottom of a ragged hole in the ground. Two men in dark
blue jumpsuits stood nearby, smoking cigarettes. When
she asked where the sniffer dogs were, McHale had told
her the handlers had to take them back to town because
they kept getting spooked by something in the woods.
A bear, probably, McHale opined.

Ryerson had come up behind the coroner's investigator and peered over his shoulder into the hole in the
earth. She'd seen more than her share of violent crimes
during her time with MCU—enough domestic violence
and rape to last a lifetime, not to mention all variety
of assaults, homicides, suicides, and even a guy who'd
been struck by a train and had his body twisted into
an hourglass—but this thing in the hole was by far the
worst. She assumed this was because it hardly looked
human—more like something that had fallen from
space, crawled into that hole, and died.

Marbled skin like blue cheese, brittle as rice paper,
with hands that looked like the scaled talons of some
predatory bird. Blessedly, the victim was still clothed,
so much of the emaciated, tendon-like flesh stretched
taut across a collection of narrow, jutting bones was
still obscured.

No, not an alien, she had thought then, staring at
that impossible and hideous thing in the hole, *but an
Egyptian mummy. The cold has mummified the flesh.*

"We've got a head here," the coroner's investigator, a middle-aged man with a neat gray beard and wire-rimmed spectacles, had announced. He pointed to what Ryerson thought was a large clod of dirt furred with roots tucked against the flannel-covered left hip bone of the corpse. "Decapitation, though I can't say if this was the cause of death."

"Decapitation. Jesus," Ryerson had said. The stink of exhaust pumping from the backhoe had begun to make her sick.

So far, they'd uncovered six of the eight bodies from that clearing up in the woods.

She was trying not to think about the dead body now, knowing full well she would be revisited by those bird-like talons and the fuzzy clod of dirt in her dreams for many nights to come, much as they had plagued her last night as she'd tried to find sleep. Instead, she needed to focus on the decrepit old house framed in her windshield now, and the search warrant. Mallory hadn't spoken about his home at all, and he refused to acknowledge whether any evidence of his crimes—or any evidence of the victims' identities—might be found there.

Captain Ericsson rapped knuckles against the window, startling her. "You ready, Ryerson?"

"Yes, sir," she said, and climbed out of the car.

Mallory's house was in the middle of the woods near the outskirts of Dread's Hand, a dilapidated structure that looked like a series of large rectangular cargo containers set one beside the other. The windowpanes were filthy and black. There was a front porch constructed out of concrete blocks and a muddy dirt driveway that looked more like a dog track that curled around toward the back of the house. There were a few old car tires nailed to the roof.

"You and McHale made the arrest on this case," Captain Ericsson said. He was a tall man with a thin, serious face and a wide gray mustache. "Is that right?"

"Yes, sir."

"All right. I want you to take the lead on this thing."

"Yes, sir."

"Get up there, Ryerson."

Ryerson hustled up the concrete steps of the front porch and queued up at the front of the line of officers. Bill Johnson stood beside her, already sweating despite the chilly temperatures. He was maybe twenty pounds overweight, with a smooth bulge of belly fat rolling out beneath the hem of his Kevlar vest. He held a ram in his hands.

"You give the word, Jill," he said.

She glanced over her shoulder at the sets of eyes staring back at her. She nodded at them, held up three fingers, then turned back to Bill. She counted down from three, and Bill Johnson drove the ram into the front door. The knob came apart in pieces and the door sprang open. Ryerson rushed into the house, her pistol out, her heart trip-hammering beneath her Kevlar vest.

She was moving so quickly that she didn't smell the place until she was already halfway down the hall—a smell that combined all the worst characteristics of rotting vegetation, unwashed flesh, and dog shit left to cook in the sun. The stink funneled up her nose and seemed to expand, hot and heavy, in her sinuses. The hallway was a narrow shaft with framed pictures on the walls, and the slender beam of her penlight, which she held against the butt of her Glock, washed along the walls like the contrail of a comet.

Two officers came up alongside her, then broke off into the first adjoining room to her right. One of them shouted, "Clear!"

Ryerson kept moving down the hall until she breached the doorway at the end, cutting around the corner, her gun out, arms extended with her elbows locked. The penlight's beam—a vague and inconsequential speck of light in so much vast darkness—dispersed to nothingness. A veil of cobwebs tickled past her face and left ashy tendrils along the front of her vest. It was late in the afternoon and it was raining, but the place shouldn't have been so dark. She could make out the outline of windows at the far end of the room, beyond the humped shapes of furniture, but it seemed like the panes had been covered with something to keep out the daylight.

"Clear!" someone yelled.

"Clear!" someone else yelled.

"All clear!" came a third voice.

"Someone get some lights on," Captain Ericsson said.

Ryerson felt along the wall. She found the light switch, jostled it, but no lights came on. "The lights don't work," she said.

"There's no power," said Mike McHale, coming up beside her. The beam of his flashlight passed along a carpet blackened by dirty boot prints. "Stinks like shit in here."

"Something's wrong with the windows," she told him. The beam of light from her penlight was insufficient to infiltrate the darkness of the room before her.

McHale lifted his flashlight and angled the beam toward one of the windows. Its pane had been painted black.

"Christ almighty," McHale said under his breath.

It wasn't just the black paint covering the window-panes, but the walls themselves, crowded with what looked like graffiti, streaks of brownish red melding to form . . . not words, but symbols, hieroglyphics. Mallory's wood-paneled walls were covered, from floor to ceiling, with these strange sigils, each one as enigmatic as the next.

"That looks like blood," Ryerson said, closing in on one wall. She trained her penlight's beam on one particular symbol that looked very much like an Egyptian glyph of an eye, only this "eye" had a vertical, catlike pupil. "Very old, dried blood."

"Then it's been here for a while," McHale said. He was running his flashlight beam along the carpet of dust on the floor. "This place has been abandoned."

Down the hallway, two state troopers brought in portable halogen lights. A moment later, the front hall was awash in bright, garish light. Shadows tilted, and it looked like the walls and the furniture moved.

Ryerson went to the nearest window. Indeed, it had also been painted over with black paint. There was the barest hint of daylight shining through tiny flecks where the dried paint had been chipped or had flaked away in places. Ryerson reached out and scratched a fingernail along the glass, widening one of the small holes, her penlight clenched between her teeth.

A shape moved on the other side of the glass.

Ryerson jumped back. She went over to where someone had propped open a rusted storm door covered in muddy handprints, and stepped out onto a short concrete staircase. She peered around the side of the house, but with the exception of two troopers guarding the back, no one was moving around the side of the house.

"Thought I saw someone," she explained to the troopers.

The troopers gave her a cursory glance. One of them—it was Alex Winsome, who'd come up from MCU's Anchorage office to partake in all the excitement—shrugged, then turned away from her. The other trooper was a young guy from her own detachment, a kid named Emery Olsen who'd joined up a little over a year ago. Olsen had been one of the troopers she'd dispatched to Dread's Hand last year when looking for that missing person. He and his partner had located the abandoned rental car.

Down among the trees, Olsen glanced back up at her, as if he could sense her thinking about him. For some reason, she thought she caught a look of contempt move across the young trooper's face. Or maybe it was apprehension.

I feel a little sick, like I'm coming down with something, and I also feel cold, she thought, gazing away from Olsen and out toward the deeper part of the woods, where a fine, rain-speckled mist hung like a gauzy curtain between the trees. *I think maybe I'm coming down with the flu, too.*

But she didn't think it was the flu.

She thought maybe it was the house.

Something about the house didn't feel right to her.

* * *

The feeling that something wasn't right was confirmed when they discovered what was in the basement.

"Jill," Captain Ericsson called to her. "I think you should come have a look at this."

At first, no one had suspected that the ramshackle old house even *had* a basement—the earth was too rocky, too hilly, and Mallory's house looked like it had been constructed decades ago by unskilled labor—but then someone noticed what looked like a trapdoor among the floorboards in the hall that led to the back bedrooms. A crowbar was procured from someone's vehicle, and the trapdoor was pried open. The smell that wafted out was terrible—a damp, heavy, cloying stench that was clearly the source of the stink throughout the house—and everyone around the hole in the floor backed away from it.

"We'll need gas masks," McHale said, and Ryerson wasn't sure whether he was joking or not.

She wended through the crowd of men who stood around the trapdoor, peering down into the darkness. Wooden stairs sank down into the earth. "Someone give me their Maglite," she said, holding out her hand. One of the troopers placed the cold metal hilt of his flashlight against her palm.

"I got your back," said McHale, coming up behind her.

"Just make sure I don't fall and break my neck."

It occurred to her as she descended the brief flight of wooden steps that the place could be booby-trapped. She'd heard terrible stories about police officers inadvertently stumbling into a house of horrors, where light switches were rigged to explosives and carpets were thrown over gaping holes in the floorboards. For all she knew, she could be stepping down into an electrified puddle of water the second her boot touched the ground . . .

But the ground was solid dirt.

"Smell's worse down here," she called back to McHale, covering her nose and mouth with one hand. That pungent, reeking scent of decay that had permeated the house upstairs was even more prevalent down here. It made her eyes water.

She cast the flashlight around the room, which wasn't a room at all, but a dirt hollow in the earth beneath the house. Pale white corkscrews of roots spiraled out of the dirt walls and finer roots—some so fine they looked like hair—sprouted in patches all around the place. She glanced up and saw the floorboards of the hallway above her head, so low she needed to remain bent forward, despite the fact that she was just five-foot-three.

"Jesus," she muttered.

It was a packrat's hole, a collection of dirt-streaked items packed against the earthen walls so that the center of the tiny underground room was the only bare space. As she passed the flashlight's beam across the items, she saw an old barn coat streaked with mildew, a pair of leather work boots, some backpacks that were crawling with large black beetles, and various other items.

"Some sort of storage cellar?" McHale suggested, his voice muffled behind his own hand. He was pressing against Ryerson's back, the room was so cramped.

"In a sense," she said, holding the beam of the flashlight on one item in particular—a large, dusty shoulder bag with a dull metal buckle and what looked like a leather strap. "That's a woman's purse," she said.

"Oh. Oh hell, Jill."

"Yeah."

She shifted the flashlight beam off the purse and along the wall of items—more clothing, shoes, a soggy-looking North Face backpack—and stopped when the beam illuminated an old steamer trunk. It was shoved up against a wall of cinder blocks with bloody crosses smeared across it, stamped almost in a straight line, the color black in the Maglite's beam. The trunk looked ancient and padded with dust, the large brass clasps along the front oxidized and green. It looked larger than a traditional steamer trunk, which for some reason troubled her. Large white stones wreathed its base. One of those strange symbols from the walls upstairs—the eye with the vertical pupil, in fact—had been painted on the lid, though she didn't notice this until she approached it and blew a layer of dust from it.

"Do we open it or call in the bomb squad?" McHale asked. Again, she couldn't tell whether he was joking or not.

Jill Ryerson opened it.

"Oh," she groaned, and turned away from the thing inside. She dropped her flashlight and pressed both hands against her nose and mouth.

Mike McHale wasn't as eloquent: He bent forward and retched onto the ground.

6

Over the course of four days, eight bodies were unearthed from unmarked graves in the woods less than two miles outside the town of Dread's Hand, Alaska. The extensive decomposition of the bodies suggested that at least five of them had been buried up there in the woods for a considerable amount of time—several years, according to the medical examiner out of Anchorage. The more recent victims weren't exactly portraits of beauty, but their levels of decomposition weren't as severe . . . although investigators still found it impossible to lift prints from their fingertips. Captain Dean Ericsson of the Fairbanks Major Crimes Unit said his officers were currently going through missing persons files to see if they could narrow down the pool of potential victims, but given that approximately 3,600 people went missing in Alaska every year, narrowing that pool promised to be a laborious and long-winded process.

Paul Gallo read about all of this online. He also

learned a bit more about the suspect, Joseph Mallory. Most of the online articles were accompanied by the same black-and-white photo of Mallory that they'd shown that first night on the news—a snapshot of a simple-looking man with a bad comb-over and the narrow, elongated face of someone not prone to smiling. He wore a flannel hunting jacket and was clean shaven. The photo did not look recent.

There was a brief bio of Mallory in each article, some only a sentence long. He was fifty-eight years old and a lifelong bachelor who'd moved up to Dread's Hand sometime in the mid-eighties. Prior to that, he'd lived in a town called Buffalo Soapstone, where he worked as a fur trapper and fisherman. He continued this career in Dread's Hand, and was known to take the occasional party into the foothills of the White Mountains to hunt sheep.

There were some cursory statements made by people who knew him from his days in Buffalo Soapstone, but, strangely, there were no statements from any of the Dread's Hand residents in any of the articles Paul read. Joseph Mallory had entered a local eatery, where he allegedly ordered hot cocoa and then confessed to killing an untold number of people to all the patrons within earshot . . . yet none of those people had been interviewed by anyone. Then, after his confession, Mallory supposedly wandered down the road and sat on a bench outside the local church to wait for the police. The local village officer arrived—no name was given in any of the articles—and this individual sat with Mallory until Major Crimes could dispatch investigators up from Fairbanks. Paul executed a quick MapQuest search and estimated that it would have taken the MCU investigators at least an hour and a half to make the drive. Yet the village officer, who had sat with Mallory for that entire time, had apparently provided no statement.

Something didn't feel right, so Paul did a little more digging. Or tried to, anyway. But there was very little information about the town of Dread's Hand online at all. It was an old mining town tucked away in the foothills of the White Mountains, ninety or so miles northwest of Fairbanks, and on the outer perimeter of the Arctic Circle. In 1916, the town's mine had collapsed, killing twenty-six men. The old prospectors' cabins still stood on the outskirts of the town, half-sunk into the fault that had been created by the collapse of the mine all those years ago. Paul learned about these from a scant few websites where people had posted about them on message boards. Other than that, it was almost as if Dread's Hand—a remote and sleepy Alaskan village, whose population had remained at around seventy-five souls since the turn of the century—didn't exist.

Over the course of that week, he dialed Investigator Jill Ryerson's desk number three more times. Each time, he was sent straight to voice mail. Each time, he hung up without leaving a message.

What is wrong with me? he wondered.

But he thought he knew.

"It's like I've lost him all over again," he said during a lunch date with Erin Sharma that Saturday. "And if I call up there and get confirmation, well . . . . well, then, that's it, isn't it?"

Erin smiled at him from across the table. She worked

in the English department with him at St. John's, a
studious-looking woman in her early thirties with an attractive smile. They'd dated a while ago, and she'd even
met Danny on a number of occasions. When Danny got
jammed up with the police and he'd asked Paul to lend
him money for an attorney, Erin had taken Danny's side,
unable to comprehend how Paul, who claimed to care
about his brother very much, could be so unsupportive.
Paul had explained that she didn't know Danny, not the
way he did. He might have even recited that pompous
old chestnut about teaching a man to fish. The situation
with Danny wasn't the reason he and Erin didn't work
out as a couple, but he felt it had forever painted him in
a negative light in Erin's eyes. He could never fully explain the situation to her, and so he gave up trying.

"Whether you call up there or not, it won't change
what happened to him," she said. "Instead, you're just
fooling yourself, Paul."

And he was, wasn't he? For the first time, he realized how all-encompassing Danny had become in his
life ever since his disappearance—even more so than
he had been when he'd been in Paul's life. There was
something sad about that.

"But do you know what I find interesting?" she said.
They were seated outside the Book & Bean in downtown Annapolis, enjoying the cool autumn weather
and watching the sailboats glide back and forth across
the bay.

"What's that?" he said.

"That he's always 'lost.' Do you realize that? Every
time you talk about him, he's always just 'lost,' and
even now, despite what you think you believe to be true

because of what some lunatic did to those poor people five thousand miles away, he's still just 'lost.' Can't you hear yourself when you talk?" She smiled. She wore thick, black-framed glasses, her eyes lucid behind the lenses. "Love, I don't think you're afraid of calling up there and finding out your brother is dead. I think you're afraid of calling up there and finding yourself back at square one, not knowing what happened to him. The same place you've been since he's gone. You've got no closure and it's changed you."

"It's changed me? How?"

She stabbed at a cucumber on her salad plate. "Little things, mostly. But there's a part of you that's different now, ever since Danny went away."

"Of course there is," he said.

"You misunderstand," she said. "Not different since he *disappeared*, but since he *went away*. Ever since he went to Alaska, I mean. Even before he disappeared. It's like some small part of you went away, too. Went away with Danny."

"So, where's this part of me now?"

"Wherever Danny is," Erin responded.

For some strange reason, this made him think of those weeks last summer, and the insufferable insomnia that had kept him up till all hours of the night, often seated with his back against the headboard of his bed, watching the sky change color as the sun rose far beyond his bedroom windows. Several times he'd nearly gotten into a car accident on his way either to or from work, his exhaustion was so great. And somewhere around day four or five—a time span during which he'd only gotten perhaps ten solid hours of restfulness—he'd hallucinated that his bedroom was a dark crypt in the middle of the earth, and that the windowpanes were covered with dirt, and that his bedroom carpet was alive and wriggling with worms. When he couldn't take it anymore, he'd gone to his doctor, who'd prescribed him sleeping pills. But the pills had only made him drowsy during the day, while he stood before a classroom of college students attempting to lecture. At night, those pills could have been jelly beans, for all their effect on him.

"He's always been a terrible brother, you know," he said, smiling but not really smiling. "He didn't mean to be. He was just always getting in trouble. Getting *me* in trouble, too." He rolled up the sleeve on his left arm and showed her the semicircular pattern of tiny divots in the flesh. "See that?"

"I remember," said Erin. "You said it was a dog bite. Now you're saying it was Danny?"

Paul laughed. "No, no—it wasn't Danny. But it was Danny's fault. He broke into an old abandoned house in our neighborhood when we were eleven years old. Somehow he convinced me to follow him. We went down into the basement and there was a dog down there. Some stray. Scared the shit out of us." Paul shrugged his shoulders as he rolled his sleeve back down. "Danny ran and I got bit. Had to get rabies shots just to be sure."

"I'll call the waiter if you start foaming at the mouth," Erin said.

"We'd always had this really weird bond when we were kids," he said. "You know I don't believe in stuff like that, but Danny and I, we were close when we were young. Sometimes it even seemed like we *knew* things about each other. Of course, now that I'm older, I can kind of put that sort of thing in perspective—I realize it had less to do with any supernatural bond between us and more to do with plain old intuition and, frankly, just playing the odds—but back then, when we were young . . . I don't know. It's like we both lived in the same head at times."

"Well, you know I'm not a believer in crystals and dream catchers and that sort of thing, either," Erin said, "but I *do* believe we carry pieces of other people around inside us. Particularly when those people are closely related to us. It's in our blood, or maybe it all comes down to genetics or whatever—some leftover instinct from when we all used to live in caves and club each other over the head with big sticks—but I believe it exists. And you guys are *twins,* for Christ's sake! You hear stories all the time about twins who . . . I don't know . . . who can feel each other's pain, or tell when the other person is hungry or scared or sick or whatever. Like, 'When the phone rang, I knew it was about my sister, two thousand miles away in Poughkeepsie, and that she'd fallen down the stairs.' That sort of thing."

"It was never like that," he said.

"Then what was it like?"

It was like a great pulsing umbilicus, he thought, the notion of it flashing across his mind for just a millisecond, like glimpsing a neon sign through the window of a speeding train. *It was like some tether uniting us, combining us to make us whole. Two halves brought together.* Instead, he said, "A gut feeling, really. The mother of all gut feelings." He pushed his thumb against his abdomen, midway between his solar plexus and his navel. "Right here."

"That's the Manipura," said Erin. "The third primary chakra."

"I thought you didn't believe in crystals and dream catchers."

"Hinduism is not crystals and dream catchers. It's not hocus-pocus."

He raised both hands in mock surrender.

"The Manipura is associated with fire," Erin said, "and also with the transformation of the body and spirit. If you learn to meditate on Manipura, you may attain the power to save or destroy the world."

"In that case, I feel like I haven't lived up to my full potential."

"You joke, but the chakras exist."

"How does it help me find Danny?"

"Ah," Erin said, smiling her rarely seen sly smile. "Find him. Because he's lost."

"You're an enigma," Paul said.

"Let's have drinks," Erin said.

Later, he would tell himself that it was the discussion with Erin Sharma that convinced him to make the call, but that wasn't the truth. It was just easier to swallow, and so he swallowed it. In truth, Paul made the call because of what happened two days later, on the following Monday, during a classroom discussion of Henry James's short story "The Jolly Corner."

"When Spencer Brydon returns to the Jolly Corner and runs into his alternate self, what is James trying to say?"

A girl in the front of the classroom whose name suddenly eluded him spoke up: "James is alluding to the 'unlived life.' Brydon's alter ego haunts the Jolly Corner, his childhood home, to show Brydon what might have become of him had he stayed in America and actually done something with his life."

"So, what do you guys think?" Paul asked. There was a distant, insect-like buzzing in the back of his head now, but he was trying to ignore it. "At the end of the story, has Spencer Brydon learned anything from the ghost of his alter ego? Will he change his life because of the experience, or will he go on being a lavish, self-centered . . . uh . . ." His thoughts became jumbled.

"They're doppelgangers," someone said. Paul could hear the voice but could not identify the speaker. "It's good versus evil. Only the reader is confused as to who is the good Brydon and who is the evil one. Brydon's alter ego ultimately overpowers him with what, in the text, is described as a 'rage of personality,' but what that really means is that Brydon is weak-willed while his alter ego—his doppelganger—has matured and succeeded, despite having not existed in the real world at all."

But Paul had stopped listening. He glanced back down at the book in his hands, a slim paperback edition of Henry James's *The Jolly Corner and Other Tales*. He blinked and brought it closer to his face. The text was visible, but the words were a jumble of nonsense. He couldn't read them. He couldn't comprehend what they meant. He felt his hand close on a piece of chalk, which felt suddenly very heavy in his palm, and as cold as a chunk of ice.

One of the female students in the first row said, "Mr. Gallo?" But her voice sounded like a record album played on slow speed, her tone deep, drawn out, discordantly masculine.

Paul dropped the book and stared at the class. He continued to squeeze the piece of chalk. At the back of the room, Rena Tremaine, his teaching assistant, glanced up from her desk, her glasses perched at the tip of her nose, a book open in front of her. Her mouth moved and she said something, but her voice was obscured by the sonic boom of his own heartbeat, steady as a bass drum in his ears—*thunk, thunk, thunk, thunk*. A fuzzy gray border framing the periphery of his vision grew thicker and thicker, until it seemed like he was gazing at the class through a pair of cartoon binoculars. The border continued to expand until all that was left of his vision were two pinpricks of dull white light. And then nothing at all.

He blinked, and found himself staring up at a gunmetal sky mottled with scudding, ash-colored clouds. A cold wind chilled his body. He was splayed out on the ground, lying immobile on his back, respiration whistling up the narrow stovepipe of his throat. When he tried to sit up, he found that he couldn't. When he tried to move at all, he found himself powerless to do so.

He sensed rather than saw a figure moving somewhere beyond the periphery of his vision—a vague and indistinct presence that nonetheless chilled him to the core. He tried to open his mouth and speak, but he was unable to do that, either.

A hand slid in front of his field of vision, blotting out the gunmetal sky and those dark clouds. He realized it was his own hand, although he had not moved it, had not brought it up in front of his face.

His palm and fingers were covered in blood.

He awoke splayed out on the floor of his classroom, a blurry and unfamiliar face staring down at him. The face's mouth moved, but no words came out. There was a warm hand against the side of his face. His entire body felt encased in a film of cold sweat.

The face above his took on the features of Rena Tremaine, and her voice filtered down to him, rising up through the octaves until it approached its normal pitch.

"Mr. Gallo? Mr. Gallo?" Her voice softened then, although the concern never left Rena's face. "There you are."

He struggled to sit up. His head throbbed.

"Maybe you should just stay put for a minute," Rena said.

"What happened?"

"You passed out."

"Where—" He managed to turn his head and found his students staring back at him, their eyes wide, a few mouths unhinged.

"Should I call an ambulance?" one of the students asked.

"Yes," said Rena.

"No," Paul said. "No, I'm okay." This time, he managed to prop himself up to a sitting position. He leaned his back against the wall, his arms buttressed on his knees. For some reason, he felt the urge to look at his right hand. He turned the hand over, and everything looked fine, except that it was powdered in chalk. Beside him on the dark green linoleum floor was a circle traced over and over again in chalk—seemingly fitfully, as if done by an angry child—with a harsh slash running through its center.

"You did that," Rena said, sounding ill.

The vision swam back to him, grainy as an old filmstrip—lying on his back, staring at the sky, the sense that someone was there with him, his right hand sliding into his field of vision coated with blood.

"At least go to the health center," Rena said.

"Yeah, okay," he said. "Can you handle the class?"

"Yes. Can *you* handle walking? I can send someone with you."

"I can manage."

"If you fall again on your way—"

"Then I'm the lucky fool who gets to claim workers' compensation."

Rena smiled down at him, though the concern was still etched across her face. She turned back to the class and said, "Okay, gang. Show's over."

The class applauded when he stood up.

That night, he called Ryerson's desk number with every intention of leaving a voice mail. He could still see that unsmiling, black-and-white visage of Joseph Mallory in his mind's eye, resonating like the afterimage of a flashbulb. The grease-parted hair and the checked flannel hunting jacket. Mallory. Mallory. And whenever he closed his eyes, he saw that bloodied hand, which he now believed was Danny's hand. However improbable that was.

Ryerson answered.

"Investigator Ryerson, this is Paul Gallo. We spoke about a year ago regarding the disappearance of my brother, Danny Gallo. You located his rental car near a town called Dread's Hand. Investigator Ryerson, I've been reading the news about what's happened out there, and I thought maybe . . . well, I thought maybe I should call."

"Of course. Yes, I remember our conversation."

"The media's been reporting that none of the victims have been identified yet."

"That's correct."

"So, how do we do this?" he asked. "Do you need me to view the bodies to make an ID? Or is it a matter of just, I guess, checking their fingerprints through some database? Danny has a criminal record."

"Well, Mr. Gallo, I'm afraid it's not that simple. Given the condition that the bodies are in, I mean . . ."

"Oh," he said.

"What we're doing now is comparing certain characteristics of the victims to any missing persons reports that have been filed in the past five years. We're also asking anyone who suspects they might be related to any of the victims to come in to the station and give a DNA sample. Given your situation, I'd recommend doing that. It's possible to do it through your local police department, though we've been expediting the results out here. I can't speak for how quick the turnaround time would be somewhere else."

"Okay," he said.

"We've also had some people come in and examine articles of clothing and some items that were seized from the suspect's residence during a search warrant. I can't send you photos of any of the items—they're proprietary—but for someone who was out here who could come—"

"Then I'll come out there," he said.

7

Jill Ryerson was outside smoking a cigarette when the unmarked car arrived. It was around 10 P.M. and the temperature had dropped considerably—it was cold enough so that Ryerson couldn't distinguish between her regular respiration and the cigarette smoke.

The electronic thermometer that hung by the side door where Ryerson stood smoking had frozen and stopped working last winter, but Ryerson knew it was somewhere in the low thirties. Snowflakes, like little filaments of pillow stuffing, floated about the atmosphere without ever touching the ground. But she was used to it.

She was born in Kennewick, Washington, but her family had relocated to Ketchikan, Alaska, when she was five years old. Hers was a large family—she was the youngest of five children—and her father, who'd worked for a logging company, found himself relocating every few years in order to get promoted and keep ahead of creditors. She'd spent her formative years in Southeast

Alaska, hiking along the banks of Lake Mahoney with her sisters, where they would often take a boat out into the center of the glacial lake, the water so clear you could see straight through to the bottom. It was a nice place to live, except during spawning season: Once the salmon had finished their run, the creeks would fill up with their flyblown corpses and the air would turn rank. Ryerson would tie a wet handkerchief around her nose and mouth and go down to the river and poke the dead fish with sticks, fascinated by the lifelessness of them. For her eighth-grade survival trip, she and her classmates were ferried out to a series of uninhabited islands by the Coast Guard and left there for three days with only a sleeping bag, a roll of Visqueen, and a coffee can filled with whatever sundry articles you saw fit to take along with you (the smart kids took matches and dried soups). Ryerson learned to build a fire and boil water to kill the parasites, lest she'd suffer from what some of her classmates called "beaver fever." While most of her classmates had found the experience to be hellish, Ryerson enjoyed it. (Her only mistake was keeping her soap in the same container in which she cooked her soup—to this day, she couldn't stomach the smell of Dial soap.) It was during this trip that thirteen-year-old Jill Ryerson became interested not only in the art of survival, but in the concept of helping *others* survive. She showed her classmates how to erect a tent of Visqueen over a tree branch and how to wrap their dry matches in a sock at night so the dampness wouldn't blunt the match heads. This interest would later bloom into a full-blooded passion that would see her through the completion of the fifteen-week DPS academy in

Sitka once she turned twenty-one. She'd only been in Fairbanks for the past three years; much like her father, who'd chased promotions for his entire career, she'd taken the transfer in order to get into Major Crimes.

But it was damn cold. Ryerson shivered inside her fur-lined parka as the unmarked vehicle rolled around the curved strip of blacktop toward the sally port. It was dark and the sedan's windows were tinted, but she didn't have to see inside to know who was being transported in the backseat.

Ryerson pitched the cigarette butt over the rail and went back inside.

Trooper Lucas Bristol was standing behind his desk in the lobby, peering down the narrow hallway that led to the sally port. He glanced at Ryerson as she came in, his baby face a mottled red from the cold. He was twenty-two years old, but in that single glance, he looked all of fifteen.

"It's McHale and Swinton back from Anchorage," she informed the younger trooper.

"With the guy?"

"Yeah. With the guy," she said. She knew he meant Mallory.

"I thought they were keeping him in Anchorage."

"Captain changed his mind." This wasn't exactly the truth: It had been Captain Dean Ericsson's plan to house Mallory at Fairbanks all along, Ryerson knew. Transferring Mallory to Anchorage Regional Hospital after his arrest from the much closer Fairbanks Memorial was a calculated misdirection on Ericsson's part. The media had incorrectly assumed Mallory would be held at the Anchorage facility following his release from the hospital instead of being transported the 350-plus miles back to Fairbanks.

"Oh," Bristol said, and Ryerson thought he looked somewhat disappointed to hear this, although she didn't know why he should. When the sally port door opened, the young trooper glanced down at his desk, where a pack of playing cards were laid out in mid-solitaire.

He doesn't look disappointed, she thought then, watching Bristol. *If I didn't know better, I'd say he looks frightened*.

Troopers McHale and Swinton came in, their faces red from the cold, ushering between them the hunched, ambling form of Joseph Mallory. Had it not been for the renovations at the far end of the detention block, they could have led Mallory straight from the sally port and into the cell block without having to cross this section of the station. Had the renovations been completed on schedule—weeks earlier, in other words—then Lucas Bristol would never have had to see McHale and Swinton leading Joseph Mallory to his holding cell.

"Starting to snow out there," McHale commented to no one in particular.

"Won't stick," Swinton responded, and Ryerson got the impression that this had been debated on much of the drive up from Anchorage.

She watched them lead Mallory across the lobby toward the large steel door that led to Puke Alley, which was what the guys called the corridor of holding cells. Mallory had one of the trooper's spare parkas draped over his shoulders, a thing that looked too heavy for the emaciated man to carry. As they went by, Mallory's head swiveled in Ryerson's direction, that curtain of long, unwashed hair swinging in front of Mallory's eyes, the top of Mallory's bald head reflecting the fluorescent ceiling fixtures. Mallory's beard looked like a tangle of dried weeds.

She looked back at Bristol, who was staring at McHale and Swinton as they ushered Mallory down Puke Alley. He continued to stare even after the steel door swung shut.

"You okay, Bristol?" she asked.

"Huh?" He jerked his gaze in her direction. "What's that?"

"Never mind. Is there any coffee?"

"Oh, uh . . . yeah. There's half a pot."

"Wonderful. Where's Johnson?"

"McDonald's run."

She nodded toward the closed steel door of Puke Alley. "They're transporting him to Spring Creek in Seward as soon as there's a bed," she said, hoping this bit of information might give Bristol some peace of mind. "Won't be long before he's their problem."

Bristol nodded but didn't say anything.

Ryerson slipped into the kitchen nook and dug a clean mug out of the cupboard. It read STUPIDITY IS NOT A CRIME, SO YOU ARE FREE TO GO on the side. She filled it with coffee that she nuked in the microwave until it was practically boiling. Her whole body felt cold, right down to her toes. Half of her coworkers were out sick, and she worried that she might be the next one in line for the flu.

I just need some sleep, that's all. A good night's sleep. Been going a hundred and ten miles an hour for the past few days, and that's not good for anyone.

As she sipped her coffee, an image of that . . . thing . . . in the steamer trunk in Mallory's cellar popped into her head. She and McHale had gotten out of there pretty quick, but not before the stink of it had crawled into her nostrils and seated itself in the center of her skull. She'd gone home that night and took a steaming shower for forty minutes, as if that could wash the memory of the stink away.

Hungry for company, she went back out into the lobby. Bristol slouched behind the duty desk, hammering a single key on the computer keyboard.

"Those bodies that were recovered up there in the hills," Bristol said, not looking up from the computer screen. "Is it true? About the heads being cut off?"

"Yes," Ryerson said. "It's not something I'll forget anytime soon."

"Postmortem or . . . ?"

"Well, we won't know about that until we hear back from the ME in Anchorage."

"Jesus. Who does something like that?"

Ryerson didn't respond. She slurped her coffee, leaned back against the wall, and tried not to think of that terrible thing in the trunk. CSI had packed the whole trunk in biohazard bags and carried it away like it was a nuclear bomb.

"Do you know anything about that place?" Bristol asked.

"What place is that?" Her mind had drawn a blank.

"Dread's Hand."

"Not really. It's just an old mining village. There are half a dozen of them out that way." But she was picturing those wooden crosses staked into the earth as she drove into town, and that peculiar child who stood on the side of the road in that fur mask, waving at her as she drove by.

"My mom's people are from Nenana," Bristol said, looking up from the laptop. "I've got uncles and cousins who used to go hunting and fishing up that way—'going up the Hand,' they called it. I had an aunt who used to tell us ghost stories about the woods out there. She used to say that the woods were haunted, and that the town itself was a bad place. She said there were bad places on earth—dark spots, like bruises—and that Dread's Hand was one of them."

"No kidding." She stared down at her reflection simmering on the surface of her coffee.

"Said there were devils up there," Bristol said. "Noonday devils, she called them. But Uncle Otto said it was the Bonewalker. 'That thing'll touch you and turn you mad,' he'd say."

"Fun guy," said Ryerson.

"I had a great-uncle who'd gone out there hunting and wound up killing himself," Bristol said.

Ryerson looked up at him. "Yeah?" she said.

"Suicide. He ate the barrel of his Remington."

"Well, shit."

"It was a long time ago. My ma's people still claim it was some bizarre hunting accident, but I don't know how you accidentally put the barrel of your rifle in your mouth, then manage to squeeze the trigger."

"Good point," Ryerson said, nodding. Suicides this far north were nothing out of the ordinary, but she could see the kid was disturbed by even the retelling of it. *He's a nice kid, but as wriggly as an ice worm,* she thought.

"My grandmother claimed it was the devil that took him," Bristol said. "That's probably where my aunt got all that devil talk. 'The devil got ahold of him, poor soul,' my grandma would say, though she didn't talk about it often. I just remember her saying it, you know? 'The devil got ahold of him.' Like it was something real, something out there in the woods with claws." He offered Ryerson a shy grin. "I guess maybe that sounds silly," he added.

"No sillier than any other superstition," she said. She pulled her car keys from her pocket and held them up so that Bristol could see the lucky rabbit's foot dangling from the key chain.

Bristol grinned, and Ryerson felt that maybe she'd helped put the kid's mind at ease, if just a little bit. Wriggly as an ice worm was an understatement.

And yet . . .

Like it was something real, something out there in the woods with claws.

Which made her think about what Mallory had said as he stood up there on that clearing in the woods the day of his arrest, his eyes closed, his face turned toward the sky—*Let's get back to town before it gets grabby again.*

She sipped her coffee and tried not to think about it.

When McHale and Swinton came back from Puke Alley, Ryerson told them to go get something to eat. Meanwhile, Bill Johnson had returned with a paper sack filled with Big Macs and McNuggets, and for the first time all evening, Ryerson saw Lucas Bristol's eyes light up.

Ryerson set her coffee mug down on Bristol's desk, then went over to the steel door. There was a small porthole window in the upper portion of the door, bulletproof and reinforced with steel wires, but it offered very little view of what was going on in Puke Alley. Ryerson selected a key on her key ring and unlocked the door.

"You want company?" Bill Johnson called over to her as he lined up burgers along the edge of Lucas Bristol's desk.

"No, thanks," she said. "I'm good. Enjoy the grub."

Other than Mallory, the holding cells were empty. There had been a few drunks and a robbery suspect in here earlier, but they had cleared them out and transported them to another wing in anticipation of Joseph Mallory's return from the hospital in Anchorage.

Mallory was sitting on the bench in his cell, his back against the cinder-block wall. Either Swinton or McHale had removed the down parka from the man's shoulders, but that was okay; it was a stifling eighty degrees in there, enough to make Ryerson break out in a sweat despite the column of cold she still felt at the center of her body.

"Can I get you anything?" she asked the man on the other side of the bars.

"No, ma'am," said Mallory. His voice was rough and abraded. He'd been dehydrated when she'd transported him to the hospital the afternoon of his arrest, and he'd had several toes removed from his left foot due to frostbite—his foot was now wrapped in a heavy gauze bandage—but he was okay. Not, of course, that Joseph Mallory *looked* okay: The skin of his face was still bright red and peeling in places, and there were dark pustules and scabs around his mouth, beneath his eyes, and around his ears. The shiny dome of his head was wind-chapped, and large blisters stood out like craters on the surface of the moon.

"Tomorrow you'll be brought before a judge to enter your plea. Has all this been explained to you?" She knew that a public defender had visited Mallory at the hospital, but she also knew that Mallory, who had already expressed his disdain for lawyers on more than one occasion since his arrest, had dummied up and not uttered a single word to the guy.

"Yes, ma'am," Mallory said. "Though I don't need no lawyer standing there getting paid while I admit to my guilt, ma'am."

"The judge will ask you why you killed those people."

"Well, now, I won't discuss that with no judge," he said. His hands were clasped together in his lap. Except for the single standardized rubber sandal he wore on his one good foot, a serial number stamped across the sole, he was still wearing his own clothes. They stank to high heaven, and even in the gloom of Puke Alley, Ryerson could see the rust-colored streaks of dried blood hardened into the fibers of the linen pants, the thermal undershirt, caked along the frayed cuffs of his sleeves. She had no doubt that they'd be able to pull a serious amount of DNA out of Mallory's lumberjack beard and greasy hair, too, if they so desired. She'd heard that some nurses had sponged him down at the hospital, and that he'd howled like a hound who'd just treed a 'coon. She'd also heard that patches of his clothes had grafted to open sores along his torso and thighs.

"How about explaining it to me?" she asked. "Who were they? The victims."

"Just some folk," Mallory said. It sounded offhand, cursory, yet not quite insolent.

"How'd you meet them?"

"That don't matter no more," he said. "Just so long as we get them to consecrated ground. It's the least that can be done for 'em now."

"It's good of you to want to see them get a proper Christian burial," she said. "But we're going to have a difficult time identifying them."

"They don't need to be identified. Just sanctified."

She frowned. "What does that mean?"

"It means their souls won't be at rest until they're properly buried. I did the best I could up there, but it ain't enough. Not to ward off eternal damnation for their souls. It's what's been weighing on me all this time."

"Is that why you confessed?"

Mallory leaned closer to the bars of his cell. "The devil's pull is a strong one, ma'am. But I just couldn't do it no more."

"We found that room beneath your house. All those items down there—the jackets and backpacks and everything. They belong to the victims, don't they?"

"Yes, ma'am."

"We've got Forensics examining those items right

now. We'll start piecing things together and learning who these people are—were—but it would go a long way with the judge if you'd just tell us."

"Ain't nothing to tell," he said. "Don't rightly know off the top of my head, to be honest, ma'am."

"How did you meet these people? Where did they come from?"

"Who can remember now?" he said back, his voice just above a whisper. He looked up, met her eyes with his—and his gaze was unexpectedly soft. "I don't mean to cause you more aggravation than necessary, ma'am, but it's been a long while with some of 'em, and my memory, it ain't so good no more."

"You painted your windows," she said. "Why?"

"So nothing could see in," he said.

"Who would be looking in? The police?"

He waved a dismissive hand at her, although even this action seemed somehow polite and timid. Yet she gathered from it that the police had never been much of a concern to this man.

"Those symbols on your walls," she went on. "Did you draw those?"

"Yes, ma'am."

"In blood?"

"Yes, ma'am."

"The victims' blood?"

"No, ma'am. My own."

"What do they mean?"

"They don't *mean* nothing," Mallory said, the first hint of exasperation in his voice now. "They there to *sanctify*. Ain't a one of you payin' any attention out here?" He leaned forward just enough so that the wooden bench creaked beneath him. "You live all your life out here, ma'am?" he asked her.

"I'm from Ketchikan."

"Ah," Mallory said, leaning back again. "The Big Stink."

"That's right," Ryerson said. It was the Tsmishian translation of the city's name. All those flyblow salmon corpses filling up the rivers during spawning season.

"Someone send you in here to ask me all these questions?" he asked.

"No, sir. I'm the lead investigator on this case."

"Seeing how you found that little hole beneath my house, ma'am, you haven't asked me the one question you really want to ask, have you?" Something about his face—not his expression, Ryerson thought, but his *face*—chilled her. He looked like a skeleton stuffed into people clothes and puppeted by a mad wizard.

She felt herself nodding, as if hypnotized by him, and she realized she was rubbing the lucky rabbit's foot on the key chain that hung from her belt.

"What's that thing in the trunk?" she asked.

Joseph Mallory offered her a sad and terrible smile.

"It's me," he said.

8

The following morning, Paul contacted Rena Tremaine and his department head, Alvin Limbeck, and told them both he had an emergency and needed to leave town for a while. Rena was at the ready to take over his classes, but the concern in her voice was palpable over the phone. She asked if it had anything to do with Paul having passed out in class the day before. He assured her that it didn't, and that he was fine. Limbeck, a dour old codger who always wore too much tweed, surprised Paul by being sympathetic and asked for no details. Paul guessed Rena had filled Limbeck in on his little fainting episode, and much like Paul's assistant, the man likely assumed that Paul was checking into the nearest hospital to undergo a battery of CT scans and MRIs.

What Paul *actually* did was board a 777 out of Baltimore-Washington International at ten thirty that morning, which ushered him into Dallas/Fort Worth at just after one o'clock in the afternoon. He'd slept very little the night before, his mind alternating between images of Joseph Mallory's black-and-white visage and that vision of the bloody hand held up against a gunmetal sky. However, at some point during his layover, and despite being contorted in an uncomfortable chair with armrests digging into his ribs, his exhaustion overtook him and shuttled him off to sleep. When he awoke sometime later, it was with a start, as if someone had just screamed into his ear. He could remember no details of what he assumed was a nightmare. At the gate, his connecting flight to Seattle was boarding.

It was around 10:30 P.M. when the Airbus's wheels touched down on the runway at Fairbanks International, which meant he'd been traveling for sixteen straight hours by that point. It also meant that it was after two in the morning back home in Maryland. Paul Gallo coasted through the airport like someone waltzing through a dream.

When he stepped out of the baggage claim area and into the night, he was struck, almost like a slap across the face, by the sudden cold. He looked around, wincing as tears threatened to freeze in the corners of his eyes. A thermometer bolted to the wall beside a set of hydraulic doors proclaimed the temperature to be 33 degrees—a world of difference from the mild autumn temperatures back home. He wondered what sadist had decided to put up a thermometer in a climate like this.

He spent that night at a Best Western, where the young woman at the reception desk served up a broad smile as he came in off the airport shuttle. He did his best to return the good cheer, but in his exhaustion, the smile felt like it was splitting the seams of his face. He felt like he'd been awake for a week straight.

His room was on the fourth floor, and there were two large windows beside the bed that looked out on a lightless landscape. A single star burned in the sky above the empty highway. He plugged in his cell phone and heard it chime as it began charging. Then he pulled the drapes closed and wandered into the bathroom.

He showered, then climbed naked into bed. The sheets felt cool and good. He closed his eyes, and must have fallen asleep quickly, given his exhaustion, because a dream seemed right there at the ready to slip unimpeded into his brain—a dream so real that he thought he wasn't dreaming at all.

He was lying in this very same bed, staring toward the foot of the bed and at a dark figure who stood there, masked in the shadows, staring back at him. Despite the fact that the figure was human, Paul had the sense that it was actually some animal—maybe a wolf, maybe a horned ungulate—crouching in the darkness across the room, watching him. The figure's eyes glowed green. As he stared at the figure, it moved around the foot of the bed until it passed in front of the large windows. Its form was silhouetted against the night sky, and even though Paul couldn't make out any details—it was a black, formless suggestion of a human being—he imagined this person to have a bushy lumberjack beard and a rifle slung over one shoulder.

Paul sat up in bed to get a better look at the figure, but the figure was no longer there, and Paul was no longer asleep. In fact, it felt as though he hadn't been asleep at all, and that the arrival of this strange bearded figure carrying a rifle hadn't been a dream at all, either. Even the drapes over the windows had been swept aside, revealing the darkened night sky—drapes that Paul had shut before going to bed. It felt so real that he leaned over to the nightstand and clicked on the lamp, flooding the room with light.

Wincing, he glanced around. Of course, he was alone. He even peered over the bed and down at the floor, half-expecting to find muddy boot prints on the carpet. But there were none.

The Fairbanks division of the Alaska Bureau of Investigation was housed in a squat brick-and-glass building with concrete planters out front. It looked more like an airport terminal than a police station, and it sat across the road from a nice-looking residential neighborhood.

Paul arrived at the station at eight in the morning, paid his cab driver fifteen bucks, then downed the rest of his Dunkin' Donuts coffee while shivering against a bone-chilling wind. He wasn't sure what he'd expected to find upon arrival, but the unpretentious nature of the building, with its diminutive parking lot slotted with a sparse number of SUVs with rack lights and shiny white police cars, did not live up to any of his expectations. If it wasn't for the large sign with the Department of Public Safety badge on it, he would have thought he was at the wrong location.

The reception area was as small as a closet and just about as festive. There were a few molded plastic chairs against one wall and a framed photo of a jowly man sporting a manicured black beard that Paul suspected was some figure of authority. Seated behind a half wall of bulletproof glass, a solemn-faced female receptionist of indeterminate age glanced up at Paul from over the rims of smudgy bifocals. Paul affected his friendliest smile and informed the woman, via an intercom inserted into the glass, that he was here to surrender some of his DNA.

"Please have a seat," the receptionist instructed, nodding toward the row of plastic chairs. "Someone will be with you shortly."

"Is Investigator Jill Ryerson available?" he asked.

"Investigator Ryerson is out on a call."

"I thought there'd be more people here," he said.

The woman arched her eyebrows, as if anticipating further commentary from him. He gave none.

He sat for several long minutes, listening to the buzz of the electric heater that vibrated against the wall in one corner. There was a smell in here, one reminiscent of locker rooms and body odor. Paul ran a shaky hand through his hair. He realized that he was nervous.

Is this it, Danny? Am I finally going to find out what happened to you? Will I finally put that all to rest?

A memory returned to him then—a memory from their shared childhood, back when the bond was still strong. Paul couldn't have been more than seven, and he was by himself in the backyard searching for carnivorous plants. He'd read a book about the Venus flytrap, and although the book assured him that Venus flytraps were only found in the subtropical wetlands of the Carolinas, seven-year-old Paul didn't think it was a stretch that some might have migrated as far north as Maryland. He didn't find a flytrap that day, but he did come across a peculiar grayish-brown sac made of brittle paperlike material dangling from a tree limb. It was the size and shape of a football, and it was honeycombed with tiny portholes, like the windows on a submarine. Bested by curiosity, he did what any boy his age might do—he found a long stick on the ground and swatted at the thing.

The cloud of hornets that spilled from the hive appeared instantly, and from every direction at once. Paul no sooner realized what they were than he felt a sharp lance of pain along his left cheekbone. He dropped the stick and howled. A second jab of pain caught him on his right forearm. A third caught him just above the right eye, and this one felt like a branding iron.

Screaming, Paul had run back to the house. By the time he came bursting through the rear patio door, he had been stung nearly a dozen times and his face had already begun to swell. Tears streamed down his face. It was a Saturday, so his father was home, and the old man examined Paul with a steady eye while Paul's mom peeled off his clothes as he stood in the bathtub. (There had been three or four more hornets twisting about inside his clothes, which his father mashed one at a time beneath the sole of a tattered bedroom slipper.) Danny had watched wide-eyed from the bathroom doorway as the stingers were extracted from Paul's flesh.

Later that night, Paul and his parents had awakened to the sound of Danny screaming from his bedroom. They all rushed in to find Danny sitting up in bed, clawing at his arms and legs, his torso, his thighs.

But nothing was wrong with Danny. Not physically,

anyway. He shrieked and said his skin was burning, and he'd raked his fingernails over his arms, his chest, this thighs, his face. But there was nothing there. Nothing.

Thinking about this now, Paul recognized this mystery for what it was: Danny stealing his thunder. He'd stood there in the bathroom doorway watching all the attention lavished on Paul by their parents, and that little fit in the middle of the night was Danny's counterbalance. Had Paul been so naïve back then to think that it had been something more? That powerful, inexplicable bond they shared, perhaps? That Danny could be capable of feeling Paul's pain was, in hindsight, preposterous.

Paul realized his leg was bouncing nervously, and that he couldn't control his breathing. He could feel the slight increase in his heartbeat, and despite the cold that he'd carried in with him from the outside, a film of perspiration had come over him. He felt amphibious with it.

Just when he was about to get up and approach the receptionist again, a side door opened and an officer in a powder-blue shirt and navy slacks came over to him. His name was Holtzman and he didn't bother shaking Paul's hand before leading him into what Paul assumed would be an office or even an interrogation room, but what turned out to be a snack lounge with Formica tables and some vending machines standing in an appropriate lineup against one wall. There were a few other people in there, most of them paired up, seated at some of the tables, while some lone stragglers paced the floor. One guy in a turban fed change into one of the vending machines with infuriating sluggishness.

"What's this?" Paul asked.

"Waiting room. Just take a seat and wait," Holtzman said. "I've got your name. Someone will call you when it's your turn."

"Are all these people—" he began, but cut himself off as Holtzman, preoccupied with his iPhone, strutted away.

There was one other person, a woman, seated at the nearest table, so Paul sat in an empty chair opposite her, hoping she would not make eye contact. But she did, and he was too slow to look away, so he smiled at her. She was maybe in her early sixties, with a braid of graying hair spilling out from beneath a knit wool cap. She might have been attractive at one time, but now she looked defeated, her eyes empty.

"The answer is yes," she said.

"Excuse me?"

"The question you were going to ask that cop. The answer is yes. We're all here for the same reason."

Paul nodded, his gaze skirting across the Formica tabletop and away from the woman. Across the room, a man in a neon-green ski jacket and headphones sat typing on a laptop. He appeared to be the only person in the room who wasn't nervous, apprehensive, unfocused. Paul watched him until the man glanced up and returned Paul's stare. The guy nodded at him and Paul nodded back. Then he redirected his gaze toward the wall of vending machines, where the guy in the turban was still feeding change into one of the machines with unflinching, methodical persistence.

"He's a reporter," said the woman at Paul's table.

"Who? The guy who thinks that thing's a slot machine?"

"No, the guy at the table typing on his laptop. I got here early and he asked me some questions about my daughter." The woman's face softened, and Paul felt pity for her. "She's missing, my daughter."

The woman got up and sat down in the empty seat beside Paul. He smiled as she placed a small photo album on the table and opened it. The album was small enough so that it only fit two photos on each page. The girl in each photograph was a stunner—brazen in her beauty, deeply tanned, every third picture showing a spaghetti-strap bikini on full display. She looked nothing like the wasted, haunted woman sitting next to him.

"Her name's Roberta Chalmers. Bobbi, we call her. Does she look familiar to you?"

"She doesn't, no. I'm sorry. But I'm not from around here."

"Oh." This didn't seem to faze the woman; she turned another page of the album and pointed to one of the photographs. "This was her college graduation. See that? Can you believe she almost dropped out?"

Paul felt ill. Was this where it ended? In some police station in the middle of goddamn Alaska waiting to get his cheek swabbed? Was he now a member of some morbid, soul-draining club, in which he'd suffer through the rest of his life showing strangers pictures of his brother and asking if he looked familiar?

"I'm sorry," said the woman. "Sometimes I don't realize what I sound like, being so forward. Maybe you aren't in the mood for conversation. I apologize." She closed the album.

"It's all right. I'm sorry to hear about your daughter. How long has she been missing?"

"Two and a half years. She's always been a free spirit, my Bobbi. She's always been too trusting, too. I worry all the time that she might fall in with bad elements. There are always bad elements around. In high school, she went with a man who was college age—not that he actually went to college, of course—and he had no job and rode a motorbike and had arms full of tattoos. He smoked *marijuana cigarettes*. Of course, I know those things don't necessarily make someone a bad person—except maybe for the marijuana part—but this guy just happened to be a bad person on top of everything else. He sometimes hit her." The sob that ratcheted out of her throat sounded like a shrill laugh, and it caused Paul to lean away from her. A few heads turned in their direction.

"How old is she?" Paul asked.

"Twenty-six. Do you have children?"

"No, I don't." He reached over and placed a hand on the photo album. "May I?"

"Please," said the woman, her face seeming to fill with some distant light. "Please do."

He turned through a few of the photographs while the woman, smiling, drew closer to him. She pointed out a few photos and explained the context, or identified other people in the pictures with her daughter.

"She's very pretty," he said, closing the album.

"A free spirit," the woman said, her voice growing distant and her eyes losing their focus on him. "Bobbi couldn't hold down a job. Got into drugs, too, but we tried to help. Do you know how hard that is? Trying to help someone who doesn't want help?" She balled her hands into fists, but her face remained soft, her eyes lost in some far-off reverie. "Do you know what that's like?"

Paul could see the pain on the woman's face. He wished he hadn't come here—not to this police station and not to Alaska. *Damn you, Danny, you son of a bitch. I wouldn't be here if it wasn't for you. You just had to pack up and take off, didn't you? Some things never change, do they? You selfish bastard.*

"We're from Bethel," the woman went on. "Spent our whole lives there. Bobbi was such a happy child. We gave her a good life, Roger and me. We were good parents. But I guess you can't stop those bad elements from sinking their claws in, can you?" She was frowning at him and wanted a serious answer. "Can you?" she repeated, more sternly.

"No," he said. "I guess you can't."

"She left home two and a half years ago. It was with some local bums. I don't mean bums as in homeless people, of course, but some older men who did nothing but drink and get drunk and shoot things. With guns, I mean. Maybe homeless people would have been better." The woman lowered her voice and added, "They all smoke *marijuana*."

Paul nodded.

The woman sob-laughed again; this time, the fellow in the turban turned and shot a disapproving eye in her direction.

"Right? Am I right?" she said. "I mean, you *see* the kind of people I'm talking about, right? Jesus, Mary, and Joseph." She genuflected.

"What makes you think she's tied up in all of this?" he asked.

"What do you mean?"

"What makes you think she didn't just go off some-place? Why do you think something . . . well, something bad happened to her?"

The woman's face went hard and cold. Her eyes narrowed, and she seemed to be seeing him now for the first time. When she spoke again, her voice was laced with palpable distrust. "It's all bad, mister. All of it. Don't you see that? Don't you know what they say about that place?"

"What place?"

"Dread's Hand."

"What do they say?"

"That it's cursed," said the woman. "That terrible things happen to people who go out there. They lose themselves. Spiritually, I mean. Their souls get corrupted."

Paul just nodded.

"The locals know, but they keep it a secret. A dark secret. I've heard all the stories. You look into that woods and something looks back at you."

"What kind of something?"

The woman didn't answer. She stared at him, her gaze growing more and more intense with the passing of each heartbeat.

"What kind of something?" Paul repeated.

A man in an oxford shirt with the sleeves cuffed to the elbows came out of a door at the far end of the room, breaking the woman's stare on Paul. She blinked and shook her head. The man in the oxford shirt examined a clipboard, then called out, "Hollister."

An elderly man and woman got up from one of the

tables and, in the slow, aggrieved waltz of the arthriti-
cally challenged, followed the man through the door.

"I'm sorry," the woman said to him. She reached out
and patted the top of his hand. Her palm was cold, her
fingers as hard and rigid as twigs. "I've got no manners.
No manners at all. Did you say you're here because of
your child?"

"My brother," he said.

"Do you have a picture of him?"

"Not with me, no."

"Not a single one? He's out here missing and you
don't carry a picture of him?"

I'm his twin, he thought, but did not say. *I walk
around with his face on.*

"Well, I have a few in my phone," he conceded.

The woman seemed to brighten. "Let's see them.
Maybe I'll recognize him."

As he dug his cell phone out of his coat, he realized
that, yes, he was now an official member of the Club
for the Hopelessly Damned. *I'm going to show this
stranger a picture of Danny on my phone, and that will
be like my gateway drug. From there, I'll start showing Danny's picture to every asshole I meet—at restau-
rants, in parks, at the movies, at the grocery store—and
then I'll start carrying whole photo albums around
with me, imparting my grief on others and gibbering
like a lunatic, until I either go mad or impose upon the
wrong person and get my goddamn nose broken.*

Astoundingly, he found he was very close to braying
laughter. It was all he could do to keep it bottled up
inside. He realized that if he *did* laugh, the spectacle
might send this poor, fragile woman shrieking like a

madwoman down the hallway and out into the street. And of course, the thought of *that* made it all the more difficult to stifle the hilarity of it.

"Is something wrong?" the woman asked. She was staring at him, one corner of her mouth turned up in her own confused half grimace.

"I guess I was just thinking about Danny," he said, and showed her the most recent photo of Danny on his phone.

It was the last picture Danny had texted to him just before all communication had ceased—a selfie of Danny standing in front of a decrepit log cabin with what looked like wooden crosses hammered against the cabin's façade. Paul had received a number of Danny's selfies during Danny's trek across Alaska, and they had reminded Paul of the Evolution of Man chart that he'd seen in a textbook as a boy, only this chart went in reverse: Danny, who had started out clean shaven and well groomed, had degenerated over time into a bearded, gaunt-faced mountain man. Paul could tell by Danny's smile in the last picture—a smile that looked too big for his brother's face, comprised of too many teeth and sharp angles—that he had lost a considerable amount of weight.

He doesn't even look like me anymore . . .

"Oh," the woman uttered, her voice toneless, flat. "Oh, God. Jesus." Then she pushed herself away from the table, the chair legs scraping along the tiled floor.

"What's wrong?" Paul asked.

"You've been playing with me," the woman said. Her voice was barely a whisper now. "You've been having fun at my expense."

"Of course not . . ."

The woman stared at the photo on Paul's phone. Her lips tightened. "You think it's funny, teasing a grieving woman?"

Paul glanced down at the photo on the phone, perhaps to divine something from it that had upset the woman, but there was nothing there except the emaciated, hollow-eyed image of his brother.

"We're twins," Paul said.

"You're a monster, is what you are," said the woman. She gathered up her photo album and stood. "Excuse me."

"Are you all right?"

"I might be sick," she said, and hurried out into the hallway.

Paul's cheek was swabbed by a burly technician with hairy arms and breath that reeked of onions. The whole thing took maybe five minutes, which included scribbling his signature on a series of forms. He asked how long it would take before the results came in, and the technician assured him they would have the results at some point tomorrow. "Someone will call you, either way," the technician said.

He stepped out of the police station feeling like a stone that had been dropped into a deep pool. The temperature had plummeted maybe ten degrees while he was inside, and he shivered as he stood there waiting for his taxi to arrive and take him back to his hotel. He could have waited in the lobby where it was warmer, but he didn't want to go back in there. The whole ordeal had left him feeling cold and exposed. He wished he was back home.

Across the parking lot, the woman who had seemed offended by the photo of Danny on his phone hustled toward a rusted Ford Escort with religious stickers crowding the rear bumper. She glanced at him over her shoulder. Even from this distance, Paul watched her expression harden. Then she genuflected, got into her car, and drove away.

9

Paul spent that evening at the hotel bar, feeling anxious and hot despite the chill in the air. The barroom was only mildly populated, the sounds of quiet conversation and the clinking of silverware the only soundtrack. Paul sat at the bar and ordered a cheeseburger and a pilsner from a young male bartender with hoop earrings and a fuzzy upper lip. There was a brief mention of the Mallory case on the muted TV. Paul read the closed-captioning as it scrolled across the screen until some ignoramus with bulging biceps in an Under Armour shirt asked the bartender to change the channel to a UFC fight.

When Paul's beer arrived, the bartender said, "This one's on your friend's tab." He jerked his head toward the opposite end of the bar, where a man sat holding up a salutatory hand in Paul's direction. The man looked familiar, though Paul didn't place him until he came over and sat on the empty stool next to him.

"You were at the police station this morning," Paul said. "You're a reporter."

"Keith Moore," the reporter said.

"Paul Gallo."

Keith extended a hand and Paul shook it.

"I'm with the *Dispatch* down in Anchorage," Keith said.

"You're covering this Joseph Mallory story? Was that why you were at the police station?"

"In part, yeah."

"Well, thanks for the beer, although I'm not sure why you felt the need to be so generous."

Keith Moore shrugged. He had a thin face haunted by the ghosts of childhood acne, and a gingery goatee that was neatly trimmed. "Looked like you could use it," Keith said.

"You're right. Many thanks."

They lifted their glasses and tapped them together. The beer was cold and infused with hops, and it seemed to carve a path down Paul's throat like an ice floe cutting through a fjord.

"You're not from around here, are you?" Keith said.

"Does it show?"

"Well, you're staying in a hotel, so I know you don't live in Fairbanks. But you don't look like you've spent much time in Alaska."

"This is my first trip," Paul acknowledged.

"So, who are you looking for? Back at the police station."

"My brother."

"How long's he been missing?"

"About a year."

"Where are you from?"

"Maryland."

Keith whistled. "You've come a long way. What makes you think your brother might be a part of this whole thing?"

"The last place I can trace my brother to before he disappeared is that town Dread's Hand, where that guy Mallory lived, and where he killed those people. I thought I should come out here and see this thing through."

"Dread's Hand," Keith murmured, grinning with one corner of his mouth. He looked at his beer as he rubbed a thumb along the rim of the glass.

"How well do you know it?" Paul asked.

"Oh, boy." Keith laughed. "So, see, I'm covering the murders, yeah, and the *Dispatch* is picking up my tab, but I'm also using this as an opportunity. I'm out here writing a book."

"About the murders?"

"About the town."

"The town? Dread's Hand? Other than the murders, what's so interesting about the town?"

"Nothing, really . . . on the surface," Keith said. "It's what's *under* the surface that I'm interested in. I've been working out here for years, and I've heard things from time to time—stories that maybe don't seem so outlandish in and of themselves . . . but then you put them all together and this bizarre sort of tapestry begins to take shape."

"What sort of stories?"

A playful smugness came over the reporter's features. Paul thought Keith Moore was going to tell him that he couldn't divulge his secrets, for fear Paul might abscond with his intellectual property and write a book of his own. Instead, Keith held up one finger and said, "In 1906, the Dread's Hand gold mine opened, and for a time, it was a flourishing little hamlet. Upwards of three hundred people were accounted for at one point. Those are big numbers for such a remote place, particularly back then. But then, in 1912, the entire population of Dread's Hand simply vanished off the face of the earth. No trace of the people, no signs of a struggle, no indication that the population picked up and went elsewhere. They were just there one day, gone the next."

"Sounds like the stories about the old Roanoke Colony," Paul said. "Raleigh and White and something like one hundred settlers vanishing into thin air."

Keith nodded his approval. "Yes! Exactly like that. Of course, Roanoke happened in the sixteenth century, in the middle of Indian country. The Roanoke settlers were most likely killed by the Croatoan Indians. Not much out by the Hand back then except wilderness."

"The Hand?"

"That's what the locals call it."

"Is that the end of your stories?"

"Not by a long shot," Keith said. "Two years after those villagers disappeared, new settlers came into town and revitalized the mine. There were far fewer people then, but they were determined to make a go of it. There was still plenty of gold up there in the hills, and things were good again—for a time. But then in 1916, the mine collapsed. Twenty-six men died down there."

"I've read about that accident online," Paul said.

"Sure," Keith said. "But ask some of the old-timers out there—the generations whose great-great-grandfathers died in that mine collapse—and they'll tell you it wasn't an accident at all."

"Then what was it?" Paul asked. "Sabotage?"

"A curse on the land," Keith said. "An evil."

Paul laughed, but when he saw that Keith wasn't laughing with him, his laughter died. "You're serious."

"Well, the old-timers are serious. I'm just interested in the facts," Keith said. "You can't deny all the facts."

"What other facts?"

Keith said, "The twenties and thirties are murky. There's not a lot of official documentation from that era, and no one was reporting any news from way out here. Maybe things happened, maybe they didn't. But my point is, no one knows for sure.

"So, let's jump ahead to 1943. A group of U.S. soldiers out of Fort Washington gets waylaid and winds up far off course—like, *way* far—and they make camp in the woods near Dread's Hand. They report strange lights in the sky, just before they get snowed in by a harsh winter. All of them died, though journals that were later discovered disclosed horrific stories—of cannibalism and of some . . . some *thing* . . . there in the forest with them, watching them from behind the trees and hiding in the shadows. A number of them went mad that winter, and one journal entry attributes this madness to that thing in the woods having touched these men while they slept. One man wrote, 'We have seen the devil and he is us.' How's that for literary gold?"

"Sounds like the legend of the wendigo."

"It does, doesn't it?"

"All of these stories sound like variations of other stories," Paul said.

Keith shrugged his shoulders. "Maybe that's how legends are spread around the globe, or maybe there's some greater meaning behind it all," he said. "Part of the beauty of legends is trying to determine what is actual fact and what has been influenced by the human element of storytelling."

"What else?" Paul asked. "What other stories are there?"

"Well, throughout the sixties, missing persons reports become prevalent in and around the area. The Alaska Bureau of Investigation has a whole file on them, and I've gotten most of them under the Freedom of Information Act, but you can Google this stuff and do your own research. Most people were never found, and there were rarely any bodies recovered. However, one party—a group of trappers who went up there in the spring and summer months—stumbled upon what was described in police reports as a mass grave of corpses half-buried in the muskeg. Witnesses reported that the bodies looked 'chewed upon,' and although I guess it's possible that animals got to them after they'd perished, the medical examiner's reports suggested that parts of their bodies had been devoured while they were still alive."

Keith had been ticking off each incident on the fingers of his left hand. He popped his thumb up now and said, "Then there's the story of Lans Lunghardt."

"Some name," Paul said.

"In 1967," Keith went on, "Lunghardt, a trapper who spent weeks on end up in the White Mountains, murdered his entire family with an ax—just chopped them up like kindling while they were still inside their home. His middle son made it out of the house, but old Lans brought the kid down with a swift drop of his ax between the boy's shoulder blades, killing him right there in the backyard. When he was done, he walked down the street, covered in their blood, sat down outside the church, and waited for the VPSO to show up."

"What's a VPSO?"

"Village public safety officer. They're not necessarily law enforcement, although they serve as a sort of de facto liaison to the state police in a lot of these remote villages where there is no actual police department. When the VPSO showed up at the church, Lunghardt admitted to slaying his entire family, and although he said he knew there was a good reason for it at the time, he suddenly couldn't remember why. And then he broke into hysterics and said he'd made a horrible, horrible mistake."

"Jesus Christ," Paul said. "That really happened?"

"Oh, absolutely. There's a record of it. Lunghardt was arrested, convicted of the murders, and sent to a state hospital down in Anchorage, where he died of pneumonia a few years later. He was never able to explain why he did what he did, and he seemed destroyed by his own actions. Those last few years of his life, he was practically a vegetable.

"If you're still with me, let's jump ahead to 1977," Keith said.

"I'm still with you."

"A man described as possessing an 'aloof demeanor' and the 'ambulatory gait of a sleepwalker' crosses the frozen Bering Strait and arrives at a small, isolated village on the island of Little Diomede. Reports say he was nothing but skin and bones, and was dressed only in a tattered pair of pants that, by all eyewitnesses' accounts, was streaked with some dark fluid that looked very much like blood. The guy wasn't even wearing shoes, for Christ's sake, and his feet were split and bleeding and frostbitten. This was at a time of year when temperatures out on the island were recorded to be around fifty below. The man said he had come all the way from Dread's Hand, where he'd 'seen terrible things,' and that much of his memory as to how he got clear across the rest of the continent and out to the island was a mystery to him. We're talking hundreds of miles here, through some of the most inhospitable terrain in subarctic temperatures. And this guy just showed up there like he'd stepped off a bus. He told one person that he had a memory—or maybe it was a dream, or maybe it was even a hallucination—of being lifted off the ground by a great wind and carried through the air for miles and miles. He said he remembered his feet scraping the treetops, which was how he lost his shoes. The wind had claws, the man told this person. This same witness later told police that the man had what appeared to be very large and obvious claw marks about the shoulders, which sort of corroborated the guy's story. The witness assumed they might have been made by a polar bear—there are polar bear attacks out on the island on occasion—though he couldn't fathom how a man could have been attacked in such a way and not be outright killed.

"Another eyewitness said the man's face was frozen

into a skeletal grin, and that he couldn't stop grinning, even though his skin was chapped from the wind and cracking and bleeding from the cold. Some of the man's teeth had shattered from the cold, too."

Paul grimaced at the thought.

"The man was given shelter until an officer could fly in from Nome," Keith continued, "but when the officer arrived, the man had vanished from the shelter—and he'd left no footprints behind in the snow."

"Was the man ever identified?"

"No," Keith said. "And no one ever saw him again. The officer who flew in from Nome interviewed a few witnesses on the island, and although everyone's story regarding the man's appearance and demeanor was the same, no one had ever gotten the man's name or knew anything about him. With the exception, of course, of an elderly Iñupiat woman, who claimed to know the name of the man. She spoke to the officer in her native dialect, which was then translated by the woman's granddaughter. The rough translation of what the old woman said was *'bone white.'* The officer took it literally, believing it to be the description of the man's pallor. But the contextual translation actually means *'demon'* or *'devil.'*"

"This is a folktale you're telling me, right? I mean, this isn't something that actually happened, is it? Is that what you're telling me?"

"There was a report filed by the officer who flew to the island. I've read it."

"Yeah, okay, but that officer was only reporting on what the villagers told him. How can you be sure that what they said was the truth? I mean, it's impossible.

Walking for hundreds of miles in subarctic temperatures in nothing but a pair of pants?"

Keith shrugged his shoulders, but the expression on his face was anything but casual. He looked pleased by Paul's skepticism. "Just think about all the seemingly impossible stuff that has happened over the course of mankind's existence," he said. "Jesus, Paul, we've sent men to the goddamn moon."

"That's different. That's science."

"But before that stuff was science, it was magic. Am I right? Tell someone in 1940 that, in just twenty years, men would be walking on the moon, and they'd call you a lunatic. Probably accused you of witchcraft in some parts of the country, I'd bet."

"There's probably a rational explanation for what happened, and over time the story just snowballed until it became this urban legend. Or arctic legend. Or whatever. That's probably how all these creepy little tales get started. Some band of settlers gets stranded in a snowy mountain pass and have to resort to cannibalism to stay alive. Next thing you know, we've got people saying it's the wendigo."

"Shit, man, it's not like I believe in these ghost stories," Keith said. "But even if you discount the possibility of any supernatural occurrences, you still can't deny that the sheer number of bizarre and inexplicable things that have happened in and around that area over the past century must cause the conclusion that there is *something* going on, that there is *something* that needs to be explored and better understood. Maybe it's ley lines or maybe it's space dust or . . . I don't know . . . radio interference making people's fillings vibrate and driving them to madness. I really have no clue. But I *do* know that anyone can take one story and rationalize it until it fits with their perception of the world. But *five* stories like that? Ten? A baker's dozen? They can't all be rationalized, and they can't all just be coincidences."

"So, how many more stories are there?" Paul asked.

"Countless," Keith said. "But we haven't even gotten to 1984 yet."

Paul grinned, sipped his beer, and said, "Okay, I'll bite. What happened in 1984?"

"A drifter named Michael Silka killed nine people in a town called Manley Hot Springs."

"Silka!" Paul said, drawing the attention of the young bartender and a few nearby patrons. He lowered his voice and said, "I've heard of him. In fact, I spoke to someone recently who ran into him back then, a few days before Silka was shot and killed by police. But none of that happened in Dread's Hand."

"No," Keith agreed, "but prior to Silka popping up in Manley Hot Springs, he spent the early part of April 1984 picking up small construction jobs along the highway and in surrounding towns, to include spending a week or so in—you guessed it—our very own Dread's Hand." Keith smiled like a Cheshire cat as he finished this anecdote.

"All right, sure, if that's what really happened, then I'll grant you that it's unusual. But what does it mean? That he contracted some mental illness or bad juju from spending a week in Dread's Hand? Or your space dust theory? Vibrating fillings?"

"Bad juju, vibrating fillings," Keith said, "or maybe something worse. Just like that old native woman told the cop from Nome back in '77—the guy had gone bone white, man. He had the devil in him."

Paul shook his head, smiling. He held up two fingers toward the bartender—two more beers.

"Like I said," Keith continued. "You can explain away any one of these incidents by itself, but it's not until you put all the pieces of the puzzle together that you start seeing the big picture. That's when it becomes more difficult to rationalize. Because there isn't anything rational about it. I don't believe in that spooky bullshit, but no place with such a small population in the middle of nowhere should have a long history of such tragic and bizarre events. Am I right?"

"I'll give you that," Paul said.

"And now we've got Joseph Mallory's story to add to the mix. Maybe fifty years from now, people just like you and me will say the whole thing is hyperbole, but you and I, we're living it right now. We know the facts. That lunatic murdered eight people and buried them in the woods on the outskirts of that town. There's nothing to rationalize there. Maybe a hundred years from now, people will question whether that ever really happened. But you and I know it's true. Just one more creepy, inexplicable link on the chain."

"So, this is what you're writing your book about? All the crazy shit that's happened in and around that place for the past hundred years?"

"It probably goes back even further than that," Keith said, "though it's pretty much impossible to find any accounts of events from that far back. Hell, Alaska wasn't even a state until 1959. And I'm sure there was some crazy shit that happened up there in the twenties and thirties—the decades after the mine collapsed and those villagers disappeared—but, like I said, there's no official record of anything, and the people who would have been alive back then are all dead now."

"So, what does this all mean?" Paul asked. "What does it all come down to? That Dread's Hand is . . . what? Haunted? Cursed?"

"Well, I guess that's the big question, isn't it?" Keith said. "I've got a book's worth of creepy, inexplicable anecdotes—*true* anecdotes—but I've got no solid hypothesis on which to hinge them all. Like I said, you can rationalize one or two events. But all of them?"

"Space dust," Paul said.

"Space dust," Keith Moore agreed. "Either that, or something ungodly walks the woods surrounding Dread's Hand."

"Joseph Mallory," Paul said.

"Mallory is just another anecdote," said Keith, finishing the last of his beer. He sucked foam from his upper lip, then said, "Have you been up there yet?"

"To Dread's Hand? No, I haven't."

"It's a different place, man," he said. "I've been up to the Hand twice—once while researching stuff for my book, and then just recently, covering the Mallory story for the paper—and it's like stepping into an alternate universe. And I'm only sort of exaggerating." Keith winked at him, and Paul raised his beer in a salute. "But really, it's like stepping across some invisible border that runs around the whole town, cutting it off from the rest of civilization. There're these huge crosses along the road just before you get into town. Some of them look so old, I'll bet they were erected by the town's original settlers."

"I've seen crosses on the side of highways before," Paul said.

"No, man, you haven't. Not like these. Not the way they're arranged, as if to form some . . . I don't know . . . some pattern that might only be understood from the sky, maybe. Who knows? But, see, it's not just the crosses. It's not any one thing in particular. I can't even describe it. It's just like this overwhelming sense of apprehension. You ever lay your ear to the ground when there are a bunch of high-tension wires around? You feel all that power shuttling through the earth? It's like a sound you can feel in your back teeth, man. It's like that. Irrational, sure, but I was there and I can't deny it. And each time, it stuck with me for the entire day, until I got back in my car and drove the hell out of there."

Paul grinned. "You don't talk much like a reporter," he said. "I thought you guys dealt with nothing but facts."

"Those *are* the facts, brother," Keith said. "But you want more? How about this? Fact—Joseph Mallory, local resident of Dread's Hand, went crazy and killed eight people over what police believe to be a five-year period. We can rationalize that any number of confluences came together to make Mallory go crazy and kill those people. But how about this? Fact—for some reason, *eight people felt compelled to go to that remote town in the first place, only to wind up dead*. Dread's Hand isn't Manhattan, man. It's not even Paris, Texas. What were those eight people doing out there? What set of circumstances caused your brother to go out there, Paul? If we can write off Mallory as crazy by sheer stupid chance, or maybe bad genes, or whatever, then how do you explain how fate brought before that lunatic eight people to murder? *What was your brother doing out there?*"

Paul didn't answer right away. The conversation had veered into territory that hit too close to home. After a moment of silence, he said, "I've been asking myself that same question since he disappeared."

Fresh beers arrived, and Paul took a healthy gulp of his.

"So, what do you think?" he asked Keith. "What's your personal opinion of Dread's Hand?"

Keith Moore sipped his beer, then sucked the beer foam off his mustache. "When I first started this project, it was purely out of curiosity. You said it, man—I'm a guy who deals in facts."

"But now?"

"But now," Keith said . . . and then his voice trailed off, as though he was no longer sure what he believed. Or maybe he was just afraid to speak it aloud. "I guess I've become a bit more open-minded, you might say."

It was at that moment that Paul realized why he was so comfortable around this stranger: Keith Moore reminded him of Danny.

"Look," Keith said, a hint of apology in his tone now, "maybe we shouldn't be talking about this stuff, given your situation with your brother, man. I mean, I hope I wasn't being insensitive. I shouldn't have brought any of this stuff up. This isn't something you want to hear. I apologize, Paul. Shit."

Paul waved him off. He wasn't offended . . . but he was thinking now, and picturing Danny staggering around some remote patch of wilderness in the middle of nowhere, just below the curvature of the Arctic Circle, his face gaunt, his chin stippled with what their father had referred to as "beardlings." What the hell *had* he been doing out there?

When Paul's cheeseburger arrived, he found that he wasn't hungry.

10

Come morning, all eight of Joseph Mallory's victims had been identified. Paul learned about this while seated at a small table by himself in the dining room of the Best Western, sipping black coffee and watching a morning news program on the TV that was bracketed to the wall above the omelet station. Police had confirmed the identities of all eight victims, the reporter said, although they wouldn't be releasing any names until the families were contacted.

Paul took out his cell phone, dialed Ryerson's desk number, and listened to the investigator's phone ring at the other end of the line. The connection was garbled, rife with static. Bad connection. No matter—her voice mail picked up, which prompted him to end the call.

When the taxicab dropped him off at the police station thirty minutes later, the same dour receptionist greeted him without interest as he approached the panel of bulletproof glass. This time, when he asked to speak with Investigator Ryerson, the receptionist said,

"I'll have to call her. She's getting coffee. Take a seat, please."

It was snowing, and Paul watched the gentle snowfall from behind a narrow window reinforced with wire mesh. The sky looked gray and terminal, and in one instant, he caught a flash of lightning far out on the horizon. He couldn't remember having ever seen lightning during a snowstorm in his life.

He waited for almost twenty-five minutes. Just when he was about to get up and approach the receptionist again, the door to the outside swung open and a woman in a bright orange knit ski cap and a puffy coat came in, stomping brown sludge off her boots. She noticed Paul sitting there and smiled. She had lucid gray eyes and the round, clear face of a college coed. Her ski cap covered all but a single raven-colored braid of hair that rested on her left shoulder like an epaulette. She wore a University of Alaska Anchorage sweatshirt beneath her coat and held a Starbucks cup in one hand.

"Mr. Gallo," she said, coming over to him while extending her free hand. "I'm Jill Ryerson. It's nice to finally meet you."

Paul stood and shook her hand, which was cold and hard, the grip firm. "Thanks for meeting me."

"Sorry about my clothes. This was supposed to be my day off."

"I hope you didn't get called in on my account," he said.

She laughed—a laugh that wasn't at all derisive, but one that suggested he was just a blip on her daily radar screen. "This place has been a madhouse, as you can imagine," she said, motioning him to follow her down a brief corridor. "Half our staff are out sick with the flu, so we're all working double and triple shifts. Looks like we've got an early snowstorm coming down from the mountains, too, so this whole thing couldn't have come at a worse time."

She opened up a door and led him down a hallway carpeted in garish blue Berber.

"Let's talk in here," she said, opening yet another door and stepping aside to allow him to enter.

It was a small office with a single desk, a few framed pictures on the walls, and an octagonal window that looked out upon a pewter sky. Covering the wall behind the desk was a huge, detailed map of Alaska. Investigator Ryerson gathered a stack of papers off of a folding chair and set them down on her desk.

"Sorry the place is such a mess. I never get around to shredding anything. I hardly spend any time in here, to be honest."

She waved a hand at the folding chair and Paul dropped down in it, an obedient dog.

"Can I get you anything?" she asked, moving behind her desk while shrugging off her coat. "Coffee or something?"

"I'm fine, thanks."

"So," she said, exhaling audibly. She pulled her ski cap off, and Paul heard the popping sounds of static electricity. What few hairs she hadn't managed to finagle into her braid lifted off her head and seemed to float around her face like an aura. When she sat down, her wooden chair squealed, catlike. "I assume you're here about the DNA test results."

"I saw on the news this morning that all the victims

have been identified," he said. "I figured I'd come out here instead of sitting there, waiting for a phone call. Cell reception's lousy, anyway."

She smiled at him again, only this time there didn't appear to be anything cheerful behind it.

"Your brother is not one of the victims," she said.

It took a second for this to resonate with him. He opened his mouth to say something, but only a rasp of air came out.

"Days ago, we executed a search warrant on Joseph Mallory's residence, where we uncovered several items that appear to have belonged to his victims. Those items were sent to a lab for tests, but we got lucky. The driver's licenses for all eight victims were still intact and with their personal belongings. We then ran their IDs against our database and were able to narrow the scope of our search to dental records. Eight positive matches. We'll be contacting the families for any additional verification, but we're certain we've identified all eight victims. Your brother, Danny, is not among them."

"That's impossible," he said.

A faint vertical line appeared between Ryerson's eyebrows. "This should be good news," she said.

"My DNA sample," he said.

"Your sample did not match any of the victims," she said. "Mr. Gallo, your brother is not among them."

"Then where is he?"

"I've recently checked with MPU—that's our Missing Persons Unit out of Anchorage—and the case on your brother is still open, with no additional leads since you and I last spoke. I know that's difficult to hear, and I understand how hearing something like this has maybe taken away any closure you might have been hoping to get, but you also should consider that this means there is still some hope for your brother being alive and well somewhere out there."

"Is there?" he said. "Is there still some hope? Because he's been gone for over a year and no one's heard anything from him. And I can't believe that something like eight dead bodies in the woods outside some rural town where my brother also went missing is just a coincidence. How do you know there aren't more victims out there?"

"Mallory confessed to murdering eight people," Ryerson said. "I was there when he did this. He even walked us up into the hills and showed us where each one was buried. Also, only eight driver's licenses were found during the search of Mallory's home. Everything matches up. There are no loose ends. We've got no reason to believe that there is anyone else buried up there in those foothills."

"So I'm supposed to just walk away from this thing, thinking it's just a coincidence? That Danny disappeared up there and his disappearance is not connected to what happened—those eight murders—in any way?"

"Missing persons cases are difficult enough back where you're from, I'm sure, but out here they're near impossible to solve. We've got over fifty million acres of wilderness out here, Mr. Gallo—we're talking inhospitable, brutal terrain. One out of every two hundred people go missing every year out here. Those are astronomical numbers. That's more than double the national average."

Ryerson leaned back in her chair and turned so that she was facing the large map of Alaska behind her. She traced a triangle that started down in the southeast region of the state, and stretched all the way up north to the Barrow mountain range.

"Not to sound hokey, Mr. Gallo, but we refer to this section of the state as Alaska's Bermuda Triangle. Inside this zone are areas of unexplored wilderness—expansive forests, mountain ranges, dried-up riverbeds, and uncounted acres of tundra. I've heard one figure estimating that sixteen thousand people have gone missing here in this region alone since 1988. *Sixteen thousand*. And I mean 'missing' in the truest sense of the word: These are people who have never been found, who have disappeared without so much as a single footprint left behind. It's almost as if they'd never existed at all. There have also been an unusual number of small aircraft that have inexplicably crashed out there or, in some cases, vanished altogether without a trace."

She turned around and leaned toward him again, her desk chair creaking—*reeeek*.

"I know this must sound like science fiction to you, Mr. Gallo, but it's really not. It's the facts of what we deal with out here. If someone picks up and wanders off into that area—we're talking maybe weeks of hiking through rugged mountain terrain or through heavy forests, crossing glacial rivers, and whatever else—and they become lost, our hands are tied. There's just very little we can do. I don't mean to sound harsh about this, Mr. Gallo, and I feel for you, I really do, but I'd be doing you a disservice if I didn't point these facts out to you. I hope you understand."

Paul leaned back in his chair, rubbing his face. "Let me ask you," he said, "was one of the victims a young woman named Roberta Chalmers?"

"Bobbi Chalmers," Ryerson said. "You met her mother here at the station yesterday." It was not a question.

"Yes."

"Her name's Peggy," Ryerson said. "Peggy and Roger Chalmers. Their daughter, Bobbi, has been missing for over two years."

"You didn't answer my question," he said.

"No," Ryerson said. "Roberta Chalmers was not one of the victims."

"Just another coincidence then, huh?" he said, not bothering to mask his irritation.

"Mr. Gallo, Roberta Chalmers is *never* among the victims."

"What's that mean?"

"It means that Peggy Chalmers has been to this police station three times in the past year. Once was for a car wreck on the interstate. We knew the victims involved right away, but she came up here anyway, insistent that one of them must have been her daughter. Another time was when we found a few homeless people dead in a building downtown. She's gone down to Anchorage, and out to Palmer, too, whenever she hears about something on the news that she thinks—or maybe even hopes—might be related to her daughter's disappearance. Point is, Mr. Gallo, she's been making the rounds ever since her daughter disappeared. Roberta Chalmers is never one of the victims. Roberta Chalmers ran away with her biker boyfriend, and her mother just can't deal with that. Plain and simple."

"Oh," Paul said, sucking on his lower lip.

"She said you tried to scare her yesterday. She told one of the other officers that you made fun of her and tried to frighten her with some picture on your phone."

"*What?*"

Ryerson didn't actually shrug her shoulders, but the expression on her face conveyed the same impression.

"She was telling me about her daughter, then she asked about my brother. She asked if I had any pictures of him. I showed her a picture of Danny from my phone. Then she just got up and ran out of the room. She was upset, but I have no idea why. I didn't do anything to her. Wait—here."

He dug his phone out of his coat and scrolled through the album of Danny's pictures. When he found the one he'd shown the Chalmers woman, he handed the phone to Ryerson.

"Striking resemblance," she said.

"We're twins."

"And this is the picture you showed Mrs. Chalmers yesterday?"

"Yes. That exact picture. The same one I sent you guys a year ago. I have no idea why she would have said I was trying to scare her. To be honest, I felt bad for her."

Ryerson handed him back the phone. "Don't let it bend you out of shape. She's got a lot of problems. My guess is, she's had them even before her daughter took off. Roberta's leaving has probably only exacerbated them."

Paul nodded.

"There is one other thing," Ryerson said. She opened one of her desk drawers and riffled through some papers. "Maybe you already know this, maybe you don't."

She produced a manila folder from a drawer, opened it, and handed Paul a stapled packet of papers. On the first page, he noticed the words SHEPPARD PRATT HEALTH SYSTEM, along with the seal for the Baltimore County Police Department. It looked like some sort of official report.

"What is this?" Paul asked.

"A petition for emergency evaluation. Those papers are from a court-mandated stay at a mental hospital in Maryland following your brother's suicide attempt."

"What? Danny?" He looked at the date of the report and noted that it was a few years old. "This can't be right."

"He tied an electrical cord around his neck and tried to hang himself. Roommate found him in the basement of their apartment building and called the paramedics."

"Not Danny. Danny wouldn't do something like that."

Ryerson said nothing. She turned away and stared out the window, her hands folded together on her ink blotter.

"I had no idea." Paul glanced down at the page of the report opened on his lap. The words "attempted suicide" leapt out at him. He closed the file. "What is this supposed to tell me? That maybe he came out here to kill himself? That we're all chasing something that doesn't exist?"

"I just thought you should know," Ryerson said. "That's all."

"This is wrong. Danny wouldn't have done something like this. I would have known."

"Why don't I give you a minute? I'll be outside in the hall."

"That's not necessary," he said.

"I need another cup of coffee. Want one?"

He sighed. "Yeah, all right. Thank you. Thanks."

Ryerson left.

Jesus, Danny.

He flipped back to the front of the report and examined it more closely. The date of Danny's supposed attempted suicide and his subsequent stay at Sheppard Pratt coincided with their parents' deaths. It would explain why he hadn't been at their funeral.

A few minutes later, he met Jill Ryerson in the hall. He felt shaky and unsteady, the medical report rolled into a cone and tucked into his coat pocket. He smiled wearily at her and she returned the smile with one of equal weariness, though tinged with compassion. She was holding two Styrofoam cups of coffee.

"You holding up?" she asked, handing him one of the steaming cups.

"Yeah, yeah. I'll be okay. Thank you, Investigator Ryerson."

"Call me Jill."

"Thank you, Jill."

They walked down the hall toward the lobby of the station, in no great rush, just savoring the silence and the taste of the strong coffee. When a door opened at the opposite end of the lobby, Ryerson froze and gripped Paul's forearm, stopping him dead in his tracks. Paul looked up and saw a prisoner, hands and feet in chains and bookended by two burly troopers in powder-blue shirts, come shambling out of the cell block doorway. He had become intimately familiar with the black-and-white photograph of Mallory that had accompanied all the newspaper articles, yet despite it being a dated photo depicting a younger man, Paul had no trouble identifying this scarecrow-thin, gaunt-faced prisoner.

"That's him," Paul said.

"I'm sorry." Ryerson sounded bitter. "I'd forgotten about his appointment with the medic. They need to evaluate his foot before he transfers down to Seward."

They were speaking in whispers and Mallory was already halfway across the lobby . . . but it was as if the sounds of their voices had reached him. Mallory's feet—one bandaged, another clad in a white sock and a rubber sandal—ceased shuffling across the floor. He turned his head and leveled his gaze on them.

On Paul.

The man's eyes were small and dark and a pinch too close together. Predator's eyes. They were also filled with some alien intelligence that sent a chill rippling down Paul's spine. But as he stared at Paul, something in those eyes changed. Disbelief turning toward fear.

He knows me, Paul thought. *He recognizes me.*

One of the troopers tugged at Mallory's arm and said, "Let's go, man."

Joseph Mallory's mouth came unhinged. He looked like he was about to start screaming.

"You," Paul said. He yanked his arm free of Ryerson's grasp and closed the distance between him and Mallory in the time span of a single heartbeat.

"Mr. Gallo!" Ryerson yelled after him.

"You," Paul repeated, coffee spilling down his hand. The two troopers turned around and looked equally puzzled, caught off guard. Paul seized the front of Mallory's shirt and pulled him forward—so close he could smell Mallory's rank breath. Mallory's head jerked on the thin stalk of his neck. "You recognize me, don't you, you son of a bitch? I can see it in your eyes. You recognize me!"

One of the troopers stepped between them, attempting to separate them, one hand on Paul's chest. A strangled gurgle rose up from Mallory's throat.

Ryerson grabbed Paul about the shoulders and pulled him away from Mallory. This seemed to snap the troopers out of their momentary stupor, as they regained their composure and gave Mallory a jerk in the opposite direction.

"Paul!" Ryerson yelled. "Paul, stop it!"

The fistful of Mallory's shirt was stripped from his hand as the troopers dragged the murderer away. Yet Mallory's terrible gaze clung to him.

"You think I'm him, don't you?" Paul bellowed as Ryerson wrestled him backward. He dropped his coffee to the floor and tried to pull himself free of her, but she was too strong. "You think I'm Danny, don't you, you bastard? You think you're looking at a ghost." He raised his voice and shouted, "What did you do to him? Where is he? Where is he?"

"Get yourself under control, goddamn it," Ryerson hollered.

"Did you see his face?" Paul said, panting. The

troopers had ushered Mallory out the door, but Paul remained staring at the spot where the killer had been just a moment before. "Did you see his *eyes*? He thought I was Danny. He thought I was Danny, and it scared the shit out of him."

"Just calm down," Ryerson said. She was still clutching his shoulder, her fingers pressing hard into his muscles.

"There's your proof," he said. "There's your proof right there."

"Please," Ryerson said. She released her grip on him. There was coffee down the front of her shirt. "Calm down."

"I'm calm. I'm calm." He glanced down at the coffee cups on the floor. "I'm sorry. I'll clean it up."

"Forget it. You burned your hand, though."

He glanced down at his hand and saw that it was a bright red from having spilled the hot coffee on it. It throbbed, as if his looking at it had summoned the pain.

"Go clean up in the restroom," Ryerson said. "I'll take care of the mess out here."

A few minutes later, he came out of the restroom to find Ryerson standing in the lobby, her arms folded over her chest as she gazed out the window at the highway. "How's your hand?"

He ignored the question. "You saw that, didn't you? He thought he recognized me. He thought I was Danny."

"His head is scrambled," Ryerson said, indifferent. "Don't let it bug you."

"He did something to my brother."

"I'll talk to him when they bring him back," Ryerson said. It was the tone she might use to placate an obstinate child. "Okay?"

"Just tell me you saw that look in his eyes."

Placating or not, Ryerson didn't lie to him. "No," she said. "I saw no look in his eyes."

In the parking lot, Paul stood beneath the concrete overhang, which kept the wind at bay, while he waited for his cab. He held the police report in his hands, and glanced down at it before tucking it into the pocket of his coat.

It no longer mattered what Investigator Ryerson said about the high number of missing persons in Alaska; it no longer mattered that she wasn't convinced that Danny was embroiled in this nightmare; it no longer mattered that there were countless acres of undeveloped wilderness out here where someone could get lost and stay lost forever; moreover, it didn't matter what some outdated police report said about his brother's mental state. Paul didn't need to search countless acres of wilderness. He knew where Danny had gone missing, and that was good enough. He knew what he had to do.

He would go to Dread's Hand and find out what had happened to his brother.

PART TWO
DREAD'S HAND

11

Blink and you'd miss it: a town, or, rather, the memory of a town, secreted away at the end of a nameless, unpaved roadway that, in the deepening half light of an Alaskan dusk, looks like it might arc straight off the surface of the planet and out into the far reaches of the cosmos. A town where the scant few roads twist like veins and the little black-roofed houses, distanced from one another as if fearful of some contagion, look as if they'd been excreted into existence, pushed up through the crust of the earth from someplace deep underground. There is snow the color of concrete in the rutted streets, dirty clumps of it packed against the sides of houses or snared in the needled boughs of steel-colored spruce. If there are ghosts here—and some say there are—then they are most clearly glimpsed in the faces of the living. No one walks the unpaved streets; no one putters around in those squalid little yards, where the soil looks like ash and the saplings all bend at curious, pained, aggrieved angles. There is a furtiveness to most of these folks, an innate distrust not just of outsiders, but even of each other. Fear has reached across generations until it is in the eyes of every newborn expelled from the womb.

If you visit, you visit alone. Some would argue that there *are* no visitors, that there have never been, and that there are only the waylaid, the shipwrecked, the lost. And once you leave—*if* you leave—this town is only remembered as a sequence of crude Neanderthal drawings glimpsed through a zoetrope, a series of snapshots all laid out of order and in random, nonsensical collages. Nightmare fuel.

The few outsiders who come here often leave in a hurry, feeling ill.

A contagion at work.

Paul Gallo departed for Dread's Hand in the late afternoon, soon after he returned from the police station, and just as a freezing rain began to shower downtown Fairbanks. The shallow forests toward the west glowed with an almost preternatural haze, and the highway blacktop shimmered beneath a slick cocktail of rainwater and motor oil. There was a smell in the air, not unpleasant, that reminded Paul somewhat of the riverbanks of his youth, and of nights spent in his backyard, gazing at the stars with Danny, their bare feet cool in the dewy grass.

After checking out of his Fairbanks hotel, he took a cab to the nearest rental car facility. There, a young female attendant was eager to help him, but she failed to locate Dread's Hand on any of the standard road maps that had been filed into the kiosk beside her desk. In the end, she located a map online, and printed it out for him. If she was aware of Joseph Mallory and of the bodies that had been excavated from the woods out that way, she did not comment on it. In fact, she seemed ignorant to anything outside of her own little world-bubble, and Paul was momentarily envious of her.

"Okay, see, you're here," she said, pointing to down-town, "and you want to go all the way out . . . *here*." The smudgy dot that represented Dread's Hand sat at the end of a circuitous roadway that stopped at the foot-hills of the White Mountains.

"This long road here, leading into the town," Paul said. "It doesn't have a name?"

"No, I guess not," said the attendant. "And it's in red. That means it's not part of the official highway system. Some of the roads in and out of those old mining towns are like that. They shut down all winter, too. No plows get out that way."

"What do people do out there in the winter?"

"Pray," said the attendant.

Paul wasn't so sure it was a joke.

"So how will I know when to turn onto this road from the highway?" he asked.

"Keep aware of your surroundings and count your mile markers," suggested the attendant. "I'm not kid-ding. Here, look. You know if you hit this intersection out here, you've gone too far. And if you're still back this way, well, then you haven't gone far enough. You'll just have to keep your eyes peeled when you get around this spot, which is really only a twenty-or-so minute drive from here. It shouldn't be too bad. At least it's not snowing."

"Thank God for small miracles," he said.

"I can get you a vehicle with a GPS system, if you think that would help."

"Couldn't hurt. Thank you."

"Sometimes they work, sometimes they don't."

Paul didn't think she sounded too hopeful.

The light rain had turned into a soupy sleet by the time he stepped outside and hustled across the macadam to pick up his vehicle, his suitcase feeling like it weighed two hundred pounds. He was exhausted, and he hadn't had a decent night's sleep since he'd been out here. He attributed this to the time change and the shrinking daylight as this part of the world moved closer toward the winter solstice. But there was no denying that Danny had been on his mind more in the past few days—it was the reason he was here. The whole thing had left him unsettled and disassociated. Last night, he'd woken around three in the morning with a scream lodged in his throat, the tendrils of some nightmare slipping off him so quickly he had no time to register anything about the dream. Except that it had to do with Danny.

It always had to do with Danny.

"Do you know where you are going?" said the young guy behind a sheet of Plexiglas as he fed the keys to a Chevy Tahoe through an opening.

"Dread's Hand," Paul said. "It's about ninety miles northwest of here, right?"

"You've seen the news, yeah?" said the guy.

"You're talking about the bodies they found?"

"That's an empty place," the man said. "A blind spot."

Paul shook his head. "What do you mean?"

"People don't go up there," said the man.

"What people? They don't go where?"

"You'd be better to go sightseeing, yeah?" The man smiled at him, exposing a mouthful of blackened, rotting teeth.

"Have a good day," Paul said, and hurried away from the window.

The Tahoe stood in a spot that looked too small for it. It was a massive vehicle, and he felt like a kid getting on a school bus as he climbed up into the thing.

Blessedly, the heater worked. He cranked it to full force, then pulled out of the lot. The strange attendant stared at him as he drove off, leaning in his chair and pressing his face against the Plexiglas in order to watch Paul go.

Up is down, down is up, he imagined Danny whispering inside his head.

Once he pulled out onto the highway, he fired up the GPS and typed in the name of the town—Dread's Hand. A little hourglass icon appeared on the GPS screen, and the sexless robotic voice informed him that the device was calculating, calculating, calculating . . . but then it informed him that the location he'd entered didn't exist.

"Great," he grumbled.

He tried it a second time. This time, a message popped up on the screen, suggesting he update his software.

Sometimes they work, sometimes they don't, indeed, he thought.

* * *

The nameless road wasn't nameless, after all.

He followed the printed map, leaving the highway for a secondary road ten minutes into his trip, and from there, he kept an eye out for a nameless cutoff road that looked like it was heading in the direction of the foothills. Although the rain had stopped, a hazy mist had gathered about the shoulders of the roadway and coiled around the bases of the surrounding trees like something alive.

He almost drove past the sharp cutoff, but stood on the Tahoe's brake at the last second. Thankfully, there were no other cars on the road, otherwise he might have been rear-ended. Spinning the wheel, he took the turn, hoping it was the right road. Judging by the position of the waning sunlight, the road headed due north, though the fog was too thick for him to make out any suggestion of the White Mountains in the distance. The sun itself was just a dim coin of light burning through the haze.

After just a few minutes of driving, he motored past a rickety wooden road sign that looked like it had been made in someone's garage. The letters had been scorched into the wood—DAMASCUS ROAD.

"You're not supposed to have a name, my friend," Paul muttered. "I just hope you're the right road."

Everything looked hard and flat and inhospitable, like the atmosphere of some foreign planet. On both sides of the unpaved road, massive lodgepole pines rose up into the atmosphere, their tops obscured by the fog, their pine boughs looking like steel brushes.

The notion of something coming in from the outside and framing his destiny latched on to him as he drove. After Danny had disappeared, Paul had taken to driving. He'd spent most of his evenings driving, usually after work, as darkness fell. He preferred the wooded secondary roads beyond the suburban neighborhoods, the ones that were so far removed from the highways and the interstate that you couldn't see the distant headlights of cars through the trees. He had cut through wooded hillsides, guided by nothing more than the iridescence of the moon. Sometimes he'd drive to the Eastern Shore, cutting across the Bay Bridge, a pair of headlights in a parade of them, the Chesapeake so expansive that he could discern the slight curvature of the earth from such a height. Cornfields, forested trails, wet and glistening blacktop—it didn't matter where. He'd kept his windows rolled up tight, the radio tuned low to some AM talk station, his eyes cutting back and forth to the shoulders while his headlamps moved through the darkness ahead. A few times, and despite the utter desolation of those secret byways and twisting, serpentine passages, he'd be convinced that he was not alone. There had been a joining presence, like warm breath on his neck, as if someone was leaning toward him from the backseat. There had even been a few occasions when he had slowed down and peered over his shoulder while driving, terrified that he might find the silhouette of another person propped up back there. But, of course, he never had.

That feeling was upon him now, again, and with full authority. There was even a moment when he thought he might turn his head, glance out the window, and see Danny standing on the shoulder of the road.

Or perhaps hanging from a tree, an electrical cord around his neck, he thought.

When his vision began to blur, Paul realized he was crying. It was the first time since that night he'd gotten drunk on Knob Creek and blared Danny's favorite Van Halen albums on the stereo.

He pulled over on the shoulder of the road and geared the Tahoe into Park. His warm breath fogged up the windows. He closed his eyes and eased his head back against the headrest. He thought of the almost-preternatural closeness they'd both shared throughout their childhood and adolescence, those brotherly transmissions that seemed to travel like radio waves between them. Those transmissions had faded over the years, though was it possible that Danny could have arrived at such a dark, dire place and had attempted to take his own life without Paul having some inkling of his brother's grief? Or worse—had the transmissions come through, only to be ignored by him?

No, there was no magical bond. We were brothers, were twins, and felt strongly for each other. That's all.

When he faced forward again, he was startled to find a large black wolf standing in the middle of the otherwise empty road. The thing was close enough so that Paul could make out the patterns in its damp, rain-slickened fur and the shimmery greenness of its eyes. Despite the shroudlike fog that blocked out the sun, the thing's shadow stretched like black taffy along the pavement behind it. Its breath steamed in the cold air.

It was staring straight at him.

Paul waited for it to move, but it seemed rooted to its spot, just a few yards in front of the Tahoe. It was motionless except for the patches of its sleek black fur that undulated like fields of wheat in the wind. The Tahoe's headlights caught the creature's eyes in just the right way so that they appeared to glow a bright swamp-gas green.

Paul shifted the Tahoe back into Drive and lifted his foot off the brake. The SUV rolled toward the creature, its shadow elongating even further along the pavement. But the wolf did not move.

Now only a few yards from the creature, Paul eased back down on the brake and watched it as it watched him. It lowered its head and looked like it might either spirit away into the woods or actually charge at the vehicle. As Paul stared at it, the beast's ears flattened to its skull, much the way a dog's would when it was preparing to attack. But the wolf did not even bare its teeth. Only stared.

Paul laid on the Tahoe's horn, the sonorous blast echoing out over the rutted dirt road and into the foothills beyond.

The wolf just stared at him.

Then it turned and, without giving Paul a second glance, trotted off into the woods. Gone.

An instant later, the robotic voice of the GPS said, "Recalculating."

Startled, Paul uttered a sharp cry, then laughed a nervous laugh.

12

The first few crosses seemed to materialize right out of the fog.

They were large structures, constructed of two sun-bleached javelins of wood tied together with string, a heavy bolt nailed through the cross section. They were staked along the right-hand shoulder of the dirt road and seemed to ghost out of the fog as he drove by.

A moment later, he could see countless others, some planted along the gravelly shoulder while others were stationed farther back from the road and partially obscured beneath the shade of the trees. They looked old and time-worn, streaked with what he deduced was bird shit and road muck and other debris, while others had fallen apart, and remained as single stakes jutting from the loam. They looked like certain doom.

Beyond the crosses, he drove past a crumbling shotgun shack off to his left. Farther up the road and on his right was a scattering of small saltbox houses with shrubs sprouting out of the gutters and boards nailed up over the windows. And even farther still, he saw what appeared to be an impromptu landfill—a conglomeration of old washing machines, truck tires, TV antennas, and even an entire discarded swing set lay in a jumbled heap in the overgrown grass, like some beast that had succumbed to the elements and left its skeleton behind. The dirt road curled around a stand of trees, and when he followed it, he saw more run-down houses there, each one like the boxcar of a locomotive, lined up against the road.

You didn't arrive in Dread's Hand, he realized, but rather Dread's Hand came at you piecemeal, a bit of itself at a time, like someone reluctant to make your acquaintance. Even the peeling wooden sign hammered into a mound of dirt welcoming travelers to the town seemed more like an admonition than a salutation. The *r* in "Dread" was missing, which made him think of all those crosses along the road on the drive in.

Unincorporated Mining Village of
D EAD'S HAND, ALASKA
SINCE 1906

*"And the devil took Him to a very high mountain
and showed Him all the kingdoms
of the world."*

I shouldn't be here, he thought.

The dirt road did not so much stop as it just sort of dispersed, tendrils of it cutting passageways past clapboard houses, through the surrounding woods and the foothills beyond. Paul continued in a straight line, assuming he'd come across the center of town eventually if he didn't veer off in any other direction. But when, after several minutes, the road dead-ended at a gravel pit that overlooked a green-gray forest, he realized that there *was* no center of town. He headed back in the direction he had come and took the first road to branch off the main thoroughfare.

He passed a feed store, a hardware store—both were dark and looked closed—and a structure that resembled an oversized outhouse around which men in heavy winter coats stood, passing around a flask of something that made their faces ruddy and their eyes glassy. They all glanced over at Paul's vehicle as he drove by, their faces expressionless, clouds of vapor unspooling from their crooked, bearded mouths. Another man in a chamois coat with wool trim was seated on a bench smoking a long, thin cigar. He watched the Tahoe roll to a stop with the slack-jawed expression of a country dullard.

Paul rolled down the passenger window and said, "Excuse me."

The man just stared at him.

"Is there a motel in town? Someplace I can stay?"

The man offered no response; his steely eyes just clung to Paul while one corner of his mouth twitched.

"Thanks," Paul said, rolling up the window. "Asshole."

He was just about to pull forward when a figure stepped out in front of the SUV. Paul jumped on the brakes and the vehicle bucked, the seat belt locking against his chest.

"Jesus," he gasped, unclenching his fingers from the steering wheel.

The person turned and looked at him, and Paul felt his whole body shudder at the sight. The figure was slight enough to be a child, although Paul couldn't be sure, because the person was wearing something over their face. It was a mask of sorts, though one crudely fashioned out of some animal's hide—or so it appeared—with ragged eyeholes cut into the grayish-brown fur.

They stared at each other through the windshield for several seconds, neither of them moving a muscle. Paul could see the small, wet eyes behind the eyeholes cut into the furry hide. Then the child—for it was a child, Paul was now certain, his mind having pieced together all the aspects of its physical character to arrive at this deduction—ran to the opposite end of the street where he or she joined two other children, both of whom wore similar masks over their faces. On the smallest child, Paul made out a single rabbit ear protruding from the side of the mask and drooping like the whisker of a catfish.

All three of them examined him from the shoulder of the road before sprinting off behind a nearby house, their sneakers kicking up clods of mud.

Paul wasn't as quick to regain his senses. He remained parked there in the middle of the road, his fingers flexing around the steering wheel, his heart break-dancing in his chest. He glanced around, wondering if there were more masked children about to dash out into the road and in front of his vehicle, and that was when he saw the Blue Moose Inn.

It was no different from the houses that stood at wide intervals along this road, an unassuming whitewashed boxcar with a pane of wavy glass beside a peeling green door. Behind the building was a squat stucco building that he would have guessed was a garage if not for a stone chimney expelling a column of smoke into the overcast sky. Dirty snow was packed against the cinder-block steps of the inn, gray as ash. A plaque over the door said BLUE MOOSE INN—EST. 1940. There was a blinking neon sign in the window that read OPEN.

Paul pulled the Tahoe up onto the gravelly lot beside the inn and got out. It was even colder up here in the hills than it had been back in Fairbanks, and he zipped up his coat as he walked around the side of the inn, stepping over the ashy mounds of old, blackened snow, and pulled open the front door.

He entered a cramped, wood-paneled room that reeked of cigarette smoke mingled with Pine-Sol disinfectant. An elderly man sat watching TV behind a mahogany desk, his feet propped up on a mini fridge, his back toward the lobby. The dusty black eyes of a taxidermied moose head gazed down at Paul from a wooden plaque fixed to the wall above the television.

There was a cramped hallway about as accommodating as a mine shaft off to the left, where Paul could make out a morose little coffee station next to a bookshelf laden with dusty hardbound tomes.

"Hello," Paul said, approaching the lobby desk.

The old man seated before the TV craned his head around, revealing a seamed face and hockey-stick sideburns the color of fresh snow. He dropped his boots down off the fridge, then grunted as he hoisted himself out of his folding chair. He had a toothpick crooked into the corner of his mouth, and he was wearing a nylon vest cinched together at the front with frayed lengths of twine. He wore an incongruous smiley-face button pinned over his left breast. The old man's age was indeterminable.

"There's kids outside wearing animal furs on their faces," Paul said.

"Who're you?" the old guy said.

Paul blinked. "I was just wondering if you had any rooms available," he said.

"Rooms?" The man just gaped at him, a cheesy clump of coagulated spittle nestled in the right corner of his mouth, opposite the toothpick. "Only got the one room," said the man.

"Is it available?"

The toothpick rolled from one corner of the old man's mouth to the other. "Who're you with, anyway?" the old man asked him. His eyes were rheumy, the sclera yellow. They were the eyes of an ancient tortoise, though somehow less wise and steeped in a haze of confusion.

"'With'?" Paul said.

"You police or newspaper man?" said the old-timer.

"Oh," Paul said. "Neither."

"Then how come you out this way?"

"I'm looking for someone. My brother, Danny Gallo. Can I show you a picture of him?"

The old man's eyes narrowed, and he made no effort to conceal either his confusion and his agitation at Paul's sudden arrival, not to mention this strange detour into photographs and missing brothers. "Ain't no one come out this way, 'cept cops. All week it's cops. Up in them woods. Bad idea. You a cop?"

"I'm not a cop." Judging by the man's demeanor, Paul

realized he'd be of no help, but he dug his cell phone out of his coat anyway, and scrolled through Danny's text messages until he found the most recent one, from over a year ago—the one he'd shown Investigator Ryerson earlier that day. Paul held out the phone so the old man could examine the photograph.

"Hmmm," said the man as he peered at the photo on the cell phone's screen. Then the man's suspicious gaze shot back up at Paul. "That's a picture of you," he said, his voice grating. "This some kind of joke?"

"We're twins," Paul said. "Like I said, his name is Danny Gallo. He came out here about a year ago. But then he disappeared."

Scrutinizing the photo once again, the old man muttered, "Uh-huh."

"So you recognize him?"

"No, sir."

"Are you sure? It was only a year ago."

"He ain't familiar. Neither are you."

Paul exhaled. He was exhausted. "How about that room?"

"What room?"

"You said . . . the room. You have a room available, don't you?"

The old man's lower lip protruded. "You with the IRS or something, fella?"

"No. No, I'm not with the IRS. Listen, is there someone else working here? I'm very tired."

"There's Igor," said the man.

"Igor?"

The old man pistoned a finger over his head and at the stuffed moose head fixed to the wall behind him, dusty black marbles for eyes. One side of the old man's mouth tightened into the approximation of a grin, which told Paul that this was some sort of joke—perhaps the only joke this old-timer knew.

"Oh. All right." Paul tucked the cell phone back into his coat pocket. "That's funny."

"You here 'cause of this brother, or are you here 'cause of them murders? Them bodies they found up in them woods?"

"I'm here because those two things might be related."

"Think your brother was killed, eh?" There was not a trace of emotion in the old man's voice. He was asking a question that could have been handed to him on an index card.

"I'm not sure what happened," Paul told him.

"Chopped off their heads. You know that?"

"What?"

"Ol' Joe Mallory from up Durham went crazy, chopped off their heads. All of 'em."

"The victims' heads? They'd been decapitated?"

"Wasn't in any of the newspapers, was it?"

"No," Paul said, feeling his stomach sink. "It wasn't."

"So don't you go printing it, neither."

"I'm not a reporter. I'm not a reporter and I'm not a cop. I'm just tired. Can I get that room?"

The inn's door opened on a gust of frigid wind and squalling hinges. A largish woman came in from the outside, her face squinty and red from the cold.

"I told you not to move from that chair, Daddy," she scolded the old man, though her stare was fixed on Paul. Her hair was tied back beneath a kerchief, and she was dressed in a man's flannel shirt and barn coat.

She went around the front desk and placed a hand on the old man's shoulder. "Go watch your TV and stop pestering folks." Then she turned to Paul. It was the old man's stoic face that stared back at him, though perhaps twenty-odd years younger, and without an ounce of femininity. A sheen of white down bristled from the woman's chin. "Can I help you?" she asked him.

"He's police," said the old man as he lowered himself back down into his lawn chair with shaky sluggishness, his hands planted on the chair's armrests, his elbows wobbling for balance.

"I'm not police," Paul said to the woman.

"Don't mind Daddy. He's got the dementia."

"Goddamn you, Janice," the old man bellowed at her, his voice hoarse and cracking. "I'm trying to watch my program here."

"Ma'am, my name's Paul Gallo. My brother came out here about a year ago, just before he went missing. Would you mind looking at a photo to see if you recognize him?"

"Don't get many people out this way, Mr. Gallo. But sure, I'll take a look."

He showed her the picture on his phone.

"That's a picture of you, ain't it?" she said.

"We're twins."

She looked back down at the photo again, this time studying it a bit closer. "Yeah, I see that now. Small differences."

"Do you recognize him?"

She shook her head. "Sorry."

"His brother's dead," barked the old man.

"All right, Daddy," the woman called to her father.

"Madman Mallory took the fella's head clean off."

"Daddy, that's enough."

"Took *all* 'em heads off. Whoop! Just like 'at."

The woman returned her gaze to Paul, her face brooding and unapologetic. "Don't pay him no mind. We've had some trouble out here lately."

"I know about the murders. That's what brought me out here."

"Well, if you're worried your brother might be messed up in all that, you're better off talking to the police down in Fairbanks. Ain't gonna do you much good prowling around out here. We're fixing to get some early snow, too. Road to the highway shuts down after the first big snowfall. The state don't plow way out here."

"I've got a police report that mentions a woman named Valerie Drammell. Is she like the town constable or something?"

"She's a he," said the woman. "He's public safety. He might help you put out a grease fire, if he ain't out at Whitehead hooking pike. That's about the extent of his policing."

"He's a lousy pissant son of a bitch," the old man commented.

"That's enough outta you," the woman called back to him over her shoulder.

"So what happens if there's an emergency?" Paul asked. "You gotta wait for the police or paramedics to drive the ninety miles up from Fairbanks?"

"We're real good at taking care of our own out here," she said. "Was there anything else I can help you with, Mr. Gallo?"

"I'd like to rent that room you've got."

"I can do that, although you might be more comfortable out by the highway."

"I prefer to stay here in town."

"Just figured I'd mention it, is all. The room's forty bucks a night, in advance. Credit card machine's busted, so it's cash."

Paul forked over two twenties and was handed a brass key affixed to a plastic fob with the inn's name printed on it in permanent marker.

"We shut the lobby down at ten," the woman said, "but your room key will get you in and out of the front door. Daddy and I stay next door, if there's anything you need in the night. And I prepare breakfast at seven sharp, if you're up and hungry come morning. I'm Jan Warren, by the way."

"Thank you, Jan. I'm Paul."

She leaned over the desk and held an arm out toward the narrow shaft of hallway beyond the lobby. "Yours is the first door on the right, just past the dining room."

"Thanks." Paul glanced up at the moose head mounted to the wall above the old man's TV. "Thanks, Igor."

He carried his bags in from the car and down the cramped little hall, passing a gloomy dining area that boasted a single rectangular table slotted up against a pair of shaded windows, and a lunch counter that accommodated two stools. It looked like a 1950s soda shop that had been evacuated following the knell of an air-raid siren.

The door to his room sported a heavy-duty dead bolt, while the wooden door itself looked about as substantial as a plank of balsa wood. The lock on the door was uncooperative, so it took some finessing with the key to get it unlocked and opened.

The room was tiny. Had it not been for the narrow little bed shoved against one wall, Paul would have thought he'd walked into a broom closet. There were just enough animal heads adorning the walls to make Paul think that Norman Bates was watching him from behind one of those sets of eyes. There were crosses on the walls, too, some of which looked as if they were handmade, carved from unpolished staves of wood or woven from lengths of dry, brittle palm. Most disturbing of all was the enormous macramé tapestry of the Virgin Mary hanging where Paul would have preferred a television to be—there was no TV in the room—and the rudimentary style of the artwork made it look almost like modern art. The eyes, Paul noted, looked unfinished; they appeared as large white orbs.

There was a peculiar gluey smell to the room, too, he noticed, stepping inside and closing the door behind him. It was as if new wallpaper had been recently put up. Researchers have said that the olfactory sense is the one most closely connected to memory, and the smell of the room brought him back to grade-school art class, and the time Danny had pulled his hands up into the overlong sleeves of his art smock, which had been one of their father's old shirts. Mrs. Proctor, the art teacher, had grabbed the sleeves and snipped them with a pair of shears. Danny had unleashed an agonized cry, and Mrs. Proctor, terrified that she had snipped Danny's fingers along with the sleeves, had turned white. But then Danny started laughing, and wiggling his fingers from the shortened sleeves. Mrs. Proctor had sent him to the principal's office, and then had spent the remainder of the class studying Paul, as if he had somehow conspired with Danny to trick her.

The memory was a strong one, yet he was still surprised to find his heart thumping in his chest. His skin felt prickly beneath his clothes.

He dumped his duffel bag and suitcase on the bed, pulled off his coat, then went to the tiny bathroom, where he washed his face and hands in a sink that was too low to the floor. Then he stared at his reflection in the mirror above the sink. Carved into the glass at the bottom of the mirror was the phrase:

YOU SHOULD NOT BE HERE

"No shit," he muttered.

For the briefest moment, he thought he saw Danny standing over his shoulder in the mirror. He didn't turn around, but instead wiped an arc through the steam. Danny was gone.

You should not be here.

His cell phone chimed in his coat pocket, startling him. He fumbled it out and saw that it was Erin Sharma.

"Hey, Erin," he said.

"Paul? You sound out of breath. Are you okay?"

"Oh, I was just working out. You know me."

Erin laughed, and the sound of it helped anchor him to reality. Until that moment, he hadn't realized just how detached he'd been feeling.

"I haven't heard from you, and I was beginning to get worried," she said.

"I'm sorry. I guess I should have called."

"Where are you?"

"Fairbanks," he said. It was a slip of the tongue—he'd answered without thinking. "No, wait. I'm in Dread's Hand."

"Where?"

"It's the town where Danny went missing."

"Have you spoken to that police detective?"

"Ryerson," he said. He crossed the room and sat down on the edge of the small bed. A headache was coming awake in his left temple. He shrugged himself out of his coat. "She's an investigator with the state troopers. Yeah, I met with her earlier today."

"And? What's going on, Paul? The news out here stopped reporting on the story. I guess they've lost interest. It's back to Justin Bieber and the Kardashians."

He cut off their heads, Erin. How's that for a news bulletin, huh? Something they didn't put in any of the newspapers, as far as I know. Heck, maybe the old bastard in the lobby was full of shit and just trying to spook me into good behavior, but I don't think he was. I don't think he was full of shit, Erin. I think that psychopath Joseph Mallory cut those people's heads off, just like the old bastard said.

"They've identified the victims. Danny's not one of them."

"What? No?" She cleared her throat. "Okay. Okay, then."

"Yeah, so . . ."

"What does that mean for you? Are you coming home?"

"In a couple of days, I think," he said. The headache had matured to a full-blown migraine in a matter of thirty seconds. He pressed the heel of his free hand against his pounding temple.

"What else is there for you to do out there?"

"Try to find out what happened," he said.

"Oh, Paul."

"What? What is it?"

"Nothing. You sound tired. Poor Paul. How are you holding up?" Her tone was more delicate now.

They'd made love on three occasions during their brief courtship, over two years ago now, but he found himself picturing her smooth, brown body, and the way she'd leave her warm scent on his pillows for days after. The way she'd set her black-framed glasses on his nightstand before bed. The pale whiteness of the soles of her feet. He missed her.

"I'm holding up just fine," he told her.

"And your Manipura? Have you used it to save the world yet?"

He smiled despite the jackhammering in his skull. "I'll get on that just as soon as I'm done pumping all this iron."

"I am not joking," she said, though he knew her well enough to sense the taunting in her voice. "You think I'm foolish, but I am praying for you, Paul."

"You're too kind to me. You worry too much."

"I have never had to worry about you before. Ever. Until now."

"Why now? What's to be worried about?"

"You have your Manipura and I have my Ajna."

"Are you talking dirty to me now?"

"The Ajna—the third-eye chakra. My woman's intuition, if you prefer your crude Western parlance."

"Erin, there's nothing to be worried about. I'll be fine. You were the one who urged me to come out here in the first place, remember?"

"Not true," she said. "I urged you to make the telephone call to that policewoman. This circumambulation to the ends of the earth was your brilliant idea, professor."

"Quit using big words. It's getting late and I'm tired."

"Yeah, well, it's four hours later here, you know. And I have work in the morning."

"Then get some sleep," he said.

"I will. Just promise me that you will be safe."

"Why wouldn't I be safe? I'm fine, Erin. Everything is fine."

"Then just promise me that whatever you find out about your brother—whatever happens out there—you'll keep in mind that you did all you could for him."

I wonder if that's true, he thought, and had even opened his mouth to say as much. But he caught himself at the last minute.

"Of course," he said into the phone. "I promise I'll keep that in mind. But please, don't worry."

"Be good, Paul."

"Good night, Erin."

He hung up.

There was a tub of Advil in his duffel bag. He dug it out now, popped two tablets into his mouth, and swallowed them dry. Also inside the duffel bag was the unlabeled box that had sat for a year on the shelf in Paul's bedroom closet—the box filled with Danny's cell phone records, credit card statements, and all the police reports that had been filed with the case. He took that box out now and opened it. The papers inside smelled stale, and the English teacher in him couldn't help wondering if their odor was symbolic.

He located the police report that had been filed soon after Paul first spoke with Investigator Ryerson over the phone, one year earlier. He reread it, noting that Ryerson had requested two state troopers, Olsen and Mannaway, to travel to Dread's Hand. There were a few photographs attached to the report that showed Danny's rental car, an aquamarine Oldsmobile Bravada, on the shoulder of a wooded dirt road. It could have been any one of the desolate roadways that traversed the country, but Paul thought it looked very much like the ninety miles of road that led from the highway outside Fairbanks out here to Dread's Hand. He could make out the mountain range at the horizon in a few of the photos, just beyond the trees, the green-black dinosaur shapes of the White Mountains.

He'd examined these countless times before, when he'd first received them in the mail, but he noticed something now in one of the photos that hadn't registered with him before. Probably because he hadn't had the context at the time to recognize it for what it was.

In one photo, there was something thin and white reflected in the Bravada's tinted rear window. Only now did Paul realize it was one of the large wooden crosses that he had passed along that nameless road—a road that was, in fact, called Damascus Road—on his drive into the village this afternoon.

What do you expect to find out here? a voice spoke up in his head. *Do you think you'll actually find something the trained professionals missed?*

But those trained professionals had no reason to believe Danny had been one of Mallory's victims. They were too narrow-minded, too focused on what they already had right in front of them. Ryerson hadn't noticed the look of recognition in Mallory's eyes. Danny had been written off. No one else would be out here looking for him.

Enough. His head hurt too much to go over this stuff right now.

He set aside the box of records and reclined on the bed. The mattress was hard and unyielding, but he realized that, in his exhaustion, he didn't care.

He was asleep in less than a minute.

13

Ryerson grabbed two cartons of beef lo mein and a bag of egg rolls from Luck Joy Beijing, then hustled back to the station beneath a light drizzle of rain.

"You'll be next to catch the flu," McHale said as she came into the squad room. He had his feet up on his desk and was hammering out a text message on his cell phone. "Isn't this supposed to be your day off, anyway?"

"Supposed to be," she said, setting one of the containers down on his desk. "Dinner."

"Ah, thank you! You're a gem. Don't let anyone tell you otherwise." McHale opened the carton of lo mein and a cloud of steam rose up in front of his face. He inhaled, grinning to himself.

"How's Mallory's foot?" Ryerson asked.

"Medic put a clean dressing on it. Says it's healing. Mallory's back in his cell now. Swinton just took him dinner. Have we heard back from Spring Creek yet?"

"Not yet. They're overcrowded. I'm sure we'll hear something soon."

"Well, we can't keep the bastard locked up in Puke Alley forever."

"I know." She was thinking of Lucas Bristol, and how uncomfortable the young trooper had been ever since they'd brought Mallory here and locked him up. Bristol, who'd told her ghost stories from his childhood about haunted forests and a great-uncle who'd taken his head apart with a hunting rifle out there in the woods beyond Dread's Hand.

"I heard there was some commotion earlier today," McHale said, peeking into the egg roll bag. "Some guy freaking out on you or something."

"No, not exactly. Guy flew in from Maryland to see if his brother was one of Mallory's victims. Did the DNA swab, but he came back negative for a match. Still, he insisted Mallory had done something to his brother. Said it was too much of a coincidence that his brother had disappeared last year from the same town where Mallory lived and killed all those people."

"Well, yeah, I can see that," McHale said.

She told him about Paul Gallo running into Mallory as she walked him through the lobby, and the exchange that had taken place.

"Guy was convinced that Mallory recognized him, and mistook him for his missing brother," Ryerson said. "Oh, I guess I left out an important part of the story— the brothers are identical twins."

"Well, shit," McHale said. He glanced up at her while in the middle of unwrapping a pair of chopsticks. "You think he's right? You think there might be more victims out there that Mallory didn't tell us about?"

Ryerson didn't answer the question. She had her own

chopsticks out of the wrapper and was tapping them against the palm of her hand.

Across the hall, Ryerson's desk phone trilled.

"That's me," she said, and set her lo mein container on McHale's desk.

"You take too long, I'm eating yours, too," McHale called after her as she jogged into her office and closed the door.

"Major Crimes," she said into the receiver. "This is Jill Ryerson."

"Hi, Jill. It's Walter Banks down in Anchorage." Banks was the medical examiner who'd been conducting the autopsies on Mallory's victims.

"Yes! Hello." She scooted around her desk, knocking some papers to the floor in the process, and dropped down into her chair.

"I've got my staff preparing an official report for your office as we speak, but I wanted to give you a courtesy call ahead of time," Banks said.

"I appreciate that."

"So, it looks like the cause of death in all eight victims is from a single gunshot wound to the head. Point-blank range from a high-velocity firearm. Probably a rifle. That's about as exact as I can get for you on that score, Jill."

"So the decapitation was postmortem," she said.

"Correct. My guess is he used an ax."

"Jesus. What in the world possesses someone to do that?"

"I assume that's a rhetorical question," Banks said.

"Yes. Sorry. I've just never seen anything like it."

"It's beyond our grasp as human beings to comprehend something like this, Jill. Don't try to understand it."

"It wasn't just one of them," she said. "He did that to all of them. Like there was a method to his—"

"His madness, yes," Banks finished. "And that's exactly what it is. Of course, I'm no psychiatrist, but I think we're capable of our own suppositions, don't you?"

"Have you ever seen anything like this before?"

There was a brief pause on the other end of the line. She could hear Walter Banks's nasally respiration.

"There was a man who killed his son and then himself back about, oh, eight or ten years ago or so," Banks said. "Family lived over in Chena Hills. Name was Rhobean. It was such an unusual name I never forgot it. Terrible case, too."

"The boy was decapitated?"

"Yes. The father took him out to the woodshed to do the deed. Then he put a pistol to his own temple. Kid's mother found them out there."

"How old was the boy?"

"Teenager. By all accounts, seemed like the kid and his old man had a fine relationship. Old man sounded like a regular guy, too, although it was a long time ago and I can't say I remember all the details. I guess it was just one of those things, huh?"

"I guess so," Ryerson said. She hoped McHale had eaten her beef lo mein after all.

"I *do* remember there was some speculation about devil worship."

She thought she'd misheard him. "Devil worship?"

"There was something about it in the newspapers. I

can't recall the details anymore. Or maybe it was something from the police report. Your unit worked the case, you know." Banks exhaled into the receiver. "My guess is those investigators are probably retired. Yet I'm still here, getting 'er done."

"And we appreciate that, Walter."

"God bless, Jill. Have a nice evening. Expect that report by the end of the week."

She was about to hang up when she remembered something. "Walter?"

"Yeah?"

"That thing we found inside that trunk in the basement. Did you have a chance to look it over?"

"I did. You wanna know what it is?"

"Absolutely," she said.

"*Ovis dalli,*" Banks said.

"What?"

"Dead sheep. The rotted carcass of a Dall sheep, to be exact. Thing's been dead for years."

"A dead sheep," she muttered to herself.

"You said this thing was in his basement? In his house?"

"Packed away in an oversized steamer trunk," she said.

"Well," Banks said. "Like I told you, Jill. Don't try to understand it. In fact, it's probably best if you forget it. Just keep going forward."

"Thanks," she said.

But she wouldn't forget it.

"That man who was here today," she said. "Did you recognize him?"

Joseph Mallory did not answer.

He was curled up in one dark corner of his cell, his food tray untouched, the clean white bandage around his foot seeming to float there in the gloom.

"Mr. Mallory?" Ryerson said, her voice rising a notch.

But Mallory would not answer. If it wasn't for his rattling respiration, she might have feared him dead.

"We've identified that thing you had in your trunk. It was a sheep."

Above Ryerson's head, a lightbulb fizzed out, dousing Mallory's cell in even more darkness.

She stood there for a few minutes longer, wondering if there was some incrimination in Mallory's silence, or if he was too unhinged to attribute any logic to his behavior.

"The devil has his tricks, but you can beat them," said Mallory.

"What does that mean?"

"That man today." But he didn't finish the thought.

"So you know him."

Mallory didn't answer.

"Do you know him? Did he look familiar to you?"

"Tricks," Mallory said. "And now I'm worried that everything I've done has been for nothing."

"Are there more bodies?"

Mallory just stared at his feet.

"Did you do something to that man's brother? Are there more bodies out there you haven't told us about? Mr. Mallory, please, if there are others, why haven't you told us?" When he didn't respond, she said, "You haven't been living in your house for some time. Pipes were frozen, no electricity. No food. Where have you been all this time?"

But Mallory was done talking.

The light above Ryerson's head blinked back on. She peered up at it, then back into Mallory's cell.

Mallory's face looked like a skull wreathed in long, greasy hair, his empty eye sockets like black pools of ink, his jaws lined with rows of elongated, vampiric teeth. A moment later, it was just Joe Mallory's face again.

Trick of the light, she thought.

Disquieted, Jill Ryerson left.

14

It was a nightmare, in which he was swept up high over the treetops by a great wind and carried off into the darkness, that caused Paul to wake. His whole body jerked as his eyes flipped open. Darkness pressed down upon him, and he sat up, disoriented. The only suggestion of light came from the stars poking through the quilt of night outside the windows beside his bed.

And then it all came back to him: He'd driven up to Dread's Hand and had checked into the Blue Moose Inn. He'd downed a few aspirin and reclined on the bed, unaware of how exhausted he'd been. Sleep had blindsided him.

But he'd fallen asleep with the lights on, hadn't he? The lights were now off. He leaned over to the nightstand and turned the switch on the lamp—*click-click-click*. The light did not come on.

The room was like an icebox, and when he exhaled, he could see his breath crystallize in the air. He wondered whether the inn had lost all power, and if so, why a place out here wouldn't have a backup generator.

The tendons in his back popping, he climbed out of bed and went over to the windows. He opened the shutters and peered out into the misty night. The moon hung above the horizon, where black trees melded with the peaks of the distant mountain range. A soft snow was falling, large, messy clumps wetting against the windowpane. The inn sat at the top of a slight incline, but there were dense conifers right outside his window, obscuring his view of the village below. The woods looked as black as a coma.

Someone was standing outside his window, blending among the dark line of trees.

Paul felt his body flush cold. He stood there staring out the window, trying to discern further details of the figure. But it was impossible to do so given that snowy darkness on the other side of the snow-wetted glass. He could make out the dome of a head and the slope of one shoulder. Paul tried to convince himself that it was a trick of the light coupled with his frazzled state of mind—that it wasn't a head at all, but one of the tumor-like burls that bulged from the trunks of the Sitka spruce—but the longer he stared at it, the more that dark silhouette was undeniable. Still, he might have been able to convince himself that his eyes were playing tricks on him and that there was no one there if a cloud of respiration hadn't been expelled from the figure's mouth, creating a blossom of fog against the outside of the windowpane.

Shit.

Paul backed away from the window, his own reflection in the windowpane momentarily superimposed over the dark figure on the other side of the glass. As he stared at it, the blossom of fog on the glass shrank, then faded away altogether. He continued to back away toward the door that led out onto the hallway, his reflection shrinking until it vanished. Not taking his eyes off the shape on the other side of the window, he brushed his hand along the door until he found the doorknob. But when he turned the knob and tugged at it, the door held fast in its frame.

A spark of panic ignited within him. He spun around and, gripping the doorknob with both hands, gave it a yank. But the door wouldn't budge.

The dead bolt was engaged, he realized, and he twisted the lock. This time, when he jerked on the knob, the door swung open.

The hallway was just as dark as his room. Paul hurried down the hall toward the lobby, one hand trailing along the wall, a rectangle of moonlight framed in the window at the front of the inn. The neon OPEN sign was now dark. The front desk was unmanned, the moose head keeping watch over an empty lobby. Paul reached the front door and shoved out into the night.

The cold struck him like a slap. He hadn't been prepared for just how sharp and bone-numbing it was outside. He was facing the rutted dirt road, which was now covered in a smooth sheet of white, and the wall of dark spruce trees beyond. The moon appeared as a massive glowing skull cleaved in half behind a gauzy black cloud, its pearl-colored light illuminating the steeple and one side of a small whitewashed church seated down in a slight valley and partially buried within the trees.

Shivering, Paul walked around the side of the inn. The proximity of the tree line to the wall of the inn made it look as if he was staring down a tunnel. He could make out the black rectangle that was his window and the footprints beneath the window in the snow.

He just stood there for several seconds, his breath misting the night air, his whole body quaking from the cold. And maybe not just the cold.

It wasn't just the footprints below the window—a trail of prints had been stamped in the fresh snow. They began below the window and wended around toward the front of the inn, keeping to the line of trees so that Paul had initially missed them. They wound down toward the snow-dusted road where they hugged the shoulder on their way down into the valley.

Paul followed them, moving through the freezing night. Even as he pursued the prints, it occurred to him that no one could have covered such a distance in so short an amount of time—less than a minute had passed from the moment he glimpsed the figure on the other side of his window until he'd rushed down the hall and out into the night. This was his rational thought, anyway; his reasoning, however, was overpowered by the urge to follow those prints as if led by an invisible tether.

Up ahead, the church came into view. It was sunken into the earth and bordered on three of its four sides by trees. It was a small whitewashed building fashioned into a perfect triangle, with a cross extending from the zenith of its steeple. Stained-glass porthole windows flanked the wooden double doors. It was as modest a church as Paul had ever seen, and its simplicity made it look like a child's drawing. There was a bench out front, its wooden slats covered in snow; Paul thought of the reporter Keith Moore, and of his story about the man named Lans Lunghardt who, in the sixties, had murdered his entire family with an ax and then sat down out in front of the church to wait for the police, his clothes covered in blood.

His middle son made it out of the house, Keith Moore had told him, *but old Lans brought the kid down with a swift drop of his ax between his shoulder blades, killing him right there in the backyard.*

Paul shivered.

The footprints curled around the side of the church and disappeared beneath the shadows of the looming spruce trees. Paul followed, the snow-covered ground beneath his feet seeming to cant at an angle. The ground beneath the snow was not level. He glanced northward and saw a wide, snow-shrouded clearing backstopped by distant mountains, where dark shapes rose up from the ground. Paul wiped the snowflakes from his eyelashes and tried to discern what it was he was seeing in that clearing, but the moon had retreated behind a wall of dark clouds, making it impossible to see with any clarity.

The footprints cut alongside the church and vanished into the woods.

Enough is enough, he thought. *Your teeth are chattering in your skull, and you're liable to break your ankle walking around out here on this sloping hillside.*

Yes, he knew he should turn back . . . but he couldn't.

There was a path leading into the woods, he saw—a path untouched by the snow that couldn't breach the heavy pine boughs of the trees. It was a rugged dirt path, black as satin in the dark, and it climbed up toward denser woods and, judging by the proximity of the mountains, the beginning of the foothills.

This is wrong, he thought. *This whole thing feels very wrong.*

He stepped onto the path . . . and felt a strange twinge in the pit of his stomach. It was like riding an elevator that was dropping floors too quickly. The feeling passed just as fast as it had come, but its eerie memory remained.

The incline was steeper than it looked, and he felt the strain in his calves as he ascended into the woods. It was too cold out here to work up a proper sweat, but after just a couple of minutes campaigning up the hillside, his heart was speed-bagging against his rib cage.

This is wr—

He groped for a branch at the same instant he saw someone—or something—shift in the darkness just a couple of yards ahead of him. The sight startled him and caused him to lose his footing while his groping hand undershot a nearby branch, missing it. The result sent him crashing down on his face onto the hard-packed earth. Stars exploded behind his eyelids and a sharp pain knifed straight up his nose and screamed like wildfire to the back of his skull.

The realization that he wasn't alone out here had him scrambling back to his feet. His eyes were watering, wet slicks freezing down his cheeks. His nose throbbed.

"Who's there?" he hissed into the darkness. He scanned the surrounding woods, but could not see anyone. "Danny?"

He realized how absurd it was, calling his brother's name, but he was no longer thinking rationally. He was no longer—

A distant, sonorous howl rose up through the night. Paul froze, his breath caught in his throat.

A wolf, he thought.

But as the howl wound down, it flattened to an unmelodious, almost human-sounding wail.

Not a wolf. Not a wolf.

Paul scanned his surroundings, but it was futile—beyond the trees in every direction was nothing but black space.

The sound came again, and this time there was no confusing it with the howl of a wolf, or any other animal, for that matter. It was a throaty, agonized shriek that rose in timbre until the voice cracked, then broke apart in a drumbeat of hitching sobs before dying altogether.

That's a person out there. Someone who's hurt.

Something moved off to his left. Paul swung his head in that direction but could see nothing in the darkness. The boughs of the spruce were heavy and pearled with moonlight, and they knitted a network of shadows beneath their branches—shadows that appeared to move and shift and betray all logic and common sense.

The shriek came a third time, and now it sounded like it was just beyond the hill. It was no animal.

Paul took a reflexive step backward, and was thrown off balance as his right foot sank into a muddy divot in the earth. He dropped to one knee, stripping a handful of pine needles from the branch he'd been clutching, and felt the icy mud inside the hole spilling over the top of his boot and soaking his foot.

When Paul glanced up, he saw a pair of pine boughs swing as if disturbed. He listened, holding his breath, and thought he could hear the inimitable sound of footfalls crunching down on a thin layer of snow close by.

Paul reached out and wrapped one arm around the thin trunk of a nearby spruce and used it for leverage as he wrenched his boot out of the muddy sinkhole. His foot had gone numb, but he managed to stand. The moon cleared the clouds and drove columns of bluish light down through the interlocking branches of the pines, throwing optical illusions at his eyes.

He swatted at the branches and cut his way through the trees. The undergrowth attempted to snare him and drag him to the ground, but somehow, in his panic, he was able to defeat it. When he fell over a deadfall and splashed down on the other side into a puddle covered with a thin shellac of ice, he realized he'd gotten disoriented and wandered too far from the path.

He crossed over to the place where the moonlight managed to permeate the trees. His heart was slamming in his throat. Snowflakes seemed to hang suspended in the air, making the blackness all around him appear as if it had been poked with holes. The darkness beyond was infinite. It was impossible to see into the spaces between the trees. How had he gotten so far off the path?

His voice carried out between the trees, as insubstantial as the swirling bits of snow that collected against his hot and sweating face: "Hello?"

Nothing.

Silence.

He backtracked through the woods, scraping himself against tree limbs, his face and hands tacky with pine sap. When he reached the path, he felt relief wash through him, though his heart was still thumping a mile a minute. He headed back down the slope at a good pace while still wary of his footing. Midway down, he became convinced that something—someone—was pursuing him. He kept checking over his shoulder, his line of sight obscured by the clouds of vapor wheezing up from his throat.

By the time he reached the bottom of the hill and crossed out of the woods, he was in a full-fledged panic. He darted around the old church and ran across the snow-covered field toward the road and the Blue Moose Inn beyond. When he reached the inn's front door, he gripped the knob with two hands, turned it, but it wouldn't budge. It had locked behind him and he'd left his key back in his room.

He took a moment to calm down. His back against the inn's door, he peered into the distance and at the place from where he'd just come. There weren't any streetlights here, so he was only able to make out the steeple of the church by the light of the moon.

He waited, expecting a figure to amble out of the darkness and onto the snowy road.

Waited.

Waited.

Nothing.

He went around the side of the inn and toward the squat, stucco building tucked behind where he'd parked the Tahoe. The flickering blue light of a television set glowed in one narrow window beneath the eaves.

Paul hammered on the door. His nerves felt like live wires. *Calm down, calm down.* A moment later, he could hear someone moving around inside. He heard the *clunk* of a dead bolt and then the door cracked open. Jan Warren's masculine face hovered in the spectral light of the TV.

"Someone's out there in the woods. Someone's hurt."

Jan Warren peered over his shoulder and into the darkness. "Huh? Where?" she said.

"Out behind the church. In the woods. I heard . . . it sounded like someone screaming."

She looked him over. "Come in here," she said, and opened the door wider.

Ten minutes later, two men showed up. The slim man with graying temples and a pinched, nervous-looking face was introduced to him as Valerie Drammell, the village safety officer. The other man—a round-shouldered woodsman with a beard and a dour disposition—was Bill Hopewell, a local mechanic and handyman. Paul, seated in a threadbare recliner in the squalid little residence Jan Warren shared with her elderly father, Merle (who had somehow slept through the ruckus), explained to Drammell and Hopewell about the figure he had seen outside his window, the footprints that led across the road and behind the church, and what he'd heard once he was in the woods.

"It was a person screaming just over the hill. Someone who was hurt. I tried to go in the direction of the sound, but I got turned around and disoriented."

"A person," Drammell said.

Jan Warren, who was standing in the hallway with her arms folded over her ample bosom, said, "I told him it was late and we didn't need to call you, Val. But he was insistent."

"If someone is hurt out there, I'd think you'd want to know," Paul countered.

Drammell and Hopewell exchanged a none-too-subtle glance.

"Listen, I know how it sounds," Paul said. "But given everything that's happened out here lately, don't you think you guys should go check it out?"

"Mallory's in jail," Drammell said. "Ain't no one else out there. Probably you just heard a wolf."

"Or a moose," Bill Hopewell added.

"It wasn't a goddamn wolf and it certainly wasn't a moose," Paul said.

"You watch your tongue," Jan chided him.

"Let's just calm down, everybody," Drammell said. "Now, where exactly did you hear this?"

Paul stood up. "I'll show you."

"Sit back down, Mr. Gallo. Bill and I'll go up and have a look around. Seems like you should just relax for a few minutes and get yourself under control."

"You won't know where to look. I'll come with you."

Drammell and Hopewell shared another conspicuous glance.

They think I'm crazy.

"You hurt your face, Mr. Gallo?" Drammell asked.

"What?"

Drammell pointed at Paul's face.

Paul touched the side of his nose, where it had felt tender ever since he'd slipped in the woods and planted his face onto the frozen ground. "Oh," he said. It seemed like the pain had returned after Drammell commented on it.

"He said he fell and hit his head," Jan Warren said.

"That's not true," Paul said.

"Did you hit your head, Mr. Gallo?" Drammell asked.

"I mean, yes, I said I slipped and hit my face, but I didn't hit my head. This wasn't some auditory hallucination or whatever, if that's what you're getting at."

"Maybe you dreamt it," Drammell said.

"Or maybe you was sleepwalking," Bill Hopewell suggested.

He realized they were poking fun at him now. He said nothing in response—just stared at them.

Drammell turned toward the door and said, "All right. We'll take a quick look, the three of us, see what we can find. Bill, you got one of them handheld kliegs out in your truck?"

"Sure do," said Hopewell.

"All right, Mr. Gallo," Drammell said, opening the door. "Giddyup."

Dressed in one of Jan Warren's oversized parkas, Paul followed them out into the night. He moved with an aggrieved limp, his right foot numb from its dunk in the frozen mudhole, his ankle sore and beginning to swell inside his frozen sock. In the ten minutes it had taken Drammell and Hopewell to arrive, the night had

grown colder. Snow was coming down with more purpose now, piling up against the sides of the inn.

Parked beside Paul's rented Tahoe was an old tow
truck with an orange emergency bubble on the roof of
the cab and a decal of the Grim Reaper clutching his
trusty scythe on the driver's door. Hopewell opened the
door and rummaged around behind the seats.

"Where's these footprints you saw, Mr. Gallo?"
Drammell asked. He had unclipped a flashlight from
his belt and was running the beam along the powdered
ground at his feet.

"On the other side of the building. But they went
down into the street and out to the church."

"Let's have a look."

He and Drammell walked around to the other side of
the inn, Drammell flipping up the fur-lined collar of his
nylon parka. When they reached the opposite side, Paul
noticed with mounting frustration that the continual
snowfall had covered up the prints.

"They were here like twenty minutes ago," Paul said,
shivering.

Drammell trained the flashlight on him. Paul raised
one hand, blocking the beam.

"Why don't you wait back in your room?" Drammell
said. "Me an' Bill can go up into the woods."

As if on cue, Bill Hopewell appeared around the corner of the inn. He carried a large battery-powered klieg
searchlight with one hand.

"I'm fine," Paul insisted. "I want to go with you."

"Suit yourself," Drammell said, and turned back
around.

The three men walked across the road, Hopewell

and Drammell kicking up clouds of powdery snow while Paul moved in a more reserved manner, favoring his one foot. When they reached the woods, they formed a single-file line with Paul in the middle. When they reached the place where Paul had been standing when he'd heard the noise—he spotted the muddy sinkhole with little difficulty, its surface shimmering with moonlight like some kind of magical stew—Hopewell turned on the handheld klieg. A bright funnel of light pierced the darkness and carved a passageway through the woods ahead of them.

"It sounded like it was coming from over there." Paul pointed through the trees and beyond a slight rise in the hillside.

Hopewell repositioned the klieg. The trees' shadows rearranged themselves in one synchronized sweep, and it was like watching the world rotate while they remained still.

Drammell pushed aside the low-hanging limbs as Hopewell advanced, training the klieg light on the deadfall that Paul had tripped over. There was a scrim of snow on it now, and flat, white mushrooms climbed up its damp, mossy bark, looking like a set of tiny stairs.

"You come through this way, Mr. Gallo?" Drammell asked. He was staring down at the disturbed ground on the other side of the deadfall.

"Yeah. I tripped over that damn tree and did a face-plant."

"Mmmm-hmmm."

"The screaming I heard came from right over there." Paul motioned with one hand past the deadfall. The woods beyond were a sightless void until Hopewell addressed it with his searchlight. Then the woods came alive, the shadows shifting and sliding and pooling in inky puddles. The snowy pine branches trembled before them.

"There's no one here," Drammell said. "It don't even look like anyone's been walking around up beyond the hill. Not even you, Mr. Gallo."

"I didn't get far. I told you, I got disoriented and turned around." He felt like an idiot, standing here with one numb foot, his clothes covered in freezing mud, and shivering inside Jan Warren's parka. No wonder they thought he was crazy.

Drammell and Hopewell crossed over to the patch of soggy ground beyond the deadfall. Hopewell's light allowed nothing to hide. But there was no evidence that anyone or anything had crossed this way. The place was desolate and undisturbed.

Drammell cupped both hands around his mouth and shouted into the night: *"Helllo!"* The echo carried out beyond the trees and over the hills—*ello, lo, lo* . . .

"Should we go up there?" Paul asked.

"Up *there*?" Drammell glanced through the interlocking branches of trees and at the darkened landscape beyond. "Hell, no."

"Why not?"

"Because it's fuckin' *cold*," Drammell said, and chuckled. "Besides, the three of us go up there now, that nice lady you're renting your room from will have to call out a search party come first light. Look, Mr. Gallo, we came out here and checked things out. But there's no one here. You heard some animal wailing off in the distance. You just got a little spooked, is all."

Paul's teeth chattered. "I'm sorry. I feel like an idiot. It's just that it didn't sound like an animal."

Drammell gave him a clap on the shoulder as he made his way out of the thicket and onto the path.

They walked back to the inn in silence, Paul too dumbfounded to speak, the other two men, judging by their lethargy, too tired to talk. By the time they reached the tow truck, Drammell was wheezing like a punctured air mattress. Hopewell went around to the driver's side, opened the door, and tossed in his klieg light. Drammell opened the passenger door, but before he hoisted himself up inside, he turned toward Paul.

"You mind me asking what you're doing out this way, Mr. Gallo?"

"My brother went missing out here just over a year ago. I'm trying to find out what happened to him."

"Gallo," Drammell said, turning the name over in his mouth. "Yeah, the name sounds kinda familiar. Couple of state troopers came up from Fairbanks sometime last fall looking for him. I remember now. You know about the murders we had up here, don't you?"

"Yes. That's why I came. That's why I thought . . ." He didn't finish the sentiment, but motioned toward the woods in the distance. In the road, their footprints were already filling with snow.

"I hear the state cops already ID'd the bodies. You might want to consult with them, if you think there might be cause to."

"My brother wasn't one of the victims."

Drammell raised his eyebrows and nodded his head.

Snow had collected in his salt-and-pepper hair. "Well," he said. "That's good news, ain't it?"

"It's not really *any* news. I'm no better off than I was when Danny first disappeared. I'd like to talk to you about that, if you've got the time, Mr. Drammell. I read the police report and know you were assisting those troopers who came out here from Fairbanks."

"Tomorrow," Drammell said. "Call me tomorrow. Janice can get you my number." He nodded toward the stucco building behind the inn, where Jan Warren's round face was framed in one of the narrow windows, backlit by the glow of her television.

"Thank you," Paul said, and shook Drammell's hand.

"In the meantime, I suggest you quit wandering around those woods, particularly at night and in a snowstorm."

"Good idea."

"Now get back inside and get warm before you freeze to death out here, Mr. Gallo. I've already logged enough hours for one night."

Drammell climbed into the cab of the tow truck just as Bill Hopewell cranked the engine. The vehicle roared to life, and expelled a cloud of black smoke from the exhaust. Paul went around to the front of the inn just as the tow truck pulled out into the street, leaving behind a helix of tire tracks in the snow. The inn's door was still locked and he still didn't have the key, so he backtracked to the Warrens' tiny residence, where he knocked on the door again, feeling like an imbecile.

Jan Warren was a mind reader—she opened the door a crack and extended a thick hand, a spare key pinched between two pudgy fingers.

"Ms. Warren, that path behind the church that goes up into the woods," he said, taking the key from her. "Where does it go?"

"Nowhere," she said. "It's one of the old abandoned mining roads. It just runs itself out halfway up the hill."

"Oh."

"But if you keep going, that's where he buried the bodies," she said, and closed the door.

Back in his room, he went to the bathroom mirror and was unnerved to see that a decent amount of blood had spurted from his nose and dried in a smear across his upper lip. He cleaned himself at the sink. The water was ice cold and refused to get warm. He glanced at least once at the YOU SHOULD NOT BE HERE scratched into the glass as he cleaned his face and hands.

After he climbed into bed, he tried to close his eyes, but they kept springing open. He kept hearing that throaty shriek rise up over the hillside, only this time it was in his head.

Just an animal. Or maybe my imagination.

His dreams were ferocious things. The only blessed part about them was that they continued to jar him awake, cutting short his suffering. Each time he woke up, he turned his head and stared at the window, wondering whether someone was still standing out there. Wondering whether someone had *ever* been standing out there.

"Stop it," he told the darkness.

Closed his eyes.

Opened them.

Closed again.

15

Alaska State Trooper Lucas Bristol, age twenty-two, was afraid.

He'd wanted nothing to do with the goings-on in Dread's Hand ever since that madman had been arrested, and he'd thought that volunteering to stay back at the station might be the best move to keep out of that whole mess. That had been when he'd thought that the madman in question, one Joseph Mallory, would be tucked away behind bars down in Anchorage until a permanent cot opened up for him in Seward. That was not the case, however. Once Mallory was released from the hospital (minus a few toes, Bristol had heard), the bastard had been shipped all the way back up to Fairbanks, in an effort to throw off any media that might come sniffing around. So now Bristol was here at his desk, with Mallory just on the other side of that giant steel door that led to Puke Alley. The only other living soul in the building was Bill Johnson, but he was down working Dispatch.

They were short-staffed, with a good number of guys out with the flu. He'd considered jumping on that bandwagon, too—faking a cough, a few sniffles. He wasn't a coward by nature, but that guy Mallory just irked the heck out of him. He knew too many stories about Dread's Hand from his childhood that made him uncomfortable having the guy under the same roof. And he certainly couldn't say this to anyone. *I open my mouth and someone even gets the hint that I'm creeped out by that guy, and the next thing I know I'll be pushing paper in Soldotna.*

So he kept up a good front.

And, for the most part, it wasn't too bad: He played solitaire and listened to music and filed papers. Pretty much just kept busy, which, in turn, kept Joseph Mallory off his mind. Every once in a while, he'd glance up at the door to Puke Alley, with its narrow, wire-mesh window at the top, and he'd think, *He's just on the other side of that door.* In these moments, for all the security Lucas Bristol felt, the steel door could have been made of balsa wood. *Besides, he's being transferred to Spring Creek first thing tomorrow morning. I just have to suffer through one more night with the guy. And, really, it isn't all that bad, is it?*

It wasn't. Not really.

The problem was the goddamn walk-throughs.

Bristol looked at the big clock face above the sally port door and saw that it was time for his first walk-through of the night. He had been dreading this since his shift started. He was required to do a walk-through of the holding cells every half hour, and that time was now.

Don't go, said a small voice in the back of his head. *You're the only one here. Who's to know whether you check in on the bastard or not?*

Chances were good that he could get away with it, too, but he'd heard too many stories about guys who'd shirked the half-hour walk-through, only to find out later that some inmate had hanged himself in his cell or had asphyxiated themselves in a pool of their own vomit while in the drunk tank. Those officers had lost their jobs. And Lucas Bristol did not want to lose his job.

He got up from his desk, knocked a few balled-up McDonald's wrappers into the wastebasket beside his chair, and sauntered down the hall to the Dispatch office. Johnson was there at the boards, trying to get Netflix to load on his laptop. There was an old bumper sticker stuck to the wall above the computer monitors that read, in a drippy ectoplasmic font, WHO YA GONNA CALL?

"I'm doing the dirty thirty," Bristol said.

"Don't stick your fingers through the bars," Bill Johnson called back to him, making a chomping sound with his teeth. It was a joke, but Lucas Bristol didn't find it funny at the moment.

He went down the hall, unlocked and opened the steel door to Puke Alley . . . then stood there, not crossing the threshold.

Those woods are haunted by the devil himself, his aunt Lin had told him and his brothers. *A man walks in there, he stands a chance of being touched by the devil. And that man, he goes sour. His mind rots. He becomes a vessel for evil, a vehicle for the devil.*

But it was all superstition and make-believe, wasn't it? Just like what he'd said to Jill Ryerson the other night, when she'd smiled at him and showed him the rabbit's foot on her key chain. It was all rabbit's feet, wasn't it?

Quit being a sissy. Why has this guy gotten under your skin?

He took a deep breath, then crossed the threshold. He moved down the corridor, conscious that he was holding his breath. He could hear Mallory moving around in his cell before he saw him—a vague, scuffing sound, like the sole of his single rubber jailhouse shoe sliding across the gritty concrete floor.

Joseph Mallory was in the third cell down, an indistinct scarecrow shape with a gleaming bald pate wreathed by strands of grimy salt-and-pepper hair. His foot—the one that had given up some toes—had been bandaged by a doctor this afternoon. The bandage was startlingly white beneath the bright bulbs in the hallway. As Lucas Bristol approached the bars of the cell, Mallory lifted his head and stared at the young trooper.

Bristol felt his bowels clench.

A long time passed, with neither man saying a word to the other. Bristol knew he could return to the squad room and not have to think about the guy in the cell for another thirty minutes, but mounting fear kept him rooted to the floor, unable to move.

After a while, Lucas Bristol said, "What happened to you in those woods, old man?"

For a long time, it seemed the man on the other side of the bars wouldn't answer. But then Mallory stood— he somehow looked much taller now than he had when he was being ushered in here the other night by Swinton and McHale—and he cleared his throat, *gruh-grrrruh!*

Lucas Bristol took a step back from the cell.

"A terrible thing," Mallory said, his voice almost . . . snakelike. "I was overcome and forced to do a hard and terrible thing."

A man walks in there, he stands a chance of being touched by the devil. And that man, he goes sour. These words shuttled through Lucas Bristol's brain.

"You cut off all their heads," Bristol said. It was as if someone else was speaking through him. He wanted to know the answer to this—it had been haunting him ever since he'd heard about it—but he wouldn't have thought he'd have the power to speak the words. Was it even a question, or was he just making a statement? The world suddenly seemed fuzzy and indistinct to him, and he found that he wasn't sure.

A low, throaty moan escaped Mallory's lips. As Bristol watched, the man eased himself back down onto the bench, that curtain of greasy hair spilling across his skull-like face.

Bristol stood staring at the man, his whole body cold despite the heat pumping through the ventilation system. After a time, Mallory lowered his whole body to the bench, resting on his side as if to sleep. But his eyes never closed; his gaze remained on Lucas Bristol.

He goes sour, Bristol thought.

A soft susurration came from the cell next to Mallory's. The front of the cells were barred, but the walls were cinder block, so when Bristol glanced over, he couldn't see anything or anyone. There was no one else back here, anyway. But still . . . he thought he caught a glimpse of a shadow pulling back from the bars of the adjacent cell.

Bristol took a step in the direction of the other cell.

"Don't look at it," Mallory said, his voice as guttural as an animal's growl.

Bristol looked into the cell just as the lightbulb in the ceiling overhead winked out. In the sudden shift of light, he thought he saw a dark shape standing in the corner of what should have been an empty holding cell. But as he stared, and as his eyes acclimated to the change in light, he realized it was only a trick played by the shadows. There was no one there.

Above his head, the second bulb fizzed, then went dark.

Lucas Bristol backed out of the hallway, Joseph Mallory's eyes blazing at him on the other side of his cell bars now.

"It's best you don't come back in here tonight, son," Mallory said.

Without saying a word, Bristol returned to the squad room. He was sweating beneath his uniform, his pulse throbbing at his temples. Maybe there was some aspirin in the break room.

There were—an economy tub of Advil, it turned out. He swallowed three tablets and washed them down with half a cup of lukewarm coffee. Then he returned to his desk. Unnerved by the silence in the squad room, he eventually got up again and went down the hall toward Dispatch. One of the hallway lights overhead blinked out as he passed by it, which caused him to hurry along.

Johnson was still there, of course, watching a pair of tits jig across the screen of his laptop. Apparently, he'd gotten Netflix to load. Johnson looked up as Bristol lingered there in the doorway.

"Everything cool?" Johnson asked.

Bristol opened his mouth, but only managed to make a creaking sound.

Bill Johnson frowned. "You okay, Luke?"

Something clicked in the back of his throat and he found his voice. "Yeah. I'm okay. Just got a headache all of a sudden, that's all."

"Wanna watch this movie with me?"

"No, thanks."

"Look at these tits. Want me to rewind it?"

"No, man. No, thanks."

He was beginning to calm down now—enough so that he couldn't remember why he had felt so unnerved just a moment earlier. Had Mallory unraveled him that much? If so, maybe he *should* be in Soldotna pushing paper . . .

He returned to his desk, plugged his iPod into a pair of portable speakers, and set it on Shuffle. Big Head Todd & the Monsters came on, singing "It All Comes Down." *Yes, it does,* Lucas Bristol thought, briefly closing his eyes and breathing through flared nostrils.

For the next thirty minutes, he busied himself with paperwork. When he looked up at the clock over the sally port door a half hour later, he saw that it was time to make his rounds again. He'd felt calmer and the Advil had gone to work on his headache, so he wasn't in any great rush to get up and revisit the holding cell of old Joseph Mallory, Puke Alley's one and only resident. In fact, the thought of having to see Mallory again caused a cool sweat to slicken the nape of his neck.

It's best you don't come back in here tonight, son.

Lucas Bristol decided that was a good goddamn idea. He turned his music up while burying his face in his paperwork.

It would prove to be a bad decision.

Bristol worked the midnight shift, which meant he was done for the day at eight in the morning. Two hours before his relief came in, he dragged himself from his desk and shuffled his heavy feet down the hall toward the men's room. At one of the urinals, he unleashed a ribbon of piss as yellow as Gatorade. As he shook off the last few drops, he liberated a fart that possessed the range and depth of a bassoon. This made him chuckle to himself as he read the bumper sticker someone— probably Bill Johnson—had stuck to the tiled wall above the urinal: MORE THAN THREE SHAKES IS PLAYING WITH YOURSELF.

It was 6 A.M. and still pitch black outside the station house windows. Lucas Bristol decided to do the dirty thirty before Swinton came in to relieve him at eight.

He unlocked the door to the holding cells and crossed down the hallway. The light fixture just outside Mallory's cell was still out, but the ones farther down the corridor provided sufficient lighting.

Something was stuck to the bars of Mallory's cell.

Bristol slowed his step. When he arrived at Mallory's cell, last night's irrational fear was replaced by a much more tangible, much more relatable distress—the fear of losing his job.

Joseph Mallory was dead. Lucas Bristol did not need to take the man's pulse or hold a mirror under his nose to know this. At some point during the night, Mallory had unwrapped the gauze bandage from his foot. He had fastened one end of the bandage to one of the bars of his cell, right where the vertical bar met the horizontal one, coming to a T. He had taken the remaining slack and wound it around his neck. And then he had simply let the dead weight of his body drop and hang. Even in his fragile, malnourished state, it was enough weight to do the job. From the crooked angle of Mallory's head—from the swollen, jellied eyes and the twisted rigor of his lips—Lucas Bristol could tell that the man's neck had been broken.

I'm going to lose my job for this, Bristol thought, panic already gripping him around the throat.

Above him, the dark bulb in the ceiling flared to brightness.

16

Paul awoke in the late morning, feeling like he had a hangover despite not having touched a sip of alcohol the night before. The window next to his bed blazed with silver daylight. In the bathroom, he washed his face, brushed his teeth, then examined his nose in the mirror. It looked fine but was still sore from his faceplant the night before.

In the light of morning, last night's impromptu escapade into the woods and his subsequent persuasion of Valerie Drammell and Bill Hopewell to do the same should have left him feeling embarrassed. Standing before the windows and gazing out at the snow-covered, forested hillside, it was easy to dismiss last night's fears. But he didn't. His only regret was that *Drammell* had dismissed him, and he still wanted to talk to Drammell about Danny. It would be easier if Drammell wasn't coming into things already thinking that Paul was out here jumping at shadows.

Jan Warren probably thought he was a dope, too—

some city boy who'd been spooked by the howl of a wolf and some pine boughs whacking against his window in the night. It didn't help that he'd locked himself out of his room in all the commotion. Thinking of this now, her voice returned to him—the comment she'd made last night as she extended the extra room key to him through the crack in the door: *That's where he buried the bodies.*

He was in the heart of it now. The last known place his brother had been before disappearing . . . and the grave site of eight victims who'd been murdered by a local psychopath named Joseph Mallory. Hallowed ground, indeed.

There was a fire burning in the hearth in the lobby. Merle Warren, the old man who had greeted him the day before, was planted in his lawn chair in front of the television set again, while Jan, his broad-shouldered, masculine-faced daughter, stood behind the registration desk, idly turning the pages of a magazine.

"Sorry for all the confusion last night," Paul said, zipping up his coat. He set the spare key on the desktop.

"I'm just glad Daddy slept through it," Jan said.

As if cued by his daughter's mention of him, the old man worked himself up out of the lawn chair and shuffled out through a doorway at the back of the room.

"Last night you said that if I kept following that path through the woods, I'd arrive at the place where Joseph Mallory buried his victims. Is that correct?"

"I don't recommend going on no hikes," Jan said.

Paul took that as confirmation.

"Last night, Mr. Drammell said you could give me

his phone number," he said. "Or . . . does he have an office in town or something?"

"If you count hanging around down at the feed store having an office, then sure, he's got an office."

Paul smiled at her. "I'll just take the number, then."

Jan Warren's left cheek bulged. She looked like she was debating whether or not to help him. Then she reached below the counter and produced a spiral-bound notebook. She flipped it open, thumbed through the pages, then tore a strip off one of the pages. She handed the curling bit of paper to Paul. It had Valerie Drammell's name and phone number written on it. Then she returned to her magazine. Paul expected it to be an issue of *Guns & Ammo* or *Soldier of Fortune,* to complete the cliché, but he was surprised to find that it was an issue of *Cosmopolitan.*

"Thank you." He tucked the slip of paper into his pocket.

The old man reappeared in the doorway, carrying a thick book in both hands. He was wearing rubber fishing waders, which seemed to hang from his thin frame no different than they would from a clothesline. His feistiness was gone, replaced by a zombielike gait and the glazed, unfocused stare of a dullard.

"Did you know Joseph Mallory?" Paul asked the woman.

"Been here my whole life. I know everyone in the village. Ain't seen Mallory in some time, though." She had been gazing at her magazine as she spoke, but she looked up and met his eyes now. "Eight bodies. Heads cut clean off, just like they do to them guys in the Middle East. You think your brother got messed up in all of that, you're better off talking with the police down in Fairbanks instead of wasting your time all the way out here, mister, just like I told you yesterday. Ain't nothing Val Drammell can do for you."

"I'll keep that in mind. Thank you."

"You mind me asking what you were doing wandering around outside last night, anyway?"

"I saw someone looking in my window. I went outside and saw footprints, so I followed them. Just what I said to Drammell and that other guy last night."

"Daddy," she called, turning around and staring at the old man, who stood in front of the TV, clutching the thick book to his chest. "Daddy, you been wandering around outside at night, peepin' in on our guest here?"

"What?" the old man barked. He didn't take his eyes from the television.

"It wasn't him," Paul said.

"Quit botherin' the guests," she said to her father anyway.

The old man turned and faced them, his mouth twisted into a knot. There was stormy confusion in his eyes. With labored steps, he approached the counter and set the book down next to his daughter's magazine.

It was a Bible. A single gold cross was embossed on the faux-leather cover.

"You being reeled in like a catfish, mister," the old man said to him. "Best take heed."

"All right, Daddy," Jan said to the old man, flapping a meaty hand at him as if he were some pesky insect. She shoved the Bible in Paul's direction. "He wants you to take this back to your room. Room's supposed to have one, anyway. It ain't law, but it's good, common decency."

"Thank you," he said to the old man.

Merle Warren stared at him for the length of two heartbeats before turning around and shuffling back to his lawn chair. It took great effort for him to fold himself back into the chair.

"One more thing," Paul said.

"Yeah?"

"Where can I get a newspaper and something to eat around here?"

"Well, Tabby's is the only place to eat. Just head out on this road and you'll see it. Little luncheonette. As for newspapers, you'll either have to go to the post office in the Springs or head east toward the highway."

"The Internet on my phone isn't working, either. The signal keeps going in and out."

"That happens." She licked her thumb and turned a page of her magazine.

He walked across the road, retracing his steps from the night before. There was still snow on the ground, but it had thinned to a shimmery crust. The old church was less ominous in the daylight, a sad, weathered structure leprous with dry rot, its stained-glass windows smudgy with grime. An industrial chain had been wound through the door handles and secured with a padlock. He hadn't noticed this last night.

He stepped around the front of the church, passing beneath the lee of the steeple. There was still some snow on the bench here, and the undeniable impression of someone having been sitting there very recently.

Strange, though, was the absence of footprints in the snow on the ground in front of the bench.

He heard a whining sound, and peered around the corner and down the length of the old church. One of the shutters creaked outward, away from the building. There was no wind—not even a slight breeze at the moment—but Paul didn't think much of it. He walked around the side of the church, his boots crunching through the crust of snow. There was another set of double doors on this side of the building, another chain looped through the handles. But one of the handles was loose and had pulled away from the door.

Paul approached the door. He reached out and gripped the cold, rusted chain. He tugged on it, and the loose handle broke away from the door with only the barest splintering of wood, like a rotten tooth extracted from diseased gums. He let the handle swing downward on the chain as he dug his fingers around the side of the door and eased it open. The hinges emitted a shrill, ratlike squeal.

It took a few seconds for his eyes to adjust to the gloom inside. When they did, he saw that it was a good thing he hadn't walked blindly into the church: There was no floor. The old warped boards had collapsed into a sinkhole, leaving a crater in the middle of the tiny church. The pews that were still visible hung slantways, tilting toward the opening where the rest of the floor should have been, the floorboards beneath them slouching at angles toward the dark pit in the center of the room.

There were perhaps three feet of sturdy floor just beyond the door, extending out over the hole in the ground like a gangplank. Paul stepped out along the planks while keeping his grip on the door frame. When the planks creaked beneath his boots, he winced and ceased all movement. He was close enough to the edge now to peer down into that dark bowel and see, beyond the spears of floorboards with their splintered edges, the bottom of the drop. It was perhaps thirty feet down, a yawning hollow filled with dirt, straw-colored fauna, and the remaining pews and floorboards all heaped together and coated in a furry gray film of dust. He heard the plinking sound of water drops, and when he glanced up, he could see a rent in the pitched ceiling, as jagged as a lightning bolt, through which a narrow channel of daylight issued. Melting snow dripped down onto the exposed rafters. Paul inhaled and caught the faint odor of animal shit.

He backed out of the church, closed the door, and fitted the handle's screws back into their screw holes. Beside his head, the loose shutter screeched, then banged against the peeling, whitewashed side of the church. At least this time there was a cold breeze to account for it.

When he turned away from the church, he found himself staring at the gradual upward slope of the narrow path that cut into the tree line and up into the woods. The path was now muddy from the melting snow that was dripping off the boughs above it. When he looked more closely, he could make out the muddy boot prints they'd made the night before. They made him feel foolish. Now, more than ever, he was convinced that he'd been imagining things last night, and that there had been nothing out here with him except his own jittery nerves and overtaxed brain.

He stepped onto the path and proceeded up the incline. The forest around him wasn't as dense as it had appeared last night in the dark; he could see a fair distance between the widely spaced Sitka trees, with those bulbous, swollen burls in the trunks that reminded him of hornets' nests, and the silvery rim of the mountains beyond.

As he walked the path, he took the curl of paper from his pocket and dialed Valerie Drammell's number. The phone rang several times before Paul was dumped into an automated voice-mailbox. He identified himself, left his contact info, then hung up.

It took about forty-five minutes for him to reach the clearing. Midway through the hike, the dirt path disappeared, and he was left to follow tromped earth toward the top of the ridge. Even more treacherous were the deadfalls and sinkholes he had to climb over or sidestep. When the trees parted and the clearing unfurled before him, Paul had worked himself into a good sweat. The muscles in his legs ached.

Tiny snowflakes spiraled in the air as Paul surveyed the acres of gray land that stretched clear out to the White Mountains. There was still a crust of snow on the ground, but not enough to cover up the trenches that had been dug in the earth, each trench marked by a system of bright orange vinyl flags staked into the ground. Police tape was strung from tree to tree around the perimeter of the clearing. It was a much larger expanse of land than he had imagined.

This is where he buried them.

He followed the police tape, walking the perimeter of the clearing and just studying the layout of the graves—how far apart they were spaced, how deep the holes, now partially filled with snow, looked. There didn't appear to be any rhyme or reason for the location of each grave—none that Paul could detect, anyway—and for a time, he just stood there, shivering in the cold. The wind skirled, blowing clouds of dusty snow across the clearing.

Despite his aching muscles and the cold that had begun to penetrate his coat, he walked clear across the glade amid a chorus of water droplets pattering down from the trees, until he'd reached the place where the forest started up again and he began to climb farther up the hillside. The trees stood closer together here, darker and fuller, the ground a muddy miasma of fluorescent-green peat moss, dried orange pine needles, sphagnum, and swampy pools of brown muskeg. There was something else back there, too, beyond the trees and obscured within the shade of the hills, that caught Paul's attention. And not just his attention—he felt a tightening in his abdomen and a vague yet somehow hostile tug forward. He wended through the trees, careful of his footing, and had only managed to traverse a few yards when he saw what it was that had garnered his curiosity.

Crosses. There were more crosses back there, similar to the ones that had been erected back on the road leading into town. These appeared much smaller—or maybe they were just farther away—but they were comprised of bleached-white wood the color of bone: a line of perfect crosses running beyond the trees, bisecting the forest from the hills. Unlike the ones back out along the road, however, these seemed to be arranged to form a line of demarcation. A boundary of some kind.

He heard movement off to his left. It was some distance away, but the sound was too distinct to be droplets of water falling from tree limbs. He looked but could see nothing—the forest was an optical illusion comprised of ramrod tree trunks and large fans of needled boughs.

He turned back to the crosses, suddenly filled with the urge to go to them. He made it a few yards into the trees until the underbrush—a vast and impassable tangle of bushes and stiff vines—halted any further advancement. The stuff was as inhospitable as barbed concertina wire. And even if he managed to get through it, he could see that the ground beyond sloped toward a narrow fault in the earth, and that the ground itself was pitched at such a severe angle that he'd risk serious injury if he attempted to traverse it.

With leaves poking at his face and a whip of brittle vine somehow wrapped around his right ankle, Paul wondered what the hell he was doing. He glanced back up at the procession of wooden crosses disappearing into the foothills. Just staring at them now, he was compelled to turn and run back to town—the exact opposite of what he'd wanted to do just moments ago. It reminded him of his conversation with Keith Moore, the reporter back in Fairbanks—how, on the reporter's two trips to Dread's Hand, he'd been aware of a nonspecific disquiet sinking into his bones, an overwhelming sense of apprehension: *It's like a sound you can feel in your back teeth*.

He tugged his arms and ankles free of the underbrush, then headed back out of the thicket. It wasn't exactly like a sound he could feel in his back teeth, but he couldn't deny the deepening sense of apprehension that was shuttling through his system just from being out here. He wasn't superstitious enough to contribute it to the town—or even to those unsettling crosses staked into the ground—but he couldn't deny that the prospect of getting out of these woods was more than just appealing to him.

He fled back down the hillside toward town.

17

He spent the next hour or so visiting the scant few establishments within Dread's Hand, and showing Danny's photo to anyone who might pay him fifteen seconds of attention. Few people even spared him that. When the two men working behind the counter at the feed store dismissed him without glancing at the photo on Paul's phone, Paul addressed the motley selection of patrons who sat around on milk crates in the rear of the store. He explained his situation to the men as they glared at him with tight-lipped indifference. He passed his phone around to them, but no one studied the photo of Danny. One grizzled old codger in a tattered hunting jacket had the audacity to scroll right past Danny's photo, curious as to what else might be on Paul's cell phone. Paul thanked the men, his tone less than genuine, and engaged in a brief tug-of-war with the old codger before he was able to wrestle his phone away from the man.

He was met with similar disinterest at the hardware

store, which was empty except for a rotund, red-faced fellow reclining in a folding chair behind the counter, watching TV. The moment Paul began to explain his situation, the guy began shaking his head, his swollen red jowls quivering like sacks of gelatin, and held up a hand for Paul to stop talking.

"No, sir," said the red-faced fellow, his eyes still glued to the TV. "I ain't getting involved."

"I'm just asking you to look at a photo."

"I ain't getting involved." He flapped a fat hand toward the door. "Now, go on. Get. Get."

Perplexed and frustrated, Paul left.

By the time he reached the small luncheonette, he was famished. Before claiming a table, he approached the woman behind the counter and showed her the photo of Danny, asked her if she'd seen him. Like many of the others, she shook her head without even looking down at the photo.

"Do you mind just taking a look anyway?" Paul urged.

With evident discomfort, the woman glanced down at the photo on Paul's phone for perhaps half a second.

"Don't know him," she said. She wore a gold crucifix on a chain around her neck, and as Paul stood there forcing a smile across his face, she gathered the crucifix between her thumb and forefinger and began rubbing it.

"You sure he didn't come in here about a year ago?"

"Ain't never seen him. God's truth."

Paul nodded. "All right." He glanced around the place and saw that the few patrons were staring at him. Yet he was too hungry to slink back out into the cold with an empty stomach, so he told the woman he'd be staying for lunch. She nodded, but did not seem at all pleased with his decision.

He was midway through a toasted ham and cheese sandwich when Valerie Drammell called him back on his cell phone. Drammell was apologetic for not getting back to him sooner. When Paul told him where he was, Drammell said he could use a bite himself, and agreed to meet Paul at the luncheonette.

Drammell arrived less than five minutes after his phone call. He walked right over to Paul's table as he tugged off his leather gloves. His rubber fire boots stamped wet tracks on the floor.

"Mr. Gallo," Drammell said, shaking Paul's hand, then sitting down opposite him at the small table. "This is nice, meeting like civilized people this time around."

"Yeah, well, I'm sorry about last night. Maybe you were right. Maybe all I'd heard was a wolf." He wasn't sure he believed that, but he figured it was best to start this meeting off on the right foot. Apologizing couldn't hurt.

"No worries. It's what I get paid for." Drammell leaned back in his chair and raised a finger into the air. The woman behind the counter nodded at him, cut her gaze toward Paul, then disappeared into the kitchen. "Ain't eaten nothing all afternoon," Drammell said.

"I guess things have been busy out here lately."

"That's the understatement of the year," Drammell said. He unzipped his coat but didn't take it off. "How's your face?"

"What?"

Drammell tapped the side of his own nose.

"Oh," Paul said. "It's fine. I'm okay. Think I'm coming down with a cold, though."

"You weren't really dressed for snowshoeing last night, that's for sure," Drammell said.

The woman from behind the counter came over and set a steaming cup of coffee in front of Drammell. "You want your usual, Val?" she asked him.

"Don't I always, Tabs?" he said, smiling up at her.

The woman nodded . . . then glanced at Paul before departing for the kitchen again.

"I feel like I've got two heads," Paul said.

Drammell's eyebrows arched. "How's that?"

"It's just that I get the impression you guys don't get many visitors out this way."

"No, not many. Ain't no reason for folks to come out here much. There's some good hunting up in the mountains and there's the national parks and rec areas nearby, but that's about it. People travel out here, they stay out along the highway or in RVs at the campsites. But folks out here are a little more on edge than usual, of course, given everything that's happened."

"Tell me about Mallory. Did you know him?"

"Everyone knew him," Drammell said. "You don't live out here and not know everybody. He'd been here for decades, an old bachelor living by himself in the woods. Would sometimes take hunters up into the foothills if they paid him, and he would do some trapping from time to time out by the river, too. Caught most of his food, I guess, though a good number of folks out here do that. He'd always pretty much kept to himself, but a lot of folks out here do that, too. The Hand ain't the kind of place you choose to live if you're a . . . I guess, a busybody or someone who likes a lot of company. Folks out here tend to keep to themselves and they know that this is a place where they can do that in peace. No one to bug 'em. That don't mean they ain't friendly, Mr. Gallo, but it's not uncommon for folks to sit in their houses, 'specially when it gets real cold in the winter, for months at a time, jus' keepin' to themselves."

"Is that what Mallory did? Sit at home for months at a time?"

"More like years," Drammell said, and sipped his coffee.

"Years?"

"Oh, someone would see him on occasion, coming through town or whatnot, and he'd even come in here from time to time. Loved Tabby's hot cocoa, is what I heard. But in the past few years, he'd holed himself up in that house of his up Durham Road and just hunkered down."

"Not just hunkered down," Paul said. "He was up to other things, too, obviously."

Valerie Drammell splayed his hands and said, "Well, yeah. Maybe he was picking up hitchhikers off the highway. Maybe he was running into them when he was up in the hills, hunting and trapping. Who can tell?"

He was hunting and trapping, all right, Paul thought.

"Were any of his victims local?"

"No," said Drammell. "None."

"My brother came out here about a year ago. You said last night that you remembered the case." Paul handed Drammell his cell phone, a photo of Danny already on the screen. "That's him. His name's Danny Gallo."

"Yeah, I remember this photo, too. Troopers brought it up with them from down Fairbanks." He glanced back up at Paul. "You fellas really look alike."

"Do you recall ever seeing my brother here in town?"

"Nope."

"Because I stick out like a fox in the henhouse out here," Paul continued. "Seems the one thing the people of Dread's Hand are attuned to is when there's a stranger among them."

Drammell just shrugged his shoulders.

"What about anyone else? Did you talk to anyone else regarding my brother's disappearance?"

"No, sir. No, I didn't."

"No one?"

"Not a soul." Drammell set Paul's phone back down on the table.

"You get a report of a missing person out here, but you don't speak to anyone besides the Warrens?"

"I'm not a police officer, Mr. Gallo. Those boys from Fairbanks, that was their job. I was just tagging along to show 'em where they could get a hot cup of coffee. Having a familiar face showing them around the village made it easier for 'em to talk to the locals, too. Folks out here don't much care for outsiders, even if they're cops. Sometimes especially if they're cops."

"Did you read the troopers' police report?"

"No, sir."

"They spoke to a few other people on their own,

showed this picture of my brother around the village. No one claimed to have seen him. Not a soul."

"All right," Drammell said, not comprehending.

"Mr. Drammell, don't you think that's odd? I just got here yesterday and every person in this restaurant has peeked at me from over their shoulder at least once since I've been sitting here. The lady working behind the counter keeps staring at me like I'm going to shoplift the silverware. Yet my brother came out here and no one can remember seeing him. Doesn't that sound implausible to you, Mr. Drammell?"

"Like I said," Drammell said, picking up his coffee, "people here are quiet. Keep to themselves."

The waitress—Tabs, Drammell had called her—brought over a tuna fish sandwich on a kaiser roll and some potato chips. She set the plate down in front of Drammell and touched his shoulder before walking away. Paul's own coffee cup was empty, but she didn't ask if he wanted a refill.

"She own this place or just work here?" Paul asked.

"That's Tabby. She's run this place since they poured the foundation, Mr. Gallo."

"This the only place to eat in town?"

"Well, I suppose. There's vending machines at the feed store. Sandwiches and sodas and whatnot."

"Because I showed her this same picture of Danny when I got here today and she didn't recognize him, either."

Drammell hoisted one shoulder in a halfhearted shrug. He picked up his sandwich and took a bite. Tuna fish glooped down onto his plate.

"So, what's your take on that?" Paul asked him. "My brother didn't eat the whole time he was here in town?"

"Maybe he ate at the Moose," Drammell suggested around a mouthful of sandwich. "Jan sometimes prepares food for the guests. She makes some killer peach cobbler. Or maybe he came into town with his own food. If he was planning to hike out into the mountains, he would have had plenty of rations. If he was smart." It must have occurred to Drammell—albeit too late—that his last comment was somewhat insensitive, given the situation. He set his sandwich down, blotted mayonnaise from the corners of his mouth with his napkin, and said, "Hey. Sorry. I didn't mean nothing by it."

Paul withdrew a few folded sheets of paper from the inner pocket of his coat. He unfolded the pages and slid them across the table and in front of Valerie Drammell. On these pages were the reproductions of the photos of Danny's rental vehicle, which had been included in the initial missing persons report.

"This was Danny's rental car. The troopers from Fairbanks found it. Were you with them at the time?"

"No, sir."

Paul tapped one of the photos with his middle finger. "This is right outside the town line, isn't it? I can see the reflection of one of those big crosses in the rear windshield."

Drammell pulled the paper closer to him and studied it. After a moment, he nodded. His cheek bulging with food, he said, "Yeah, looks it."

"That's the only road in and out of town, isn't it?"

"That's right."

"So, no one noticed that big SUV sitting up there in

the grass until the police from Fairbanks came up this way?"

"Maybe someone did but didn't think nothing of it. Or maybe no one had any reason to leave town in all that time. That old road ain't exactly the interstate, you know. Remember, Mr. Gallo, we didn't know your brother was missing until those boys from Fairbanks showed up here. We had no reason to *look* for a car."

This made sense, but Paul still felt some piece of the puzzle was missing. He also felt that Valerie Drammell was being evasive with him.

"What's out there?" he asked. "What reason would my brother have for driving out that way, parking his car, and getting out?"

"Mr. Gallo, you're asking me questions I can't answer. There ain't *nothing* out there. Not a blessed thing but wilderness. Maybe he was bird-watching. Maybe he wanted to walk some of the old mining trails. Maybe he just stopped to take a piss. You'd know your brother better'n anyone, I'd think. You tell me—what was he doin' out there?"

That's the question, isn't it? Paul thought. *That's what this whole thing keeps coming back to. What the hell was Danny doing out here in the first place?*

He handed Drammell his cell phone again, this time showing him the last picture he'd received from Danny. The one with Danny in front of the cabin.

"That him? Because he looks different in this one," Drammell commented. "Looks . . ." His voice trailed off, and Paul thought he saw the faint lines of concern tighten around his mouth and eyes.

"What?" Paul said. "What is it?"

After a moment, Drammell said, "Nothing. Just a brain fart."

"That cabin in the background. Do you recognize it?"

"You seen one cabin, you seen 'em all."

Somehow I doubt that, Paul thought. *Somehow I think the quiet, reclusive people of Dread's Hand—or just the Hand, as it's known—would know one cabin from another just like a mother can tell her twin children apart.*

"There's a line of crosses standing up in front of the cabin, on either side of that door. See them?"

Drammell sucked at his lower lip, then said, "It's a small picture . . ."

"Come on." Paul leaned over the table and tapped the cell phone's screen, enlarging the photo. "You see?"

"Yes. But so what?"

"This is the last bit of communication I received from my brother. I want to find that cabin. For all I know, it's the last place he'd been before he disappeared."

"All right," Drammell said, though his tone was less agreeable.

"How do I get to the old mining town from here?" Paul asked.

"Oh." Drammell's mouth tightened into a small knot. "Well, it's a hike, unless you've got four-wheel drive. But that don't look like any of the old shacks out by the mine. Don't recall any crosses like that on any of those buildings."

"How do I get there?"

"People just don't go out there no more, is the thing," Drammell said.

"Then I guess I won't be disturbing anyone."

"The ground isn't too sturdy, either. Feel I should warn you."

"Is there some reason I can't go out there, Mr. Drammell? Is it . . . I don't know . . . private property or something?"

Drammell shrugged. He seemed bored. "Ain't private property. Ain't *no one's* property. Not no more."

"Then tell me how to get there."

"Your brother didn't disappear up near the mine, Mr. Gallo."

"How do you know? Did you look for him there? Because there's nothing about it in the police report."

"There would be no reason for him to go out that way, that's all," Drammell said. His voice was calm in the face of Paul's mounting irritation.

"How many other people have gone missing from here over the last few years?" Paul asked. "How many hikers have come into town only to disappear without a trace?"

Drammell had his coffee cup halfway to his mouth when Paul asked the questions. It hovered there now, and Drammell looked unsure whether he wanted to drink it or set it back down on the table.

"Eight bodies were found buried in those woods, Mr. Drammell," Paul continued. "My brother wasn't among them. But those eight people had to come from somewhere. Did they stay here in this town? Who would have seen them? And maybe there were more than eight. Maybe Mallory had a second plot of land somewhere— a second site—where he buried the others. Because my brother has got to be somewhere, Mr. Drammell. Do you understand me? My brother has got to be *somewhere*."

Drammell didn't respond. After a moment of silence, as Paul felt his aggravation dissipate from his body, Valerie Drammell got up from his chair and ambled over to the lunch counter.

The son of a bitch is going to pay his bill and walk out on me. Unbelievable. What's wrong with this place?

Drammell *did* pay his bill, but he returned to the table with a Styrofoam container and a to-go cup for his coffee. "Let's talk about this stuff someplace else," he said, dumping his half-eaten sandwich into the container.

"Yeah, all right."

Paul got up and went to the counter to pay his own bill. When he handed Tabby his credit card, she shook her head and, in a mousy, almost inaudible voice, said, "Cash."

He'd watched Valerie Drammell swipe a credit card just moments ago, but he didn't feel like arguing with the woman. Instead, he dug a twenty from his wallet and handed it over. By the time she handed him back his change, Valerie Drammell was already standing outside.

Paul joined him, zipping up his coat.

"Take a ride with me," Drammell said, and before Paul could respond, the man was already crossing the road, the soles of his rubber boots leaving deep impressions in the mud. He approached a mud-splattered pickup truck with a decal on the driver's door that said Public Safety and Drammell's phone number beneath it. Below that, incongruously, was a skull and crossbones.

*   *   *

"Where are we going?" Paul asked.

They had left the main road and taken one of the secondary dirt channels that whipped around the snowy hills and stunted trees toward the mountains. Judging by the position of the sun, Paul could tell they were heading northwest. He thought of that story the guy back at Telluride had told him and Luther Parnell, about running into a man somewhere out here who turned out to be a mass murderer, and how that man could have killed him and dumped his body in the woods, where no one would ever find him. Paul didn't think Valerie Drammell was the type, although this impromptu truck ride through the wooded hillside did not make him feel too warm and toasty.

If Joseph Mallory never confessed to those murders, those poor souls would have never been found, either.

"You wanted to go to the mine," Drammell said. He drove with one hand while trying not to spill his coffee, which he held in the other. Tabby back at the luncheonette had neglected to provide a lid for his to-go cup. "Well, I'm taking you there."

They were heading for a dense copse of trees. The road—what still remained of it out this far from the village—ended right at the tree line, and unless this was like a secret passage in a haunted house and that veil of trees was going to part to reveal that the road continued just as they approached it, they were going to crash.

"Jesus, Drammell. Look out."

Unfazed, Drammell spun the steering wheel, a teardrop of coffee spilling over the lip of the cup and onto his knuckles.

Suddenly, they were on . . . not a road, but a passageway that wove through the trees and up toward the foothills. The pickup thumped and rattled and the assortment of air fresheners that hung from the truck's rearview mirror swung wildly. Paul braced himself against the dashboard with one hand while his other hand searched for a seat belt that was nonexistent.

When Paul glimpsed a line of wooden crosses through the trees off to his right, he said, "What's with the crosses out here, Drammell? They're beginning to creep me out."

"Folks out here tend to be religious," Drammell said.

"One or two would have sufficed. These look more like they're lined up like some kind of boundary."

Drammell said nothing.

They arrived less than five minutes later, Valerie Drammell's pickup truck cresting a barren plateau, where much of the snow had melted to runoff that drained down into a narrow chasm at the center of the pitched basin. Paul saw the remains of old slapdash wooden shacks, arranged in the rough approximation of a semicircle around the snow-covered clearing. The largest building looked like an old barn, boards missing from its walls like absent teeth in a diseased mouth. There was some sort of silo or chute at the top, where the remains of what looked like a conveyor belt projected out like a tongue. Below that was what looked like a large wooden barrel with a number of staves missing. Beyond the hovels was a sparkling silver creek that shone like jewels in the sun.

There was no reverence here: Drammell drove right down into the center of the semicircle of buildings, keeping to the right side of the fault line that cut straight down the center of the valley—a concavity in the earth several yards deep and dusted with snow. Even the buildings slouched at angles toward the crevasse in the center of the plateau.

Drammell pulled up alongside the first in a half circle of shacks and turned off the ignition. "Come on out with me," he said, popping open his door and stepping out.

Paul got out, his boots breaking through the hard crust of snow. He could feel the pitch of the ground even where he stood, where the earth tilted toward that jagged fault line at the center of the hilltop. He walked around the front of the pickup truck and followed Valerie Drammell out into the center of the semicircle. There were maybe two dozen shacks out here, including the large barnlike structure, some of them as small as old wooden outhouses. A few were no longer structures at all, only vertical wooden struts climbing toward the overcast sky, their walls reduced to rubble all around them. The structures all faced the gaping hole in the ground, as well as a collection of ancient stone grave markers.

Drammell stood on the edge of the fault line, sipping his coffee while peering down into the crack in the earth. Paul joined him, gazed down into the cut in the earth, and found himself looking into the mouth of a mine shaft. The mine's opening was crisscrossed with old two-by-fours that were bolted into place with nails the size of railroad spikes. Leafy vines spooled out from the hole like the tentacular arms of some underwater creature. Beyond the opening and across the face of the plateau, the ground formed a concave chasm, several yards deep in some places, although the snow made it difficult to tell just how deep.

"This is the village behind the village," Drammell said. "The ghost village, you could say. The Hand's alter ego. This place right here is why Dread's Hand exists today."

"How far down does it go?" Paul asked, still peering down into that narrow chasm in the earth. It was maybe a few yards wide but there was something terrible about it, something dangerous. He took an unconscious step back from it.

"Far enough," Drammell said. "Twenty-six men died down there when the mine collapsed back in . . . oh, 1916 or thereabouts." He raised a hand, acknowledging the rows of stone crosses that served as grave markers. Twenty-six of them.

Paul turned toward the semicircle of run-down shacks that stood within a stone's throw of them. They looked about as stable as buildings fashioned out of matchsticks, making the patina of fresh snow on their cantilevered roofs appear dangerously heavy. How these buildings had remained standing for one hundred years was a mystery, particularly since they now resided around the rim of a massive sinkhole. If it wasn't for the snow and for the expanse of coniferous forestry in the background, they might have been structures straight out of an old Technicolor Western.

"Listen, Gallo, I'm gonna level with you. Folks out here are superstitious. Look around you. Our winters are black, and in the summer it's just one long stretch of perpetual daylight. People around here don't have much. They drink and they hunt and they sit around telling ghost stories."

Drammell hocked a glob of phlegm onto the ground and continued. "Back at Tabby's, you asked about how many people had gone missing out here. Answer is, Mr. Gallo, no one really knows. And things like that just tend to fuel their superstition. And now we've got Joe Mallory, one of their own, doing what he did. I guess I'm trying to let you see why people might behave a little strangely toward you out here. They're afraid, is all."

"And what exactly are they afraid of?"

"Oh," said Drammell, taking a step back from the edge of the fault and scanning the tree-studded horizon. "The forest. The foothills. And what's in it."

"I'm not following you. What do you mean?" Paul asked. He had taken his phone out now and was holding up Danny's most recent photo, studying the cabin in the background of the picture and comparing it to the ones that stood just a few yards from him now, farther up the slope. None of them possessed that unusual pattern of crosses bracketing their doorways.

Drammell sipped his coffee and said, "These people think the woods are cursed. That if you go in there, you run the risk of being touched by evil and having your mind turned dark and twisted. And what Joe Mallory had done only confirms the superstition."

Paul lowered his phone and glanced back at Drammell from over his shoulder. "They think Joseph Mallory was possessed by some evil spirit, and that's why he killed those people?"

"Not just some spirit, Mr. Gallo," Drammell said. He wiggled a set of fingers at him, as if they were claws.

"But the devil himself. 'Bone white,' they call it. When a man loses everything inside him that makes him human, and gets taken over by the devil. Possessed."

"Well, then, the people of this town are bat-shit crazy," Paul said, shaking his head.

He turned away from Drammell and scanned the horizon and the semicircle of shacks again. Then he glanced again at Danny's selfie on his phone—Danny's bearded face standing in front of a similar cabin, great twisting vines spiraling off the roof and moss climbing the dark, wooden walls. It looked *similar,* yes, but Paul didn't think this cabin matched any of these. There was something . . . earthy . . . about the one in Danny's photo. Something organic about it that Paul couldn't put his finger on.

"I'd be the first to admit the folks around here are a little off the reservation," Drammell said. "Hikers come out here and go missing, it's the devil that got 'em. Some stir-crazy mountain man shoots his old lady in the face with a shotgun, or that fella Mallory gets a hankering to go people-hunting up in the hills one day, folks say they've gone bone white. They *believe* this shit, you understand? Even the kids, they wear animal fur masks whenever something bad happens, thinking they'll trick the devil into thinking they're forest critters and leave 'em alone. But then you come sniffing around asking about a missing brother, and it's gonna set them all on edge. And it certainly don't help that you fellas are twins."

"Why does that matter?"

"Because you look just like him. If there's anyone here in town who recognizes your brother, they're apt to think you're him, coming through the woods like a ghost."

"You've got to be shitting me."

"They say that's how old Mr. Splitfoot gets you. He holds up a mirror image of yourself to confuse your spirit. That's when he moves in, replacing your soul with evil. There've been folks who have claimed to have glimpsed themselves out there in those woods. My daddy told me of a man who shot and killed his mirror-double, but when he went to collect the body, it was a dead sheep. It's all fairy tales, Mr. Gallo—a myth to make sense of the senselessness of living out here. Something that can explain away the madness and the violence that are by-products of rampant alcoholism, domestic violence, suicides."

Paul was thinking of Peggy Chalmers, the pitiful woman he'd met at the police station who'd been frightened by Danny's photograph. Had she heard the stories about Dread's Hand? Had their twinness come across to her as some arcane evil?

"So, how come you don't believe this stuff?" he asked Drammell.

"Shit, Gallo, you think I've lived my whole life out here, in this shithole? I was born here and now I'm back, but I've been around enough so that I ain't spent my life in a bubble. But most of these sad bastards, they've never left the Hand. Most of these families been here for generations. You raise a baby in a room with no windows, and they're apt to grow up thinking that there ain't nothing beyond those four walls. It's no different out here, 'cept maybe our walls are trees and mountains. I came back to take care of my daddy after he got the cancer. He died some years back now, and I just stayed put. It's quiet out here and that's all right by me. But even my old man believed these old ghost stories."

"You think the people out here are distrustful enough of strangers to do something to one of them?"

"Like what?"

"Like doing something bad to them to prevent them from wandering off into the woods and pissing off the devil, for starters."

"You're asking me whether these folks have done something to your brother."

"It wouldn't be hard."

"You sound about as loopy as they do," Drammell said.

"No one wants me going off into the woods. Including you last night."

Drammell laughed. "That's because it was colder than a witch's tit, Gallo. You wanna go for a hike, be my guest."

"I'm just saying it would be pretty damn easy to get rid of me out here, if that would put their minds at ease."

Drammell grunted. "That's some imagination. You don't actually believe that, do you?"

Paul waved a hand at him. "Never mind," he said. Yet he was thinking about Drammell's baby-in-a-room metaphor, and of that baby as an adult, its mind ruined from years in a windowless box, its eyes wild and crazy and attuned to nothing but absolute blackness, blind as a mole, its fingernails grown into claws. What does that baby-turned-adult do when, for the first time in forever, a hole is punched through that wall and the sun shines through? What does that baby-turned-adult do to the first stranger who comes walking through that hole?

"You just about satisfied out here, Mr. Gallo?"

"Just about," he said, turning away from Drammell and walking around the inside perimeter of the cabins. There were no doors on any of the shacks, just the crude, warped doorways. As Paul passed before one of the doorways, he noticed something carved into the wood of the shack's rear wall.

Paul crossed the threshold and entered the shack. The floor was comprised of warped, creaking boards, the walls bowing inward from age and the elements. Bands of sunlight bled through the cracks.

The carving was of a giant eye with a vertical pupil. Paul went to it and traced it with his index finger. Whoever had carved it had wanted it to stay for a good long time, for the carving was deep.

It shouldn't have bothered him. He'd gone into Baltimore enough times in his life to become accustomed and immune to all varieties of graffito—from the profound to the profane, the vulgar to the enigmatic—but this simple wood-carved glyph unleashed in him a sense of unease bordering on dread. And despite his certainty that he had never seen anything like it before, he felt a sense of familiarity with it, of near déjà vu. As if the animal part of his human brain knew what this was deep down on some base level.

Something passed along the rear outside wall of the shack, moving in front of the bands of daylight that glowed through the cracks and splits in the boards. Whatever it was, it was dark and moved close to the ground.

"That you, Drammell?" he said.

The figure paused . . . then continued its languid, fluid passage around to the far side of the cabin.

Paul took a step back . . . and that was when the boards beneath his feet gave way.

He heard the dry, brittle *pop* followed by the splintering of old wood. A second later, he felt the floor give out from under him. Gravity tugged at his legs. He went down through a manhole-size aperture in the rotting floorboards, jagged splinters snagging at his coat and cutting into his exposed flesh. As he slid down into the hole, he managed to dig his fingernails in between the seams of two floorboards and arrest his fall.

"Drammell! Drammell!"

Somewhere down below, his feet cycled in midair. He would have thought there'd be nothing but solid earth beneath the cabin, but that wasn't the case—God knew how deep a drop it was to the bottom of that black chasm.

"Drammell!"

The safety officer's shadow fell over him, his breath wheezing. "Jesus, boy," Drammell huffed. "Hold tight."

Drammell dropped to his knees and reached down the curve of Paul's back, down past the splintery harpoons of rotted wood, and grabbed hold of Paul's belt.

"Count of three," Drammell said, then he counted out loud. On three, Drammell pulled while Paul scrambled out of the hole.

Rolling over on his back, Paul lay there staring at the pattern of sunlight shining through the fissures in the cabin roof. His heart ached, it was beating so fast. Drammell was kneeling beside him, his face pale, his large hands planted on his thighs.

"I warned you this place was dangerous," Drammell wheezed.

"Duly noted," Paul said, his own breath hot and ragged in his throat.

Drammell climbed to his feet. He extended a hand and Paul used it to pull himself up. Glancing down, he saw ragged tears through which tufts of cotton purled in the fabric of his coat. When he lifted up his coat and the layer of clothing underneath, he saw a series of bloody striations running along the left side of his rib cage, like shark gills.

"Your face is cut, too," said Drammell, still panting. "You're bleeding." He tapped one of the jagged boards that formed the perimeter of the hole in the floor. "Lucky it didn't take an eye out of your head."

Paul touched two fingers to a tender spot on his left cheekbone. "I'm lucky I didn't fall down there and break my goddamn neck," he said, wincing at the hot throb of pain that had bloomed along the left side of his face. He peered over the side and down into the chasm. It was pitch black down there. He couldn't see the bottom. "Is this what happened to the church back in town?"

"The church," Drammell said. He took an inhaler from his pocket and triggered off two blasts into his mouth.

"I poked my head inside and noticed the floor was gone."

"Wasn't exactly the same thing," Drammell said. "That hole didn't open up beneath the church. Church was built over top of it. Floor just gave way over time."

"That makes no sense." Paul followed him out, careful now of where he placed his boots. "Why would they build a church over a massive hole in the ground?"

"They thought sticking a church over top that hole might keep the devil from climbing out." Drammell nodded back toward the cabin doorway and at the sunken mine in the center of the plateau. "The devil had used up this place and was working his way toward the town."

"What about this?" Paul said, pointing at the eye-shaped symbol carved into the wood. "Another part of the superstition?"

"It's the mark of the Keeper," Drammell says. "That story I heard as a kid, straight from my old man. Legend has it that someone from town was designated as a lookout of sorts. Someone to keep any eye out for any evil that might try to infiltrate the village."

"I've seen this somewhere before," Paul said.

"Yeah?"

"Not sure where." For some reason, his mind slipped back to his fainting spell at the front of his classroom, and that circle with the line through it that he had scrawled in chalk on the floor while he was unconscious.

"Come on," Drammell said, snapping Paul from his reverie. "I'm freezing my ass off out here."

18

They drove back down from the old mine and through the woods in silence. Paul had no patience for any more ghost stories—or devil stories, or whatever the case might be—and Valerie Drammell seemed content to remain quiet. It wasn't until they were back on the main road—that muddy brown strip of roadway whose shoulders were crowded with dirty snow—that Paul spoke.

"Where's Mallory's house?"

"Huh?" Drammell looked at him, a cigarette drooping from his lower lip.

"Mallory's house. Is it close?"

"Close, yeah," Drammell said. He was still staring at Paul, yet his truck seemed to stay on the winding road. He turned the steering wheel as if by rote memory. "But what do you want to do up at Mallory's place?"

"I thought I might talk to some of the neighbors, see if any of them can identify Danny from his photo."

Drammell turned his gaze back to the road. "You

just choosing to ignore that whole conversation we just had?"

"I'm not trying to spook anyone. I just want some answers."

Drammell tossed his smoke out the window, then sucked on his lower lip. The truck slowed to a crawl as he downshifted, the gears grinding. The collection of plastic deodorizers dangling from the rearview mirror clacked together like broken wind chimes.

"All right," Drammell conceded. "I'll take you up Durham myself."

"That's not necessary."

"It's my job." He pointed to a ball cap that was wedged between the truck's windshield and its dashboard, the title SAFETY OFFICER stenciled across the front panel. There was a large brass fishing hook bent around the bill of the hat.

"I appreciate your concern, but I don't think I'm in any serious danger."

"Nearly got yourself killed back at the mine."

"Yeah, well, is the ground going to disappear beneath my feet along Durham Road, too?"

"Well," Drammell said, his face serious. "Guess you never can tell."

"A police escort," he said, reclining back in the passenger seat. "I feel like a celebrity."

"I ain't no police," Drammell reminded him.

Durham Road looked like a dirt go-kart track carved into the wooded hillside. There was a sign for it, though half the letters had been rubbed off, and it bent at such an angle that suggested it had been struck by more than one motor vehicle in its time. The houses here, tucked away from the road and back among the trees, looked like large rectangular shipping containers. Tar paper covered the windows, and the porches had been cobbled together from cinder blocks. Plaster lawn ornaments were in abundance. Moose antlers hung over a number of front doors.

Drammell pulled his truck up onto the shoulder, which was just a sloping hillock of shrubbery, and shifted into Park. When he twisted the key out of the ignition, the entire chassis shuddered, then went still.

"Do you know any of these people?" Paul asked.

"Remember back at Tabby's I said that most folks here keep to themselves? Well, these are most folks." He cranked open the driver's door.

"You're coming with me?"

"Safety first," Drammell said, and chuckled. It was the closest to a joke the man had come all afternoon.

It was colder out here, the trees taller and more densely packed together. They were on the verge of the true forest out here, and midway up into the foothills. It was just the slightest shift in altitude, but Paul could feel it. He expected Drammell to lead the way, seeing as how he had insisted on coming out here with him, but he didn't; he jammed another cigarette into his mouth and, leaning against the hood of his pickup, chased the tip with a match.

Paul stepped over great spools of weeds on his campaign up to the first house. He could see lights on behind the tar paper covering the windows, but still, the place looked about as hospitable as a snake pit. Plastic sunflowers lined the nonexistent walkway leading up to

the cinder-block porch, and somehow even their simple
existence suggested some level of foreboding, as if they
had once been travelers on a similar mission, witched
into plastic sentinels.

"Keep an eye out for dogs," Drammell called to him.
He was hanging back a few feet, standing on the edge
of the property by the road and smoking.

"Dogs?" That decades-old dog bite on his left arm
suddenly itched.

Drammell waved him toward the house.

Paul knocked. He heard movement inside, thought
maybe there were footfalls approaching the door . . .
and then nothing. No one came to the door. No one
peeked out between the gaps in the tar paper over the
windows. Whatever dogs Drammell had warned him
about were determined to remain just as elusive as their
owners.

He knocked again, and this time he heard a TV being turned off.

It's like they're hiding from me.

After another thirty seconds, he turned toward
Drammell and raised his hands in mock surrender.

"Someone's in there, but they're not answering."

Drammell shrugged.

"Is this going to happen at every house?" Paul asked.

Drammell laughed.

It happened at every house.

It was a quarter after six by the time they climbed
back into Drammell's truck, but civil twilight had already colored the sky a deep lavender in preparation

for the long night. Paul had knocked on about eight or nine doors, but no one had answered, despite Paul's certainty that everyone was at home. At two of the houses, dogs *had* barked, and Paul could even hear their owners chastising them from behind their closed doors. Still, these doors were not opened. The people here pretended not to be at home.

As Drammell cranked the ignition and the pickup jangled to life, Paul said, "Which house is Mallory's?"

"He didn't live down by the road," Drammell said. He pointed toward a slight dip in the hillside, where a dense black forest rose up to touch the purpling sky. The trees were twice as large back there than they were here alongside the road.

"Can we check it out?"

"Nothing to check out. Anyway, it's a crime scene. Can't take you up there."

"You knew this was going to happen before we even came out here," Paul commented. "These people not answering their doors."

"Figured it might," said Drammell as he pulled back onto the go-kart track of a road. "It's coming on dark. No one out here opens their doors at night."

Paul grunted his displeasure.

"So, where to now? Or are you done sightseeing for the night?"

Paul didn't answer right away. There promised to be no positive outcome out here. *Had* Mallory murdered Danny? Or maybe the xenophobes of Dread's Hand had done something to him, like those creepy villagers who burned Christopher Lee alive in that old movie. And somehow worse than both of those scenarios was the troubling possibility that maybe Danny had come out here and done something to himself . . .

"What's it gonna be, Gallo?"

"You can take me back to my room, thanks," he said. Then he turned away and stared out the passenger window so Valerie Drammell wouldn't see the look of composure sloughing from his face. He felt sick. He felt like he was way off course and spinning haplessly in a void. The nights would grow longer and colder, and he'd just keep on spinning, spinning, spinning.

You can still cast an anchor, he told himself, peering into the rearview mirror and at the approximate location where Drammell had pointed out Mallory's house. Back there. In the woods.

"Listen," Drammell said as he pulled up outside the Blue Moose. They sat there idling, the truck's cab filling with the stink of burning motor oil. "I know you gotta do what you feel is right. But if you want my advice, you should call the cops. Let Fairbanks deal with this. No offense, Gallo, but you don't really strike me as the type of guy who'd appreciate getting snowed in out here all winter. Take a powder. I find out anything about your brother, I'll call you personally. You have my word on that."

"Yeah, you're probably right," he said, and stepped out of the truck.

"And let's not do any midnight gallivanting tonight, huh?" Drammell grinned good-naturedly.

"Yeah. All right."

He slammed the door then watched as Drammell made a U-turn in the road. The pickup shuddered and belched gray smog from its tailpipe, and Paul watched it go until the truck disappeared behind an outcrop of pines.

He turned toward the inn and was mounting the front steps when he heard a sharp metallic ding resonate in the air. It was very close—on the other side of the inn, or so it sounded. Before he could even step down from the steps, he heard a second metallic bang, this one deeper, like a mallet to a gong. This was followed by a shrill peal of laughter.

He stepped around the side of the inn to find three kids chucking rocks at the Tahoe. He saw that the rear windshield was a meshwork of cracks and that the body of the vehicle looked like it had been sprayed with buckshot.

"Hey!" he shouted.

All three kids whirled to face him, grins dropping from their pale faces. At the sight of him, their eyes bugged out. Their gloved hands dropped the remaining stones to the ground. The youngest was maybe seven years old, the other two maybe nine or ten. They all looked terrified.

"What the hell are you guys doing?"

All three kids had their fur masks propped up on the tops of their heads. The two older kids tugged theirs down over their faces before taking to their heels: They sprinted across the road, their sneakers kicking up clumps of muddy snow, and they did not slow down when Paul shouted for them to come back.

The remaining kid managed to swipe his own fur mask down over his face, but he failed to line up the eye-holes. He turned to run, too, but got only a couple of feet before one of his oversized boots collided with a downed tree limb. The kid went sprawling to the ground. His hands were up to brace for the fall, but Paul watched as the side of the kid's head collided with the pile of stones the kids had been using as ammo against the Tahoe.

The fact that the kid didn't start shrieking concerned Paul. He rushed to the boy's side and helped roll him over onto his back. The kid wasn't unconscious—his teeth were clenched, his lips drawn back in pain. Paul stripped the mask off the kid's face and could see a bruise already beginning to form on the right side of the boy's forehead.

"You okay?"

The kid blinked up at him. A soundless wheeze escaped his clenched teeth. A look of fear replaced the confusion that fled from his eyes. He swung an arm at Paul and struggled to sit up.

"Relax, kid."

"Get away!" the kid cried. He rolled onto his side, then sobbed. He drew his right knee up to his chest and clutched at his ankle.

"Easy," Paul soothed. He placed a hand on the boy's shoulder and the kid whipped his head around, staring at him. There was undeniable terror in his eyes. Paul lifted his hand off the kid's shoulder and held both hands up in surrender. "I'm not gonna hurt you."

"Yes," said the boy. "You will."

Paul shook his head. He glanced at the Tahoe, with its cracked rear windshield and dented quarter panels. The kid was patting the top of his head, searching for the furry animal mask that was no longer there.

"Let me see that ankle," Paul said, reaching for the boy's foot.

The kid slid his leg away from him.

"It's okay," Paul said. "Just let me have a look."

The kid's leg stilled and Paul took the foot in one hand. He lifted the pants leg and saw that the flesh around the ankle was already beginning to balloon.

"Can you wiggle your foot?"

"Hurts."

"Give it a try."

The kid rotated his foot, wincing.

"It's not broken," Paul said. "Just sprained. But you're lucky you didn't knock yourself unconscious. What's your name?"

"Toby," the kid said. His voice was small and his eyes, which were still glued to Paul, were still simmering with fear.

"How come you and your friends were throwing rocks at my car?"

"So you'd leave."

"Why do you want me to leave?"

"Because you're white."

Paul frowned. This kid was paler than he was. "I don't understand."

"Are you gonna take me away?" the kid said.

"Of course not. Why would you think that?"

"That's what the other kids said."

"That I'd take you away?"

"That you'd take any of us away. If we got too close. That you'd hurt us."

"Why would you think I'd do anything like that?"

The boy's breath stuttered from his mouth in bursts of vapor. "Because you're *white*," he repeated.

"So are you."

The boy shook his head.

Paul glanced across the road in the direction where the other kids had run off. "Some friends," he said. "Where do you live?"

The boy pointed across the road and toward a dilapidated tract house nestled along the tree line. A light burned in one window.

"Let me help you over there."

The kid's eyes went wide.

"It's okay," Paul assured him.

"W-w-why'd you come back?" Toby asked, shivering.

"What do you mean? Back from where?"

Toby's eyes flitted in the direction of the woods beyond the church before settling back on Paul. "Out there," he said. "The forest. I saw you come out."

Paul realized the kid had seen him coming down the path behind the church earlier that day. Why it frightened the kid so much, he wasn't sure. More superstitions, he supposed. Or maybe the kid had bumped his head harder than he thought.

"What did you mean when you said I'm 'white'?" Paul asked.

"Bone white," the kid said. "The devil's inside you."

"Yeah? Why do you think that?"

"Because you went away and now you came back." The kid was starting to cry.

"I just walked up the hill this morning," he said, nodding across the street toward the path behind the church. "Those are just ghost stories, kid."

"Not this morning," Toby said, sniffling.

"When?"

"Last year," Toby said. "You went away last year and

now you're back." Toby wiped the tears from his cheeks with two trembling hands.

"My brother," Paul said. "You saw my brother."

Toby just stared at him, his eyes sloppy with tears.

"That wasn't me. Look." He took his cell phone from his pocket and scrolled through a series of photos until he found one—a rare one—of him and Danny together, Danny's arm around Paul's shoulder.

"You're twin brothers," Toby said, staring at the photo.

"Yes. Yes."

"This isn't a trick?"

"No, son. That's my brother. Danny—his name's Danny. You saw him here last year? You saw him here in town?"

Toby nodded.

"Did you talk to him?"

"No."

"Where did you see him?"

"Just here. Around. Here." He pointed at the Blue Moose.

"He stayed here?"

"I don't know," said the boy. "He was here. He was here."

"What happened to him? Do you know what happened to him? Did you see him go somewhere? Did he walk off into the woods?"

Toby's eyes kept volleying between Paul and the photo on his phone. "We thought you were him. I . . . I'm sorry about your car, mister." He began to weep.

"Don't worry about the car. It's okay." He squeezed the boy's shoulder.

"It was a different car, anyway," Toby said. "I should have known it wasn't you. Your brother had a different car. I'm sorry for breaking your window, mister. Please don't tell my mom."

"My brother had a blue car." Paul remembered the printout from the police report that he had in his pocket. He took it out, unfolded it, and showed Toby the photos of Danny's rental vehicle. "This right here, right?"

Toby nodded.

"Do you know what happened to that car?"

Toby looked at him. "They took it away," he said.

"Took it away," Paul repeated, the words sinking in. "Who?"

"Mr. Hopewell."

"Who's that?" The name sounded familiar, though he couldn't place it.

"He drives the tow truck," Toby said.

"Mr. Hopewell towed my brother's car away?"

The boy nodded.

"From where?"

"From right here," Toby said, looking now at the Tahoe. "From right where you're parked."

Son of a bitch, Paul thought.

"Am I in trouble?" Toby said. His lower lip was quivering again. He was close to spilling more tears. "For throwing those rocks?"

"I won't say anything if you won't," Paul said.

"I won't," Toby said. "I really won't. I'm sorry."

"It's okay. I paid for the insurance. Just do me a favor and tell your friends they don't need to be afraid of me, okay?"

Toby smiled. "Okay."

"And no more rocks."

"Yeah. Okay. I promise."

"Let me help you back home," Paul said.

Toby glanced at his injured ankle, then back up at his house in the distance. He was weighing his options, Paul saw. In the end, the kid nodded, then held out his hand so Paul could help hoist him off the ground.

"Hurts," Toby said as he took his first step.

"We'll make it," Paul assured him.

They campaigned across the road and over the frozen ground on the other side toward the small tract house. A shape moved behind the lighted window. A moment later, the side door of the house opened and a woman came out, clutching an ankle-length coat about her thin frame.

"Who are you?" she barked at Paul. "What are you doing with my son?"

"My name's Paul Gallo. I'm staying at the Blue Moose. Your son tripped and sprained his ankle, and I wanted to make sure he got back home safe—"

"Come," she called to Toby.

The boy released his grip on Paul's arm and hobbled over to his mother.

"You know better," she said to her son. Then she looked back up at Paul. "He's home now. Thank you." But there was no gratitude in her voice.

"All right." He looked at Toby. "Go ice that ankle, okay?"

Toby nodded and raised a hand.

"Get inside," his mother scolded him. She watched

as he hobbled up the stairs and disappeared into the lighted doorway. "Who are you?" she asked him again after the boy had shut the door.

"Paul Gallo," he repeated.

"What are you doing here?"

"I just wanted to make sure your son was okay."

"He's okay. So thank you. And please leave. Please." In the darkness, Paul could not make out the expression on her face. But he imagined it wasn't a pleasant one.

"Good night," he said, and headed back toward the inn.

19

The inn's lobby was empty when he returned, though a fire burned in the hearth and the old man's TV was tuned to an old John Wayne war movie. The vest with the smiley-face button hung from the back of the chair. Paul was hungry again, but exhaustion had settled down on his shoulders, making him feel as though he was carrying a heavy load.

"Hello?" he called, and waited. But no one came out of the back room.

Bill Hopewell, he thought, walking down the hall toward his room. It was the guy who had shown up last night with Valerie Drammell. The guy who drove the goddamn tow truck. *Drammell, you lying son of a bitch. What's going on around here?*

He opened the door to his room to find Merle Warren seated on his bed, staring at him. Only the small lamp beside the bed was on, casting half of the old man's features in pools of black shadow.

"Mr. Warren," he said, and it was like the man's name stuck like adhesive at the back of his throat.

"You read the Good Book?" Merle Warren said, his speech slurred but direct.

"What?" Paul said.

"You read how he took Him to the highest mountaintop and tempted Him with material things?" Merle was holding something in his lap—something metallic that glinted in the room's dim light.

"Where's your daughter, Mr. Warren?" Paul asked him.

"No," Merle said, a tone of disappointment in his voice. "No, of course you haven't. You think you can walk among us, that you can fool us, but you're wrong. You're wrong."

"Mr. Warren . . ."

Merle Warren stood from the bed and charged at Paul. The item that glinted in his hand was the blade of a hunting knife. Eyes blazing with a terrible madness, he lunged at Paul, swinging the knife blade in a clumsy arc. It was a lumbering and onerous attempt, but Paul's instinct was to raise his hands in front of his face instead of jumping back to avoid the blade altogether. The blade bit into the soft meat of his right hand, just below the pinkie. Only then did Paul sidestep the old man's second attempt at cutting him. Merle Warren's forward momentum sent the old man sprawling to the floor. The old man cried out as the knife skittered out into the hallway.

"Janice! Janice!" Paul shouted. He backed against the far wall of the hallway, and when he spotted the knife on the floor, he pressed the sole of his boot down on it. Inside the room, Merle moaned and rolled on his side. When his eyes caught Paul's gaze, he sent one liver-spotted hand groping for Paul's ankle, his fingers like blunt dowels. But he was too far away to reach him.

Janice Warren appeared at the far end of the hallway, an apron twisted halfway around her ample waist. She hustled past Paul and entered the room, pausing at the sight of her father sprawled out on the floor.

"What happened?" she demanded.

"He came at me with a knife," Paul said.

"Daddy," Janice said, bending down beside her father. She sounded like a disappointed parent. "I thought you were asleep in front of the TV. You could have hurt yourself."

Paul barked a sour laugh, cradling his injured hand. "Hurt himself, huh?"

Ignoring him, Jan Warren proceeded to help her father up off the floor.

Paul bent down and picked up the knife. It had a four-inch blade, and could have easily done more damage than it had to Paul's hand. The wound didn't even hurt—not yet, anyway—but blood was pooling in his hand and streaming down his arm.

Janice ushered her father out into the hallway while the old man mumbled nonsense under his breath. She glanced over at Paul, who stood holding the knife in one hand while staring at the runnels of blood trailing up his arm. She looked irritated with him.

"Come on with me," she said to him. "I'll take a look at it after I get Daddy settled down."

He followed them down the hall, keeping a healthy distance from the old man. When they reached the lobby, Janice ushered her father behind the desk. Then she glanced over at Paul. "There's paper towels under the counter," she instructed. "Try not to bleed on the floor."

Well, fuck you, too, he thought, and went around behind the desk to search for the paper towels.

When Janice Warren returned ten minutes later from getting her father settled next door, Paul was in the old man's lawn chair watching John Wayne swagger across the TV screen. He'd wrapped paper towels around his hand to staunch the bleeding, but the pressure on the wound was causing the pain to flare up.

"You think you need stitches?" Janice asked, setting a first-aid kit on the desktop.

"I don't know."

"If so, I can call Galen Provost from up the road. He's stitched plenty folks up before."

"He's a doctor?"

"Taxidermist."

Wonderful, Paul thought.

"I'll take a look, see what I can see," Janice said, laying out a series of paper towels on the desktop. "Come on over here and prop your hand up. Let's have a look."

He set his hand down on the desk and peeled the paper towels away from his wound. The gash was maybe an inch and a half long, and although it had bled with zeal, the cut didn't appear to be very deep.

Janice gripped his hand with pincer-like fingers. Paul winced. She rolled the hand first one way, then the other. "Hurts?"

"Just a little," he said.

"Can you flex that little finger there?"

"Yes." He showed her.

"All right. I think a couple of butterfly bandages will do it." She addressed the first-aid kit, rummaged through it. "Where'd you put the knife?"

He nodded at the edge of the counter, where the knife rested on an issue of *Cosmo*. "That's a pretty hefty knife for your dad to be carrying around."

"Probably got it from the kitchen."

"A hunting knife?"

Janice said nothing. She took a bandage from the kit and peeled the paper from it.

"Shouldn't we sterilize the wound first?" he suggested.

Janice's eyes slid over to him. Her lips tightened. She set the bandage down, then reached under the counter. She rooted around for what Paul expected to be a bottle of peroxide, but instead produced a small bottle of Jack Daniel's. She unscrewed the cap and told him to hold still.

"Is that—" He hissed, the pain surging up his arm as Janice poured the cold whiskey over the wound. It felt like she'd set his hand on fire.

"Better'n penicillin," she said.

"Yeah, I think that's their motto," he groused.

Janice took a swig from the bottle before screwing the cap back on and stowing it back beneath the counter.

"I spoke to some kid outside who said he saw Danny's car being towed away from here sometime last year."

"Danny?"

"My brother."

Janice said nothing.

"Bill Hopewell," Paul said. "He was the guy who showed up last night with Valerie Drammell, wasn't he?"

Busying herself with rearranging the items inside
the first-aid kit, Janice said, "Was him, yeah."

"Are you sure you don't recall my brother staying
here? Because if his car was here—"

"I don't recall."

"Did you have Bill Hopewell tow my brother's car?"

She slammed the lid of the first-aid kit, startling
him. "Are you accusing me of something, Mr. Gallo? If
so, I'd appreciate it if you'd just spit it out."

"I just want to know what happened to my brother."

"I don't *know* what happened to your brother. And
now you've worked up my daddy, just like you've been
working up the good folks in this town."

He frowned at her.

"Oh, that's right," she continued. "Don't think I
haven't heard about you going all over the Hand, botherin' folks with these stories about your brother. Don't
you think we've been through enough lately? We don't
need you hanging around, causing trouble."

Paul was too taken aback by her outburst to summon
a response.

"I'm heading next door," Janice continued. "There's
coffee in the kitchen, if you're interested. Heat it up in
the microwave. Some leftover cobbler, too. Daddy will
sleep through the night. Best to keep your door locked,
though, just the same."

"You bet I will," he said.

"Come tomorrow, I think you'd better consider moving on from here, Mr. Gallo."

Without waiting for a response from him, she moved
across the lobby toward the door. She shrugged on her
coat, then stepped out into the night.

Paul went into the kitchen, located the percolator, and poured some black sludge into a mug. The microwave looked like it had been scavenged from the *Titanic,* but it did the job. He carried the mug in his one good hand while balancing a plate of peach cobbler in the other as he went back out into the hall. Behind the front desk, the television was still on, though it sounded like the John Wayne movie had been replaced by the news. He caught a snippet of it as he walked by.

"In other news, authorities report that Joseph Mallory, the man who confessed to the murders of eight hikers over a five-year period in the foothills of Alaska's White Mountains, has taken his own life . . ."

Paul darted around the front desk, sloshing coffee onto the floor in his haste.

"Mallory was in police custody when he was discovered early this morning having . . ."

Paul watched the entire news segment while holding his breath. It was only a thirty-second report, but by the time it was over, he felt as though he had just run a marathon.

Back in his room, he dialed Jill Ryerson's desk number but was dumped straight into her voice mail. He called the main line and was routed to an administrator, who told him that Ryerson was out on sick leave. He started to speak, but the administrator could no longer hear him: The signal was dying. Shaky and unsettled, he disconnected the call. He only hoped that Ryerson had gotten a chance to speak with Mallory about his brother prior to Mallory taking his own life.

Exhausted and with his hand throbbing, he reclined on the bed, his back propped up against the headboard.

The tapestry of the Virgin Mary stared at him from the opposite wall. He had the heater cranked on high, and the blowing hot air was causing bits of wallpaper to peel away at the corners and curl around the collection of crucifixes hanging on the walls. The smell of the wallpaper glue was strong. He ate his cobbler and sipped his coffee while he watched the section of wallpaper closest to the heater slowly ripple and peel away from the wall. It gave him childish satisfaction. The wall beneath was wood paneling, and he could see the bits of wallpaper glue stuck to it. He could see something else, too—a perfect capital *Y* and part of the letter *O* gouged into the paneling. It had to be part of some word.

Paul set down his coffee and cobbler, got up from the bed, and crossed over to the peeling section of wallpaper. He pinched the unfurled corner between his thumb and forefinger and gave it a good tug. Given the warm air that he'd had pumping nonstop from the heating unit since his arrival, the glue unstuck without protest and the section of wallpaper came away in a complete sheet.

"Jesus Christ . . ."

Someone had carved the same phrase over and over again into the wood paneling, in varying sizes. Paul ran his fingers across one of the carvings, as if to touch it, to feel it, would quash any disbelief he might have upon making such a discovery.

YOU SHOULD NOT BE HERE

Over and over again. Carved in elongated, spidery capital letters.

YOU SHOULD NOT BE HERE
YOU SHOULD NOT BE HERE
YOU SHOULD NOT BE HERE

He went to the next wall and proceeded to pull all the decorations away from it—the crucifixes, the animal heads, the tapestry of the Virgin Mary, all of it. Once the wall was bare, he urgently stripped each section of wallpaper·from the paneling, exposing an entire collage of that same unsettling phrase.

Shaking, Paul sat on the edge of the bed and stared at the walls that surrounded him. After a time, he shut his eyes. His whole body was trembling.

Was this you, Danny? Was this some warning you'd left behind for me to find? And if so, how did you know I'd come out here looking for you?

But, of course, Danny would know what he would do. They were one and the same, weren't they? Always had been since childhood. Since birth.

Which begged the next question: Why did Danny feel the need to warn him in the first place? What terrible thing was encroaching upon him?

You should not be here, Danny whispered in his ear.

"Too late," Paul said to the empty room.

It would be another long night in the Hand.

20

Hopewell's Garage was an old barn that had been converted to accommodate a hydraulic lift, a wall of automotive tools and accessories, and two bored-looking young men in coveralls with grease on their faces. There were about six or seven junkers around the property—the carcasses of ancient automobiles that no longer resembled any known make or model—and several oil drums filled with discarded mechanical innards. A muscular dog was chained to a post, and as Paul approached the barn, it began barking and salivating all over the place. Paul, who'd maintained an unease around dogs ever since he'd been bitten by one when he was a child, steered a wide berth around the creature.

It was a quarter after ten in the morning, and the sun was a dim bulb beyond the distant trees. Last night, he'd been unable to sleep after the discovery he'd made beneath the wallpaper. He'd paced the room, made repeated phone calls to Jill Ryerson's desk, then hung up in frustration when the call went to voice mail. After a while, he'd forced himself to take a shower, then, trembling, he crawled into bed. The few times he actually fell asleep, he was soon jarred awake by either some terrible nightmare or by the sound of the wind blowing through the trees outside the window. At one point, he dragged the nightstand in front of the door, in case old Merle Warren decided to return for an encore performance. It had been around five in the morning before exhaustion dragged him into unconsciousness, and he'd slept undisturbed till the first bands of sunlight slid through the slats on the shuttered window.

He didn't feel right. Something was off, and it wasn't just his internal clock trying to adjust to the time difference out here. It wasn't just the fleeting hours of daylight bookended by the lengthening periods of darkness. He couldn't get settled, couldn't relax. He felt like Danny's shadow . . . or like Danny himself, doomed to repeat the actions that had caused his brother's disappearance the year before. It was crazy, but he felt caught in some echo, some loop. That he was his brother and his brother was him.

The prospect of eating breakfast at the luncheonette that morning had made him uncomfortable, so he opted to go down to the feed store and grab a chicken salad sandwich from a vending machine. And even that hasty exercise caused a look of suspicion bordering on distrust to wash across the proprietor's face. Paul had gotten his sandwich and a cup of coffee, set a ten-dollar bill on the counter, and hurried out the door.

Now Paul peered into the garage bay and squinted

into the gloom. One of the young men in coveralls looked up and said, "Can I help you?"

"I'm looking for Bill Hopewell."

"Around back." The guy jerked a thumb over his shoulder.

Bill Hopewell was behind the barn, his head and shoulders buried beneath the hood of a 1962 Ford Thunderbird.

"Mr. Hopewell," Paul said.

Bill Hopewell held up one grease-streaked finger as he finished fiddling with something beneath the hood of the car. When he extracted himself from beneath the hood, he wore an irritated expression. Behind him, Paul could see his tow truck parked beneath the shade of the barn.

Wiping his hands on a dirty rag, Hopewell said, "Gallo, ain't it?"

"That's right."

"Having car trouble?"

"Having trouble," Paul said. "Not necessarily with my car. I'm out here looking for my brother. He went miss—"

"I know the story," Hopewell said, cutting him off. "Pretty much everyone around town knows the story. What do you want from me?"

Paul extended a stapled packet of papers toward the mechanic. "Those are some pictures of my brother's rental car. Oldsmobile Bravada. Aquamarine. You recognize it?"

Bill Hopewell twisted his mouth as if he was chewing on something. After a long silence, he handed the pages back to Paul. "Not sure."

"I heard you towed that vehicle from the Blue Moose sometime last year."

"All right," Hopewell said.

"I'd really appreciate a 'yes' or 'no' from you."

"Let's settle for a 'maybe,'" Hopewell said. He folded his arms and leaned against the Thunderbird.

"Is there some reason you don't want to be straight with me? You say everyone in town knows why I'm here, but no one's willing to cut me any slack. No one's willing to help me out."

"Ain't nothing no one can do for you," he said. "Or your brother."

"No," Paul said. "I want you to tell me what the hell is going on around here. You towed my brother's car and dumped it along the road outside of town. I want to know why."

"Because it's my *job*, Gallo." Hopewell extended a hand toward the tow truck. "The car was abandoned in the Moose's lot. I got it out of there. I didn't know who the hell it belonged to."

"And dumped it on the side of the road outside of town?"

"Well, I wasn't going to tow the thing all the way back to Fairbanks, was I?"

"What happened to my brother?"

"I don't *know*," Hopewell said. His gaze was hard. "Nobody knows. He vanished, Gallo. Disappeared. You're getting so messed up, you're out here suggesting I did something to him? Is that it? You here accusing me of doing something to your brother?"

"Why didn't you tell the police that you'd towed the car?"

"Because the police never spoke to me. Had they, I would have told them."

"When did you do it?"

"What?"

"Tow the car to the road and leave it there?"

"I don't know, man. What do you want from me, huh?"

"Because I doubt you towed it straight from the Blue Moose's lot and out to the road on the same day. I think maybe you towed it here first. My guess is you figured on keeping it for parts, like some of those other cars out there. I think maybe you didn't tow it out to the road until you heard that a couple of state troopers were coming up from Fairbanks to investigate my brother's disappearance."

"What the fuck difference does it make? You with the rental car police?"

"It makes a difference because you're covering something up."

"Listen to me," Hopewell said, advancing toward him. He slung the greasy rag over one shoulder and, jabbing a finger at Paul's face, said, "I don't know what happened to your brother. All I know is that SUV sat outside the Moose for two weeks and no one knew who it belonged to, so I hauled it away. Maybe I was gonna sell the parts, maybe I wasn't. You wanna get pissy about the details, let's get pissy. But it ain't gonna help you find your brother. I don't know what happened to him. Never fucking laid eyes on him. Okay?"

"You can tell that to the police when I call them," Paul said.

Hopewell laughed. "Call whoever the fuck you want," he said, then turned and peered down at the Thunderbird's engine block.

"I think my brother was here," Paul said. "I think he stayed at the Blue Moose, and everyone here knows he did. But then something happened to him, and now everyone's conspiring to cover it up. You're all trying to erase him."

"You've got some imagination," Hopewell said.

"Last night," Paul said, "you didn't want to go up into those woods."

"It was freezing," Hopewell countered, not looking at him.

"No. No, you didn't want to go up there. Why? What were you so afraid of?"

Hopewell glanced over at him, his jaw firm. "You don't belong here, Gallo. Your brother didn't belong here, either. His SUV was parked there for two weeks when I towed it, okay? He disappeared and never came back. But I'm telling you, I had nothing to do with it. He just wandered off, man. He just vanished. My advice to you is to get back in your vehicle and get the hell out of this town."

"You're all crazy," Paul said. "This whole goddamn town. You're all fucking insane."

Hopewell disappeared under the hood of the Thunderbird.

Paul walked back around to the front of the barn. He could feel his anger rising off of him like steam. He would get no help from the people of Dread's Hand. There was only one place left to go where he stood a

slim chance of finding some answer to Danny's disappearance, and he'd go there now. It was the only thing
left to do.

As he climbed into the Tahoe, the dog tied to the
post barked at him with manic agitation. Paul blared
the Tahoe's horn at the mangy thing as he drove away.

21

Paul drove across town to Durham Road. It had begun to snow again, and the snowflakes made wet asterisks on the windshield. The looming black trees swaying in the pale daylight seemed to beckon him, their spruced boughs weighty and tinged with the silvery breath of frost. Wind scattered the snow like confetti.

He was a jangle of nerves. His body felt hot and feverish, yet there was a pit of ice at the core of his being that would not thaw. At one point, he glanced up at the rearview mirror, wondering whether Danny's reflection would be there, sitting in the backseat. That ball of ice rolled over in his belly, buoyant on a sea of stomach acid.

Up ahead, he saw the bent sign for Durham Road. Paul took the turn and crawled up into the forested hills. Even at this time of day, no one was out, no one was stirring. The Durham Road tract houses looked like they had been evacuated.

He stopped when he came to the place along the hill where Drammell had pointed yesterday. There was no house here, but the trees stepped aside to create a passageway. It was a dirt road and it wound farther up into the hills. Paul took it.

What minimal daylight there was in the sky was obscured. The Tahoe carved through a deepening mist that clung to the ground. The deeper he went, the more the trees encroached upon the dirt roadway; pine boughs slapped against the Tahoe's windshield and hoary branches clawed at the roof.

Just as he began to wonder whether he had taken the wrong road after all, the trees parted and Joseph Mallory's house appeared before him. A black abandoned relic, it stood silently in the middle of the woods, unwieldy tree limbs intersecting over the roof as if in an embrace. Police tape was garlanded across the cement porch where it rippled, bullied by the wind. Paul saw moss-covered siding and rail posts twisted out of shape by both time and the elements. The front door was closed, but it was askew in its frame, strips of yellow police tape running together to form an X across it.

Paul climbed out of the Tahoe, his boots crunching through a crust of snow. It was much colder up here than it had been back in town. His fever-hot skin felt as if it might crack like ice.

He went up the concrete porch steps and crossed a soggy wooden plank toward the front door. In a sudden gust of wind, the police tape made a *thwap!* sound against the door.

Are you in here, Danny? Have you left some clue behind?

Paul kicked in the door.

It swung open without protest, bands of police tape fluttering to the ground like parade streamers. A black maw was revealed to him. He thought of the old abandoned house on Euclid Street in the neighborhood where he'd grown up. At Danny's insistence, they had broken in to that house when they were eleven years old, and had gone down into that cellar. What they hadn't known was that there was a *thing* down there, and the *thing* had sprung out of the shadows at them. Danny had fled up the stairs while Paul had been bit on the arm. It had been a stray dog, and it had run away, much as Danny had, while Paul sat alone in that cold, dark cellar, crying and holding his injured arm.

Some things don't change, he thought now.

Paul went into the black.

The smell struck him first—the unmistakable stench of death, heady and assaultive. Something had died in this house.

The lights didn't work, so he took out his cell phone and activated the flashlight app. A thin white beam of light washed along the narrow corridor. The walls were a collage of framed photos behind cracked and broken glass, crooked and caked in gray dust. Cobwebs hung like tassels from the ceiling.

It was a short hallway that led to a small living area. The flashlight app's insufficient beam could only illuminate small puzzle pieces of the room, one section at a time. He saw a soggy couch shoved against a mold-blackened wall, one armrest furry with mildew and sprouting a cluster of tiny white mushrooms. There were water stains on the floor and palettes of plaster missing from the ceiling. A toppled wooden chair and an empty bookcase, its shelves slanting at broken angles. There was a door there that could have been a closet or could have opened up to the back of the house, a half-dozen handprints stamped across its dust-laden surface. When the flashlight beam struck the windows along the far wall, the light was not reflected in the glass, but instead reduced to a dull cataract of illumination. The window-panes had been lathered in black paint.

He crossed into the room, the floorboards creaking beneath his boots. It was only a few degrees warmer in here than it was outside, and his breath rained down like a mist. He ran the flashlight beam along the walls and saw the parade of crosses smeared there in a dark, coppery brown. It looked like dried blood. There were symbols among the crosses, too. One symbol was a crude spiral, and it reminded Paul of the curling horn of a ram. Another looked like two crosses placed next to each other so that it resembled a capital *H*. He followed the line of crosses down a second hallway that Paul supposed led to the rear of the house. They formed a straight line at eye level before the artist— the madman—lost momentum midway down the wall, curving the line of crosses in an arc toward the floor. Errant streaks of dried muck were splattered all over the peeling, mossy Sheetrock and there were blood-stains on the hardwood floor.

He peered into a dank, foul-smelling bathroom with black water simmering in the toilet and a shower stall so heavily coated with mildew that it looked like something that had grown out of the earth. There was no shower curtain, but a spiderweb extended from one side of the shower stall to the other. The web glistened like gossamer in the glow of the cell phone's flashlight.

He stared down and saw what looked like a trapdoor inserted into the planks of the hallway floor, a metal ring inlaid in the door.

Jesus.

His first instinct was to not open it. This was followed by the very strong urge to get the hell out of there.

He bent down and tugged on the metal ring. The trapdoor screeched open, revealing a perfect square of infinite black space below. The smell of death wafted up out of the hole, so pungent that it caused Paul's eyes to water.

He cast the beam of light down into the hole.

I'm going down there, Danny had said back at the house on Euclid Street, peering down into the cellar, when they were eleven years old.

"So am I," Paul whispered now, as if his brother was standing right next to him, speaking to him, listening to him. His headache was in full force now.

The narrow beam of light illuminated only a small section of dirt floor at the bottom of a set of rickety wooden steps. He took a deep breath in an attempt to ease his nerves . . . and his stomach threatened to revolt at the stench, moist and thick, roiling up out of the hole.

He took the steps slowly, skeptical about their ability to support his weight. But he made it to the bottom without incident, and found himself in a dank, underground pit that looked disconcertingly like a grave.

There was nothing down here. It looked like Mallory had dug this hole himself, had perhaps used it as a root cellar . . . or maybe for more nefarious purposes. The wall opposite the stairs was shored up with cinder blocks and there were more crosses painted on them. However, these were not arranged in as slapdash a fashion as they had been upstairs. In fact, these seemed perfectly centered on the cinder-block wall, a pattern of three crosses on either side of another symbol—the strange eye with the slashed pupil.

And in that instant, Paul realized what he was looking at.

"Holy shit." The words rasped out of his constricted throat. "Holy fucking shit."

With his bandaged right hand, he scrolled through the photos on his phone that Danny had sent him during his trek through Alaska. Scrolled until he came upon the last photo—of Danny in the foreground with the cabin behind him taking up most of the background.

He had looked at the picture countless times, and while he had noticed the crosses flanking the cabin door, he had never paid much attention to the pattern of them—three crosses on both sides of the cabin door— and that there was something in the center of the door. He enlarged the photo and stared at the symbol. It was the eye with the vertical pupil.

"I don't believe it . . ."

It was the exact pattern that was painted on the cinder-block wall in front of him right now.

It was surreal; he felt almost giddy. His hand holding the phone began to shake, the narrow beam of light jittering along the collection of symbols painted on the cinder blocks.

He took a step back and ran the beam of light along the wall and back toward the rickety stairwell. More crosses were painted along the other walls in a single-file line, much as they had been upstairs. He looked up and saw a single cross, more faded than the others, on one of the ceiling joists.

And that was when he realized that the pattern of crosses painted down here—and on the walls upstairs—were not random or haphazard at all. They were—

"It's a goddamn map," he said.

One of the floorboards creaked above his head. He glanced up, shining the flashlight toward the run of exposed boards and joists that made up the ceiling of the cellar but which were, in fact, the underside of the hallway floor. A light sprinkle of dust rained down from between two of the boards. There came a second creak from above, and more dust puffed out and settled to the dirt floor. A *third* creak—

Someone's up there. Someone's standing right above me, looking at the trapdoor in the floor that I left open.

In his sudden terror, he didn't even possess the wherewithal to wonder what would happen to him if whoever was up there closed that trapdoor and locked him down there; he just listened, aware that whoever was up there was standing directly above him. His eyes shifted toward the stairs that led back up through the trapdoor, expecting to see a boot descend through the opening and plant itself on the first step. He wanted to shine the beam of light over there, but he resisted; instead, he covered the light with one hand, dousing the room in darkness.

Overhead, the floorboards creaked again. Sweat stung Paul's left eye. He imagined he could hear someone breathing up there.

He wasn't sure how long he stood there in the dark, too frightened to move and make a sound, but after enough time had passed he began to wonder if he hadn't just imagined the whole thing. It was possible that it had just been the creaking of the house in the wind, wasn't it?

He slid his hand off the beam, spilling that cold, pencil-thin light back into the cramped, underground room. The cell phone shook in his hand. Even the throbbing of his headache ceased, leaving nothing inside his skull but the sonorous moan of an arctic wind.

There's no one up there.

He took the stairs two at a time, then stood, panting, in the hall, the cell phone's narrow beam boring a tunnel of ponderous light down the corridor. Beyond the reach of the light, the living room was a black pool of shadow. He stood there listening, but could hear nothing.

The flashlight's beam trembled. He kept expecting a pale figure to step into the tenuous conical of light—a ghost-pale visage that moved with the fluid mobility of something propelled through dark water. But nothing happened.

He walked down the hall to the living room. The room was just as he'd left it, except that the door with the half-dozen handprints on it was now partway open, exposing a sliver of gray daylight. A cold draft circulated throughout the room.

Paul angled the flashlight beam toward the floor.

There were muddy footprints emblazoned on the buckling floorboards—footprints that glistened with mois-
ture and looked fresh. Footprints, it seemed, of bare
feet.

Paul went to the door and shoved it open. He hadn't
realized how much he'd been perspiring until the cold
air struck his damp flesh. He edged out onto a constricted square of concrete that served as the rear porch,
and he stared out across the wooded back lot. The rear
lot had been cleared of trees, the shorn stumps of cut
trees at staggered intervals like land mines poking up
through the crust of snow. Beyond, the Sitka spruce,
pine trees, and hemlocks wove together in a tapestry,
their boughs swaying while interlocked, like parish-
ioners joining hands. Wind whistled through their
branches.

There was no one out there. The muddy footprints
descended the concrete steps of the porch, but there
was no evidence of them continuing along the ground,
no impressions of them in the snow.

He stood there shivering in the cold for an indeterminate amount of time, staring off into the shadowy
spaces between the trees. That darkness seemed bottomless, infinite. Snow twirled and spiraled and seemed
to float up and never touch the ground. He was overcome by the urge to step off the porch and walk straight
into those trees. To see where they'd lead him. He could
almost feel the hook in his mouth, reeling him in . . .

He stepped down off the porch and took three long
strides across the yard toward the cusp of the forest. A
gust of wind funneled through the trees and blew the
hair from his sweaty forehead.

This is where—

But the spell was broken at the sound of an approaching vehicle. Paul blinked, clearing his head. He walked around to the front of the house, where he was frozen by the sight of headlights trundling through the woods toward the house. Paul crossed over to the Tahoe and watched as Valerie Drammell's truck came to a stop.

"You've got a real thing about wandering around in the woods, don't you, Gallo?" Drammell said, climbing out from behind the wheel. "Must be an East Coast thing."

"I had to see the place."

"That's called breaking and entering," Drammell said. "Trespassing, too. And I already told you this place is a crime scene. I thought we were clear on that."

"Your pal Bill Hopewell towed my brother's vehicle," Paul said. "Were you aware of that?"

"I'm not sure I know what you're talking about." Drammell lit a cigarette, then leaned against the grille of his truck.

"You people are covering something up out here."

"Don't be melodramatic, Gallo. No one's covering anything up. You're beginning to fall apart on me, is what I think. Could be the solstice." He glanced toward the gunmetal sky. "Days getting shorter and shorter."

"I think the police need to come back out here. Ask you some more questions."

"Good idea," Drammell said, blowing a stream of smoke out of the corner of his mouth. "Go back to Fairbanks and tell 'em to get their butts on up here. What happened to your hand?"

Paul glanced down, having forgotten about the bandage. "Mr. Warren back at the inn came at me with a knife last night."

"Making friends everywhere you go, I guess." Drammell sighed. "I think it's best you leave the Hand, Mr. Gallo. What do you say?"

"I'll leave when I'm ready." He tried to sound tough, but his voice hitched on the last word.

"Come on, Gallo," Drammell said, folding his arms over his chest. He sounded bored. "I'm just doing my job. You go wandering around out here and hurt yourself, I'm the guy who's gotta deal with it. You get me? I feel bad about your brother, I really do, but I can't have you bumbling around a crime scene. Am I right?"

"You're not gonna bully me out of town."

"Yeah, well, I spoke to Jan Warren this morning. Says you tore apart your room. Stripped the wallpaper right off, then slashed up the walls underneath. That true?"

"No. I mean, I took the paper down, but I didn't do anything to the walls. That was already there. I think Danny may have—"

"Enough," Drammell interrupted, his voice raised and echoing across the hillside like the report of a pistol. In a much more tempered tone, he said, "She won't be renting that room to you another night, so it ain't me bullying you out of town, okay? She wants you to get your stuff and hit the road. Right now."

Paul just stood there, his whole body vibrating, unsure what he should say or do next.

"You go on back to Fairbanks and talk to whatever

cops you want. I'll be happy to speak with 'em myself. But we're done here, you and me. There's no grand conspiracy. There's nothing. Got that? We're all done here."

"Right." The word came out of him in a croak. He climbed back into the Tahoe, cranked the engine, then had to execute a clumsy three-point turn to navigate the vehicle around Drammell's truck. He drove back down the hillside toward Durham Road, glancing only once at the Tahoe's rearview mirror to see whether Valerie Drammell would follow him or not. But Drammell seemed content to remain propped against the grille of his truck, smoking his cigarette as a dusting of snow collected on his shoulders.

22

He returned to the Blue Moose Inn to find Jan Warren watching a game show on the TV behind the front desk. She stiffened visibly at his approach.

"I'm just gonna get my stuff and leave," he said, moving down the hall to his room.

"You'll be charged extra for the damage," she called after him.

He packed up his things while the wind blew clouds of snow in front of the single window beside the bed. Back out in the lobby, Jan Warren was standing behind the counter writing something down in a small notepad. Paul placed his room key on the counter.

"Printer's not working," she said, not looking up. "I'm writing you up a receipt by hand."

"Never mind."

Jan ripped a sheet of paper from the notebook anyway, and slid it over to him. He left it there, untouched. She then took the key and hung it on a pegboard that was mostly empty.

"Who carved up the walls in there?" he asked.

She froze, her back toward him. "Some guest," she said after several seconds.

"Some guest, huh? Some guest from last year, maybe? Some guest who looked exactly like me?"

She faced him. He was taken aback to see the stricken look on her face. It was almost as if she was afraid of him all of a sudden. "It's for the best, you know," she said.

"What's that?"

"You leaving."

He let his gaze linger on her for the span of several heartbeats before turning and heading out the door.

He loaded his bags into the Tahoe, then glanced over at the small building behind the inn where the Warrens lived. Merle Warren stood in the open doorway, staring at him. The old man was dressed in a double layer of long johns and had a ridiculous hunting cap with earflaps cocked askew on his head. His bowed legs appeared to quake in the cold.

"There's no getting away from here now," the old man said. "The devil's already locked on to you."

"Take care, Mr. Warren," Paul said, and opened the driver's side door.

"You're already dead," Merle Warren said. The blast of laughter that followed this statement erupted from the old man's throat with enough force to conclude with a coughing fit.

Paul got in the Tahoe, turned over the engine, and pulled out onto the road.

* * *

As Paul had anticipated, Valerie Drammell was in his truck near the outskirts of town. Propped up on the snow-crusted shoulder, the ancient truck coughed plumes of black exhaust into the air. Drammell was sitting in the cab with the window down, smoking a cigarette. As Paul drove by, he slowed the Tahoe so that Drammell could get an eyeful of his departure. Drammell raised a lethargic hand through the cloud of cigarette smoke that wafted about his head like an aura and waved at him.

Paul lowered his foot on the accelerator and watched Drammell's truck shrink in the rearview mirror. The line of crosses on either side of the road whizzed by as he sped toward the main highway, leaving Dread's Hand behind him.

If for just a little while.

He stopped at a diner off the highway and ate a large meal—an omelet loaded with cheddar cheese, onions, bits of ground sausage, tomatoes, and with a healthy dusting of salt and pepper on top; several strips of bacon; wheat toast, liberally buttered; hash browns dressed in A.1. steak sauce; and a banana bread muffin packed with walnuts that looked like tiny meteors. He put away three steaming cups of black coffee and fed quarters into the tableside jukebox while he ate. He wasted some time.

The sun sat framed in the passenger window of the Tahoe as he coasted up the highway. He'd become accustomed to the sight of the sun simmering just below the distant trees, never fully rising in the sky, never fully arching across that deepening expanse; it merely peeked over the far-off horizon, sailed low above the trees, then sank down again in the early evening, taking the day's minimal heat and all of its light with it.

He took the Damascus Road exit off the highway and headed back toward Dread's Hand. When the large white crosses marched toward him out of the haze, Paul felt like he was waltzing back into a dream. Valerie Drammell's truck was no longer parked at the border of the town; like some character in an old spy film, Paul had given Drammell the slip, and the acknowledgment of this brought with it a fleeting sense of satisfaction.

He pulled the Tahoe off the road and drove up onto the snow. A line of large white crosses flanked the right-hand side of the vehicle, jutting at crude angles from the ground. They ran up the hillside and vanished into the trees. He drove alongside them, bringing the SUV to rest just within the cusp of the forest. The vehicle wouldn't be fully concealed from anyone who happened to pass along the road, but it would have to suffice.

Paul turned off the Tahoe's engine. His breath fogged up the windshield; his respiration was whooshing out of him in nervous, staccato bleats. He gazed up at the massive cross that stood beside the vehicle. It was overwhelming, being so close to the thing.

He got out of the Tahoe, his boots crunching through a crust of snow. The line of crosses entered the trees, but from this vantage point he could see where they continued up into the foothills. They were enormous— at least eight feet high and maybe four inches in diameter. They were dappled with bird shit and bleached to the color of bone.

He had approximately three hours before the sun vanished below the horizon. If he couldn't find the cabin in half that time, he'd drive to Fairbanks and tell Jill Ryerson all that he'd discovered while out here in the Hand.

Zipping up his coat, he advanced through the snow toward the forest, following the trail of crosses, leaving the last vestige of civilization behind.

23

Jill Ryerson, who'd spent the past forty-eight hours in bed with a temperature that spiked at 103 degrees, thought she might be dying. Hers wasn't just an autumn cold or a twelve-hour stomach virus—she was laid up with the goddamn flu. Given that half the Fairbanks division of the ABI had succumbed to the crippling crud over the past several weeks, she figured it had been inevitable. Everyone eventually had to pay the piper, right? It hadn't helped that she'd been overworking herself and losing sleep. She felt like a petri dish, perpetually germinating.

It couldn't have happened at a worse time. Or, depending on your outlook, it couldn't have happened at a *better* time. She had been fighting the chills and ignoring the cottony feeling in her head for a number of days. But when she could fight it and ignore it no longer, she'd requested sick leave and crawled into bed, where she slept for ten hours straight. It was the first stretch of undisrupted sleep she'd had in about a month. At some point during this ten-hour sleep marathon, Joseph Mallory had unraveled the bandage from his foot. He'd tied one end to the crossbars of his cell and wound the other end around his neck. When Trooper Lucas Bristol discovered Mallory's strangulated corpse the following morning, Jill Ryerson was still lost in a feverish dreamland.

The first phone call was from Mike McHale, informing her of what had happened. A whip of Kleenex corkscrewing from one nostril and a steaming mug of Theraflu on the counter, she'd listened to McHale's voice in disbelief. It was suicide, McHale had said, but there would be an inquiry, and Bristol might be on the hook.

The second phone call came from Captain Ericsson, who relayed to her the district attorney's great displeasure at this unfortunate turn of events. Ericsson sounded demoralized over the phone. When Ryerson asked what she could do to help alleviate some of his heartburn, Ericsson just told her to rest, get better, then get back to work.

She watched the rest of the story unfold on the news. Bristol was put on paid administrative leave pending the results of an internal inquiry into Mallory's death. Mallory's body was shipped to Anchorage for an autopsy. The district attorney addressed a crowd of reporters outside her office on a gray, dreary afternoon.

The identities of Mallory's victims were each made public as the families were notified. Some of the families appeared on television, including one from Miami whose twenty-nine-year-old son had been one of Mallory's earlier victims, according to the medical examiner's report. The irate father with his doughy congressman's face thrust a fist against a podium while his brood huddled together behind him, weeping in each other's arms. Another family consisted of just the father and younger brother of the deceased, who came in from Canada, said nothing to the press, and were photographed leaving the police station before they fled back home.

Her fever broke for good in the afternoon of the second day, although she still felt like she'd been run over by a Mack truck. For breakfast, she managed to force down some eggs and toast—the first solid things she'd eaten since going on sick leave—and washed them down with two full glasses of orange juice. Later, around lunchtime, she had just settled into a comfortable spot on the sofa and cued up Netflix when her doorbell rang.

She pulled on her robe, shoved her feet into a pair of threadbare slippers, and answered the door.

Mike McHale stood there in an Aces hockey jersey with a brown paper bag held out before him. The smile fell from his face when he saw her.

"Jesus Christ, Ryerson, you look like death warmed over."

"What the hell are you doing here? I'm contagious."

"Yeah, well, my hazmat suit is at the dry cleaner's." He held out the brown paper bag. "I brought you some chicken soup."

"No kidding? Homemade?"

"Caribou Café," McHale said. He handed her the bag, then scraped the grime from his boots onto the welcome mat in the hall. "Can't beat it for a cold. I'm pretty sure this stuff cures cancer, too."

McHale followed her into the kitchen, where she opened the brown bag on the counter and inhaled—as best she could—the cloud of steam that billowed out.

"Smells delicious." She took one bowl down from the cupboard, then, reaching for a second, said, "You want to share?"

"I'm good. Just had some pizza. Wanted to check up on you, that's all."

"You're too kind." She opened the soup container and poured some into a bowl. "How's Bristol holding up?"

"He's a nervous wreck. Looks like he failed to make rounds a few times that night."

"That's not good," she said.

"Yeah, well, at least he didn't try to falsify it in the ledger."

Ryerson nodded. They kept a ledger that needed to be signed, dated, and time-stamped after each walk-through of the holding cells. Ryerson had heard stories of officers in the past having fudged these entries to cover up some problem, only to be caught later and fired. As long as Bristol hadn't done something stupid like that, he'd make it through this thing without any serious problems. That was good.

"Also, Emery Olsen quit," said McHale.

Ryerson froze with her soup spoon halfway to her mouth. *"What?* He's only a year out of the Academy! What happened?"

"He said he wanted to move down southeast to be

closer to his family. But I spoke to Mannaway, and he said Olsen had been acting funny ever since the search warrant on Mallory's place. Said something had spooked him."

"What?"

"Beats me. But he and Mannaway were close. I think they went through the Academy together."

She recalled the look of contempt Olsen had given her when she'd met his eyes during the search warrant at Mallory's place. She'd gone out the side door of the house and Olsen had been standing in the back lot, staring into the woods. Olsen and Mannaway had been up to Dread's Hand a year earlier, and had found Danny Gallo's rental vehicle on the side of the road.

"Well, that sucks," she said.

"Some people just aren't cut out for this stuff."

Ryerson spooned soup into her mouth. "Jesus, you're right. This stuff might just cure cancer after all. Thanks, Mike." She nodded at the folder he now held in both hands. He'd had it tucked under his arm when she'd opened the door for him moments ago, but only now recognized it as one of their case files from the office. "What's that?"

"It's that old file you asked me to get before you wimped out and got sick."

McHale set the file on the counter, and Ryerson could see the subject's name typed on the tab—RHOBEAN, DENNIS. She'd forgotten about it.

"Did you look at it?" she asked, setting her soup aside and picking up the folder. She opened the file and looked at the cover page of the report. It was dated nine years ago.

"Hell, no," McHale said. "We've got enough stuff going on right now that I don't need to read about ancient murders, too. What's the big deal with it, anyway? Why're you so interested?"

"It's probably nothing," she said, scanning the report, "but something the ME said to me on the phone the other day piqued my curiosity. I'm sure it's just a dead end, but I wanted to check it out."

"This have to do with the Mallory case?"

"I don't know. Probably not. It's really nothing. Forget it." She closed the folder and tossed it onto the counter.

"Well, in that case, I'm so glad I wasted an afternoon digging that thing up for you." But McHale's smile was genuine. "Hey, you feel better, okay? I'm gonna take off."

"Keep me posted on Bristol," she said, walking him to the door.

"I will."

"And thanks again for the soup."

"Cures what ails ya," he said, and clomped out into the hall. Next door, the widow Tannis poked her gloomy old face out of her apartment and scrutinized McHale like a housemother in a girls' dormitory. McHale saluted her, said, "M'lady," and caused her to withdraw back into her apartment with a twisted scowl on her face.

Grinning to herself, Ryerson closed the door and slid the chain lock into place.

Back in the living room, she finished her soup while watching the third season of *Orange Is the New Black*, but she lost interest halfway through the second episode. She was thinking about the Rhobean folder sitting on the kitchen countertop. She told herself she'd lay her eyes on it, if only because McHale had gone through the trouble of digging it up for her from the old hard-copy file cabinets in the basement. But as she got up, set her empty soup bowl in the sink, and picked up the Rhobean case file off of the counter, she knew that wasn't the reason. She'd scrounged around in the station-house basement in the past herself, pulling old case files—those that had existed prior to the conversion to the electronic case management system—but in those instances, she had pulled cold-case files to see if they were in any way related to any of her current investigations. That was not the case here. The Dennis Rhobean investigation wasn't unsolved. Moreover, the Joseph Mallory case was . . . well, Mallory's suicide had seen to it that that was driven to a swift and final conclusion, too.

That's because they both killed themselves, she thought, taking the case file into the living room. She powered off the TV and used the remote to switch to the stereo. A Lovedrug CD came through the wall-mounted speakers. *Both suspects took their own lives. Also, both suspects cut off the heads of their victims. I'm not looking for a correlation here, and I don't even expect to find one . . . except for maybe a peek into the psyche of the type of person—the type of madman— who would do something so heinous.*

She started with the police report. She did not recognize the investigator's name, but it was written in the terse and workmanlike style with which she was familiar.

The Rhobeans were from Chena Hills. The father, Dennis, was a millworker. Gwendolyn, the mother, was a middle-school teacher. They had one child between them, a boy, named Kip. Kip was fourteen years old when his father walked him out to the woodshed behind their property, placed the barrel of a Glock 9mm to his head, and pulled the trigger. He then proceeded to separate the boy's head from the rest of his body with an ax Dennis had kept in the woodshed. Based on the coroner's report, it had taken Dennis three attempts to get all the way through the neck bone and spinal column. Once the job was done, Dennis Rhobean wrapped his teenage son's head in a sheet of tarpaulin, then shot himself in the temple with the same handgun. The coroner opined that Mr. Rhobean had lived for two hours on the floor of the woodshed beside his son's decapitated body, the bullet having penetrated the right hemisphere of the brain before cutting to a sharp ninety-degree angle and exiting out the top of Dennis Rhobean's skull. Rhobean's cause of death was listed by the coroner as exsanguination—loss of blood.

The report contained no statement from the wife and mother, Gwendolyn Rhobean, although the investigator mentioned that it had been Mrs. Rhobean who had discovered the carnage in the woodshed later that evening. Ryerson couldn't begin to imagine what something like that might do to a person. When she was younger, she'd heard about a woman who'd rolled her SUV into a lake in South Carolina with her two young children strapped inside. The woman had lied and told police that she'd been carjacked, but she was ultimately found guilty of filicide. The worst part, for Ryerson, were the images of the father of that South Carolina woman, sobbing on TV, so filled with grief and terror and a black, rancid sorrow that Ryerson had never been able to forget that doomed and tortured man, whom she had never met, except in a scant few nightmares. How did someone continue with their life after something like that?

Ryerson turned the last page of the report, unprepared for what followed.

Photographs of the crime scene had been scanned into the report. Her only solace was that they were poor reproductions, grainy and black-and-white. Much of the detail had been washed out by a lousy Xerox machine. Nonetheless, they were terrible. The photos of the bodies were bad enough, but the single shot of the sheet of tarpaulin folded over and twisted at the top like it was a Christmas gift was, for some reason, the most disturbing of all.

She turned the page and froze.

The report said nothing about this, she thought, staring at these additional photos of the crime scene.

They were photographs of the woodshed's interior walls. Perhaps an average person looking at these photographs wouldn't understand what they were seeing, but Ryerson was bringing some context to it. Even in black and white, she could tell that the strange hieroglyphic symbol streaking the woodshed wall had been painted there in blood. Moreover, she recognized it. The eyeball with the vertical pupil.

She stared at the symbol until the CD stopped playing on the stereo.

How is that possible?

She flipped back to the first page and checked the

date of the investigation again. It *was* nine years ago. Nine years ago in Chena Hills, Alaska.

So, how is that possible?

It wasn't. That was the only sensible answer—it *wasn't* possible. Yet there it was, reproduced in shitty Xeroxed photos tagged on to the end of a police report that was roughly a decade old.

Maybe it means something. Maybe I should have an expert look at it, an expert in symbols.

But she wouldn't even know where to begin.

She closed the file and set it on the coffee table. The stereo's disc changer rotated to the next CD, and when Trent Reznor's static-laden guitar riff burst through the speakers, she nearly jumped out of her skin.

24

After an hour of campaigning through the forest following the trail of crosses up into the foothills, Paul came upon a clearing that he didn't recognize until he saw the vinyl flags staked into the ground, the streamers of yellow police tape tied to tree trunks blowing in the wind, the excavated craters in the earth from which the bodies of Mallory's victims had been exhumed. The crosses had led him to the mass grave site by way of the forest, which meant he was back inside the border of Dread's Hand.

But no—that wasn't exactly true. He was on the *other side* of the border this time, on the opposite side of the line of crosses forming the boundary around the tiny village. He looked up toward the foothills, where the woods grew darker and more dense and where the sky was a muddy smear above the treetops, and he could see the crosses at intervals between the trees. The crosses were smaller out here, only a few feet high and as thin as broomsticks, but he could still see them. The pattern also matched the pattern on Mallory's walls—larger crosses to smaller ones, arcing high with the incline of the land. But how far did he have left to go? He didn't want to get caught out here after the sun had gone down.

He continued on, sweating despite the cold, the muscles in his legs getting a strenuous workout. Only when his shadow repositioned itself on the ground did he realize he kept changing direction. His increasing weariness notwithstanding, he began to feel invigorated by the climb. The burn in his muscles felt good. Moreover, there was a sense of certainty bordering on giddiness that washed over him with each step he took. This was the right thing. He was on the right path.

But when he looked around, he realized there *was* no path. Somewhere during his trek the crosses had vanished, or perhaps he had wandered away from them without realizing it. He walked in a complete circle, peering through the interlocked boughs of the trees, but he could no longer see the crosses. How long had he been traveling blind?

He laughed nervously, a plume of vapor rising in front of his face.

Wait a minute. Just wait . . .

He took his cell phone out, checked the time—3:55 P.M. How the hell had it gotten that late? It would be dark in less than two hours.

"Shit."

He found his footprints in the snow and retraced them, hoping to come upon the place where he had inadvertently parted ways with the line of crosses. Yet after about twenty minutes, he found himself coming upon a second set of his own footprints. He realized that he'd been walking in circles.

"Goddamn it." He rubbed some warmth back into his cheeks. The cold was beginning to get to him. Or maybe it was just nerves.

The shadows of the trees grew long, and the woods began to darken all around him.

He pushed on, heading in the direction that felt right . . . although he'd never been one whose internal compass could be trusted. He questioned his decision with every step, and wondered if it didn't make more sense to just follow the slope of the land downward. He'd reach either Damascus Road or Dread's Hand that way, wouldn't he?

The color of the snow on the ground went from white to purple to a deepening gray. For a time, Paul stared at his shadow as it gradually faded. When he looked up again, the daylight had been leeched from the horizon.

A figure stood maybe twenty yards away, partially obscured behind skeletal tree limbs, staring at him.

It was Danny.

Paul felt his throat tighten. He called out his brother's name, and it came out in a hoarse, restrictive cry—"Danny!"

Danny turned away from him and stepped over a deadfall, moving with the lassitude of a sleepwalker. He walked off into the woods, where he was quickly eclipsed by shadow.

"Danny!"

Paul pushed himself forward despite his aching leg muscles. In his haste, his boot snagged on a tree stump, sending him sprawling to the ground. He scrambled to his feet and ran after his brother, scanning the darkness for Danny's pale shape. After a moment, he discerned a figure cresting an incline several more yards ahead. Paul pursued, not pausing to realize that there was no way Danny could have covered such a distance in so few seconds.

His face was whipped by pine boughs and scratched by branches as he ran. He fell a second time when he slammed both shins against a massive deadfall that, in his urgency to catch up with his brother, he had overlooked. He rolled over the deadfall and slammed against the cold, solid earth. The pain in his shins flooded through him a moment later. But by then, he was already up and racing through the trees, desperate to catch sight of Danny again.

25

He did not know how deep into the woods he had gone—or how long it had taken him to do so—when, exhausted, he sank to the earth. He leaned his back against a tree and pulled his knees up to his chest. He was out of breath, and his muscles felt rubbery and loose. The headache was back, a jackhammer driving through shelves of gray matter, and he still felt ill at the pit of his stomach. Each exhalation felt like he was breathing fire. He guessed he had a full-blown fever now, too.

Beyond the canopy of trees, the moon crept behind a scudding train of dark cloud. A wavy band of greenish light bisected the night sky, shifting dreamlike. Paul watched the green turn to a cool aquamarine, to a pale indigo, to an impossible alien color that appeared to spread like a stain across the bowl of sky. Occasional stars would poke through the veil, like small, uninhabitable islands within a river, their usual cold-white brilliance tinted to a hazy bronze.

It began to snow. As Paul stared up past the interlocking tree branches and at the river of impossible light traversing across the sky, snowflakes cooled his face and collected in his eyelashes.

If there was ever a true connection between us, Danny, let me connect with you now. Please. Please, Danny.

He closed his eyes and tried to grasp at a connection he'd never believed existed before, but, like an operator ringing a dead line over and over again, he received no answer. He felt hollow and untethered, and he wondered if that was because of the fever he could now feel circulating throughout his system. He coughed out great billows of vapor. Snot trickled from one nostril.

He remembered his cell phone, and fished through the pockets of his coat for it. With numb fingers, he dug it out and pressed the Power button, but nothing happened. The cold had killed the battery.

His hands began to tremble. He felt like chucking the cell phone at the nearest tree, but instead, he fumbled it back inside his pocket.

Sure, he thought. *Just in case I happen to find a power outlet on the side of a pine tree. That would be perfect.*

The laugh that followed this thought scorched his throat.

He closed his eyes for just a second—

—but when he opened them, he felt different. His entire body was overcome by a strange combination of frigid numbness and slick, burning heat. He held one hand up in front of his face, expecting to see steam rise off his flesh.

Something watched him from a high tree branch. It was a figure—a silhouette—of a human being, though it was perched in an impossible crouch on a high branch with seemingly perfect balance. Paul stared at it, unable to discern anything more than its indistinct, humanoid outline. After a time, it rose to its full height, a black figure silhouetted against the shimmery green aurora that formed a winding ribbon across the night sky. The figure's eyes blazed with a dazzling emerald-green light.

That isn't real. I'm hallucinating.

It crouched behind the trunk of the tree, then proceeded to crawl down, its movements simultaneously reptilian and insect-like. When it touched the ground, it moved partway out from behind the tree. It was too well hidden in the dark now for Paul to make out anything more than ambiguous, ill-defined movements. It shifted around him counterclockwise, its footfalls soundless on the wet ground. Paul turned his head to watch it go, and swore he heard the creaking of the tendons in his neck.

The figure lowered itself to all fours, its back arching, and assumed the shape of a large black wolf. Those green eyes flashed again. Then the wolf disappeared into the forest.

None of that just happened. I'm hallucinating. I've got a fever, and I'm freezing out here. That wasn't real. I did not just see that.

He closed his eyes for what felt like just a minute or two, but when he opened them, the moon had repositioned itself halfway across the sky. The Northern

Lights were still there, now as a pulsing purple artery overhead. A sheen of snow now covered the ground. The quality of the light was different now, too, and when he looked around, he didn't recognize his surroundings. He was no longer crouched on the ground leaning against a tree, but perched on a large boulder surrounded by twiggy saplings.

He sensed that the figure—the wolf—was still somewhere in the vicinity, watching him. But he couldn't see it. It hurt to turn his head on his neck now.

He closed his eyes.

Inhaled.

The freezing air burned his lungs.

At one point, he opened his eyes to find himself sitting on a deadfall, watching himself from a close distance. This alternate version of himself wore no shirt or shoes, only a tattered, blood-streaked pair of chinos. The blood looked black in the moonlight.

As Paul stared at himself, the figure who was him stared back. Other-Paul leaned forward, revealing eyes blazing with madness and a wide grin filled with too many teeth. This alternate version of himself then stood and cut a path around him. Paul could no longer turn his head to follow the thing's progress. He felt it moving behind him, very close now. Close enough so that he could feel the thing's hot breath against the frozen nape of his neck.

It whispered something to him, but he couldn't make it out.

He thought maybe he screamed.

* * *

All of a sudden, he and Danny were eleven years old again, and breaking into an abandoned house in their neighborhood. It had been abandoned for years, and no one could recall who the family had been who'd once lived there, or whether anything tragic had ever taken place within those walls to account for its vacancy. There were birds' nests bristling and bulging beneath the eaves; the sharp green, weedy shoots sprouting from the cracks in the slate walkway; the busted carriage lights bookending the front door, with its peeling paint and curse words sprayed in garish neon colors across it. A large piece of flagstone had been used to smash one of the rear windows. Yet before they crawled inside, eleven-year-old Danny looked at him, and Paul was terrified to find that there was a massive gash bisecting his brother's neck, and that the blood that dribbled down from the wound had soaked the front of his bright white T-shirt. There was a bullet hole in the side of Danny's head, too, the hair tacky with gore and small bits of skull. His brother's face was—

(bone white)

—drained of color. And when Danny's mouth opened, Paul saw that it was black inside, as if Danny had ingested some terrible poison that was rotting him from the inside out.

—You're dying, Paul. You're dying.

"That's okay, Danny," he said. "You're dead, too."

The words were like nails scraping along his throat.

And then there was a blaze of heat—a fireball exploding just beyond the trees, turning the night into a dazzling, brilliant orange. Paul staggered toward it, the heat from the great conflagration wringing sweat from his pores and stinging his eyes. When he inhaled, he tasted smoke; it coated his tongue and made his mouth feel as if it had been upholstered in flannel.

When he arrived on the scene, he saw the tail section of a Cessna jutting at a 45-degree angle from the burning ground. Behind it, a fiery contrail blazed on the surface of the snow. Thick columns of smoke rose up beyond the trees and into the multicolored sky. Something continued to watch him from high up in a tree—a thing whose eyes blazed an unnatural green.

Paul ran toward the inferno and, through the flames, could make out the crushed cockpit and a shower of glass. The cockpit's door hung at an angle and smoke purled out of the opening. With his boot, he kicked the door aside. It struck the shattered windshield of the cockpit, then surrendered itself into the steaming snow.

A figure lurched out of the opening, a man with his face and hair on fire, his clothes nothing but smoldering, charred tatters. The figure's mouth opened, and a banner of black smoke spiraled up and into the air.

"Paul . . ."

Paul grabbed the man and dragged him free of the flames. Paul's own hands burned and the sleeves of his shirt caught fire, while between his fingers, pieces of the man's burned flesh sloughed off in ribbons.

He shoved the man into the snow and rolled him around, rolled him around, rolled him around, until the black husk of him was left steaming and smoldering in a muddy crater in the earth. Paul could smell the man's burning flesh—a stink that singed the hairs in his nose.

"Paul . . ."

"No," Paul groaned, shaking his head while backing away from the blackened skeleton leaving smoke trails in the air. "No. No."

You were supposed to look out for him, Paul. You were supposed to look after your brother.

Paul screamed.

When he opened his eyes again, it was morning. Pale gray daylight filtered down through the tree branches above. He was no longer perched on a boulder or leaning against a tree, but sprawled out on the snowy ground, as if he'd fallen asleep in the middle of making a snow angel.

He knew this wasn't a hallucination because he was in pain. His whole body burned with fever. The snow around him should have been steaming. When he sat up, he felt a terminal weakness at his core. His muscles were twisted into painful knots. His throat felt abraded. The headache was gone, having once more been replaced by a hollowness, the distant susurration of desert wind. He didn't feel all there.

Somehow he managed to stagger to his feet, maintaining his balance by leaning all his weight against a nearby tree. The lack of need to urinate told him that he was dehydrated. The overheated, prickly sensation of his flesh beneath his clothes warned him that he was close to hypothermia. Though it was tempting, he resisted the urge to strip off his coat, unbutton his shirt, and roll around in the snow.

Shivering, he lowered himself to the ground, cupped some snow in his numb, shaking hands, and sucked it into his mouth. He did this over and over again.

Hugging himself, his teeth rattling in his skull from the cold, he managed to rise to his feet and plod a few yards in no discernible direction. Snow had managed to permeate his boots, and his feet were now wet and starting to grow numb. He could no longer feel his toes. Yet despite the cold, he was burning up. Droplets of sweat wrung from his pores and glistened across his forehead. His mouth tasted like pulverized rock.

A figure, blurry and indistinct, materialized out of the white. It was a man, and he moved toward Paul. At one point, the figure doubled . . . then tripled . . . but then Paul's vision realigned itself.

Paul was maybe ten feet from the man when his legs gave out and he crumpled to the snow. His head was thudding to an inaudible rhythm, and he tasted blood now in his mouth, mixed with that powdery, pulverized-rock taste. He had dropped onto his back, his legs bent at awkward angles beneath him. Above, the sky was a meshwork of intermingled tree branches. He raised his right hand and saw it was slick with blood.

The figure appeared, standing over him—a dark, featureless blur that swam in and out of focus.

Paul tried to speak, but could only manage a dull clicking sound near the back of his throat.

"Don't talk," said the figure.

The visage became clear again, and this time Paul could see that the man had the barrel of a rifle pointed down at him. The man's breath steamed the air, his face hidden behind a mop of hair and a bristling black beard. Yet the man's eyes were clear, lucid.

Paul just lay there, incapable of movement. His heartbeat pulsed in his ears.

The figure lowered the gun a fraction of an inch. He lifted his head from the stock.

Paul tried to raise his hands again, but the muscles in his arms felt frozen. His teeth wouldn't stop chattering.

"Paul," said the mountain man. The barrel of the gun lowered by increments as the wind whipped the man's long hair across his face. "Paul, is that you?"

Paul couldn't respond. He couldn't move. He thought he just might close his eyes and sleep for a while.

The figure approached him, circled partway around him, pausing just a few feet away from him.

"Jesus Christ," said the man.

The wind blew the man's hair off his face.

It was Danny.

PART THREE

KEEPER OF THE GATE

26

There was pain, and there was sound. The pain was all-encompassing, like a storm raging within the fibers of his muscles and along the rigid bands of his tendons. He felt himself contract and pull in on himself—a tightening at the center of his body that consisted not just of muscles but (it felt like) a collapse of bones. A breaking; a death.

The pain became cyclic, in that it beat like a pulse, with breathy pauses of soundlessness between the beats. In these spaces, these pauses, between the contractions of his body, he glimpsed a dewy and dimly lit peacefulness. Golden. Warm. It was like running past a fence and glimpsing a beautiful flower garden in the spaces between the rotting, splintered boards. He found himself diving for those spaces when they came, ejecting himself into that garden. Sometimes he made it. Sometimes he didn't.

Whuh-WHUMP-whuh-WHUMP-whuh-WHUMP!

The sound was unreliable. He sometimes heard a man

speaking through a fuzzy PA speaker (or so it seemed), while other times—most of the time—there was nothing but the empty howl of the wind, both near and far at the same time, in tandem with the rhythmic *whuh-WHUMP* of his heartbeat. The creaking of old wood shuddering in the throes of a terrible storm. The gritty tap dance of small, hard pellets flung against a sideboard.

The sound said, *doon nokay yore doon nokay.* A record played at the wrong speed.

Glimpses of that garden. Lilac petals. Palm fronds. Cadres of tiny, multicolored birds taking flight across an azure sky. There was a sun that burned like ice. A sparkle of gold atop a fishpond. And he was—

—*doon nokay yore*—

—sometimes there, sometimes not.

Floating in the memory of memory.

A cool hand on his burning forehead—

"Doing okay. You're doing okay."

He awoke to a dim orange light floating in spectral darkness. Sensation filtered back into his arms and legs, his fingers and toes. His body felt like a pincushion. At the center of his head pulsed a throbbing heartbeat, each beat underscored by bright flashes of light behind his eyes; each pulse seemed to stretch the bones of his skull out of proportion, as if his bones were made of rubber. And even given all of these very real sensations, Paul wasn't sure whether he was awake or snared in the midst of some panicked, irrational unconsciousness.

It took some effort to turn his head. The motion caused the pounding in his skull to advance to a steady hammer-strike that made his back teeth ache. He focused on the gaseous shimmer of orange light somewhere in all that blackness with him—a tiny sun bleeding its energy out into the cosmos. Bands of light radiated from it, paling to a wan yellow before the light was devoured by the darkness.

Erin Sharma was here with him, although he couldn't see her. She stood off to the side of that dazzling orange sun, her body turned into a living absence of light by contrast. Other times, she *was* the sun, and this, for whatever reason, comforted him. When he looked at her, he could see she was trying to tell him something, but he couldn't hear her. Her mouth moved, but no words came out. Whatever she was saying was lost to him. This troubled him on some deep, spiritual level, because he believed that what she was saying was important. Was a warning.

Yet he wasn't floating in space. Erin Sharma was *not* there. There was something hard yet yielding beneath him. Something he had been lying on. He ran a hand along it and felt a springy coverlet that was gritty and porous. Like foam. He lifted a corner of the foam and felt rough wooden planks beneath it. His hand trembled.

When his vision cleared, he saw that the burning orange sun was actually the smoldering embers of a fire. As his eyes adjusted to the limited light, he saw that he was in a room with a barren, wooden floor of twisted and splintered boards. The embers glowed from within a potbellied stove in the middle of the room, its cast-iron grate swung open. He could smell the fire . . . and he could smell an earthier smell beneath it, dark and ripe like unwashed flesh. As caustic as a chemical spill.

More details were coming to him now. He was in a room just slightly larger than a toolshed. Thin staves of moonlight slid through cracks and gaps and poked through knotholes in the wall at the opposite side of the room, creating a zebra-like pattern of alternating light and shadow on the buckling floorboards and in the corners where the stove fire did not reach. There was a door rimmed in silver moonlight, but no windows. He leaned his head back and felt the wall behind him covered in silken fur. He wondered whether or not he was dreaming. A moment later, he discerned figures standing in a lineup along the opposite wall. They didn't so much frighten him as rouse a sense of deep perplexity in him. A moment after that, he realized they were just heavy woolen coats hanging from wall pegs.

He tried to sit up, but a wave of nausea and stomach cramps crippled him. He leaned over on his side, coherent enough to know that he didn't want to choke on his own vomit. But all he did was dry heave, his agonized moans sounding like a sea lion's dissonant bark, his fevered breath blossoming into great magnolias of cloudy vapor in the cold air of the room. He couldn't hear himself. It was as if someone had packed his ears full of cotton.

A figure materialized in front of him. Blurry.

"Can you hear me? Can you hear my voice?"

He wasn't sure whether he answered the man or not. His eyelids eased closed and there it was again—that magical garden between the slats in the fence. Animated Disney animals capering on green lawns. Birdsong like angels' trumpets.

And just like that, he was gone again.

* * *

And then he was standing outside in the snow, shaking against the cold. His face numb, the tears at the corners of his eyes frozen to diamonds. Beyond the trees and the crescents of snowcapped hills, dawn broke in a ribbon of pastel hues.

He looked down and saw footprints leading away from him in the snow.

He blinked his eyes, and found that he'd followed the footprints to the cusp of a rocky ledge. He peered down into a ravine and saw that the footprints continued down there. They led straight to the hillside, and vanished into a yawning dark maw in the face of the hill. It looked like a mouth. It looked like an eye. He stared at it for an impossible length of time, his whole body growing numb, the frozen tears at the corners of his eyes spearing into his flesh every time he blinked. Drawing blood.

There was a figure standing down there. It was a sheep-headed boy. Dead black eyes stared up at him. The prints in the snow around the thing were small, circular divots. Hoofprints.

"No," said a man's voice, very near to him. He felt a strong hand tighten around one bicep. The sensation of being pulled—being dragged—backward. He shut his eyes and heard nothing but the grinding of footfalls on hard snow. Nothing but the clicking of his own teeth.

When he opened his eyes, he saw the tiny sun again. Maybe he smiled. At least he was warm now. A little, anyway.

"Doing okay. You're doing okay. Stay with me for a second longer, Paul."

He felt something touch his lips. Cold. *Wet*. He didn't so much drink as open his mouth to allow a brilliant stream of water to sear a passageway down the heated, constricted pipe of his throat.

He gagged. Sputtered. Fireworks went off behind his eyes. The sound of his cries sent the Disney animals scattering like bowling pins.

"Drink slow," said the voice.

Air hissed out of his lungs. He felt his entire body deflate. He thought maybe he could open his eyes and sit up—that he could use those burning embers in the potbellied stove as an anchor to keep the room from spinning—but just as he had this thought, he felt his mind plummet back down into a dark and bottomless sea.

The tiny orange sun was back again. He made a life inside it. Stayed there, warm and protected. It was better than the garden. It was safer: a mother's embrace.

Paul stared at it for a countless amount of time before he realized that he wasn't dreaming. There was still a symphony warming up in his head, but he found that he had better control over his motor functions now. He lifted a hand in front of his face. Flexed the fingers. Felt a sinister numbness along the back of his hand, dull pain beneath it. The joints were stiff. There were two butterfly bandages covering up a wound on the palm of his hand.

He sat up like someone waking from a coma. He was still in that dark room with the burning sun at its center, so he kept his eyes trained on that smoldering orange ember to maintain his balance. He managed to stiffen into a sitting position, his head resting against the fur-lined wall at his back. Small, strange trinkets hung from the ceiling joists, indecipherable in the firelight.

Oh Jesus oh God oh Jesus my feet . . .

He rolled his legs over the side of the makeshift bed and planted his feet on the floor. His boots were off, but his feet were wrapped in something warm enough to cause them to sweat. He realized that his entire body was a conundrum—simultaneously sweating and shivering, achy yet numb, swollen but emaciated. He tried to stand, but vertigo struck him back down on his buttocks, his heartbeat in competition with the *thump-thump-thump* of his headache. *Strike up the band, kids!* His entire body felt cold while the center of his guts boiled within some sludgy stew.

Don't move too quickly. One neat little baby step at a time.

The door opened, revealing a widening rectangle of pearl-colored light. Frigid air followed, and the beads of sweat along Paul's forehead froze. He could see the snowy ground on the other side of that door and, beyond, a dark veil of pines. He looked up and could see that the trinkets hanging from the joists were little wooden crosses made from twigs, so many crosses of various sizes, hanging like cured meats in a deli. A figure appeared in the doorway. It was a man, and he entered the cabin and shut the door behind him.

He stood there, a black silhouette. Staring at Paul.

"You're awake," the man said. "I thought so. Good. Good."

"Where—" Paul began, but his throat clamped shut on the rest of the sentence. His mouth was parched, his tongue swollen. The simple utterance of that single word felt like razor blades were slicing down the length of his esophagus. He began to cough, which hurt even more than speaking.

The man lit a Coleman lantern that was hanging from a low ceiling joist. The room brightened, and the canopy of hanging crosses trembled like living things.

Paul's coughing fit having subsided, he swiped at the nonexistent tears he imagined were burning down his cheeks and stared at the figure, who now stood within the glow of the lantern.

The figure's hair was long and damp, with dark black ringlets curling across his forehead and near the corners of his eyes. His beard was thick and black, too, and climbed up the man's cheekbones. He was dressed in a heavy coat with a fur collar, and there was a rifle propped against one shoulder. Despite the unfamiliarity of all those elements, Paul had no trouble recognizing the man who stood before him.

"Danny," he managed, ignoring the agony in his throat now. "Danny." He struggled to his feet, but the world seemed to want to shake him off into space, and he nearly lost his footing.

"Don't try to get up," Danny said, rushing to his side. He set the rifle on the floor and slipped an arm around Paul's chest, arresting his downward momentum just as Paul's legs gave out. Danny pulled him back toward the makeshift bed and helped him sit back down. Before letting him go, Danny's one-armed embrace tightened in a tenuous squeeze . . . and then Danny kissed the top of Paul's head. He was already stepping away and picking up the rifle before Paul realized what had just happened.

"How—" Paul began, but then winced at the pain in his throat.

"Don't talk right now, either," Danny said. He hung the rifle on the wall, then slipped through the shadows toward the rear of the cabin. In the commingled light of the stove and the lantern, Paul was able to inventory more details of his surroundings—an ax leaning against the wall in one shaded corner; a plaid bedroll laid out on the floor against the far wall; a six-shot revolver resting on a flattened pillow. Other items revealed themselves to him more slowly, their presence less disconcerting—some pots and pans and an old coffee percolator; several pairs of heavy boots lined up beneath the row of coats hanging on the opposite wall; a few paperback novels assembled in tidy little stacks on the floor; various animal furs nailed to the walls, some so large that Paul wondered if they'd once belonged to bears; more clothing hanging from wall pegs with other clothes overflowing from a wooden box. The potbellied stove had a multi-elbowed stovepipe extending from it, which ran straight up through the vaulted ceiling. He saw that the bed he was on was just a collection of wooden boxes covered in yellow egg-crate foam.

"Where are we?" Paul rasped. His saliva felt like steel wool going down his throat.

"I said don't talk," Danny called back from the shadows. He was moving items around back there, although Paul couldn't see what they were. "You're safe. That's all that matters right now. But when I found you two days ago, you were burning up with a fever. Dehydrated and hypothermic, too. You were talking nonsense and probably delirious. My God, I thought I was imagining things, seeing you stumble out of the woods like that. I still can't believe it."

Memories filtered back to him. He remembered breaking in to someone's house. He remembered chasing some figure through the woods and getting lost. He remembered a sky that changed color, and that a pennant of light coursed like a river through the heavens— light so beautiful that his eyes had had difficulty seeing it. He recalled a sleek black figure crouched high in a tree, its mouth rimmed with shark's teeth and eyes like supernovas. But after that, his memory failed him.

"You were too weak to walk," Danny continued, "and I knew I couldn't carry you. But we were close enough to the cabin for me to come back here, get the sledge, and load you up. You passed out as I pulled you here through the snow. Do you remember any of it?"

Paul shook his head. But then he realized that Danny couldn't see him, so he murmured, "No." His throat felt like it was lined with rebar.

Danny advanced into the firelight. He was holding a tin cup, which he handed to Paul. "Drink it. You're still dehydrated." He slapped a frigid hand to Paul's sweaty forehead and added, "You've still got a fever, too."

Paul gulped down half the water, then gagged.

"Go slow, bro," Danny said. "You're parched."

Paul cleared his throat, then brought the cup back up to his lips. He sipped it now. This time, it was like heaven going down.

"You've been in and out of consciousness for two

days," Danny said. He went over to the wooden crate overflowing with clothes and began rifling through it. "I kept feeding you water by sticking a damp rag in your mouth so you wouldn't choke. Powdering Tylenol tablets, too, and rubbing the powder against the insides of your cheeks to get the fever down. Shit would be a lot easier if I had an IV and a saline drip, but this ain't Johns Hopkins, huh?"

"Two days," Paul mused. The water had made his throat feel somewhat better, but his headache was still jackhammering away at him. He couldn't stop shivering, either, despite the extra layers Danny had dressed him in while he'd been unconscious. There was a blanket made of animal furs at his feet, which he grabbed and pulled up over his thighs.

"It's just lucky I found you when I did," Danny said. He ceased rummaging through the wooden box and peered at Paul from over one fur-lined shoulder. It was as if something had just occurred to him, something important that he'd missed until now. But he said no more about it.

Paul raised one shoulder. His muscles were sore and tight. He felt like he'd just had the shit kicked out of him.

From the wooden crate, Danny pulled out a backpack that looked large enough to haul around a set of golf clubs. He unzipped one of the compartments and upended the backpack, dumping random items onto the warped floorboards of the cabin—one of which was a pill bottle that Danny scooped up and carried over to Paul. He shook two tablets into his hand.

"Aspirin," he said.

Paul took them, put them in his mouth, and swallowed them with some difficulty. Even with the water as a lubricant, they felt like two large stones bullying their way down his throat.

"We'll just have to keep you hydrated," Danny said, taking Paul's cup and refilling it from a dented aluminum teapot. "It's the best we can do."

Paul took the cup from him but remained staring at his brother. Danny stared back, his head cocked, that broad smile now replaced with a melancholic half grin. He leaned in and planted another kiss on Paul's sweat-slickened forehead while squeezing the back of Paul's neck. Then he dragged over one of the wooden crates and sat down on it.

"I thought you were dead," Paul rasped. It hurt his throat, but he could feel a frenzy of anger welling up inside him. "It's been over a year. I thought you'd died out here. I filed police reports; I talked to investigators. I dropped everything and flew out here because I thought . . . I mean, I just. . . . Christ, I don't . . . I don't even know where to begin. It's been over a *year*."

"Don't get excited. Please, Paul. You just need to rest right now."

Paul clapped a hand over his eyes. He felt the sob ratchet its way up through his chest and spring from his throat on a hot expulsion of air. He was too dehydrated for tears, but the emotion was all there, and it shook him. Hurt him. The hand holding the tin cup trembled until the cup clanged to the floor. He didn't know how long he sat like that, digging his fingernails into the burning flesh of his face and smelling his own rank breath while Danny watched him, but when he stopped and looked up, he felt drained.

Danny was smiling at him, and nodding his shaggy head. But his own eyes were glassy.

"I can't believe you're alive," Paul said. "Holy shit, Danny, I can't believe it . . ."

"And I can't believe you're here," Danny countered. "Seriously, Paul. I don't believe it. It's almost frightening that you're here. You have no idea."

"What's going on here, Dan?"

Danny stood up from the crate. "I'm sorry, man. You should rest. No talking. We'll have plenty of time to talk when you're feeling better. When you're stronger." He went over and took the rifle down from the wall brackets.

"Where are you going?" Paul asked.

"Out. Just for a bit. I'll be back."

"Where exactly are we, Danny?"

"We're up in the foothills."

"Whose cabin is this?"

"Mine, now."

"How'd you get it?"

"That's a story for later. You need your rest."

"Have you been out here for the past year? What are you *doing* out here? Are you in some kind of trouble? Tell me." His mind raced along with his heartbeat.

Danny didn't answer right away. Paul could see his lips twitching behind his beard. He could see the slight narrowing of his eyes, too. Despite the distance that had grown between them over the past year—both actual and spiritual—Paul knew his brother well enough to know that whatever he was about to say wasn't going to answer his question.

"Important work," Danny said. "I'm doing important work." Then he smiled. "Let's leave it at that for now, all right? Tomorrow's another day. And you need your rest." He doused the hanging lantern, dropping the room back into a coma-like blackness, with only the simmering orange coals in the stove for illumination.

Danny slipped the rifle's shoulder strap over an arm as he moved toward the door. "You stay put, okay? You're too sick to get up and wander around. No more going outside. I mean that—no matter what you hear or think you hear, you stay inside this cabin. There's a bedpan on the floor at the foot of your bed, in case you gotta pee. But I'm guessing you're as dry as a desert right now."

"How far are we from town?" Paul asked.

"Town? You mean the Hand? Far enough. Not really sure. Haven't thought about it in a while."

The Hand, Paul thought, and shivered. It was as if Danny had been . . . what? Indoctrinated? All of a sudden, he felt more than just uncomfortable. He felt extremely vulnerable—almost infantile in his helplessness. *Far enough. Not really sure. Haven't thought about it in a while*. He didn't like that answer, either.

"You know, it's funny," Danny said. "You spent your whole life taking care of me, Paul. And now I'm taking care of you." It looked like he smiled again, but his face was masked in shadows and Paul couldn't be sure. "I think it's good that you're here, Paul."

"Are we the only people out here?"

Again, there was a slight hesitation before Danny answered. "Let's hope so," he said, then walked out into the night. The door was tugged closed, and bits of dust and dirt showered down from the ceiling. The crosses swung and spun around on their strings like party decorations. There were dozens of them.

Paul stared at the closed cabin door for several minutes after Danny left. He wasn't sure what he wanted to do—get up and look around the cabin or maybe even crack open the cabin door and see if he could catch a glimpse of Danny doing whatever it was he was doing—but before he could arrive at a decision, his eyelids began sagging and that aching in his head was ushering him toward some black, dreamless void. He wasn't sure whether he should welcome it or fight it.

Far enough. Not really sure . . .

He closed his eyes and reclined on the mattress of egg-crate foam. He worked the fur blanket up over his body with one clumsy hand, tugging the hide right up under his chin. It helped a little, but the shivers refused to leave. His body shuddered like a dying engine. The wall he was lying against was covered in animal furs, but he could still feel the cold outside, pressed up against the boards of the cabin like some large, black predator eager to get at him. In fact, he imagined he could hear it moving around out there, separated by maybe two inches of wood, scrounging in the snow and snorting hot breath into the cold night air.

No matter what you hear or think you hear, you stay inside this cabin . . .

He might freeze to death if he fell asleep, he realized, but he was also too exhausted to care.

It won't matter, because this is a dream. I'm not with

Danny in some cabin in the woods. Yes, this is just a dream. Or another hallucination. Maybe I'm still out there in the woods, freezing beneath a layer of fresh snow, and these are my last dying thoughts before my soul is shuttled off to that great teachers' lounge in the sky.

But that tugging at his navel was there, telling him this wasn't a dream, and that he wasn't dead. Erin Sharma's Manipura. Call it what you liked, the thing spoke. And just before Paul was ushered off to sleep, it whispered to him that perhaps—just perhaps—those hadn't been aspirin Danny had given him, but something much stronger. Something that would knock him out. Something that would keep him here, unconscious, until Danny returned.

What are you doing out here, Danny?

Important work. Now, go to sleep, Paul. Tomorrow's another day. Let's hope you live to see it.

27

According to the ABI's database, the last known address for Gwendolyn Rhobean was the house in Chena Hills where her husband had murdered her son and then committed suicide nine years earlier. Jill Ryerson doubted the woman still lived there, but she drove the sixty miles to the remote little town nonetheless. She still had a slight fever and could have used one more day in bed, but she found that she couldn't get the Rhobean case out of her mind. The inexplicable similarities between the Rhobean and Mallory cases haunted her—decapitations and bloody symbols smeared on walls.

A 2011 census listed Chena Hills's population at fifty-one people. It had a grocery store, a gas station, and a collection of drinking establishments with names like the Pissing Mongrel and the Dutch Oven. Men in heavy winter coats sat on benches outside the gas station, smoking cigarettes.

When she arrived at the Rhobean house, she realized

that her assumption was correct—Gwendolyn Rhobean no longer lived there. In fact, *no one* lived there. The quaint single-family home had fallen into disrepair, with a section of its roof having caved in and its doors and windows boarded up. The whole thing was covered in so much spray-painted graffiti that it looked like a subway station wall.

She got out of the car and walked up to the porch anyway. Someone had sprayed the phrase DEVIL HOUSE across the boards that had been nailed over the front door. Broken bottles and empty beer cans littered the front stoop. Sensing that someone was watching her, she turned around and saw an elderly woman standing on the porch of the house across the street, staring at her.

Ryerson went around to the side of the house. A fence surrounded the property, but a good number of the staves had fallen away, so that she was able to squeeze through and gain access to the backyard. There was an overturned picnic table dusted with snow, a concrete birdbath tipped on its side, and a population of garden gnomes scattered about the overgrown yard. The blazing red face of the devil, complete with horns and a black goatee, had been painted across the rear of the house. Below that, someone had spray painted the phrase BURN IN HELL, MUTHAFUCKA!

The place had become a refuge for the homeless or bored teenagers—probably both. The house's foundation had been turned into a graveyard for discarded beer bottles and boxes of condoms. The rear door of the house looked like it had been pried open on more than one occasion, and she could see that it wasn't seated properly against the jamb, although two-by-fours had been hammered across the frame. She approached one of the garden gnomes, only to realize that it wasn't a gnome at all, but a child's doll half-buried in the ground, its eyes missing from its plastic skull.

She looked around for the woodshed, but didn't find it. She wondered whether Gwendolyn Rhobean or maybe even the police had had it removed after the incident. But then she saw what had become of it—a wooden palette with a single wall still rising from it intact, tucked in the far corner of the yard and overrun by a complex system of brown vines and holly. A pile of wooden planks were stacked against the fence beside it, while others lay in a heap on the lawn. She approached what remained of the thing, for some reason ashamed of the conspicuous footprints she left behind her in the thin layer of snow.

Much like the house itself, the upright boards were covered in graffiti. She made out various song lyrics, crude cartoons, foul language, and even a variety of symbols, though nothing that had been left behind by Dennis Rhobean. This was the work of teenagers, coming to the local haunted house to drink beer and tell ghost stories about the man who went mad and murdered his own son. Indeed, there were several more empty beer bottles scattered about the area.

An icy wind blew her hair out of her eyes. Ryerson shivered. Despite the rabbit's foot she kept on her key chain, she wasn't a superstitious person. Yet standing here in this yard, she felt a cold finger of unease prod against the small of her back. Suddenly, she just wanted to get back home and crawl into bed.

She went back around to the front of the house. The woman was still watching her from across the street, the only neighbor in sight.

"Hello," Ryerson said, smiling as she crossed the street and mounted the slate steps that climbed the slight hill of the woman's property. "My name's Jill Ryerson." She showed the woman her badge. "I'm trying to find a current address for Gwendolyn Rhobean."

"She in some kind of trouble?" asked the old woman. She had her hair in curlers tucked beneath a hairnet and wore a floral housedress beneath her heavy overcoat. Her stocking feet were shoved into tattered bedroom slippers.

"No, ma'am. I just had some information for her and have no way of reaching her." She glanced at the rundown house across the street and made a disapproving face. "I figured it was a long shot coming out here."

"She left soon after it happened," said the woman.

"You were living here back then? When it happened?"

"Been living here my whole life. Grew up in this house."

"Would you happen to have a forwarding address for Mrs. Rhobean?"

"Kids did that," the old woman said. She had followed Ryerson's gaze and was still staring at the house across the street. "Defaced the property, I mean."

"It's terrible."

"Started doing it before the poor woman even had a chance to move out."

"Is that right?" She wasn't too surprised; bored teen-agers had no sense of compassion.

"It'll be Halloween soon, and they'll be throwing their little midnight parties," the woman went on. "I keep calling the cops on them, but no one fixes the problem."

"How could we fix it?" Ryerson asked.

"Tear down that house," said the woman. Her eyes—wintry gray—focused on her. A milky cataract covered the left eye in a film. "Raze it to the ground. It's an abomination."

Ryerson could only nod her head. It had been point-less coming out here.

"She went to stay with her brother," the old woman said.

"She did?"

"I've got an address written down inside. Give me a minute."

The woman turned and vanished behind the smudgy pane of her storm door. A pair of eyes watched Ryer-son from behind the glass—a black cat with a crooked red bow around its neck. As Ryerson stared at it, a sec-ond set of eyes materialized out of the gloom and joined the black cat. This one was a calico. Both felines eyed her through the door. Paw prints had been stamped like commendations on the glass.

The old woman returned clutching a folded bit of paper in one arthritic hand. "It's been almost ten years. Not sure if she's even there anymore. We used to send Christmas cards, but that stopped a few years back. She lost her mind, as you can probably imagine."

Ryerson took the slip of paper and tucked it into

her pocket. "I can imagine, yes," she said, and glanced at the Rhobean house one last time. "I'll make a call, see if someone can come out here and put up some No Trespassing signs. For what it's worth. See if someone can do a few drive-bys on Halloween night, too."

"The kids will still come. They always do. Some of the older ones remember when it all happened. Their families knew the Rhobeans. It's become this fairy tale about devil possession. They tell ghost stories about him, you know. And not just the kids—they talk about him in town sometimes, too. But I lived here, and I saw the change in him. A sweet child who turned dark."

Ryerson frowned. "You're talking about Dennis Rhobean? The father?"

"No, ma'am," said the old woman. "I'm talking about the boy."

Ryerson glanced down and saw a third set of eyes appear behind the glass—a brown tabby who stretched out next to the other cats. It yawned like a lion, then stared at her with unwavering stoicism.

"I don't understand," Ryerson said. "What about the boy?"

The old woman hugged herself and shivered. "It's nothing we should be talking about."

"The ghost stories the kids tell are about the son? Not the father?"

"Nothing that we should talk about," the old woman repeated. She opened the storm door and stepped inside. The cats at her feet did not move. "Have a good day, Ms. Ryerson. Safe travels."

The storm door was closed, followed by the heavy wooden door behind it. Ryerson heard the bolt turn.

In the window beside the door, the gauzy curtain was brushed aside to accommodate the three sets of eyes that appeared behind the glass, staring at her as if to accuse her of some terrible crime.

Ryerson's departure from Chena Hills felt like she was fleeing something unnamable.

28

Daylight broke like an arterial bleed. Paul awoke as if kicked, his eyes springing open, his entire body achy and tense. He was sweating beneath the fur blanket, though he thought that maybe his fever had broken in the night. Still, his nose was leaking like a sieve and the headache was still there, too, although greatly diminished now and lurking somewhere in the far back rows of his mind-theater. His entire body felt bruised and battered. But at least he was able to sit up on his makeshift bed without feeling like the planet was trying to jostle him off into space.

He was alone in the cabin. The fire in the potbellied stove had been reduced to a dull orange glow, but bands of daylight stood between the wooden staves of the opposite wall, bright as molten silver.

He counted silently to ten before hoisting himself up off the foam-covered crates. His legs wobbled and his knees felt like they might give out. Worst of all were his feet. They felt like clumsy, inarticulate bricks swaddled in furs that were tied above the ankles with lengths of leather string. His left foot in particular ached when he put pressure on it. He wondered if that was a good thing or a bad thing. At least there was some feeling there.

While he'd slept, a tree stump had been rolled beside his makeshift bed. On it was the dented teakettle and the tin cup. Paul filled the cup with water from the kettle, drank it in two greedy swallows, then refilled it and repeated the process.

He stood and stretched his muscles, feeling the tightness of his joints and the tendons that ran down the backs of his legs. How far had he walked last night through the woods? But then he realized it hadn't been *last* night—it had been two or three nights ago, hadn't it? He couldn't remember what Danny had told him, and he certainly couldn't rely on his own memory.

I feel like I've been hit by a train. Then on the heels of that: *Where the hell am I?*

He tried to remember whether Danny had answered any of his questions last night during their brief conversation. But it was futile. He couldn't even be certain that he had *asked* Danny any questions. Had it even *been* last night? Christ, maybe it had all been another dream.

Just crawl back into your sun and go to sleep.

He wanted to. It was ridiculous, but a part of him longed for that semiconscious delirium. All was golden in that gossamer web.

He took a single step, then winced. The pain in his left foot was bad, but at least it was *something*. His right foot was numb, and it was difficult to walk on it. He recalled a student whose leg had fallen asleep during a lecture, and how, at the end of class, the kid had stood, then immediately collapsed to the floor. His foot had been twisted at an unnatural angle—broken.

The memory made him cautious. He leaned against the nearest crate as he hobbled around the room, getting familiar with the disquieting numbness of his feet. After a few minutes, he felt confident enough to move toward the back of the cabin.

How has he been surviving out here for a year?

At the rear of the cabin stood a wall of rickety wooden shelves. Various items were crammed on each shelf, no order to their arrangement—several containers of lighter fluid next to a chipped coffee mug; spools of twine beside what looked like a transistor radio with its faceplate removed; a box of galvanized nails alongside a tub of Folger's coffee; drinking glasses and an REI medical kit. One whole shelf was dedicated to ammunition, Paul realized amid a throng of concern. He knew nothing about guns, but he could tell just by looking at the boxes of ammo that they were for at least two or three different types of firearms—rounds for the rifle Danny had been hefting about last night, and rounds for the six-shot revolver Paul had noticed resting on the pillow beside the plaid bedroll on the floor. He peered over his shoulder and at the bedroll now, only to find that the revolver was gone. So was the rifle, missing from its wall brackets. *So is the ax,* he noticed, glancing into the empty corner where it had stood the night before. *He's removed anything that could be used as a weapon.* He felt like Jack in that fairy tale, having successfully climbed the bean stalk and was now tiptoeing about the giant's castle. Only this was the opposite of a giant's castle; this was a Morlock's fetid dwelling. And he wasn't up in the clouds, but flung into the far reaches of the middle of goddamn snowy nowhere.

Packed beneath the shelves were a cooktop that ran off propane (but no propane, as far as Paul could see), various tools, soap detergent in a bright orange box, scouring pads, several long rolls of polyethylene sheeting, a pair of binoculars, a small fire extinguisher, and various other items. There were also what, to Paul's untrained eye, looked like animal traps: several metal boxes with leveraged doors and two jagged-tooth half moons he recognized as bear traps. Paul knelt down and examined one of the bear traps. There was dark fur and what looked like dried blood caught between the rusted iron teeth.

He stood, wondering what sort of hallucination he had walked into. Back when Danny had been living with him for those brief months after getting out of prison, the guy ate nothing he couldn't pop into the microwave. Was he actually out here hunting for his own food now? The notion was preposterous.

There was a doorway cut into the side wall, covered by a patchwork quilt of multicolored animal furs hanging from what looked like a shower curtain rod. He pushed aside the furs and peered into a small, dark cutout no larger than a shower stall, which was packed nearly to the ceiling with unwashed clothes. They reeked of perspiration.

"Mom would be proud," he uttered, feeling lightheaded and giddy. He was about to let the fur curtain swing back over the doorway when he noticed that strange eye-sigil branded into the wood of the back wall. This one was much more elaborate than the crude renditions that had been streaked in dried blood on the walls of Mallory's house or the one carved into the wooden shack at the old Dread's Hand mine. The branding was filigreed and the pupil was comprised of two slightly bowed vertical lines that gave it a three-dimensional appearance. The light-headed delirium Paul had felt only a moment before fled from him, replaced with a cool disquiet. He pulled the fur curtain back across the curtain rod.

He looked around for his boots but couldn't find them. However, Danny had a couple of extra pairs lined up against one wall. He sat back down on his makeshift cot and unwrapped the fur lining from his feet. A pair of thick woolen socks were underneath. They reeked of mildew but at least they were dry. He squeezed his right foot and then his left. There was feeling there in the soles of his feet, but the pins-and-needles sensation in his toes troubled him.

Don't look.

He had to look.

This is a bad dream.

True. But it was also real.

Sucking at his lower lip, he peeled the wool sock off his right foot. His flesh looked fish-belly white, and somehow more naked than naked. His toes looked okay. He commanded them to wiggle and they complied. He flicked one and felt a dull pain. That was good.

Yes, but what about the other one? The one that feels as if it's currently being used as a butcher block?

He dropped his right foot onto the floor and propped his left ankle on his right knee. He was halfway through removing the sock when the wool protested. He tugged at it with a bit more strength and felt a searing pain as a fresh wound opened up along the arch of his foot.

"Shit."

Do it like a Band-Aid.

He did. He tore the sock clean off his foot, and heard the frizzy ripping sound as the wool separated itself from the wound. The sock had begun to fuse to a foot wound as it healed; shearing it from his foot had set the wound bleeding again.

But that wasn't the worst part. The worst part was his toes—the two smallest ones. They were purple and swollen, as if pumped full of air. The taut flesh had overgrown both toenails. He didn't flick them as he'd done to the toe on his right foot; instead, he gently prodded his smallest toe with his index finger, and just that simple act drove a dozen knife blades into the toe.

Paul winced, leaned over, and cradled his foot in both hands until the pain subsided.

I need to get to a hospital.

"Danny!" His voice echoed in the small chamber of the cabin. He waited, but his brother did not come.

He hobbled over to the medical kit, opened it, and found a fresh roll of gauze bandage. He tore into it, wrapped up the wound along his frostbitten foot, and clamped the bandage into place with two pins. He then maneuvered his way back to the makeshift bed, pulled his socks back on, then slipped his feet into a pair of Danny's boots. They were too large, even with the thick socks and the bandage on his foot. Paul found this odd. He and Danny had always had the same size feet.

Things are changing, old Jack. Grab that goose that lays the golden eggs and skedaddle the hell back down that beanstalk before you wind up on the giant's dinner plate.

He grabbed one of the winter coats from the wall peg and skedaddled into the daylight.

A white, untouched landscape was laid out before him. Trees shimmered in the sunlight, and the snow, now several inches thick, sparkled as if beaded with diamonds. Danny's footprints were the only disturbance in the smooth whiteness, carving passages back and forth between the cabin and the trees and around the perimeter of the cabin itself. A small fire burned within a circle of stones just outside the cabin. There was no sign of Danny.

Quaking from the cold, he took a few steps out from beneath the shade of the cabin and stared up at it. There was a crust of fresh snow on its pitched roof, and its fascia was comprised of ashy wooden planks the color of bone, so that it blended with its snow-covered surroundings. Just like in the photo Danny had texted him, there was the eye symbol carved into the door. Those unusual wooden crosses stood on either side of the door, serving as trusses for the overhanging roof . . . yet there was something beyond their simple functionality that seemed to resonate from them.

A strange notion occurred to him then, one that was as terrifying as it was implausible: that Danny was not really Danny at all, and that his brother had died out here shortly after texting him that photo last year. The Danny-like figure whom he had spoken with last night in the cabin, half his face shielded in shadow while the other half danced in the firelight—the Danny who had

rescued him as he lay half-unconscious in the snow—
was some other creature entirely. One that wore the
mask of Daniel Gallo, like the children from Dread's
Hand who wore the masks of animals to fool the devil.

The notion was preposterous.

The urge to urinate struck him—a strained throb at
his groin. He was relieved to feel it. Paul limped around
one side of the cabin, unzipped his pants, and liberated
a pungent ribbon of hot urine into the snow. It turned
the snow a bright orange. He couldn't remember the last
time he'd urinated.

He looked up and saw a series of wooden crosses running around the perimeter of the cabin. These were even
more rudimentary than the ones he'd followed through
the woods, each comprised of two hefty sticks tied together by twine to form a cross. He followed them with
his eyes. In one direction, they cut around to the rear of
the cabin and disappeared behind a stand of pines. In
the other direction, they formed a fence line that wound
around toward the front of the cabin, completing the cir-
cuit.

The sight made him feel ill.

He followed the procession of crosses around the rear
of the cabin, coming around the far side. Here, against
the side of the cabin, was a stack of firewood beneath
a blue tarp. A wooden sledge was propped up beside
it. He stepped around the woodpile and nearly walked
face-first into what he initially thought was a tangle of
loose tree limbs that hadn't fallen to the ground. When
he backed up, he saw that it was actually the skeleton
of some large horned mammal. It was suspended from
a tree by two steel cables, its bones picked clean, its

rib cage like an intricate bit of alien machinery. There was still some whitish-yellow hair wreathed around its splayed, marrow-colored hooves. Its skull, with its spiraling ram horns and blunt rows of teeth, looked like something that should be on display in a museum.

He stared at it awhile, watching its limbs sway in the breeze. The bones clattered together like bamboo wind chimes.

Jesus Christ . . .

Beyond the hanging skeleton and the few sparse trees, the ground fell away to a deep ravine. Paul peered over the side and saw large, slate-colored stones rising like the humps of whales from the snow. It was maybe a twenty-foot drop, but those rocks cresting out of the snow made it look deadly. The disturbed snow and the random footprints suggested that someone—Danny?—had been moving around down there.

Something about a boy, he thought, unable to focus on what it meant. Yet the thought was sharp and determined and had the flavor of memory. *Something about a boy with the face of an animal . . .*

Unable to stop shaking, he crept back through the trees and around to the front of the cabin. When the wind picked up again, he could hear those hanging bones whisper as they clacked together.

"I thought I told you not to leave the cabin." Danny's voice echoed out over the clearing. "I wasn't kidding about that."

Paul turned and saw his brother, rifle strap clinging to one shoulder of his fur-collared coat, advancing toward him through the trees. He was holding one of the box-shaped traps, and there was something large and furry shifting irritably inside.

"Where were you?" Speaking still caused his throat to burn, but he was able to power through it now.

"Getting breakfast," Danny said, hoisting the cage as he approached so that Paul could see the critter inside. It looked like a marmot. "You feeling okay?"

"Danny, what the hell are you doing out here? What's going on?"

Danny set the cage down beside a tree stump, the stump's flattened surface dusted with snow. He slid the rifle strap from his shoulder and leaned the gun against the stump so that the barrel pointed skyward. He looked at Paul, seeming to study him. "It's complicated," Danny said.

"Complicated? Have you actually been living out here?"

Danny didn't respond. He pulled off his gloves, then, kneeling in the snow, pressed one palm against the top panel of the cage. He applied pressure and the top panel lowered on springs, closing in on the large rodent inside. The marmot began to squeal like a pig as Danny lowered the spring-loaded roof of the cage onto it, its claws clacking against the aluminum bars, its frantic breath misting the air.

"Have you been living out here for the past year, Dan?"

"For a while, yeah," Danny said. He pulled a long, serrated hunting knife from a scabbard at his hip and, in one practical thrust, rammed the blade through the bars of the cage and into the marmot.

"Jesus Christ, Danny . . ."

Danny looked up at him. The pupils of his eyes were as small as pinheads.

The thing in the cage started making a terrible clicking sound that, to Paul, sounded like the engine of a lawn mower conking out. A spurt of blood had shot out and arced across the snow. Danny withdrew the knife and thrust the blade into the ground. There was blood on his knuckles.

"There's some firewood beneath a tarp on the far side of the cabin," Danny said, laying both hands down on the top panel of the trap now and squeezing the life out of the dying critter. "Grab a couple of logs and toss them on the fire, will you?"

"Are you fucking serious?"

Danny glanced up at him again.

"I want to know what the hell you're doing out here, Danny. I thought you were dead. I came out here ready to identify your goddamn corpse in some morgue, and here you are, playing Robinson fucking Crusoe in the middle of the goddamn woods."

Danny just stared at him, his face expressionless.

"I've been through hell because of you. I've had a knot in my goddamn stomach ever since you disappeared. How could you just cut off all ties with me like that?"

"You need to calm down," Danny said.

"Calm *down*? Are you kidding me? I think you'd better start explaining yourself."

"We should go inside." Danny glanced over his shoulder and through the meshwork of tree branches beyond the line of crosses.

"I'm not going back in there," Paul said. "Start talking. What's going on?"

Danny took off his knit cap and stuffed it into the pocket of his coat. His long hair draped down over his shoulders, damp and flecked with snow. He rubbed his bare hands down his face, then propped them on his hips. Paul could see the scabbard of the hunting knife hanging from Danny's belt. It was stained with dried blood.

"Remember when we were kids," Danny said, "and we used to take turns skateboarding down Penniman Hill Road? One of us would stand at the bottom of the hill to make sure there were no cars coming through the intersection, because you couldn't see them from the top of the hill. You'd wave to me when the coast was clear, and I'd skate down the hill and burn right through the intersection. Then we'd switch, and I'd wave to you when there was a break in traffic, and you'd do the same. Remember?"

"Yeah," Paul said.

"Well, this is like that. I'm at the bottom of the hill and I'm waving at you. I'm telling you I can see things you can't, and that it's okay to come on down. But you gotta trust me."

"Yeah, all right," Paul said. "I'm trusting you. I'm listening."

"Past few years, my life's been shit, man. I mean, yeah, I've always been a little all over the place, but I hit some real dark times. You have no idea. I came out here hoping to catch a new beginning for myself, maybe find myself. Maybe put some of the pieces back together, you know? And if I couldn't, then that was it.

There would be no going back if I couldn't get my shit together."

"You came out here to die," Paul said. It was not a question. "To kill yourself."

"My head wasn't so clear about anything back then, so I can't say for sure what I would have done. I think I was just gonna keep going until I hit the goddamn North Pole, I guess. By the end of last summer, I'd heard about this place—Dread's Hand. I dug the creepy name and I thought it might make as good a last stop as any before oblivion, so I drove out here and stayed a couple of days in town. I went up to the old mine on the hill, and I walked the trails. But I got lost. I was wandering around out here in the woods for a day and a half, dehydrated and sick. At one point, I sat down under a tree to rest and I guess I fell asleep. When I woke up, I was lying on the ground. I had a nosebleed. My head hurt, too, and I wasn't sure where I was. Next thing I know, this old guy came out of the woods. He took me to this cabin and gave me some food and water. He let me stay awhile. I even took a selfie and sent it to you."

"Tell me about it," Paul said. "It was the last I heard from you."

"I didn't know it then, but we were setting things in motion," Danny said.

A strong wind funneled down from the mountains and rattled the tree branches. The boughs of the firs shook, raining snow down onto the ground. Danny cast his eyes in the direction of the wind, his long hair billowing back off his face, as if to interpret something in it. In that moment, he looked every bit the isolated survivalist he had become.

"Where's this guy now?" Paul asked.

"Like I said, it's complicated."

"How's that complicated? Is he coming back? Is he living here, too? This is his place?"

Another gust of wind shook loose branches down from the trees; they clattered down the trunks, some getting snared in the pine boughs below. Others planted themselves like spears in the snow.

"Yeah, this was his place," Danny said. "But it's mine now."

"What's this guy's name?"

"Joe," Danny said. "Joe Mallory."

"Mallory!" Paul cried. "Are you fucking *kidding* me? Do you know who the guy was? He was a goddamn serial killer, Danny! He killed a bunch of people out here, then turned himself over to the cops. That monster is the reason I came out here looking for you."

"You've got it all wrong," Danny said. He was shaking his head, but his voice was calm, steady. "Joe Mallory is no monster."

"Mallory was a *murderer*!" Paul shouted. "He killed eight people, Danny. He cut their goddamn heads off and buried them in the woods."

"Yeah, I know about the bodies," Danny said.

Paul opened his mouth but then shut it again. His headache pulsed like a beacon. Almost in a whisper, he said, "Tell me you had nothing to do with those people buried out there. Tell me that, Dan."

"I had nothing to do with it," Danny said. "That all happened long before I came out here. But the impression you have of this whole thing is wrong, Paul. Mallory wasn't a monster. Mallory wasn't a serial killer."

"Are you out of your mind? That guy killed innocent people."

"No." The word launched out like a slap, yet Danny's face remained stoic, impassive. "You're wrong, Paul. They were *not* innocent. They weren't even people."

"What does that mean?"

"They were evil," Danny said. "They'd been *corrupted* by evil. This has been going on for years out here, Paul. Centuries, even. It's nothing I can explain, and even if I could, you'd just think I was nuts. But this place is evil, and there's something out here that can touch a man and corrupt him. Possess and poison him."

"Please," Paul said, shaking his head.

"There's always been someone—a gatekeeper—out here to fight that evil. It's a calling. Joe Mallory was chosen, and he prevented those monsters from leaving this forest and going back to civilization, where they would have done heinous things."

Paul took a step in Danny's direction, pointing a finger at him. "Listen to me. This guy was a self-confessed serial killer, and you're saying he was some kind of savior. Do you know what you sound like right now?"

"You don't understand."

"What's there to understand? You meet some psychopath out here in the woods who tells you ghost stories . . . *and you believe them.* And now you've been out here . . . what? House-sitting for a year? Listen to me, Danny—Joseph Mallory is dead. He was arrested, and he killed himself in his jail cell. Whatever you're doing out here is unhealthy, and you need to come home with me."

The look on Danny's face wasn't one of surprise, or

anger, or shock, or even resignation. In fact, there was hardly an expression on his face at all. "I don't expect you to understand, Paul. I didn't understand at first, either. And I'm not an idiot. I don't just believe whatever people tell me. But I stayed out here and I've *seen* things. I've seen things that have convinced me beyond a shadow of a doubt."

"Like what?"

Danny waved a dismissive hand. "It doesn't matter what I tell you, because you'll just think I'm crazy. I would, too. There's nothing I can say that will make sense to you, or clear any of this up in your mind for you. I know that. All I can say is that I've seen things that have made me understand all of this, and accept it. I've become a true believer."

"So, what does that mean?" Paul asked. "You can't believe this stuff back in Maryland?"

"I'm not going back to Maryland."

"What have you been doing out here for a year, Danny?"

"I told you," Danny said. "Important work."

"Danny." He took another step closer to his brother. He could see the crow's-feet in the corners of Danny's eyes, the scant few silver hairs in his beard. He could smell the sour perspiration on his unwashed flesh. "Have you killed anyone, Danny?" The words juddered out of Paul's constricted throat.

Calmly, Danny said, "I believe everyone has a calling. I think I was destined to come to this place and do what I have to do."

"Jesus Christ," Paul muttered. "Jesus Christ, what have you done? What have you *done*?"

"You're upset because you don't understand. You don't believe."

"Who are you to play God and pass judgment on people?"

"They're not people."

"You've killed people, haven't you? Haven't you, Danny? My God . . ."

"They're not people," Danny repeated.

"Those bodies the police dug up were human fucking beings, Danny. They had families who were out there looking for them, just like I was looking for you. They were *people*!"

"That's how they looked to you," Danny said. "I see them differently. I can tell a regular person from someone who is bone white."

"Bone white! Danny, you don't think that this sounds crazy? Look at it realistically, from my point of view. You come out here and disappear for over a year and cut off all contact with me. No rational person does that. You say you're out here fighting evil, but I say spending a year out here in the woods by yourself has screwed up your head. This place—this town—is only exacerbating your problems. I've only been out here a few days, and it's messing with my head, too. It's a freaky goddamn place, Danny. So let's just go home. We'll work all this out at home."

"I'm not leaving, Paul. I've been in turmoil my entire life, and now I'm at peace. I've finally found my place. I'm doing good work out here. I won't leave."

"You have never committed yourself to a single goddamn thing in your entire life," Paul said, "and now *this* is the thing you choose? Some backwoods psychopath convinces you to sit up here and watch for demons, to fucking *kill people,* and you *do it*?"

"I used to be just as lost and confused as you," Danny said. "But once I understood, I found inner peace. It made sense. My eyes were opened. I feel better than I ever have in my whole life."

"Then tell me what you saw that convinced you," Paul said.

"Nothing I can say will convince you, Paul. Just like there's nothing you can say that will convince me that *I'm* wrong."

"Then *show* me. Show me what you saw that convinced you. I want to see it, too."

"It doesn't work like that."

"Mallory convinced you, but you can't convince me?"

"It's not a magic trick," Danny said. "I can't snap my fingers and make you a believer. It wasn't anything Mallory showed me. It was stuff I witnessed on my own after staying out here awhile."

Paul turned away from him, running his shaky hands through his hair. He realized he was breathing as if he'd just run a marathon.

"You've known me my entire life," Danny said. "I know I've always been a little flaky, but I'm not an idiot, Paul. I didn't just walk into this thing blindly. It didn't happen overnight and it didn't happen all at once. It's not one big thing but a combination of many little things. I could sit down and tell you every little nuance of what I saw, but it would mean nothing to you. In fact, it'll only reinforce your belief that I'm nuts and need to get out of here."

"You're right," Paul said, turning and facing him again. "Your words won't change my mind. I need to be shown these things."

"Then you have to stay here with me," Danny said.

It was a laugh that erupted from Paul's throat, but there was no humor in it. It was a sad, defeated wail, and it had come from deep inside him where all the soft things were easily hurt. "Yeah," he uttered. "Yeah, sure."

"I was brought here for a reason," Danny said. "I think you were brought here for a reason, too."

"I wasn't *brought* here. I came out here looking for you."

"No," Danny said. "That's wrong. You were brought out here to help me on my journey. You're needed here, just like I am. You're meant to help me fulfill my destiny here."

"Ah, Dan. Goddamn it."

"No one else knew I was out here except Mallory. Yet you came out here and you found me. And it wasn't just dumb luck that I happened to come across you out here, either, half-dead in the woods. Isn't that miraculous? It's all part of the plan."

"Come home with me."

"Stay here and see this thing through with me."

"For what? A week? A month? So I can eat barbecued groundhogs and wipe my ass with pine needles?" Another humorless laugh erupted out of him.

"I'm not going home with you," Danny said. He pulled the knit hat out of his coat pocket and tugged it back down on his head. "If you want to leave, I won't stop you. But these woods aren't safe. You're be-ing watched right now." Danny turned from him and looked at the surrounding woods. He gestured toward the circle of crosses that formed a perimeter around the cabin. "If you leave here, you risk exposing your-self again to the evil. It came close to taking you last time."

"Jesus Christ." Paul swiped at his eyes, but he was too dehydrated for tears. His palms were cracked and dry, like old shoe leather. "You've lost your mind. You're lost, Dan."

The wind gusted through the trees again. Powdery clouds of snow blew off the pine boughs and swirled around them. Paul could hear the bones of the skeleton-ized beast hanging from the tree clatter together, fore-boding as a death knell.

"I'm perfectly found." And then there it was—the trademark Danny Gallo grin. Only there had been an alteration to it over the past year. There was a stark assuredness to it that looked foreign yet comfortable on Danny Gallo's face. "I'm not going back with you. What you do from here is up to you, Paul. What will you do?"

Paul said nothing. His entire body quaked.

"At least get some food in you before you make up your mind," Danny suggested.

"You're gonna cook that big rat?" Paul said, sud-denly desperate for levity. "Probably tastes like chicken, huh?"

"More like duck," said Danny. "I love you, Paul. You know that, right?"

Paul could only stare at him. His face felt stiff and inarticulate. The marching band in his head was going around the block yet one more time.

"Love you, too," he said, then went around to the side of the cabin to get some firewood.

29

Paul was sitting on his makeshift cot, an animal hide draped over his shoulders like a shawl. The potbellied stove at the center of the room pumped heat into the air, but his bones felt like they were made of ice. His left foot was soaking in a pail of warm water, which Danny had prepared for him.

Paul had choked down a few gamey chunks of marmot before his stomach threatened to betray him. Danny kept coming into the cabin to check on him, insisting that he eat some more, but he mostly stayed outside.

Paul used the silence to formulate some game plan in his head, and wondered if he could come up with a scenario that would enable him to take Danny away from this place with him. He didn't think that was possible. And if he tried to find his way back to town on his own, could he call the cops and have them haul his brother to some mental institution? What if there was a struggle and Danny was killed? Could he live with himself if something like that happened?

What about all the things he's been doing up here for the past year? How many more bodies are buried in these woods and beneath these hills? How many more families crowding into police stations, year after year, searching for their loved ones? Danny is my brother and he's lost his mind, but that doesn't mean those people should have to suffer.

It was his father he thought of then, and his instruction that Paul look out for Danny after they had gone.

Bang-up job there, he thought, and found his vision growing blurry. He fought off his grief and instead focused on the pain in his feet. If they didn't get better, he doubted he could walk out of here at all.

Danny came into the cabin carrying a large pot of water. "Did you have enough to eat?"

"Yes."

"How's the foot?"

"Hurts."

"You shouldn't walk on it for a while. Once your toes start looking better, I'll wrap it up for you."

With his boot, Danny kicked aside some items on a shelf at the back of the cabin. He set the pot of water on it, then shrugged off his coat and unbuttoned his shirt. He had lost a lot of weight. His ribs and muscles were clearly defined. There was also a handful of pinkish scars running along his back. The largest one must have been six inches long, and it curled down Danny's left flank, a puckered Frankenstein contrail that still looked tender.

"You get in a fight with a bobcat?" Paul asked.

"Something like that." Danny soaked a rag in the pot, then proceeded to wash his chest, his armpits, his arms. Paul watched as he scrubbed the grime off his face.

"Where are they? The people you've killed." The words were out of his mouth before he realized he had said them.

Danny wrung the rag out over the pot. When he turned to look at Paul, there was no animosity in his eyes. In fact, the look there was so foreign that at first Paul didn't recognize it for what it was: pity. The man who'd spent a year of his life out here steeped in madness was looking at him with pity in his eyes. As if Paul was the madman.

"That part doesn't matter," Danny said. "Anyway, there are more important things we can talk about."

"Like what?"

"Like why you're here," Danny said. "The reason you were summoned here."

"I already told you that. I wasn't summoned. I came out here looking for you."

That look of pity simmered in Danny's eyes. "Last week," he said, "I was out checking the traps when I fell down the side of the ravine out there. I hit my head and was knocked out for a couple of minutes. But for a split second, just before everything went dark, I was lying not on the ground out there, but on the floor of a classroom with a bunch of kids staring at me. Suddenly I had a book in my hand and I think my nose was bleeding. The vision was so clear to me that when I got back to the cabin, I wrote down the title of the book."

He dried his hands on his shirt then went over to the small tower of paperback novels that stood on the floor beside his bedroll. He opened one of the novels to the title page—it was some garish bodice-ripper with a distressed female on the cover—and he held it out so that Paul could see what had been hand-printed just above the author's name in Danny's inimitable handwriting:

THE JOLLY CORNER

Paul felt a finger of ice trace down his spine at the sight of it. He handed the book back to Danny.

"I wasn't sure what that vision meant until you showed up out here. And then I thought maybe it was some sort of premonition. That maybe the vision of the classroom was a vision of my twin brother, the big college professor. My other half." Danny smiled at him, then glanced down at his own handwriting on the book's title page. "Do you know what *The Jolly Corner* is? Is that a real book?"

"It's a story. I teach it in class. You must have heard me talk about it before."

Yet Paul's actual thought was that he had been talking in his sleep, or that he'd had some conversation with Danny while still in the throes of a feverish delirium. If that was the case, why would Danny want to trick him now? What did it all mean?

Nothing. It means nothing.

"I'm not sure exactly what it is yet," Danny went on, "but I know things are coming together. We're meant to do something out here—something even greater than what I've been doing all along, maybe. I think . . ." His voice trailed off.

"What do you think?" Paul prompted.

"I think we're here to end this thing. Somehow. For good."

Paul didn't like the finality he heard in his brother's voice. *He's killed people out here. He's lost his mind and committed murders. What makes you think you're any safer than any of them?*

"So, what's the plan, then?" he asked Danny.

"I don't know yet. I'm not sure."

"Maybe the plan is for me to take you home. Maybe that's how I help you, how I fit into all of this. Maybe the whole point of us finding each other out here is to help us get back to where we're supposed to be."

The pity in Danny's eyes turned to stone. "I'm not so sure it's about us at all, Paul. I'm not so sure it's about you and me helping each other. I think we're here on some greater mission. We're just the conduits."

We are both going to die out here. The thought rang through Paul's head like a Klaxon. All of a sudden, it was too easy to imagine Danny shooting him in the head, then killing himself. And just thinking this made him think of the police report that Jill Ryerson had given him.

"I read that police report. The one where they sent you to Sheppard Pratt for evaluation."

"How'd you find that?" Danny asked. He didn't seem the least bit bothered by it. He swept aside the fur curtain over the cutout in the wall and rummaged around until he found another shirt.

"Doesn't matter," Paul said. "How come you didn't talk to me about it?"

"That's not something you talk about."

"I'm your brother."

"That's all behind me now. I'm not that man anymore."

"Yeah," Paul said, and his eyes skirted away from his brother's oddly satisfied face.

"I just hit a low point. I wasn't thinking clearly."

"You could have come to me if you were in that much pain. To do something that drastic . . ."

"It doesn't matter anymore," Danny said, buttoning his shirt.

"It does to me," Paul said.

"I love you, Paul," Danny said. "You were always a good brother to me. I'm sorry I was always such a shit."

"Not always. You had a good week in the fall of 2002."

Danny laughed, and just like that, Paul was transported to those summers spent swimming in the river behind their house, just him and Danny, mirror images of each other, splashing and diving off piers and seeing who could hold their breath the longest underwater.

He's going to win this time around, Paul thought, and the thought sobered him up. *He's going to outlast me out here unless I think of something.*

Danny's laughter subsided. "I was in the hospital when Mom and Dad died. I didn't even know about the funeral. You think they forgive me for not going?"

"I think they'd understand."

"Thanks for handling all that stuff back then. I always looked up to you for it."

"I'm your big brother," Paul said.

"By seven minutes," said Danny.

"Well, you're handling things now." The words simmered between them. Paul lifted his foot out of the pail of water. The water had grown cold.

Danny replaced the water with a pot that had been simmering over the fire outside. It wasn't hot—it was just barely warm—yet it hurt like hell to sink his ruined toes back into it. He wondered how long it took for frostbite to turn gangrenous.

"It's good that you're here," Danny said, smiling at him through the gloom.

Just until I can figure out a way to get us both out of here, Paul thought.

He hoped that epiphany would come sooner than later.

30

Gwendolyn Rhobean now lived with her brother, Gordon Boutillier, in a small fishing community called Winsock. According to the background info Ryerson was able to pull up on the woman, she had never remarried and had never made a public appearance or even released any public statements following the murder-suicide of her husband and teenage son.

Ryerson had called Boutillier that morning and had explained her interest in wanting to speak with his sister. There was a long pause on the other end of the line before Boutillier asked her to hold on for a second. She expected him to refuse her request, but when he returned on the line, he said his sister was willing to meet with her. She thought that even he sounded surprised. Gordon Boutillier invited her out to the house.

She left Fairbanks around two thirty, her head still aching from her battle with the flu. The sky to the north looked like hammered tin. Swollen gray storm clouds were creeping down from the mountains, and halfway through the drive, a frozen drizzle speckled her car's windshield.

You're chasing ghosts, she thought, unable to silence that head-voice throughout the duration of the hour-long drive out to Winsock. *What connection could there possibly be between Rhobean and Mallory? The only thing you're going to accomplish is to upset a poor woman who has already had more than her share of grief.*

She silenced the head-voice by sliding a Marilyn Manson disc into the CD player. She still wasn't feeling a hundred percent—far from it, in fact—but sitting in the house for days on end had made her restless and nervy. At night, doped up on NyQuil, she slept hard and deep, plummeting into her nightmares headlong like someone shoved into the dark sea strapped to an anchor. There was no logic to her nightmares, but the random clutter of images—the ones she could remember upon waking, anyway—carried with them a grave and unsettling aura. Last night, after having read the Rhobean file again, cover to cover, she'd awoken from a weighty sleep to the sound of someone screaming. It wasn't until she came fully awake and bolted upright in bed that she realized she was the one screaming.

By the time she arrived in Winsock, her body was racked with chills and her muscles were sore. There were only about a dozen homes here along the river—dilapidated double-wides with massive red oil tanks in their yards. The land was flat, and as Ryerson entered the community, driving past a wooden sign that showed two wooden carp jumping toward each other, she could see for many miles across a brownish-yellow tundra, straight out to the hills. The shores of the river were made of black sand and white stones, and the water itself glittered and shone like crystal.

She had anticipated some difficulty locating Gordon Boutillier's residence upon arriving in Winsock—her GPS worked for shit out here—but the guy's name was stenciled on a mailbox at the end of a stone driveway. Ryerson turned into the driveway and parked her car behind an old Ford Super Duty and two mud-splattered ATVs. The vehicles looked more expensive than the house.

Ryerson got out of the car and was immediately struck by the fishy scent of the air. It sent her mind reeling back to her childhood in Ketchikan, and of the dead salmon that would stink up the air at the close of spawning season.

As she approached the trailer's door, a large Alaskan malamute appeared from around the corner of the trailer. Malamutes were normally beautiful dogs, but this one, despite its healthy size, looked mangy and malnourished. It locked Jill Ryerson in an ice-blue stare.

A woman came around the side of the trailer after the dog. She was calling to it and didn't notice Ryerson until Ryerson called out to her.

"Hello," Ryerson said. "I'm looking for Gordon Boutillier."

The woman was short and thick around the middle, with dark features and a severe widow's peak. Ryerson had gotten Gwendolyn Rhobean's photo from the DMV, and this woman looked nothing like her.

"Are you that cop?" the woman said.

"I am. I spoke to Mr. Boutillier earlier this morning. He's expecting me."

"Yeah, he said you'd be coming around." The woman bent down and looped her fingers around the malamute's collar. Yet the girl looked more feral than the dog. "I'm Claire, his daughter. My dad's around back." She nodded toward the rear of the trailer. "Go on. Gunnar won't hurt you."

At the mention of his name, Gunnar growled deep in his throat.

Ryerson had shot and killed a dog once, when responding to a domestic at some squalid little trailer park not much different from this place. She knew that the average citizen was appalled whenever they heard stories like that, but it was easy to criticize when you didn't have some hundred-pound monster with snapping jaws and teeth like spear hooks eager to rip out your jugular.

"Seriously, lady, he's cool," said Claire.

"I must look like a Milk-Bone." But she approached anyway, that stupid, phony smile still stuck to her face.

This close, she could see that Claire was close to her own age, though the weatherworn look of her face was deceiving. She wore a diamond stud at the side of her nose, and when she spoke, Ryerson could see that some of her teeth were silver.

"You state police?"

"Yes."

"Ever kill anybody?"

"Huh?"

Claire made a gun shape with her thumb and forefinger. "You know," she said. "Ever shoot anyone?"

Just a dog, sweetheart, so keep your hand on old Gunnar's collar.

"Not yet," she said.

"Right on," said Claire.

She gave the malamute a wide berth as she turned the corner of the trailer. Wind chimes jangled from the eaves. The rear lawn was a field that stretched out toward the river maybe fifty yards out. Fronds and tall grass rippled in the cool breeze. Ryerson felt that chill straight down to the marrow. She wondered whether her fever was creeping back up on her.

A large man stood on a concrete slab, either assembling or taking apart a large wire cage that reminded Ryerson of the crab pots back home. The guy had his back toward her, his expansive girth covered in a camouflaged hunting jacket. He wore rubber waders that looked wide enough to fit around an oil drum.

"Gordon Boutillier?"

The man turned around, startled. He was maybe in his sixties, with a sparse beard the color of beach sand. His eyes were shaded by the bill of a ConocoPhillips ball cap.

"Ryerson, right?" Boutillier said. His wasn't the gruff longshoreman's voice Ryerson had been expecting, based on their brief conversation earlier that morning on the phone. The tone was smooth, almost musical. The guy could have been an opera singer.

"Hello." She extended a hand and he stripped off one rubber glove and shook it. "I truly appreciate this."

"It ain't me who's doing you any favors," Boutillier said. "It's been almost ten years, Ms. Ryerson. But I don't think time heals a thing like that. Do you?"

He seemed to be genuinely asking the question, so she said, "No. I don't think so, either." Photographs of the crime scene slid through her brain. "Is she still willing to talk?"

"Well, she baked cookies." He hitched his shoulders in an expression that said he was done trying to understand the mind-set of his grief-stricken sister. "We don't get a lot of visitors, and Gwen, she don't go out much."

"I see."

"Do you mind me asking, Ms. Ryerson, what's the sudden interest in this thing now, after all these years?"

There was no sense in being evasive. She said, "I've come across some similarities between your brother-in-law's case and one that I've been working. It's probably a long shot, Mr. Boutillier, but there might be a chance your sister might know something that could help me connect some dots. Something so minor that it may mean nothing to her, but might help me."

"It's that Mallory fella, ain't it?" Boutillier said. He tugged off his other glove, then dug a pack of Marlboros out of his breast pocket.

"I'm not really at liberty to talk about it."

"You don't have to. I've seen the news." He stuck a cigarette in his mouth, then waved her toward the set of sliding doors at the back of the trailer. "Come on. She's inside."

She followed him into a cramped little room that seemed to serve as both the living room and kitchen nook. The furniture looked like it had been salvaged from a fire sale, and the carpet was so worn in places, Ryerson could see the nylon stitching. There was an enormous flat-screen TV balanced on a rolling cart in one corner of the room, *The Price Is Right* on the screen. At the kitchen table, a woman sat in pressed slacks and a handsome cable-knit sweater before a laptop, her fingers clattering away at the keys. She turned her head in their direction as they came into the room.

"Gwen, this is Ms. Ryerson, the investigator from the state police," Boutillier announced in his operatic voice.

"Call me Jill," she said.

"Oh, you're a peach," said Gwendolyn Rhobean.

Ryerson smiled and said, "I'm sorry?"

"Look at her, Gordon. She's so young."

The woman pulled herself out of her chair and extended both hands toward Ryerson. Not knowing what to do, Ryerson gripped both hands in her own and found herself a participant in some awkward double handshake.

"So young," repeated Gwendolyn Rhobean. "But you have a smart face. A smart face." She turned toward her brother. "We're okay in here."

Boutillier nodded, though most of his focus was on lighting the tip of his cigarette with a plastic lighter. Once he got it lit, he strolled back out into the yard, sliding the door closed behind him.

"Have a seat inside on the sofa," Mrs. Rhobean said, closing her laptop.

Ryerson sat on the sofa. There were tufts of stuffing spooling out of the armrest and the cushions were so worn and thin, she could feel the springs pressing against her ass. *They could probably sell that TV and move into a nice condo,* she thought. If she had a nickel for every shithole apartment she'd been in where the TV took up the entirety of one wall, she'd be a very rich woman.

"Can I get you something to drink?" Mrs. Rhobean called from the nook.

"Water's fine. Thank you."

"Are you sure? I'm having a cocktail."

"Just water," Ryerson said.

On the television, a King Kong version of Drew Carey laughed good-naturedly at one of the contestants. Ryerson thought she could see the camera crew reflected in the lenses of Carey's oversized glasses.

Gwendolyn Rhobean returned with a glass of water, a vodka tonic, and a plate of chocolate chip cookies. She set the drinks and cookies on the wobbly table in front of the sofa, then turned a rattan rocking chair around so she could face Ryerson. The woman was sixty, and Ryerson had been expecting someone who looked much older, prematurely aged by the darkness that had taken away her son and husband. But Gwendolyn Rhobean looked spry and almost jubilant, her face done up in blush and eye shadow, her nails freshly polished.

"I appreciate you meeting with me, Mrs. Rhobean."

"Call me Gwen."

Ryerson smiled and picked up her glass of water. She glanced down and saw a dog hair stuck to one of the ice cubes.

"I've recently read the police report, the file on your husband and son. I had a question about an odd symbol that was left at the crime scene. Do you remember anything about it?"

Gwen furrowed her brows. "A symbol? What kind of symbol?"

"Just like this," Ryerson said, setting the glass of water back down on the table and producing a folded index card from the inside pocket of her coat. On it, she had reproduced in red marker the symbol of the eye with the vertical pupil. She would have preferred to have shown Gwen the actual photograph taken from the crime scene, as some of her fellow troopers might have done, but she couldn't be so crass.

Gwen took the card from her and examined it.

"This symbol was discovered on the interior walls of the toolshed where the . . . when the police arrived."

"It wasn't just in the toolshed." She handed Ryerson back the index card. "Dennis became obsessed with it near the . . . well, near the end."

"Obsessed how?"

"He carved it onto our bedroom door. He . . . he . . . he'd scribble it on sheets of newspapers or on old bills that were left around the house. I saw him sitting in a chair one morning, staring out the kitchen window, his finger working furiously on his thigh—making circles over and over with his finger. He never realized he was doing it, and he couldn't explain what it meant."

"Had he seen it somewhere before?"

"Only in his head. He didn't know what it meant."

"In the months before the incident, had your husband joined any new organizations? Had he maybe started going places, or maybe to any one place in particular, that he'd never gone to before?"

Gwen shook her head, an absurd smile stretching her bright red lips. There was lipstick on her upper teeth.

"How about any new friends? Had he been hanging around with any new people?"

"No, dear. We'd lived in Chena Hills our entire married lives. There *were* no new people."

"Any other changes in his behavior leading up to the incident, Mrs. Rhobean?" It was an unconscious shift back to using the woman's surname—a habit of her profession.

"Well, he became possessed," said Gwendolyn Rhobean, matter-of-factly. "This . . . obsession . . . gripped him and wouldn't let him go. It tormented him, day and night. He wept about it. He stopped going to work."

"What obsession?"

"Well, with Kip," said Gwen, that clownlike smile still plastered on her face. "He became obsessed with our boy."

"Your son?"

Gwendolyn Rhobean's smile faltered. "He became tormented by what he believed he had to do. You see, Dennis's change was only a result of what had happened to Kip."

"What happened to Kip?"

"His behavior. He'd begun to change. We thought maybe it was drugs at first."

"Was it?" It so often was out here—drugs or alcohol. A toxicology report on the father was included in the file—Dennis Rhobean had not been under the influence of any illicit narcotics or alcohol at the time of the incident—but there hadn't been such a report completed on the son.

"No," Gwen said. She was struggling to maintain that false smile now, and it was a battle she was losing.

She blinked rapidly, and that seemed to rejuvenate the smile. Gwendolyn Rhobean's whole face brightened. "Do you have any children, Jill?"

"No, ma'am."

"Oh." That brightness fled from her face. For the first time, Gwen Rhobean looked her age—looked much older, in fact. She hid a dark grief behind that mask of rouge, eye shadow, and lipstick.

"Tell me about your son," Ryerson said. "What had changed with him?"

Gwen Rhobean's eyes grew distant. Her gaze left Ryerson's face and skirted across the room. Behind her, Drew Carey helped a giddy female contestant spin the giant wheel.

"It was both of them, really. Something happened to both of them." She cleared her throat, then said, "Twice a year, Dennis would take Kip on a hunting trip. It was a way for them to bond. They always came back refreshed and excited. But that last trip . . ." Her voice grew solemn. "I could see a change in both of them the moment they returned. Kip was withdrawn. I thought he might be sick. Dennis did, too. And Dennis, he was . . . unsettled. Restless. I don't know how else to describe it."

Ryerson nodded.

"I could tell that something had happened to them on that hunting trip, but neither of them would talk to me about it. It changed both of them. Dennis started sleepwalking. One night I woke to the sound of something scraping against our bedroom door. It was Dennis, scratching that symbol onto the door with a kitchen knife. He was disoriented when I woke him. He didn't recognize the symbol he had carved, although he said that he sometimes dreamed about it. When I asked him what it meant, he refused to talk to me about it.

"Kip began to change, too, only in different ways. Worse ways. He wasn't himself anymore. He'd become . . . darker."

"What do you mean?"

"He'd defecate on the floor of his bedroom," Gwen said.

Ryerson cocked her head. "What?"

"It was to be spiteful. He claimed that he'd started sleepwalking, too, and that he wasn't in control of himself when he'd do these terrible things. But I could tell that he was lying to me. It was one of his . . . his changes. Sometimes I'd wake up in the middle of the night and he'd be standing at the foot of our bed. Just standing there in the dark, staring at us. Watching us sleep. 'Hey, Mom,' he'd say, when he realized I was awake and looking at him. I asked him what he was doing and he'd always say, 'I'm sleepwalking, Mom. Don't worry about it. Go back to sleep.' But let me ask you, Jill—do sleepwalkers know when they're sleepwalking?"

Ryerson shook her head. "I don't know."

"They were lies. They were games. 'Go back to your room,' I'd tell him. Sometimes he did. Other times, he kept standing there. I'd wake up Dennis, but Dennis wouldn't know what to do. He seemed . . . I don't know . . . afraid of Kip by this point. They were both changing around me, living under the same roof but becoming . . . different. It's like that movie where the aliens replace real people with evil versions of themselves."

It was at that moment Gwen Rhobean seemed to remember that she had a cocktail sitting on the table in front of her. That eerie clown smile situated back on her face, she picked up her rocks glass. She brought the drink so quickly to her mouth that some vodka and tonic sloshed onto her knuckles and spattered onto the carpet. Ryerson heard the glass *clink* against the woman's teeth. When she set the drink back down, her hand was shaking.

"Other nights, he'd just stand there at the foot of the bed and not say a word. Even when I saw him and said something to him, he'd not say a word. I remember one night I woke up to find him standing there with an old stuffed sheep's head on his own head, wearing it like a mask or a headdress or something."

"A—what?"

"Sheep's head. One of the sheep he and his father had shot on a hunting trip. It was mounted on the wall in the den, but Kip had taken it down, and he was wearing it over his head that night. Like a mask. He started wearing it more and more toward the end."

Ryerson suddenly felt very cold.

"He started hurting people, too," Gwen Rhobean went on. "Kids at school. He'd fight them for no reason. Even kids who were older and bigger than him—even if that meant he would get hurt in the process. He just wanted to hurt them. And he laughed about it. All the time, he laughed about it."

Gwen's eyes grew glassy.

Ryerson reached out and touched one of the woman's knees. "It's okay," she said.

"We had some trouble," Gwen went on. "There was a family who lived down the road from us. The Pecks. Allison Peck was a few years younger than Kip. They used to play together when they were small. When they got older, Kip acted like a big brother to her. She was . . . she was a little slow." Gwen's shaky hand tapped the side of her own head. "One night, her parents came over to our house. Allison's mom had been crying. Her dad was so angry his face was the color of a tomato. They said . . . they said that *Allison* said that Kip had . . . that he'd . . ."

She made some gesture with her hands in the air that suggested nothing and everything all at once.

Ryerson nodded.

"Kip denied it. We stood up for our son. Allison wasn't all there, you know? We thought maybe she'd misunderstood something that had happened. It was possible. Somehow, we convinced the Pecks. They went home. But then the second we shut the door, Kip started laughing. Laughing like a madman, so much so that it frightened me. Dennis was frightened, too, but he was also angry. He slapped Kip across the face. It was to get him to stop laughing. And he did, he stopped. But then something changed behind his eyes, and he was on Dennis and clawing at him like some wild animal. Biting. Scratching. I pounded Kip on the back to get him off of Dennis. When he stopped, he stood there panting like a dog. He'd bitten Dennis so hard on the arm that there was blood on his lips. And when he looked at me, he smiled. A dark spot spread across the front of his pants, too. He'd wet himself in all the excitement."

Gwen Rhobean used both hands to pick up her drink this time. Three swallows drained it.

"That night, I woke to find him standing at the foot of our bed again. He was naked and . . . and he . . ." Gwen shook her head, ridding it of the image. Her eyes were still glassy but no tears had fallen yet. "You know what he said to me, Jill? Standing there in the dark, you know what he said?"

"What's that?"

"He said, 'We got them good, didn't we, Mom?' He meant the Pecks—that we'd fooled the parents and that he'd done something terrible to their daughter after all. 'We got them good, didn't we, Mom?'"

For several moments, the only sound in the room was the TV.

"It's been almost a decade, Ms. Ryerson, and I need to confess something to you now."

"All right."

"About a week or so after that confrontation with the Pecks, Allison Peck disappeared. She never returned home from school. Police questioned all the neighbors, but no one knew anything. And maybe in their grief, the Pecks never made the connection to what Allison had accused Kip of doing, because they never came back to our house to ask any more questions. But, you see, Dennis and I knew. Not because we had any hard evidence—only Kip, and Kip's behavior. When the police came to our house and asked if we had any information that might help them find Allison, Kip stayed up in his room. Once the police left, I went upstairs and found Kip sitting at the foot of his bed. He had that sheep's head on, and he turned and stared at me as I came into the room. I knew he couldn't see through that thing, but at the same time, I knew he *could*. 'What did you do?' I asked him. And for a long time, that sheep's head just stared at me. I began to feel sick standing there in that room. 'I know you did something to that girl.' And he just started to laugh—muffled beneath the sheep's head, but loud and mocking, too. And then . . . and then he sort of rolled back onto the bed in slow motion until his legs were up over his head. He rolled back until his back was flat against the headboard and that sheep's head thumped against the wall. And then he just . . . he climbed the wall. He just sort of crawled up the wall like a spider, and hung there, laughing beneath that sheep's head mask, his hands and feet flat against the wall, his body just . . . just hanging there."

Ryerson opened her mouth but no words came out.

"I know how it sounds," Gwen said quickly. Perspiration had dampened her upper lip. "I've never spoken about this before, not even to Dennis. I just . . . I just ran out of his room crying."

"He . . . he was just—"

"He was just hanging there," Gwen said. "And I never told the police about it. I never told them that Kip was probably the one who did something to that poor girl. They never found her, Ms. Ryerson, and her poor parents never knew what became of her. Because I was scared. I was so scared. But Dennis and I, we *knew*. It sounds terrible, doesn't it? We *knew*, and we were too scared to say anything."

Outside, a dog bark caused Ryerson's heart to skip a beat.

"It was two nights later that Dennis told me what happened on that hunting trip," Gwen continued. "They'd gone out to the forest and spent the first night sleeping in a tent, just like they always did. But something woke Dennis in the middle of the night, and when he looked around, Kip wasn't in the tent with him anymore. He went outside and saw Kip crouched down among the trees, staring off into the darkness. He had stripped all his clothes off and he was out there, shivering and naked. Dennis went to him, shook him, but Kip didn't respond. It was like he was in some sort of trance. Dennis said there was a large red handprint on Kip's back, as if he'd been slapped by someone. When he bent down to meet Kip's eyes, he could see bruises around his neck, as if someone had been choking him.

"He got Kip back inside the tent, covered him up, then went back outside with his rifle. It was the middle of the night. He couldn't see anything, but he could hear something moving around their camp, just beyond the trees.

"He saw a shape move through the trees behind the tent. He went toward it, and in the light of the lantern, he saw a man standing there, just a few yards away, but mostly hidden in shadow behind the trees. He raised the rifle and called to the man, but the man didn't respond—he just stood there.

"And then a second later, the man charged at him. He just ran straight for Dennis, coming right out of the trees, and Dennis pulled the trigger and fired a shot at

him. But then . . . when the man hit the ground, Dennis
saw that it wasn't a man at all. It was a sheep. The thing
had come charging at him out of the trees, but it was
just a sheep.

"He convinced himself it was a trick of the light, a
trick of the shadows, combined with his nervousness—
that it had never been a man. Yet he said that when
the man had first come through the trees at him, he'd
caught a glimpse of his face, and it was . . ."

"Was what?"

"The man had Dennis's face. Dennis said the man
looked just like him—a mirror image, right down to the
clothes he was wearing. The whole thing happened in
less than a second, and of course it hadn't been a man
after all, but Dennis had been so *certain* at the time.

"The next morning, they packed up their gear and
came home. Kip didn't say a word on the drive home.
The bruises on his neck were no longer there, either,
and Dennis began to wonder if he had imagined the
whole thing. 'But I know now that I didn't imagine it,'
Dennis told me that night. 'I know that the boy down
the hall is not our son. And I know what I have to do
about it. It came to me in a vision.' And then . . . then
the next day . . ." Her voice trailed off with a hitch. A
moment later, Gwen sprang up from her rattan rocker
and said, "Time for a refill." She fled into the kitchen
nook.

Ryerson stared at the dog hair stuck to the ice cube
floating in her glass. She heard something rattle off to
her left. She looked and saw a blue parakeet in a wire
cage in one corner of the room. She looked behind her

and out the window, and saw Gordon Boutillier weaving a thick rope between the latticework of the large crab pot.

"I wasn't trying to hide any of this from the police at the time," Gwen said, returning with a fresh drink. "I just didn't know what to believe back then. It's been almost ten years, Ms. Ryerson, and I'm able to look back on things now with more clarity. Even through my grief." She smiled at Ryerson. "The grief, it never goes away, you know."

"I guess not," Ryerson said. "I'm so sorry."

"That wasn't our son that my husband killed. My son never came out of those woods. My husband knew it, and I knew it near the end, too. My husband did what he had to do, yet his grief was too great. He blamed himself for losing our boy up there in that forest. And that's why he killed himself, too." Gwen smiled, and Ryerson found it impossible not to stare at the bright red streak of lipstick across her front teeth.

"Where did they go on this hunting trip?"

"The same place they always went. Up the Hand."

"The Hand?"

"Dread's Hand. It's a small village about two hours north of here."

The interior of the trailer felt too hot. Each breath Ryerson took was like breathing through a face mask. She reached up and pressed a palm to her forehead. It was burning up and damp with perspiration. In her rocking chair, Gwen Rhobean's face had revealed itself, even beneath all that makeup; the woman who looked at her now wore a withered, angry, grief-stricken mask, half her mind lost in the past and focused for all eternity on one terrible day.

"Excuse me for a moment, will you?" Gwen said, and left the room.

Outside, the dog continued to bark. Ryerson peered back out the window. Boutillier was gone, but the malamute was out there, staring at the trailer. Barking at it.

"Well," Gwen said when she came back, swiping an index finger beneath her eyes. She had reapplied her eye shadow. She sat back in the rocking chair, then frowned as she peered past Ryerson's shoulder and out the window. "Goddamn dog." Then her eyes jittered over to Ryerson, and just like magic, that forced smile was back on her face.

"I'm sorry," Ryerson said. "I think I've taken up enough of your time."

Gwen Rhobean continued to smile at her, the look in her eyes one of confusion. "You haven't had any cookies. They're just out of the oven."

Ryerson took a cookie from the plate, but the thought of eating it made her want to vomit. Instead, she thanked Gwendolyn Rhobean, and carried the cookie with her toward the door. Ten seconds later, she had chucked the cookie into the bushes and was hurrying around the side of the trailer, worried that she might throw up on her way to her car. Boutillier was gone, as was the woman named Claire. But the malamute was standing beside her vehicle when she reached the front of the house. The dog growled at her and bared its teeth.

"I'll shoot you, motherfucker," she uttered, tasting acid at the back of her throat.

The dog turned and padded around the far side of the trailer, leaving her alone.

She backed out of the driveway and sped out of Winsock, the windows down despite the cold. Her entire body felt feverish again. It wasn't until Winsock was a tiny dot in the rearview mirror did she begin to calm down.

31

He didn't realize he was asleep until Danny was standing above him, shaking him awake. It was night, the interior of the cabin lit only by the glow of the stove's embers behind the iron grate in the middle of the room. Danny's face looked like a mask, his wild hair and unkempt beard part of some elaborate disguise.

"Come with me," Danny breathed into his face. "Get up."

Paul slid his legs over the side of the makeshift bed, wincing at the pain in his toes and the stiffness of his legs. His left foot felt like it was filled with shards of broken glass. Danny draped a coat over him and helped him to his feet.

"The hell's going on? Where are we going?"

"Outside," said Danny.

"What's outside?"

Danny crossed the cabin and flung open the door. Icy wind flooded the interior of the cabin, and doused the embers in the stove. The cold struck Paul with solid force, so strong and invasive and all-encompassing that he forgot about the agony in his left foot.

Danny hurried outside into the night. Snow swirled around the open doorway. Paul campaigned toward the doorway at a slow pace, bells and whistles going off in his head. Something wasn't right here. Something was off. He slipped his arms into the sleeves of the loose coat Danny had draped over him and buttoned it up. Above his head, the contingent of little wooden crosses fluttered and spun and spiraled in the wind.

Stepping out into the night was like jumping into ice water. An agonized cry crawled from his throat. His aching feet, covered in multiple layers of animal furs, cried right along with him. He took a few steps out into the clearing, his rabbit-hide boots cleaving through the snow.

The night sky looked like the bottom of an underwater trench. There were no stars. Wind howled and whipped the trees into a frenzy. With each gust, tornadoes of snow spiraled across the ground. Ice pellets struck his face and burned against his flesh.

Danny stood in the center of the clearing, his rifle in his hands. He was scanning the nearby tree line, his hair rippling behind him in the wind.

"Danny! Danny!"

Danny turned and waved him forward. Paul thought it was easier said than done: It felt like it was twenty below out here, and despite the multiple layers, he could feel the frigid air permeating his flesh straight down to the marrow of his bones. Gritting his teeth, he advanced toward Danny, the icy wind searing the dry pockets of flesh below his cheeks. He began to shake. His feet felt like they each weighed three hundred pounds.

Danny stepped toward the perimeter of crosses, his rifle aimed at the chasm of darkness that filled the gaps between the trees. He paused on this side of the crosses, with only the barrel of the gun extended beyond the barrier. A moment later, there was a loud *crack*. A large pine bough dropped from a nearby tree, crashing through other branches on its way down. It struck the ground in an expulsion of white powder.

"Danny!" Paul shouted over the wind.

Danny held up one hand in his direction—the universal gesture for *stop*—but he did not turn around and look at him. He didn't take his eyes off of that dark patch of forest.

Paul heard a hollow chattering around the far side of the cabin. He looked and saw the ram skeleton dancing wildly in the tree.

Danny came up alongside him. There was a runner of snot crystalizing in his mustache and his eyes were narrowed to slits. The steel barrel of the rifle gleamed a bright blue in the moonlight. He pointed toward the spot where he'd been staring just a moment ago.

"There's something there."

"What?"

"There's something *there*," Danny repeated. "Go see. But stay behind the crosses."

"What's going on?"

"Just go and take a look."

Holding one hand up in front of his face to block out the driving sleet, Paul hobbled through the snow and stopped before the line of wooden crosses.

Paul looked up at the black forest that loomed before him. He could hear more branches falling from the trees. In the periphery of his vision, he thought he saw movement in the darkness all around him.

"Stay," Danny called to him. "Stay there."

Snow crystals peppered his face like buckshot. The pain in his feet had lulled to a dull nothingness, and Paul didn't know whether this was a blessing or if it signaled certain doom.

"Stay," Danny commanded.

"I'm not a fucking dog!" Paul shouted back.

Something darted through the blackness beyond the trees. Paul caught it at the very last second. It was just a glimpse, yet he couldn't deny that something was there. It wasn't just another falling tree limb.

"Did you see it?" Danny called to him.

"What am I looking for?" When Danny didn't answer, he raised his voice and repeated the question: "What the hell am I looking for?"

There came the dry, brittle cracks of a tree trunk breaking against the strength of the wind. It sounded so close that Paul took a step backward and glanced up, half-expecting a large pine tree to come barreling down on him through the darkness. A tree *did* come down, shearing tree limbs and kicking up clouds of snow in its descent, but this one crashed to the earth maybe twenty feet from him, falling very close to the outer perimeter of the crosses. Clouds of snow roiled out of the woods like smoke from a fire.

After a moment, Paul realized that the wind had died down, and that the rush of air that filled his ears was his own labored respiration.

Danny came up behind him and clapped a hand on his shoulder.

"What the hell was all that?" Paul gasped.

"Did you see it?" Danny said. "It was out there. It moved around the clearing and cut down into the ravine."

"What did?"

"The devil. The devil, Paul." Danny surveyed the dark forest all around them. "It's not setting any traps for you. No tricks this time around. It's coming straight for you. It's already got a handhold around your heart." Danny turned to him, and Paul was startled to find tears standing in his brother's eyes. "I'm not gonna let it get you, Paul. I promise. I'm not gonna let it get you."

Danny's hand dropped off his shoulder. Paul watched as Danny went over to make sure the crosses closest to the fallen tree were still secure in the ground. The wind had died, but there were still little whirlwinds of snow spiraling across the clearing. On the far side of the cabin, the sheep skeleton danced its terrible dance.

I'm not gonna let it get you, Paul. I promise.

Yet Paul couldn't shake the feeling that Danny had just used him as bait.

32

The solution came to him two days later, as he helped Danny build a fire for their breakfast. Danny only checked his traps in the mornings, and whatever he'd caught was what they ate for all three meals of the day. But twice a day—in the early morning and again just before dusk—Danny would disappear for an hour or two into the woods by himself, his rifle hanging over one shoulder, his revolver tucked into the rear waistband of his pants. These were perimeter checks, Danny informed him; he'd circle the cabin in a widening gyre that sometimes covered several miles. Paul didn't ask him what the purpose of these checks was, mainly because he was afraid of the answer. Before he left, Danny would suggest that Paul read a book and keep off his aching feet while he was away, and usually Paul did . . . although he always had one ear cocked for the sound of gunfire in the distance.

Danny was adamant that Paul remain within the circle of crosses, particularly when Danny was out on one of his perimeter checks. It was safer that way, Danny said. So Paul remained behind in what he came to think of as the Cross Corral, like a puppy with nothing better to do than stare off into the forest and wait for his master to come home. On the two occasions when Danny taught Paul how to shoot the rifle, Paul remained behind the Cross Corral while Danny traipsed into the forest to hang targets.

Having never fired a gun before, Paul took to these lessons with reluctant assiduousness. Danny instructed him on what to do and Paul did it. The rifle's shoulder-stock stamped purple-green bruises along his right shoulder, and after only a half hour of shooting, there wasn't enough water in the world to wash the acrid taste of gunpowder from the back of his mouth.

Paul never asked why it was so important he learn to shoot, mainly because he thought he knew the answer. He just narrowed the focus of his mind and got through it, ignoring the larger picture all around him. He'd only broached the subject once. He had just finished firing at a target fifteen yards away, and had a nice grouping to show for it, when he lowered the barrel of the gun and said, "How will I know which ones to shoot when the time comes?"

Danny hadn't required elaboration. And his response, as simple as it was, chilled Paul down to the core: "I'll tell you."

Paul began to grow frightened by the prospect of some stranger coming through the woods and happening upon the cabin. Every time he heard movement beyond the trees, he prayed it was an animal. He was terrified that some waylaid hunter might come stumbling into the clearing, looking for directions or trying to get better cell phone reception, only to have half his face sheared off by a .30-06 Springfield cartridge.

It was over the course of these two days that Paul began formulating various plans on how to get Danny back to civilization. The easiest scenario would be for Paul to leave the cabin on his own while Danny was away on one of his perimeter checks, and hike down through the woods toward Dread's Hand. He could call Jill Ryerson and say he found his brother and that Danny was in need of medical attention. Yet Paul was tormented by the vision of his brother rotting away in some prison cell for his crimes. Did Alaska have the death penalty? He wondered if he could talk Ryerson into recommending psychiatric institutionalization over a prison cell. But was that really any better?

For a time, Paul considered striking Danny over the head and knocking him unconscious. People in movies made it look easy, but Paul worried that striking Danny over the head might result in dire and even fatal complications. Instead, he thought he might be able to drug him and render him unconscious. There were enough pills in the arsenal Danny kept in the cabin. Once Danny was unconscious, Paul could load him onto the sledge and drag him down through the foothills, much like Danny had dragged him here when he found him semiconscious in the woods.

The main problem with all of those scenarios was that they required Paul to navigate the forest and make it back to Dread's Hand on his own. He'd already gotten lost once out there. What would happen if he knocked Danny unconscious and started dragging him away,

only to get lost out there again? They were in the foothills, and logic dictated that if he continued walking at
a downward slope, he'd ultimately reach the town or the
road that ran through it from the highway. But that logic
had only gotten him lost all those nights ago. It hadn't
worked. Also, could he even pull Danny on the sledge
with his ruined feet?

*There hasn't been a single airplane overhead. I
haven't heard the gunshots from hunters' rifles out
here, either. It's almost as if we're in an entirely different world, the only two living human beings.* All
of a sudden, he could picture himself walking down
through the woods for days, weeks, months at a time,
and never coming upon civilization, or even flat land for
that matter—that the rest of his life was doomed to be
one continual downward trek through the mountains.

The day before, he had commented on the state of
his two purpled toes. "They're frostbitten," he had explained to Danny. "They're gonna cause trouble. I need
to go to a hospital, Dan."

But Danny hadn't been swayed. "They're not gangrenous. I've been keeping an eye on them."

"They hurt."

"I can take care of it," Danny said, and Paul wondered just how Danny might do that.

Amputation, Paul thought, shivering in the corner of
the cabin. *He'll dope me up and take them off with his
hunting knife. Easy as pie.*

It just showed how adamant Danny was about staying put. Even Paul's own deteriorating health wasn't
enough to coax Danny back to civilization.

It was on that second morning, while he prepared a

fire inside a wreath of rocks so that Danny could cook their breakfast, that the solution came to him. The second he thought of it, he knew it was the only plan that would work. It was so simple that it should have been staring him in the face all along, and he began trembling at the prospect of it.

I'll set the goddamn cabin on fire and burn it to the ground. There's enough accelerant in there to do the job, and once these old tinder walls go up, there'll be no stopping it. Winter's almost here, and it's already around twenty below at night. Without shelter, he'll have no choice but to come back down out of the woods with me.

It would have to work.

He decided to wait until Danny left for his morning perimeter check, which meant he was a bundle of nerves during their breakfast of whatever rat-like thing Danny had managed to snare in one of his cages. Talk was minimal and Danny looked exhausted. There had been another midnight rousing the night before, Danny shaking him awake and ushering him outside into the cold. There had been no wind this time, and the night had been as silent and still as a crypt. Danny had urged him to walk around the perimeter of the Cross Corral, and Paul had complied, his entire body aching, his feet like two hollow cinder blocks attached to his ankles. He had seen nothing, and after a time, Danny allowed him to go back to sleep. But Danny had remained awake, sitting outside by a campfire, his rifle across his legs, staring out into the darkness.

"What's with the skeleton of that animal hanging in the tree?" Paul asked midway through breakfast. It was still as black as night outside, without even the barest shimmer of daylight glowing through the cracks of the cabin walls.

"It's me," Danny said. He was scraping the remainder of his meal from a tin pot and shoveling it into his mouth. When he looked up at Paul, he must have seen the dour expression on his brother's face. "I'd been here at the cabin for three days, and Mallory wouldn't let me leave. He said I was being stalked, just like you are now. He said it would come for me in the night. And it did. But I got it. Mallory showed me how."

"What exactly did you get?"

"It's funny," Danny said, "but I thought it was you at first. I went out into the woods and there was this guy standing right there, a few feet away, in the trees. A stranger, I thought, somehow out here with us in the middle of nowhere. It was dark, but when he took a step toward me and the moonlight struck his face, it looked just like you, Paul."

"Or you," Paul said.

"Yeah," Danny said. "That's the point, though, right?"

"Is it?" Paul said. "I have no idea."

Danny set his food down on the cabin floor. "It tries to trick you. It shows you an image of yourself to confuse you. But Mallory had warned me, and I wasn't confused. I shot it and killed it."

"A man?"

"No. Just a trick. It wasn't a man. Not really. After I shot it, I saw it was just a sheep. I skinned it, cleaned the bones, and hung it out back as a reminder."

"A reminder of what?"

"That I'm here for a reason. That I'm on this mission now."

"Because you shot a sheep . . ."

"Because I beat it at its own game," Danny said. "Everything became clear once I killed it. I broke the spell. I began having these vivid dreams. Sleepwalking a little, too. I'd make these circles in the ground outside, digging with my hands while I slept. Circles with a line through them."

"A symbol of the Keepers," Paul said.

Danny's eyes widened. "Yes. How'd you know that? Have you dreamed it, too?"

He was thinking about the afternoon he'd passed out in the classroom and how he'd scribbled the circle with the slash through it on the floor in chalk. But he chased the thought away just as quickly as it had arrived.

"Someone back in the village told me about it," he said instead.

"Well," Danny continued, "Mallory told me how it worked—how it had been working for more than a hundred years. He said that the Inuit people out here had done it since the beginning of time, and that he was going to teach me." Danny's lips went tight. "I think he was starting to go crazy out here by the time I came along."

"You think?" Paul said, unable to restrain the sarcasm in his voice.

"I had my doubts that I'd be able to tell if someone was . . . well, bone white . . . in the very beginning. Just like you. But Mallory said I'd know when I came upon the right person. And he was right."

"How many people have you killed out here, Dan?"

"I told you," he said. "They're not people. They're husks of people with something black and evil walking around inside them. That's why killing them isn't enough. You have to remove the heads, too, and bury them. For a while, it's okay to just . . . just bury them where you can . . . but Mallory began wondering toward the end if those bodies shouldn't be buried in consecrated ground. A holy cemetery somewhere."

"How many of these . . . these devils have you killed?"

"It's only one devil. Poisons you by touch. A spiritual touch. He almost got me, you know."

Paul said nothing. The greasy marmot meat was turning over in his stomach, feeling like a lump of sod.

"That night when I shot the man who looked like me—who looked like you—there was a moment when the beast almost overtook me." Danny leaned forward on his knees, his eyes bright. "It was looking at me through the trees, and then for one split second, my perspective shifted. All of a sudden I was standing where *it* was standing . . . or at least seeing through the thing's eyes, because I was staring at myself again, only this time it was my *real* self, the one holding the gun and looking terrified. But then a second later I was back in my own body again. That's when I knew what it was and what it was trying to do. So I pulled the trigger and brought it down. After that, I could see things for what they really were." He leaned back down on his buttocks. "Maybe you will, too."

"Maybe," Paul said, incapable of continuing this conversation. He wanted to crawl into a fetal ball and hide in some dark corner. *I'm getting you out of here today, Danny, whether you like it or not. Not another day longer.*

After they ate, Danny cleaned up while Paul soaked his left foot in another pail of warm water. The swelling had gone down, but the two smallest toes of his left foot remained a disconcerting purple, and they ached whenever he put pressure on them.

After Danny put out the fire outside, he came into the cabin and took his rifle down from the wall. He glanced at Paul, who sat on the edge of his egg-crate bed reading one of the paperback romance novels, his left foot soaking in the pail of water. Paul stared back. "What?" he said.

Danny didn't respond. But then he shrugged his shoulders and said, "Nothing. Enjoy your book. I won't be long."

When he left, Paul set the book down but didn't get up right away. He thought about that connection that had seemingly always existed between them, a near-clairvoyance that, if he were to believe such a thing, caused Danny to write down Henry James story titles and Paul to sketch out eye shapes in chalk on the floor of his classroom.

Danny is not reading my mind. We have no supernatural bond. I'm just paranoid.

Yet for some reason the old dog-bite scar along his left arm began to itch. He scratched at it and stared at the countless crosses that hung like bunting from the rafters. His heart was beating a mile a minute.

He climbed down off the egg-crate bed, dried his foot, then pulled on two pairs of socks and some boots.

An extra shirt from the clothes box and a Marlboro Man coat from a peg on the wall. He realized he was sweating as he hurried around the place, dressing quickly and staving off full-fledged panic.

Take some supplies, just in case. You don't know how far from town you are.

He snatched a backpack from the closet with the animal-hide fur over the doorway and proceeded to fill it with extra pairs of socks, the first-aid kit, a box of matches and one of the smaller Coleman lanterns, gloves and knit caps, two extra pairs of boots. He zippered the backpack closed, then slipped his arms through the shoulder straps. It shouldn't have felt as heavy as it did, but he figured he'd lost about fifteen or more pounds out here over the past week, and much of his muscle mass had atrophied.

Will you even be able to make it back to town? What if it's five miles? Ten?

There was no way they were ten miles from civilization. He wouldn't have made it this far to begin with.

Quit stalling.

The plastic containers of lighter fluid were lined up on the shelf at the rear of the cabin. On the shelf below was a tin of Coleman lantern fluid. He took the lantern fluid and sprayed it in shimmery ribbons across the floor. Then he doused the walls, too, and the pile of clothes in the wooden clothes box. He soaked the stack of paperback bodice-rippers, as well, before the container ran dry. He tossed the canister aside, then worked his way through each of the containers of lighter fluid. He sprayed the ceiling joists and the count-

less wooden crosses that hung from them. He soaked
the yellow mattress of egg-crate foam and the wooden
boxes underneath. He drenched the furs that hung on
the walls for insulation. When he was done, he tossed
the empty bottles aside. He was breathing heavily, having overexerted himself. Too many deep breaths and
the pungent odor of the lighter fluid stung his nostrils.

Do it and get out.

He grabbed a box of wooden matches as he backed
out the cabin door. The early morning was still as dark
as night, and there was a parade of stars overhead, but
daylight would prevail soon enough, giving them light
by which to see for their trek back to civilization.

Go! the voice shouted in his head.

He backed out of the cabin, struck the wooden match
against the flint strip on the side of the box. A ball of
yellow flame blossomed at the head of the match. He
stared at it for a second before tossing it into the open
doorway of the cabin. An instant later, a dorsal fin of
flame shot up from the floorboards and raced toward
the rear of the cabin. Fiery tributaries branched off
from the main artery, trailing up the walls and across
the ceiling. The wooden box of clothes went up like
dry tinder. Wooden crosses dropped from the rafters
as their strings snapped. Framed in the center of the
doorway was the potbellied stove, like a squat, black
martyr.

Paul backed away from the cabin, unable to take his
eyes off of it. Flames licked out between the boards
and shot like fiery fingers through the knotholes in
the wood. The crosses flanking the door went up, and
it was almost as if the whole thing had been choreo-

graphed. A black column of smoke billowed up into the sky, obscuring that parade of stars and blotting out the three-quarter moon.

There was a cracking, grinding sound, as one wall of the cabin collapsed. A ball of fire belched into the air as the roof slid down and onto the snow. Several wooden crosses that formed the Cross Corral went up, as well.

When Paul turned around, he saw Danny standing among the trees, staring at the conflagration. Danny's eyes met his, and instead of the rage Paul expected to find there, he saw only a deepening terror that made him feel very cold.

"What did you do?" Danny shouted. He came through the woods but froze midway across the clearing, his body gilded in firelight. The look on his face was one of abject horror.

"Danny—"

"What did you *do*?" Danny cried. It came out almost as a plea.

"Come," Paul said, holding out a hand to his brother. "Let's leave here."

But Danny wasn't looking at him; he was watching the crosses burn. Several had already fallen over and were burning in the snow while others were nothing but smoldering black ash.

Paul went to him, the weight of the backpack on his shoulders causing his muscles to strain. He gripped Danny by the forearms and shook him. Over the roar of the fire, he said, "I won't leave you. Come with me and we'll get through this togeth—"

But the look on Danny's face killed the words in Paul's mouth.

Paul turned around just as a strong wind bowed the trees. Branches snapped and clouds of snow rolled out into the clearing. A resounding wail, mournful as a ghost's lament, was borne on the wind.

Danny placed a hand against Paul's chest. "Stay right behind me," he said. He was staring into the forest.

Paul looked but could see nothing. It was too dark and the wind was blowing too hard now, icy torrents coming down from the White Mountains. Paul's heart slammed in his chest.

Danny raised the rifle and scanned the tree line, his exhalations crystallizing in the air. Their shadows were stretched out on the snow in front of them, long and distorted by the firelight at their backs; Paul watched them merge, then separate again as Danny crossed in front of him, the rifle scanning the black cusp of forest.

That ungodly wail again . . . and then something came flying around the side of the burning cabin, trailing a streamer of flame. Danny whirled around and peeled off two shots, the rifle cracks echoing through the forest. Something fell to the snow.

Danny reached back and grabbed a fistful of Paul's shirt before advancing toward the thing. Their shadows walked alongside them now, long-legged boogeymen striding across the snow. The burning cabin created a black chasm of shadow in the nearby ravine. At the edge of the ravine, the thing that had come around the side of the cabin lay in a heap of snow. It looked alive in the dancing flames.

It was the sheep skeleton. The branch that it had been hanging from was on fire.

Danny's fist was still clutching at Paul's shirt like a

heavy stone pressed against his chest. Paul hardly noticed: He was staring at their shadows, and at the way they repositioned themselves in the snow as the fire moved, and how it looked for a moment as if there were more than two shadows there . . .

Paul's gaze rose to the tree line. A nebulous black shape crouched in the darkness between the trees, staring at them.

"Danny—"

The thing burst into the firelight, a formless black monstrosity with flashing green eyes and a mouth ringed with teeth.

The thing in the tree! Paul's mind shrieked. *The thing in the tree!*

Danny shoved him out of the way, knocking him off his feet. The wind was punched out of his lungs as he struck the ground, the items in the backpack driving into his spine like shrapnel. He saw Danny with his legs planted wide in the snow as the rifle barked and a flash erupted from the barrel. An instant later, Danny was knocked to the ground as some dark shape collided with him, the rifle sailing off into the darkness.

Paul crawled through the snow in the direction of the gun as Danny let out a scream. His fingers found the rifle stock, and he was able to drag the weapon into his lap while propping himself into a seated position in the snow.

He managed to swing the barrel around just as those luminous green eyes filled his field of vision. He pulled the trigger a moment before it felt like he was struck by a locomotive, driving him back down into the snow. Something heavy and hot gashed across his abdomen—

knife blades clawing at his guts. A black shroud surrounded him, an impossible weight pinning him down.

But then the thing was off of him. Paul gasped for air and tried to roll over in the snow while fiery embers rained down around him. He managed to turn his head and saw Danny outlined in firelight. Danny staggered backward, clutching at one arm. His agonized cries sounded like the hiss of a flare gun over the treetops.

Whatever the thing was, it circled around them and paused before the blazing cabin, an amorphous stain of darkness that glistened like ichor in the firelight, green eyes blazing from a shapeless black skull. It was nothing but a silhouette against the fire, humanoid and animal all at once, great clouds of its breath steaming the air. It focused its shimmering green eyes on Paul.

"Here!" Danny shouted, waving his arms above his head. "Here!"

But the thing just stared at Paul.

Paul looked down and saw the palm of his hand covered in blood. His guts ached . . . but there was another sensation there, too—a tenuous pulsing of his and Danny's shared umbilicus, their Manipura. He waved his bloodied hand through the air in front of his chest, expecting to feel it strumming there like an electrical cable, but there was nothing except the sensation, the sensation, the sensation—

—and then Paul was watching himself from Danny's eyes, seeing himself there in the snow, his face pale and streaked with sharp daggers of blood, his eyes as wide as saucers. It was Danny who spoke, but Paul could feel the words coming out of his brother's body—

"I'm here," Danny said. "Here."

Those terrible green eyes swung in Danny's direction. The thing ratcheted up on its hind legs, a black devil against the backdrop of the burning cabin. It pivoted its body so that Danny was now in its direct path, its movements grotesquely human. And before he was ejected from Danny's body and back into his own, Paul could hear the roaring thunder of Danny's thoughts: *I love you*.

The cold rushed back to him, as did the burning sensation across his chest and abdomen, and when he opened his eyes, he found he was back on the snowy ground with a scream lodged in his throat. He rolled onto his side, white-hot agony exploding at the center of his body.

He looked up just in time to see the thing rush at Danny. Danny could have rolled away, but he didn't—his legs were planted in the ground and something in his hand glinted with firelight. He ran at the thing and met it halfway—

"Danny!"

An inhuman howl rose into the night as Danny and the creature collided, then disappeared over the edge of the ravine.

Paul tried to scream, but all that came out was an agonized sob. His lungs burned, but he could no longer feel anything below the waist. He glanced down at his stomach and saw that he was bleeding. The thing had sliced through the layers of his clothes and had carved into his belly. He touched a hand to the wound and was astounded to feel just how warm his blood was, soaking through his shirts and spilling down toward the crotch of his pants.

That's my Manipura, he thought crazily, his mind unraveling. *That's it right there. Spilling right out of my guts. Good-bye.*

He dropped his head back down in the snow. His vision faded in and out. His heartbeat was like thunder in his skull. He blinked his eyes to fight off the darkness that was clouding them and filling them with smoke. After a time, the only thing he could see was a crack of light bisecting the early morning sky—green and purple, lavender and indigo, a widening curtain of light that was lanced with stars and spread across Paul's waning field of vision like some holy salvation.

And the world fell away.

33

Valerie Drammell was standing in the middle of the road, waving his arms. It was a frigid morning, and the clouds that had gathered around the distant mountaintops looked like they might be carved from ice.

Ryerson slowed the cruiser to a stop and rolled down her window.

"It's right over here," Drammell said, pointing to where the Sitka spruce wore their snowy shawls and the crosses rose up into the bone-colored sky. Paul Gallo's Chevy Tahoe was hidden among the trees off the shoulder of the road and coated in a blanket of fresh snow.

Ryerson pulled the cruiser behind the Tahoe and got out. She went to the Tahoe and tried the door, but it was locked. She cleared snow off the driver's side window and peered inside. She could see luggage in the back.

"How long has it been here?" she asked.

"I don't know," said Drammell. "He checked out of the inn maybe a week ago."

"And he just went off into the woods?"

"I have no idea."

She glanced around but saw no fresh footprints in the snow.

"Why would he come here?" Drammell asked. He took a pack of smokes from the liner pocket of his winter coat. He was wearing fingerless gloves, which helped him finagle a cigarette out of the pack and prop it up in the corner of his mouth. "Can't figure what he might've been doing."

"I know what he was doing," Ryerson said.

Valerie Drammell arched an eyebrow. "Yeah?"

"He went looking for his brother," she said.

"You ain't planning to go after him, are you?" Drammell asked.

She removed a business card from her commission book and scribbled Mike McHale's number on the back of it. "That's smoke, isn't it?" she said, nodding toward the horizon.

Drammell squinted. "Looks it," he said.

"What's out there?"

"Nothing. Trees."

"Something's burning," she said, and handed the business card to Drammell. "Go back to your place and call this guy. Tell him where I am, and that I'm requesting K-9s and a helicopter. My cell phone's not getting a signal out here."

Drammell just stared at the business card. When he looked back up at her, he only repeated his question. "You ain't going out there, are you?"

"Just a little ways," she said, pulling on a pair of wool gloves.

Drammell just stood there.

"The sooner the better," she said.

Drammell tossed his cigarette to the ground, then turned and headed back to his truck, which was parked in the middle of the road. Ryerson watched him go, then turned her attention back to the woods and that faint finger of smoke on the horizon.

Just a little ways, she told herself.

She walked for a while, thinking, *I'll just go a little bit farther,* each time she considered turning back. Before she knew it, however, she'd been out there for over an hour and was meandering through the narrow passageways and crooked, twisting ravines of the foothills of the White Mountains.

The sky was a silver band arching over the mountains. She caught sight of a stand of barren trees that rimmed the nearest slope. Beyond that, she saw the drift of black smoke spiraling into the air. She was closer to it than she thought. She hiked.

What had once been a cabin was now a charred, blackened heap of wooden boards, with sections of a standing wall still ablaze. The whole pile steamed and sent streamers of smoke and fingers of flame into the sky. Ryerson stared at it, struggling to accept its existence here in the middle of nowhere. After a time, she looked down and saw patches of red atop the snow. When she turned and looked across the clearing, she saw a figure lying there on the ground.

She approached the figure, thinking that whoever it might be was dead. But as she came down on one knee to examine the body, the person rolled over and blinked at her. The man's face was a pallid blue and there was blood saturating his clothes and along the side of his coat. Large clumps of snow had gathered in his eyelashes.

And then she recognized him.

"Paul," she said. "Paul Gallo."

Something akin to a sob erupted from Paul's lungs. He was clutching something under one arm, and he seemed to be trying to push it over his body in her direction. It was a backpack, damp from the snow and grimy with mud. Paul's lips—split and caked in dried blood—moved but no sounds came out.

"Just relax," she said, taking the backpack from him. "It's okay. You're gonna be okay."

He held on to the backpack, clutching it in one pale blue fist. He shook it until she looked back down at it.

"Okay," she said, not understanding.

He tugged at the backpack again.

She just shook her head, still not comprehending . . . but then she looked down at the backpack. Stitched to the front of it was a small white card tucked into a clear plastic window. It was a luggage tag, and there was what appeared to be a name and address printed on it.

It read:

ROBERTA CHALMERS
5 WINTERCREST LANE
BETHEL, ALASKA

"Jesus Christ," she said.

Paul released his grip on the backpack and pointed across the clearing. His hand was covered in blood. Ryerson followed the gesture and saw that there were splotches of blood in the snow leading all the way to the edge of a cliff. The snow had been disturbed. There were strange tracks all over the place. There was a rifle on the ground, too.

"Okay," she said, patting Paul's shoulder. She stood and followed the bloody snow toward the edge of the cliff. It overlooked a ravine, and she peered down into it.

There was a man dead at the bottom, his torn and bloodied body powdered in places with snow. There were deep wounds and gouges across the man's chest, his arms, and a deep slice along the one cheek that had flayed the skin away so that Ryerson could see the man's teeth in a neat, white row. The man's single exposed eye socket was filled with bloody snow.

A few feet away from the man was the largest goddamn wolf Ryerson had ever seen. Its matted, blood-streaked fur was as dark and smooth as velvet, and its paws were the size of catcher's mitts. She could see one of its dull green eyes staring up at nothing. A large buck knife protruded from the animal's belly, the hilt of which was only a few inches from the man's bloodied, outstretched hand. There was a ragged tear that ran the length of the creature's belly, from which ropes of pinkish-purple intestines had unspooled out onto the snowy ground like a nest of wet, iridescent snakes.

It was the sound of churning helicopter rotors that ultimately snapped her out of her stupor. Ryerson looked up and saw a helicopter carving a wide berth across the sky, nearly touching the treetops.

She went into the center of the snowy clearing and began waving her arms.

34

That he would suffer nightmares for the weeks and months to come, there was no doubt. He would move through the daylight hours with the grim certainty that everything he had ever believed to be real and true was only a dazzling light show in the night sky. And whenever he looked in the mirror, it was Danny's face that looked back at him. That, of course, had always been the case. But it was even more so now.

He awoke in a hospital bed with gauze wrappings on both feet, a large square bandage across his navel, and an IV drip in his right arm. He was cold. There was only a starchy white bedsheet draped over him, but he thought they could outfit him in a space suit and ship him to the equator and his teeth would continue to chatter. He wondered if it was a sensation he would ever get rid of.

The doctor who managed to save his life was named Epstein. He was less successful in saving the two small toes on Paul's left foot. They had been amputated, and Paul was told that he would be walking with a cane for a while until he got used to it. He took the news with minimal emotion, and the tears he shed during the night were not for himself but for his brother.

That first night in the hospital, as he drifted in and out of consciousness, he opened his eyes to find Danny seated in one of the molded plastic chairs at the foot of his bed. He was cleanly shaven and had cut his hair. He smiled at Paul, and Paul smiled back. Then Danny got up and walked out of the room. Paul could hear his footfalls recede down the hallway. It was too real to be a dream.

On his second day of consciousness, he was visited by Jill Ryerson. She was dressed in jeans and a UAA Seawolves sweatshirt. She smiled at him and asked how he was feeling.

"Like I've been through hell and back," he told her . . . and then brayed uncontrollable laughter. After a time, the laughter turned into sobs. Jill Ryerson slipped out of the room and left him to it.

A few days later, he found himself leaning on his walking cane in the doorway of Jill Ryerson's office. When she looked up, he could tell by her expression just how terrible he looked. He *felt* terrible. He thought it would be a long time before he felt normal again. If he ever did.

"Hello," he said. "Is this a bad time?"

"Not at all," she said, getting up and moving around her desk. "Come in, Paul." She closed the door as he hobbled into the office with his cane and sat in the chair in front of her desk. She rolled her desk chair around and sat down next to him. "You look better. How're you feeling?"

"Twenty-nine stitches across my gut, plus I'll be heading home tomorrow with two toes less than I came here with." He smiled at her, but there was still much grief there. He could feel it hanging from his face like counterweights, and he could see it reflected in Jill Ryerson's face, too. "Some cops came by the hospital the other day and said I needed to give a statement before I went home. I told them what Danny told me. I told them there are other victims out there."

"Yes. We've already got men doing a preliminary search of the woods up where the cabin had been. Unless they find something right away, we may have to put things off till spring. Snow's moving in and the roads will be closed soon."

"The road," Paul corrected. "Just one. In and out."

Ryerson nodded. "I notified Peggy Chalmers about the backpack you found with your brother's stuff in that cabin, too."

"Good."

"Paul, how did you find your brother out there? How'd you know where to look?"

"Actually, he found me. I just got lost out there. He saved my life."

Ryerson opened a drawer and took out a small digital recorder. She showed it to him. "For your statement, if that's okay."

"That's fine," he said. "But I guess I'm just wondering what statement I should give."

"What do you mean?"

"Well," he said, "I can tell you a story you'll believe. One you'll be satisfied with. Or I can tell you what really happened out there, and leave you to come to your own conclusion."

"I want to hear what really happened."

"Okay. But first, about the wolf . . ."

"I thought your doctor would have told you. It was sent to the lab and tested for rabies. You're all clear."

"They cut off the head when they test an animal for rabies, right?"

If Ryerson found this to be an unusual question, she didn't let it show. "They do. Yes."

He nodded, satisfied. "It wasn't really a wolf, you know," he said. "But I won't start there. I'll start at the beginning. In hindsight, it's all a lot clearer to me now."

Ryerson turned on the digital recorder, then set it on the edge of her desk. She was still smiling at him, but Paul noticed that something had sharpened in her eyes now. *She's no dummy,* he thought.

"Have you heard the stories about that place?" he asked. "Dread's Hand?"

"About the devil, you mean," Ryerson said.

Paul forced a smile. "I saw something out there that I can't explain. I'm still trying to process it, even though I know what really happened."

"What really happened?" asked Ryerson.

"My brother tricked the devil," Paul said, then told her everything. And twenty minutes later, when he was done, a silence fell between them. Ryerson had turned and was staring out the window at the snow falling in the parking lot. After a moment, she leaned over, picked up the recorder, and turned it off.

"Maybe I'll just handwrite this one," she said.

"I know how it sounds. I won't ask you to believe me. That's not important. But I just wanted you to know what really happened. Keep it in mind when you think of my brother, and what he did out there."

"That's for a higher power to judge," Ryerson said. "I'm just a cop."

And I'm just a man who has lost part of himself. I'm one-half of a set. The rest of me is gone, gone.

"Anyway, I don't think there'll be any more horror stories about Dread's Hand. You can believe what you like, Ms. Ryerson, but you can rest easy on that score."

"How do you know?"

"It's just something I feel." He considered this, then added, "Or maybe it's something I felt through Danny. Right at the end."

He grunted as he rose up from the chair, the walking cane wobbling back and forth like a loose post in soft ground. "Take care," he said, and made his way toward the door.

"Don't be so quick to judge," Ryerson said.

He turned and looked at her.

"I've heard a few stories lately that I can't explain," she said. "One of which has to do with that wolf."

"What about it?"

"The report we received from the lab," she said. "DNA test said the wolf was over a hundred years old."

Paul said nothing, only stared at her.

"That's impossible, of course. Thing is, they couldn't

retest it because the animal had already been destroyed. I've seen plenty of those tests come back with bogus results before. It's no big deal. I guess this one's no different." She looked at him. "Right?"

"I guess so," he said.

Ryerson nodded. "That's what I thought," she said. "You have a good flight home, Mr. Gallo."

"Thank you," he said, and shuffled out into the hallway.

Outside, he limped through the parking lot toward his rental car as clumps of snow fell all around him. At one point, he glanced up at the station house and thought he saw Jill Ryerson watching him from her office window.

He realized he was crying when his cheeks began to freeze. He wiped away the tears and exhaled a shuddery breath. Just before he reached the car, he thought he felt a tightening at the center of his stomach.

Your Manipura. It was Erin Sharma's voice whispering in his head. *It grants you the power to save or destroy the world.* For the first time in his life, Paul Gallo realized that those things are sometimes one and the same.

You were right, Erin. Only thing is, you were right about the wrong brother.

He climbed into his car, cranked the ignition, and sat there while the windshield wipers swiped away the snow. Only once did he give in to the temptation and peer up at the rearview mirror, not expecting yet still hoping that he might see Danny's reflection staring back at him. And in a way, he did.

He pulled out of the parking lot and onto the highway, heading toward downtown. At the horizon, the foothills rose until they turned white and faded into the sky.

Winter was coming, and it promised to be a cold one.

ACKNOWLEDGMENTS

With the risk of sounding nepotistic, my primary thanks go to my dad, Ron Sr., and my wife, Deb, for their tireless support and advice during the writing of this novel. They were both still providing input and support up until the day this manuscript was due on my editor's desk. Thanks also to my friend Jim Braswell for his editorial suggestions; he took time away from his own writing to assist me with mine, and I cannot think of a more selfless act.

Many thanks to my editor, Peter Senftleben, whose suggestions improved this novel, and to Michaela Hamilton for picking up the torch. It's an author's great pleasure to work with a conscientious and caring editor, so in that regard, I have been doubly blessed.

Thanks to my tireless agent, Cameron McClure, whose efforts always go beyond that of an agent— you wouldn't be reading this right now if it wasn't for her.

In seeking details that would make this book realistic, I relied on input from some wonderful folks who have lived in Alaska—Richard Larrabee, Claire L. Fishback (another generous author), and Melissa Sirevog.

Lastly, my heartfelt gratitude to the hardworking men and women of the Alaska State Troopers. They were always eager to answer my questions and to provide information that helped make the investigative elements of this story as realistic as possible. My gratitude goes out to them, not only for their willingness to help with my book, but for putting their lives on the line every single day.

Don't miss Ronald Malfi's hair-raising ghost story

LITTLE GIRLS

Available from Pinnacle Books,
an imprint of Kensington Publishing Corp.

Keep reading to enjoy a sample excerpt . . .

1

They had been expecting a woman, Dora Lorton, to greet them upon their arrival, but as Ted finessed the Volvo station wagon up the long driveway toward the house, they could see there was a man on the porch. Tall and gaunt, he had a face like a withered apple core and wore a long black overcoat that looked incongruous in the stirrings of an early summer. The man watched them as Ted pulled the station wagon up beside a dusty gray Cadillac that was parked in front of the porch. For one perplexing instant, Laurie Genarro thought the man on the porch was her father, so newly dead that his orphaned spirit still lingered at the house on Annapolis Road.

"Glad to see Lurch from *The Addams Family* has found work," Ted commented as he shut off the car.

"It looks like a haunted house," Susan spoke up from the backseat, a comment that seemed to underscore Laurie's initial impression of the ghostlike man who stood beneath the partial shade of the porch alcove.

Susan was ten and had just begun vocalizing her critical observations to anyone within earshot. "And who's Lurch?"

"Ah," said Ted. "When did popular culture cease being popular?"

"I'm only ten," Susan reminded him, closing the Harry Potter book she had been reading for much of the drive down from Connecticut. She had been brooding and sullen for the majority of the trip, having already pitched a fit back in Hartford about having to spend summer vacation away from her friends and in a strange city, all of it because of a grandfather she had never known.

Who could blame her? Laurie thought now, still staring out the passenger window at the man on the porch. *I'd pitch a fit, too. In fact, I just might do it yet.*

Ted cupped his hands around his mouth. "Thank you for flying Genarro Airlines! Please make sure your tray tables are up before debarking."

Susan giggled, her mood having changed for the better somewhere along Interstate 95. "Barking!" she cried happily, misinterpreting her father's comment, then proceeded to bark like a dog. Ted wasted no time barking right along with her.

Laurie got out of the car and shivered despite the afternoon's mild temperature. In the wake of her father's passing, and for no grounded reason, she had expected her old childhood home to look different—empty, perhaps, like the molted skin of a reptile left behind in the dirt, as if the old house had nothing left to do but wither and die just as its master had done. But no, it was still the same house it had always been: the redbrick frame beneath a slouching mansard roof; Italianate cornices of a design suggestive of great pinwheels cleaved in half; a trio of arched windows on either side of the buckling front porch; all of which was capped by a functional belvedere that stood up against the cloudy June sky like the turret of a tiny castle. *That's where it happened,* Laurie thought with a chill as her eyes clung to the belvedere. It looked like a tiny bell tower sans bell, but was really a little room with windows on all four sides. Her parents had used it mostly for storage back when they had all still lived here together, before her parents' separation. Laurie had been forbidden to go up there as a child.

Trees crowded close to the house and intermittent slashes of sunlight came through the branches and danced along the east wall. The lawn was unruly and thick cords of ivy climbed the brickwork. Many windows on the ground floor stood open, perhaps to air out the old house, and the darkness inside looked cold and bottomless.

Laurie waved timidly at the man on the porch. She thought she saw his head bow to her. Images of old gothic horrors bombarded her head. Then she looked over her shoulder to where Ted and Susan stood at the edge of a small stone well that rose up nearly a foot from a wild patch of grass and early summer flowers on the front lawn. *Yes, I remember the well.* Back when she had been a child, the well had been housed beneath a wooden portico where, in the springtime, sparrows nested. She recalled tossing stones into its murky depths and how it sometimes smelled funny in the dead heat of late summer. Now, the wooden portico was gone and the well was nothing but a crumbling stone pit in the earth, covered by a large plank of wood.

Without waiting for Ted and Susan to catch up, Laurie climbed the creaky steps of the porch, a firm smile already on her face. The ride down to Maryland from Connecticut had exhausted her and the prospect of all that lay ahead in the house and with the lawyer left her empty and unfeeling. She extended one hand to the man in the black overcoat and tried not to let her emotions show. "Hello. I'm Laurie Genarro."

A pale hand with very long fingers withdrew from one of the pockets of the overcoat. The hand was cold and smooth in Laurie's own. "The daughter," the man said. His face was narrow but large, with a great prognathous jaw, a jutting chin, and the rheumy, downturned eyes of a basset hound. With the exception of a wispy sweep of colorless hair across the forehead, his scalp was bald. Laurie thought him to be in his late sixties.

"Yes," Laurie said. "Mr. Brashear was my father."

"I'm sorry for your loss."

"Thank you." She withdrew her hand from his, thankful to be rid of the cold, bloodless grasp. "I was expecting Ms. Lorton. . . ."

"I'm Dora's brother, Felix Lorton. Dora's inside, straightening up the place for you and your family. She was uncomfortable returning here alone after . . . well, after what happened. My sister can be foolishly superstitious. I apologize if I've frightened you."

"Not at all. Don't be silly." But he *had* frightened her, if just a little.

Across the front yard, Susan squealed with pleasure. Ted had lifted the corner of the plank of wood covering the well, and they were both peering down into it. Susan said something inaudible and Ted put back his head and laughed.

"My husband and daughter," Laurie said. She recognized a curious hint of apology in her tone and was quickly embarrassed by it.

"Splendid," Felix Lorton said with little emotion. Then he held out a brass key for her.

"I have my own." David Cushing, her father's lawyer, had mailed her a copy of the key along with the paperwork last week.

"The locks have been changed recently," said Felix Lorton.

"Oh." She extended her hand and opened it, allowing Lorton to drop the key onto her palm. She was silently thankful she didn't have to touch the older man's flesh again. It had been like touching the flesh of a corpse.

"Hi, there!" It was Ted, peering up at them through the slats in the porch railing while sliding his hands into the pockets of his linen trousers. There was the old heartiness in Ted's voice now. It was something he affected when in the company of a stranger whom he'd had scarce little time to assess. Ted was two years past his fortieth birthday but could pass for nearly a full decade younger. His teeth were white and straight, his skin unblemished and healthy-looking, and his eyes were both youthful and soulful at the same time, a combination many would have deemed otherwise incompatible. He kept himself in good shape, running a few miles every morning before retiring to his home office for the bulk of the afternoon where he worked. He could work for hours upon end in that home office back in Hartford without becoming fidgety or agitated, classical music issuing from the Bose speakers his only companion. Laurie envied his discipline.

"That's my husband, Ted," Laurie said, "and our daughter, Susan."

Susan sidled up beside her father, her sneakers crunching over loose gravel. Her big hearty smile was eerily similar to his. She had on a long-sleeved cotton jersey and lacrosse shorts. At ten, her legs were already slim and bronze, and she liked to run and play sports and had many friends back in Hartford. She was certainly her father's daughter.

"Nice to meet you folks. I'm Felix Lorton."

"There are frogs in the well," Susan said excitedly.

Lorton smiled. It was like watching a cadaver come alive on an autopsy table, and the sight of that smile chilled Laurie's bones. "I suppose there are," Lorton said to Susan. He leaned over the railing to address the girl, his profile stark and angular and suggestive of some predatory bird peering down from a tree branch at some blissfully unaware prey. "Snakes, sometimes, too."

Susan's eyes widened. "Snakes?"

"Oh, yes. After a heavy rain, and if it's not covered properly, that well fills up and it's possible to see all sorts of critters moving about down there."

"Neat!" Susan chirped. "Do they bite?"

"Only if you bite first." Lorton chomped his teeth hollowly. Then he turned his cadaverous grin onto Laurie. "I suppose I should take you folks inside now and introduce you to Dora."

"Yes, please," Laurie said, and they followed Felix Lorton into the house.

She had grown up here, though the time spent within these shadowed rooms and narrow hallways seemed so long ago that it was now as foreign to her as some childhood nightmare, or perhaps a threaded segment of some other person's life. Her parents had divorced when she was not much older than Susan, and she and her mother had left this house and Maryland altogether to live with her mother's family in Norfolk, Virginia. Subsequent visits to the house were sporadic at best, dictated by the whim of a father who had been distant and cold even when they had lived beneath the same roof. Her mother had never accompanied her on those visits, and when they stopped altogether, Laurie felt a warm relief wash over her. In her adult life, Laurie had chosen to maintain her distance, and she had never returned to this unwelcoming, tomblike place. Why should she force a relationship on a father who clearly had no interest in one? Even now, despite the horrors that had allegedly befallen her father, Laurie felt little guilt about her prolonged absence from his life.

"This place could be a stunner if it was renovated properly," Ted commented as Lorton led them through a grand entranceway. "I didn't realize the house was so big."

"Is it a mansion?" Susan asked no one in particular.

"No," Ted answered, a wry grin on his face now, "but it's close."

The foyer itself was large and circular, from which various hallways speared off like spokes on a wheel.

There was an immense crystal chandelier directly above the entranceway and a set of stairs against one wall leading to the second story. The floors were scuffed and dulled mahogany, with some noticeable gashes dug into the dark wood. Some of the floorboards creaked.

Laurie paused at the foot of the stairs. She felt Lorton hovering close behind her. A cool sweat rose to the surface of her skin and the nape of her neck prickled hotly. "I'm sorry," she said, reaching out and grasping the decorative head of the newel post for support. "I just need a minute."

Ted asked if she was okay.

"It's just a bit overwhelming, that's all."

Frightened, Susan said, "Mommy?"

Laurie offered the girl a tepid smile, which Susan returned wholeheartedly. "Mommy's okay, sweetheart," she said, and was glad when her voice did not waver.

Ted came up behind Laurie and squeezed her shoulder with one firm hand.

"It has been a while since you were last here, Mrs. Genarro?" Felix Lorton asked.

"It has, yes," she confirmed. "I spent my childhood here but haven't been back in many years."

Felix Lorton nodded. "Understandable."

After Laurie regained her composure, Felix Lorton led them into the parlor. The walls were drab, the paint cracked and peeling. A comfortable sofa and loveseat sat corralled on a threadbare oriental carpet before a dark stone hearth. A few books stood on a bookshelf, while an ancient Victrola cabinet squatted in one corner, its lacquered hood raised. Beside the phonograph was a small upright piano, shiny and black. A tarnished candelabrum stood on the piano's hood. At the opposite end of the room, a liquor cabinet with a mesh screen for a door displayed a collection of antediluvian bottles. The windows in this part of the house faced a green yard and, beyond, a wooden fence that separated the side of the house and backyard from the neighboring property which, from what Laurie was able to glimpse, looked overgrown with heavy trees and unkempt shrubbery. The whole room smelled unsparingly of Pine-Sol.

"Strange," commented Ted. He was staring at a large gilded frame on one wall. The frame held no lithograph, no portrait, though bits of it still clung to the inside of the frame. Aside from that, it framed nothing but the blank wall on which it sat. "What happened to the picture?"

Felix Lorton cleared his throat and said, "I wouldn't know, sir."

"Did you work for my father as well, Mr. Lorton?" Laurie asked as she walked slowly around the room. Beneath the cloying smell of Pine-Sol, she could detect the stale odor of cigar smoke, and for a brief moment she was suddenly ushered back to her youth. Her father had often smoked the horrid things. The parlor had been arranged differently back then, her mother having brought to it a domestic femininity it now sorely lacked. Cigar smoking had not been permitted in the house, and Laurie recalled a sudden image of her father standing just beyond the windows of this room, firmly planted in the strip of lawn that ran alongside the fence while he puffed away on one of his cigars. The vision was so distant, Laurie wondered if it was a real memory or some nonsense she had just conjured from thin air.

"No, ma'am, I did not. My sister was assigned to take care of your father from the service. When things got . . . more difficult . . . the service brought on another girl to assist with the caretaking responsibilities. A night nurse. You're aware of this, I presume?"

"Yes."

"I had been coming around on occasion in the past few months, Mrs. Genarro, mostly to do minor repairs. Old houses like these . . ." There was no need for him to complete the thought. "When Dora said the locks needed to be changed, I came and changed them. That sort of thing."

"Why *were* the locks changed?" she asked.

"You'll have to speak with Dora about that."

Laurie frowned. "If it was necessary to have someone maintain the property, I wish the service would have told me. I don't like the idea of you having to take care of my father's things for free."

"It wasn't like that at all, ma'am. My sister had simply requested I come with her so she wouldn't have to be here alone."

"What about the other girl?" Laurie asked. "The night nurse?"

"They were never here at the same time. They worked in shifts. Toward the end, your father required around-the-clock care, as I've been told. I presume you were kept up to date on all of this?"

"Yes. I was aware of my father's condition." Then she frowned. "Why wouldn't Dora want to be here alone?"

"You'll have to ask her, ma'am," said Lorton. It was becoming his automatic response. "If you don't mind my asking, where do you folks currently reside?"

"Hartford, Connecticut," Laurie said. She feigned interest in the crumbling mortar of the fireplace mantel. As a child, there had been framed photographs and various other items on the mantelpiece. Now, it was barren. "It took us longer to get here than we thought," she added, as if the distance excused her absence from this place and her father's life.

What do I have to feel guilty about? she wondered. *He was never there for me; why should I have been there for him? Anyway, what business is it of Felix Lorton's?*

"Understandable. Please have a seat and I'll go fetch my sister," Lorton said, extending a hand toward the sofa and loveseat. "Would any of you like something to drink?"

"Ice water would be great," Ted said. He was examining the spines of the few books on the bookshelf.

"Do you have any grape juice, please?" Susan asked.

The question caused Felix Lorton to suck on his lower lip while his eyes narrowed to slits. A sound like a frog's croak rumbled at the back of the man's throat.

"Water will be fine for her, too," Laurie assured him.

"Very well," Lorton said, then disappeared down the hall that led to the kitchen.

"All these books have pages torn out of them," Ted said, replacing one of the leather-bound editions back on the shelf. "How strange."

Laurie went to one of the windows and looked out onto the side yard. The lawn was spangled with sunlight and the wooden fence was green and furry with mildew. Tree branches drooped over the fence from the neighboring yard, the trees themselves all but blotting out the house next door. She could make out shuttered windows and dark, peeling siding. A green car of indeterminable make and model was parked in the neighbor's driveway and there was another vehicle with some sort of emblem on the door parked on the street. The Russ family had lived there when she was a girl. Laurie wondered who lived there now.

"This house smells funny," Susan said. She was crouching down to peer into the black, sooty maw of the hearth. "It reminds me of Miss Tannis's house back home." Bertha Tannis was the elderly widow who lived two houses down from the Genarros in Hartford. When she was younger, Susan would sometimes go there after school if both Laurie and Ted weren't home to greet her.

Ted went over and sat on the loveseat. He sighed dramatically as he draped an arm over the high back. "I should have asked the old *galantuomo* for a scotch and soda."

"Is this where bats live?" Susan asked, still peering into the fireplace. She was trying to look up into the chimney, but there was a tri-panel screen in the way blocking her view.

"It's a fireplace, Snoozin," Ted said, using their daughter's much hated nickname. "You know what that is."

"I know what it *is*," she retorted, "but there's *animals* out here. Not like we have at home. Didn't you hear what the man said about the snakes in the well?"

"There are no snakes in the well," Ted assured her. He sounded bored, tired. It had been a long drive down from Connecticut for him, too. "He was just pulling your leg."

"What does 'pulling your leg' mean?"

"It means he was joking."

"I know it means *that,* Daddy, but *why* does it mean that?"

"I don't know. That's a good question."

Felix Lorton returned with two tall glasses of ice water. He set them on the coffee table between the sofa and the loveseat. Laurie caught Lorton eyeing Ted ruefully, as if he did not approve of the man lounging on the loveseat in such a casual fashion.

"Thank you," Ted said, picking up his glass and taking a healthy drink from it.

"Why does someone say 'pulling your leg' when they're telling you a joke?" Susan asked Felix Lorton.

The man straightened his back and lifted his head just enough so that the bands of loose flesh beneath his neck hung like a dewlap. He cleared his throat. "To pull one's leg is to make a fool of them, as in to trip them up and make them fall down." Felix Lorton spoke with an authority Laurie found comical, particularly when addressing a ten-year-old girl. Laurie bit the inside of her cheek to keep from laughing.

"Neat," Susan said.

"Yeah, neat," Ted added. "I didn't know that, either."

"My sister will be with you folks shortly. If you'll excuse me, there are some things I need to attend to before we leave."

Laurie thanked him and Lorton effected a slight bow. His black coat flared out around his ankles as he shuffled quickly down the hallway. *Blood thinners,* it occurred to Laurie. *That's why he's wearing the coat and that's why his hand was so cold. He must be on blood thinners for medical reasons.* A moment later, Laurie heard a door far off in the house squeal open and then close again. With little carpeting to dull the noise, the sound echoed throughout the house.

Susan skipped over to the coffee table and scooped up her glass of water. She hummed a soft melody under her breath.

"Don't spill it," warned her father.

Susan scowled and, for a moment, she looked to Laurie like a grown woman. Those dark eyes, that lustrous black hair, the copper-colored skin and long, coltish legs . . . at times, the girl looked so much like her father that Laurie felt like an outsider among them, an interloper in some other family's life. Laurie was the fair-skinned freckled one with a plain face and eyes that were maybe a hair too far apart. Summertime, while her husband and daughter tanned with the luxuriance of Roman gods, Laurie burned a fiery red, then shed semitransparent sheets of peeled skin for the next several days.

"How come you didn't tell me it was such a nice house, Laurie?" Ted asked from the loveseat.

"Didn't I?"

"A house like this could go for top dollar, even in this lousy economy. I'll bet it's worth a fortune. It just needs a little TLC, that's all."

"I guess we'll find out when we speak to the lawyer."

"What's 'TLC'?" Susan asked.

"You're dripping water on the rug," Ted told the girl.

Susan set her drink down on the coffee table, then went over to the piano.

"B-flat," Ted said.

Susan pecked out the correct key. It rang in the stillness of the otherwise silent room.

"D-sharp," Ted said.

Susan said, "Oh," and her index finger moved up and down the keyboard like a dowsing rod, counting the keys silently, but with her mouth moving. She tapped another key, lower on the fingerboard.

"Yuck," Ted said from the loveseat. "Are you sure? D-sharp? Try again."

Under her breath, Susan mumbled, "Sharp is . . . *up.* . . ." Her lithe fingers walked up a series of notes until she rested on one. She hammered the note a few times, smiling to herself.

Ted stuck his tongue out between his lips and produced a sound that approximated flatulence. This set Susan to giggling. She turned around, her face red, her eyes squinting in her laughter. Laurie watched her daughter, smiling a little herself now. She was glad to have Susan back to her old cheerful self again, after the sullenness of the long car ride down from Connecticut. Then Susan's laughter died and the girl's smile quickly faded from her face. Laurie followed her daughter's gaze to the alcove that led out into the main hall. A woman stood in the doorway. Her face was sharp and white, her iron-colored hair cropped short like a boy's. She wore a paisley-patterned frock and was in the process of wiping her hands on a dishtowel when Laurie spotted her and offered the woman a somewhat conciliatory smile.

"You must be Dora," Laurie said, moving swiftly across the room with her hand extended.

"That's right," said the woman. She had a clipped,

parochial voice. She stuffed the dishtowel partway into a pocket of her frock and shook Laurie's hand with just the tips of her fingers. She looked to be in her early fifties. There were faint lines bracketing her mouth and crow's feet at the corners of her eyes. The eyes themselves were an icy gray.

"It's so nice to finally meet you. I'm Laurie Genarro. That's my husband, Ted, and my daughter, Susan."

"I'm sorry we must meet under these circumstances," Dora Lorton said as she nodded her head at each of them curtly. "My condolences, Mrs. Genarro."

"Thank you."

"If you've got bags with you, Felix can help bring them in from the car."

"That isn't necessary," Laurie told her. "We haven't decided whether we're staying here or not."

"Why wouldn't you stay? It's your house now."

The thought chilled her.

Ted stood from the sofa, straightening the creases in his linen pants. "There's supposed to be an historic inn downtown. It sounded interesting."

"George Washington stayed there!" Susan chimed in.

Dora's brow furrowed. "Downtown?"

"Annapolis," clarified Ted.

"Well, it's your house now," Dora Lorton repeated, and not without a hint of exasperation. "I suppose you folks can do as you like."

Ted shot Laurie a look, one that she interpreted as, *Cheerful old coot, isn't she?* Once again, Laurie had to fight off spontaneous laughter.

"The house is clean and everything in it is functional," Dora went on in her parochial tone. "Your father was not a man of excesses, Mrs. Genarro, as I'm sure you can see, so you'll find very little items of a frivolous nature in the house. There are no televisions, no radios, nothing like that. What items there are—Mr. Brashear's personal items, as opposed to *house* items, I mean—have been relocated to his study. When was the last time you were here at the house, Mrs. Genarro?"

"Not since I was a teenager, and that was just for a brief visit. I can hardly remember. And, please, call me Laurie."

"Do you recall where the study is?"

Laurie considered and then pointed down one of the corridors that branched off the main hall. It had been a small library when she had been a child, and she could easily imagine it as a study now. "Is it the room just at the end of that hall?"

"Yes. Do you require a rundown of the rest of the house?"

"A rundown?"

"A tour of it, in other words. Seeing how it's been such a long time."

"Oh, I don't think that will be necessary. I remember it well enough. And what I don't remember, I can figure out."

"Nonetheless, there are a few things I feel I should show you." Dora's chilly gray eyes volleyed between Laurie and Ted. "Which one of you does the cooking?"

"Mostly, it's me," Laurie said.

"Laurie's a splendid cook," Ted added. His smile was charming, but Laurie could see that it held no influence over Dora. "I can hardly microwave a salad."

"I figured I would ask nonetheless, just so my assumptions wouldn't offend anyone," Dora said, marching right past Ted's attempt at humor.

"Oh," Laurie said, "not at all."

"Very well," said Dora, those cold eyes settling back on Laurie. "You'll come with me then?"

"Of course."

"Can I go play outside?" Susan chirped to her mother.

"Not just yet, Susan."

"But I'm bored!"

"I'll go with her," Ted said, taking up Susan's hand.

"All right," Laurie said. She shared a look with her husband then . . . and wondered if he could decipher the clutter of emotions behind her eyes. Not that she could decipher them herself. She was weak, tired, troubled, overwhelmed. There was a darkness here in this house, she knew—something cold and widespread, like black water gradually filling up behind the walls—and she thought it might have been the residual ghost of her parents' divorce and Laurie's subsequent extraction from this place. *Extraction,* she thought, summoning the image of a diseased tooth being liberated from purpling gums. *That's good.*

Laurie followed Dora into the kitchen. It was a spacious room with brick walls and stainless-steel appliances. A small circular table stood before a bay window that looked out on the backyard and the moldy green fence that separated the property from the house next door. There were plenty of windows and the room was generously bright.

"You lived here as a child?" Dora said. She led Laurie over to the stovetop.

"I did, yes."

"It's a gas range. The appliances are in fair working order, though I can't be certain how old they are. You've cooked on a gas range before?"

"We have a gas range back home."

"Let me show you, anyway," said Dora. She turned the knob and let the burner tick until a blue flame ignited. The smell of gas rose up to greet them. Dora turned the stove off and moved to the refrigerator. She opened the refrigerator door. It was stocked, but not obnoxiously so. Laurie could see many of the items within hadn't yet been opened, and it occurred to her that either Dora or Felix Lorton had recently gone to the supermarket in anticipation of their arrival. "You'll find it is stocked with milk, cheese, bread, juices, and plenty of condiments. There are frozen meats and poultry in the freezer as well, Mrs. Genarro, and the pantry is sufficiently stocked with cereals, pastas, and canned goods. I didn't bother getting any fruits or vegetables or other perishables from the market, as they tend to go bad quickly in the summer if not eaten right away. I wasn't sure how long you folks planned to stay."

"I'm not sure we know yet, either."

"It's understandable," Dora intoned, sounding just then like her brother. Next, Dora led her over to the dishwasher. "Standard functions, quite easy to use. There is detergent beneath the sink."

Beyond the curved bay windows, Laurie saw Ted and Susan galloping across the green lawn. They raced along the fence and up the lawn's slight incline to where the trees grew denser and wild blackberry bushes and honeysuckle exploded like fireworks from the ground. The tree limbs that overhung the fence waved sleepily in the breeze, throwing moving shadows against the mossy pickets.

"There's a list of emergency numbers beside the telephone," Dora went on. "For your convenience I've included the number for Mr. Brashear's lawyer, a Mr. Cushing, I believe, though I presume you already have his contact information."

"Yes, but thank you."

"I've left my home number for you as well, in the event you have any further need of me."

"That's very thoughtful of you. Thank you." It seemed all she was capable of saying to the woman. Also, it occurred to Laurie that Dora Lorton hadn't looked at her a single time since they'd entered the kitchen. "Have you been working here the whole time, since I called the care service?"

"Yes. It had just been me for a while, until Mr. Brashear's condition worsened and we had to bring on more help. I was assisted by a younger woman named Ms. Larosche. Do you know of her?"

"No, I don't. I mean, I was aware the service had added a second caretaker because of the need for twenty-four-hour care, but I'd never spoken to her."

"Nor will you need to. She only worked nights. I handled the household chores. Any questions you might have can be answered by me."

"And Felix, your brother? He had been helping out around here, too?"

At last, Dora's eyes ticked up in Laurie's direction. "That's just been recently."

"Did my father get terribly out of hand? I haven't heard the extent of it. I mean, given the way things ended, I could only imagine what it must have been like."

"You've spoken with Mr. Claiborne?"

"Yes," said Laurie. Mr. Claiborne was the managing director of Mid-Atlantic Homecare Services. Their conversations on the phone had been strained but polite. The last call she had received from him had been to inform her that her father had killed himself. While he had offered his sympathy, Laurie could tell Mr. Claiborne's primary concern was toward any potential lawsuit his company might be facing in the wake of such tragedy. Laurie had assured him she would take no legal action against him or his employees. "He explained the situation as best he could," Laurie continued. "Nonetheless, Ms. Lorton, I feel I owe you some sense of gratitude for looking after my father."

"It was my job."

"I just wanted to thank you. And Ms. Larosche, too."

"What's done is done." As if to brush away crumbs, Dora swept a hand across the Formica countertop, though Laurie hadn't seen anything there. "Come along and I'll show you the rest," said Dora.

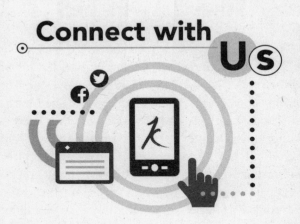